FRED VARG

This Night's Foul Work

TRANSLATED BY
Sîan Reynolds

VINTAGE BOOKS
London

Published by Vintage 2009

2 4 6 8 10 9 7 5 3 1

Copyright © Éditions Viviane Hamy, Paris 2006
English translation copyright © Siân Reynolds 2008

First published with the title *Dans les bois éternels* in 2006 by
Éditions Viviane Hamy, Paris

First published in Great Britain in 2008 by
Harvill Secker

Vintage
Random House, 20 Vauxhall Bridge Road,
London SW1V 2SA

www.vintage-books.co.uk

Addresses for companies within The Random House Group Limited can be
found at: www.randomhouse.co.uk/offices.htm
The Random House Group Limited Reg. No. 954009

A CIP catalogue record for this book is available from the British Library

ISBN 9780099507628

This book is supported by the French Ministry of Foreign Affairs, as part of
the Burgess Programme headed for the French embassy in London by the
Institut Français du Royaume-Uni

ïi institut français

Ouvrage publié avec le concours du ministère français chargé de la
Culture – Centre National du Livre

This book is published with support from the French Ministry of
Culture – Centre National du Livre

The Random House Group Limited supports The Forest Stewardship
Council (FSC), the leading international forest certification organisation.
All our titles that are printed on Greenpeace approved FSC certified paper
carry the FSC logo. Our paper procurement policy can be found at
www.rbooks.co.uk/environment

Printed in the UK by CPI Bookmarque, Croydon, CR0 4TD

THIS NIGHT'S FOUL WORK

I

BY FIXING HIS CURTAIN TO ONE SIDE WITH A CLOTHES-PEG, LUCIO COULD better observe the new neighbour at his leisure. The newcomer, who was small and dark, had stripped to the waist despite the chilly March breeze and was building a wall of breeze-blocks without using a plumb line. After an hour's watching, Lucio shook his head abruptly, like a lizard emerging from its motionless siesta. He removed his unlit cigarette from his mouth.

'That one,' he said, pronouncing his final diagnosis, 'has no more ballast in his head than in his hands. He's going his own sweet way without the rule book. Pleasing himself.'

'Let him get on with it, then,' said his daughter, without conviction.

'I know what I have to do, Maria.'

'You just enjoy upsetting other people, don't you, with your old wives' tales?'

Her father clicked his tongue disapprovingly.

'You wouldn't talk like that if you had trouble sleeping. The other night I saw her, clear as I see you.'

'Yes, you told me.'

'She went past the windows on the first floor, slowly like the ghost.'

'Yes,' Maria said again, with indifference.

The old man had risen to his feet and was leaning on his stick.

'It's as if she was waiting for the new owner to arrive, as if she was

1

getting ready to stalk her prey. That man over there, I mean,' he added, jerking his chin at the window.

'The neighbour?' said Maria. 'It'll just go in one ear and out the other, you know.'

'What he does after that's up to him. Pass me a cigarette – I'm going over there.'

Maria placed the cigarette in her father's mouth and lit it.

'Maria, for the love of God, take off the filter.'

Doing as she was asked, Maria helped her father on with his coat. Then she slipped into his pocket a little radio, from which a hiss of background noise and muffled voices emerged. The old man wouldn't be parted from it.

'Don't go scaring the neighbour now, will you,' she said, knotting his scarf.

'Oh, the neighbour's had worse than this to cope with, believe me.'

Jean-Baptiste Adamsberg had been working on his wall, unperturbed by the watchful gaze of the old man across the way but wondering when he would be coming over to test him out in person. He watched as a tall figure with striking, deeply scored features and a shock of white hair walked across the little garden at a dignified pace. He was about to hold out his hand to shake when he saw that the man's right arm stopped short at the elbow. Adamsberg raised his trowel as a sign of welcome, and looked at him with a calm and neutral expression.

'I could lend you my plumb line,' the old man said civilly.

'I'll manage,' said Adamsberg, fitting another breeze-block into place. 'Where I come from, we always put up walls by guesswork, and they haven't fallen down yet. They might lean sometimes, but they don't fall down.'

'Are you a bricklayer?'

'No. I'm a cop. *Commissaire de police.*'

The old man leaned his stick against the new wall and buttoned his inner jacket up to his chin, giving himself time to absorb the information.

'You go after drug dealers? Stuff like that?'

'No, corpses. I work in the Serious Crime Squad.'

'I see,' said the old man, after registering a slight shock. 'My speciality was the bench.'

He winked.

'Not the Judge's Bench, wooden benches. I used to sell them.'

A joker in days gone by, thought Adamsberg, smiling at his new neighbour with understanding. The old man seemed well able to amuse himself without any help from anyone else. A joker, yes, a man with a sense of humour, but those dark eyes saw right through you.

'Parquet floors too. Oak, beech, pine. If you need anything, let me know. Your house has nothing but tiles on the floor.'

'That's right.'

'Not as warm as wood. Velasco's the name. Lucio Velasco Paz. The shop's called Velasco Paz and Daughter.'

Lucio Velasco smiled broadly, but his gaze did not leave Adamsberg's face, inspecting it thoroughly. The old man was working up to an announcement. He had something to tell him.

'Maria runs the business now. She's got a good head on her shoulders, so don't go running to her with stories, she doesn't like it.'

'What sort of stories would those be?'

'Ghost stories, for instance,' said the old man, screwing up his dark eyes.

'No chance. I don't know any ghost stories.'

'People say that, and then one day they do know one.'

'Maybe. For all I know. Your radio isn't tuned properly, *monsieur*. Would you like me to fix it?'

'What for?'

'To listen to the programmes.'

'No, *hombre*. I don't want to listen to their rubbish. At my age, you've earned the right not to put up with it.'

'Yes, of course,' said Adamsberg.

If the neighbour wanted to carry around in his pocket a radio that wasn't tuned to any programme, and call him 'hombre', that was up to him.

The old man staged another pause as he watched Adamsberg line up his breeze-blocks.

'Like the house, do you?'

'Yes, very much.'

Lucio made a joke under his breath and burst out laughing. Adamsberg smiled politely. There was something youthful about Lucio's laughter, whereas the rest of his demeanour suggested that he was more or less responsible for the destiny of mankind.

'A hundred and fifty square metres.' The old man was speaking again. 'With a garden, an open fireplace, a cellar, and a woodshed. You can't find anything like this in Paris nowadays. Did you ever ask yourself why it was going so cheap?'

'Because it's old and run-down, I suppose.'

'And did you never wonder why it hadn't been demolished either?'

'Well, it's at the end of a cul-de-sac – it's not in anyone's way.'

'All the same, *hombre*. No buyer in the six years it's been on the market. Didn't that bother you?'

'Monsieur Velasco, it takes a lot to bother me.'

Adamsberg scraped off the surplus cement with his trowel.

'Well, just suppose for a moment that it *did* bother you,' insisted the old man. 'Suppose you asked yourself why nobody had bought this house.'

'Let me see. It's got an outside privy. People don't like that these days.'

'They could have built an extension to reach it, as you're doing now.'

'I'm not doing it for myself. It's for my wife and son.'

'God's sakes, you're not going to bring a woman to live here, are you?'

'No, I don't think so. They'll just come now and then.'

'But this woman, your wife. She's not proposing to *sleep* here, is she?'

Adamsberg frowned as the old man gripped his arm to gain his attention.

'Don't go thinking you're stronger than anyone else,' said the old man, more calmly. 'Sell up. These are things that pass our understanding. They're beyond our knowing.'

'What things?'

Lucio shifted his now extinguished cigarette in his mouth.

'See this?' he said raising his right arm, which ended in a stump.

'Yes,' said Adamsberg, with respect.

'I lost that when I was nine years old, during the Civil War.'

'Yes.'

'And sometimes it still itches. It itches on the part of my arm that isn't there, sixty-nine years later. In the same place, always the same place,' said the old man, pointing to a space in the air. 'My mother knew why. It was the spider's bite. When I lost my arm, I hadn't finished scratching. So it goes on itching.'

'Yes, I see,' said Adamsberg, mixing his cement quietly.

'Because the spider's bite hadn't finished its life – do you understand what I'm saying? It wants its dues, it's taking its revenge. Does that remind you of anything?'

'The stars,' Adamsberg suggested. 'They go on shining long after they're dead.'

'All right, yes,' admitted the old man, surprised. 'Or feelings. If a fellow goes on loving a girl, or the other way round, when it's all over, see what I mean?'

'Yes.'

'But why does he go on loving the girl, or the other way round? What explains it?'

'I don't know,' said Adamsberg patiently.

Between gusts of wind, the hesitant March sunshine was warming his back, and he was quite happy to be there, building his wall in this overgrown garden. Lucio Velasco Paz could go on talking all he wanted, it wouldn't bother Adamsberg.

'It's quite simple. It's because the feeling hasn't run its course. It's beyond our control, that kind of thing. You have to wait for it to finish, go on scratching till the end. And if you die before you've run your life's course, same thing. People who've been murdered, they go on hanging about, their presence makes you itch non-stop.'

'Like spider bites,' said Adamsberg, bringing the conversation back full circle.

'Like ghosts,' said the old man, seriously. 'Now do you understand why nobody wanted your house? Because it's haunted, *hombre*.'

Adamsberg finished cleaning his cement board and wiped his hands.

'Well, why not?' he said. 'Doesn't bother me. I'm used to things that pass my understanding.'

Lucio tilted his chin and looked at Adamsberg sadly. 'It's you, *hombre*, who won't get past her, if you try to be clever. What is it with you? You reckon you're stronger than her?'

'Her? You're talking about a woman, then?'

'Yes, a ghostly woman from the century before the one before, the time before the Revolution. Ancient wickedness, a shade from the past.'

The *commissaire* ran his hand slowly over the rough surface of the breeze-blocks.

'Indeed,' he said, suddenly pensive. 'A shade, you said?'

II

ADAMSBERG WAS MAKING COFFEE IN THE LARGE KITCHEN-LIVING ROOM OF his new house, still feeling unaccustomed to the space. The light glanced in through the small window-panes, and shone on the ancient red floor-tiles dating from the century before the one before. The room smelled of damp, of woodsmoke, of the new oilcloth on the table, an atmosphere that reminded him of his childhood home in the mountains, when he thought about it. He put two cups without saucers on the table, in a rectangular patch of sunlight. His neighbour was sitting bolt upright, clasping his knee with his good hand. That hand was large enough to strangle an ox between its thumb and index finger, having apparently doubled in size to compensate for the absence of the other.

'You wouldn't have anything to pep up the coffee, by any chance? If that's not too much trouble.'

Lucio looked suspiciously at the garden, while Adamsberg searched for something alcoholic in the cases he had not yet unpacked.

'Your daughter wouldn't like a drink, would she?' asked the *commissaire*.

'She doesn't encourage me.'

'Now what's this one?' asked Adamsberg, pulling out a bottle from a tea chest.

'A Sauternes, I'd say,' was the opinion of the old man, screwing up his eyes like an ornithologist identifying a bird from a distance. 'It's a bit early in the day for a Sauternes.'

'Doesn't seem to be anything else here.'

'We'll settle for that, then,' decreed the old man.

Adamsberg poured him a glass and sat down alongside, letting his back feel the patch of sunlight.

'How much do you know about the house?' Lucio asked.

'That the last owner hanged herself in the upstairs room,' said Adamsberg, pointing at the ceiling. 'And that's why nobody wanted the house. But that doesn't worry me.'

'Because you've seen plenty of hanged people?'

'I've seen a few. But it's not the dead who've ever troubled me. It's their killers.'

'We're not talking about the real dead here, *hombre*, we're talking about the others, the ones who won't go away. And she's never gone away.'

'The one who hanged herself?'

'No, the one who hanged herself *did* go away,' explained Lucio, swallowing a gulp of wine, as if to recognise the event. 'Do you know why she hanged herself?'

'No.'

'It was the house that made her go mad. All the women who've lived here have been troubled by the ghost. And then they die.'

'What ghost?'

'The convent ghost. A silent one. That's why the street is called the rue des Mouettes.'

'I don't follow,' said Adamsberg, pouring out coffee.

'There used to be a convent here, in the century before the one before. Nuns who were forbidden to speak.'

'A silent order.'

'Right. It used to be called the rue des Muettes, the Street of Silent Women, but as people forgot the real name, and said it wrong, they started to call it the rue des Mouettes, which just means the Street of Seagulls.'

'Nothing to do with birds, then,' said Adamsberg, disappointed.

'No, they were nuns, but the old name was harder to pronounce. Anyway, one of these silent sisters dishonoured the house. With the devil, they say. Well, I have to admit, there isn't any evidence for that bit.'

'So what *do* you have evidence of, Monsieur Velasco?' asked Adamsberg, smiling.

'You can call me Lucio. Oh yes, there's evidence all right. There was a trial at the time, in 1771. The convent was closed and the house had to be purified. The wicked Silent Sister had managed to get herself called Saint Clarisse. She promised any women prepared to come up with a sum of money and go through a ceremony that they would have a place in paradise. What these poor women didn't know was that they were going straight there. When they turned up with their purses full of cash, she cut their throats. Seven of them she killed. Seven, *hombre*. But one night, she got her come-uppance.'

Lucio laughed like a boy, then gathered himself once more.

'We shouldn't laugh at anyone so wicked,' he said. 'The spider bite's itching again, that's my punishment.'

Adamsberg watched as Lucio scratched in the air with his left hand, waiting placidly for the rest of the story.

'Does it help when you scratch it?'

'Just for a moment, then it starts up again. Well, on the night of 3 January 1771, one more old woman turned up to see Saint Clarisse, hoping to buy her way into paradise. But this time the woman's son, who was suspicious, and mean, came along with her. He was a tanner. And he killed the so-called saint. Like that,' said Lucio, crashing his fist down in the table. 'He beat her to pulp with his huge hands. Are you with me so far?'

'Yes.'

'Because if not, I can start again.'

'No, no, Lucio, carry on.'

'Only the thing was, this wicked Sister Clarisse never really went away. Because she was only twenty-six, do you see? And since then, every woman who's ever lived here after her has left the house feet first, after meeting a violent death. Before Madeleine, that's the one who hanged herself, there was a Madame Jeunet in the 1960s. She fell out of a top-floor window. No reason. Before Madame Jeunet, there was a Marie-Louise who put her head in the oven during the war. My father knew them both. Nothing but tragedy.'

The two men nodded simultaneously. Lucio Velasco with gravity, Adamsberg with a certain pleasure. The *commissaire* didn't want to offend the old man. And to tell the truth, this satisfying ghost story suited both of them, so they savoured it, making it last as long as the sugar took to dissolve in their coffee. The horrors of Saint Clarisse made Lucio's life more exciting, and the tale diverted Adamsberg momentarily from the mundane murders he was investigating at the time. This female phantom was more poetic than the two petty criminals who had been slashed to death the previous week at Porte de la Chapelle. He almost decided to tell Lucio about the case, since the old Spaniard seemed to have a definite view about everything. He warmed to this one-armed humorist, though he could have done without the radio buzzing away uninterruptedly in his trouser pocket. At a sign from Lucio, he filled his glass again.

'If everyone who's ever been murdered was still trailing around in the ether,' Adamsberg said, 'how many ghosts would I have on my hands in this building? Saint Clarisse, plus her seven victims. Plus the two your father knew, plus Madeleine. That makes eleven. Any more?'

'No, no, it's just Clarisse,' Lucio pronounced. 'Her victims were all too old, they didn't come back. Unless they went to their own houses – that's possible.'

'OK.'

'And the other three women, they're different. They weren't murdered, they were possessed. But Saint Clarisse hadn't finished her life when the tanner beat her to death. Now do you see why the house was never demolished? Because if it had been, Clarisse would have moved somewhere else. To my house, for instance. And round here, we'd rather know exactly where she is.'

'Right here.'

Lucio agreed with a wink. 'And here, so long as nobody comes to disturb her, there's no harm done.'

'She likes the spot, you're saying.'

'She doesn't even go into the garden. She just waits for her victims up there in your attic. But now she's got company again.'

'Me.'

'You,' Lucio agreed. 'But you're a man, so she won't trouble you much. It's the women she drives crazy. Don't bring your wife here. Take my advice. Or else just sell up.'

'No, Lucio, I like this house.'

'Pig-headed, aren't you. Where are you from?'

'The Pyrenees.'

'High mountains,' said Lucio, with respect. 'So it's no good my trying to convince you.'

'You know the Pyrenees?'

'I was born the other side of them, *hombre*. In Jaca.'

'And the bodies of the seven old women? Did they look for them when they held the trial?'

'No, in the century before the one before, the police didn't search the way they do now. I dare say the bodies are still under there,' said Lucio, pointing to the garden with his stick. 'That's why people haven't dug it too deeply. You wouldn't want to disturb the devil.'

'No, no point.'

'You're like Maria,' said the old man, with a smile. 'You think it's funny. But I've seen her often, *hombre*. Mist, vapour, then her breath,

11

cold as winter on the high peaks. And last week I was out taking a leak under the hazel tree in my garden one night, and I really saw her.'

Lucio drained his glass of Sauternes and scratched the spider's bite.

'She's got a lot older,' he said, almost with disgust.

'It *is* a long time, after all,' said Adamsberg.

'Yes. Well, Sister Clarisse's face is as wrinkled as a walnut.'

'And where was she?'

'On the first floor. She was walking up and down in the upstairs room.'

'That's going to be my study.'

'And where will you sleep?'

'The room next to it.'

'You're not easily scared, are you?' said Lucio, getting to his feet. 'I hope you don't think I was too blunt? Maria thinks I'm wrong to come in and tell you all this straight off.'

'No, not at all,' said Adamsberg, who had unexpectedly acquired seven corpses in the garden and a ghost with a face like a walnut.

'Good. Well, perhaps you'll manage to calm her down. Though they say that only a very old man can get the better of her now. But that's just fancy. You don't want to believe everything you hear.'

Left to himself, Adamsberg drank the dregs of his lukewarm coffee. Then he looked up at the ceiling, and listened.

III

After a peaceful night spent in the silent company of Saint Clarisse, *Commissaire* Adamsberg pushed open the door of the Medico-Legal Institute, which housed the pathology lab. Nine days earlier, at Porte de la Chapelle, in northern Paris, two men had been found a few hundred metres apart, each with his throat cut. According to the local police inspector, they were both small-time crooks, who'd been dealing drugs in the Flea Market. Adamsberg was keen to see them again, since *Commissaire* Mortier from the Drug Squad wanted to take over the investigation.

'Two lowlifes who got their throats cut at La Chapelle? They're on my patch, Adamsberg,' Mortier had declared. 'And one of them's black, what's more. Just hand them over. What the devil are you waiting for?'

'I'm waiting to find out why they've got earth under their finger-nails.'

'Because they didn't take a bath too often.'

'Because they'd been digging somewhere. And if there's digging going on, it's a matter for the Crime Squad.'

'Have you never seen these characters hide drugs in window boxes? You're wasting your time, Adamsberg.'

'That's OK by me. I like wasting time.'

The two bodies were stretched out, unclothed, alongside each other: one very big white man, one very big black man, one with a hairy torso, the other smooth, both harshly illuminated by the strip lighting in the morgue. With their feet neatly together and their hands at their sides, they seemed in death to have turned abruptly into docile schoolboys. In fact, Adamsberg thought, as he considered their sober appearance, the two men had led lives of classic regularity, since there's not a great deal of originality in human existence. Their days had followed an unchanging pattern: mornings asleep, then afternoons devoted to dealing, evenings to women, and Sundays to their mothers. On the margins of society, as elsewhere, routine imposes its rules. Their brutal murder had cut abnormally short the thread of their uneventful lives.

The pathologist was watching Adamsberg as he walked round the two bodies.

'What do you want me to do with them?' she asked, her hand resting negligently on the black corpse's thigh, idly patting it as if in ultimate consolation. 'Two dealers from the wrong side of town, slashed with a knife – looks like the Drug Squad had better take care of it.'

'Yes, they're shouting for them.'

'So what's the problem?'

'Me. *I*'m the problem. I don't want to hand them over. And I'm hoping you'll help me hang on to them. Find some excuse.'

'Why?' asked the pathologist. Her hand was still resting on the black corpse's thigh, signifying that for the moment the man was still under her jurisdiction, in a free zone, and she alone would make any decision about sending him either to the Drug Squad or the Crime Squad.

'They had newly dug earth under their fingernails.'

'I expect the drugs people have their reasons too. Do they have files on these two?'

'No, not at all. So these two are mine, full stop.'

'They told me about you,' said the pathologist calmly.

'What did they tell you?'

'That you're sometimes on a different wavelength from everyone else. It causes trouble.'

'It wouldn't be the first time, would it, Ariane?'

With her foot the doctor pulled over a stool. She sat down on it and crossed her legs. Twenty-three years earlier, Adamsberg had thought her a beautiful woman and, at sixty, she still was as she posed elegantly on her perch in the mortuary.

'Gracious me!' she said. 'You know my name.'

'Yes.'

'But I don't know *you*.'

The doctor lit a cigarette and thought for a few seconds.

'No,' she said at last. 'I can't say I remember you. I'm sorry.'

'It was twenty-three years ago, and we were only in contact for a few months. I remember your surname and your first name, and indeed that we were on first-name terms.'

'Were we now?' she said, without enthusiasm. 'And what were we doing to be on such familiar terms?'

'We had an almighty quarrel.'

'A lovers' tiff? I'd be devastated if I'd forgotten something like that.'

'No, it was professional.'

'Gracious me,' said the doctor again, frowning.

Adamsberg inclined his head, distracted by the memories that her high-pitched voice and cutting tone brought up for him. He recognised the ambiguity which had both attracted and disconcerted the young man he had been then: her severe way of dressing combined with a mane of tousled hair, her haughty manner but familiar way of speaking, her elaborate pose but spontaneous gestures. He had never been quite sure whether he was dealing with a superior but absent-minded specialist, or a workaholic who cared nothing for appearances. He even recalled the way she said 'Gracious me!' at the start of a sentence, without being able to work out whether this was an expression of scorn or simply a provincial mannerism. He was not the only policeman to be wary of

15

her. Dr Ariane Lagarde was the most eminent pathologist in France, an unrivalled forensic expert.

'So we were on first-name terms, were we?' she went on, letting the ash from her cigarette fall to the floor. 'Twenty-three years ago I would have been in mid-career, but you would have been just a junior policeman.'

'As you say, a very junior policeman.'

'Well, you surprise me. As a rule, I'm not on familiar terms with my junior colleagues.'

'We got on pretty well. Until a big bust-up that caused a stir in a café in Le Havre. The door slammed and we never met again. I never got to finish my beer.'

Ariane stubbed out her cigarette underfoot, then sat back on the metal stool as a smile hesitantly returned to her face.

'The beer,' she said. 'I wouldn't by any chance have thrown it on the floor, would I?'

'You did indeed.'

'Jean-Baptiste,' she said, detaching each syllable. 'That young idiot Jean-Baptiste Adamsberg, who thought he knew better than everyone else.'

'Yes. That's what you said when you smashed my glass.'

'Jean-Baptiste,' Ariane repeated more slowly.

The doctor slipped off her stool and put her hand on Adamsberg's shoulder. She seemed on the point of kissing him, then put her hand back in the pocket of her overall.

'I did like you, Jean-Baptiste. You upset the apple-cart without even noticing. And according to what people say about *Commissaire* Adamsberg, you haven't changed. Now I see: that was you, you're him.'

'Sort of.'

Ariane leaned her elbows on the dissecting table where the white corpse lay, pushing the body aside to make more room. Like most pathologists, Ariane showed little respect for the dead. On the other hand, she investigated the enigma of their bodies with unrivalled talent, thus paying homage in her own way to the immense and singular complexity of each one. Dr Lagarde's analyses had made the corpses of some quite ordinary mortals famous. If you passed through her hands, you had a good chance of going down in history. After your death, unfortunately.

'It was an exceptional corpse,' she remembered. 'We found him in his bedroom, with a sophisticated farewell letter. A local councillor, compromised and ruined, and he had killed himself with a sword, hara-kiri style.'

'Having drunk a lot of gin first, to give himself courage.'

'I remember it clearly,' said Ariane, in the mild tone of someone recalling a pleasant story. 'A straightforward case of suicide, on the part of a subject with a history of depression and compulsion. The local council was glad the matter went no further, do you remember, Jean-Baptiste? I had put in my report, which was impeccable. You were just the junior who used to make photocopies, run errands, sort out my paperwork, though you didn't always stick to instructions. We used to go and have a drink sometimes by the harbour. I was about to be promoted, and you were daydreaming and going nowhere. In those days, I used to put pomegranate juice in beer to make it fizz.'

'Do you still mix crazy drinks?'

'Yes, lots,' said Ariane, sounding disappointed, 'but I haven't found the perfect mixture yet. Remember the *violine*? An egg whipped up in crème de menthe and Malaga.'

'Awful drink, I never went for that one.'

'I stopped making the *violine*. OK for the nerves but a bit too strong. We experimented with a lot of things in Le Havre.'

'Except one.'

'Gracious me.'

'A bedroom experiment. We never tried that.'

'No, I was married in those days, and a very devoted wife. On the other hand, we worked well together on the police reports.'

'Until the day.'

'Until the day a little idiot of a Jean-Baptiste got it into his head that the local councillor in Le Havre had been murdered. Why? Because you found ten dead rats in a warehouse in the port.'

'Twelve, Ariane. Twelve rats, all slashed across the belly with a blade.'

'All right, twelve, if you say so. And you concluded that a murderer had been testing his courage before the attack. And there was something else. You thought the wound was too horizontal. You said the councillor would have had to hold the sword at more of an angle. While he was blind drunk.'

'And you threw my glass of beer on the floor.'

'I had a name for that beer-grenadine mixture, for heaven's sake.'

'*La grenaille*. You had me transferred away from Le Havre, and put in your report without me: suicide.'

'What did you know about forensics? Nothing.'

'Nothing at all,' Adamsberg admitted.

'Come and have a coffee. And tell me what's bothering you about these two corpses.'

IV

LIEUTENANT VEYRENC HAD BEEN ASSIGNED THIS MISSION FOR THE PAST THREE weeks, stuck in a broom cupboard one metre square, providing protection for a young woman whom he saw go past on the landing a dozen times a day.[1] He found the young woman rather touching, and this feeling disturbed him. He shifted on his chair, trying to find another position.

He shouldn't have been troubled by this – it was just a little grain of sand in the machinery, a splinter in the foot, a bird in the engine. The myth according to which a small bird, however exotic, could make an aeroplane engine explode was complete nonsense, one of the many ways people find to scare each other. As if there weren't enough problems in the world already. Veyrenc expelled the bird with a twitch of his brain, took the top off his fountain pen and set about cleaning the nib. Nothing else to bloody do anyway. The building was completely silent.

He screwed the top back on, replaced it in his inside pocket and closed his eyes. It was fifteen years to the day since he had defied the old wives' tales and gone to sleep in the forbidden shade of the walnut

[1] The events in Canada which prompted this protection, and are referred to occasionally hereafter, are described in *Wash This Blood Clean from My Hand* (Harvill Secker, 2007).

tree. Fifteen years of determined effort that nobody could take away from him. When he had woken up, he had used the sap of the tree to cure his allergy, and over time, he had tamed his furies, worked his way backwards through the torments he had endured, and exorcised his demons. It had taken fifteen years of persistence to transform a skinny youth, who took care to keep his hair hidden, into a sturdy body attached to a solid psyche. Fifteen years of applied energy to learn not to be tossed like a cork on the seas of love, something that had left him disillusioned with sensations and sickened with complications. When Veyrenc had straightened up under the walnut tree, he had taken the decision to go on strike, like an exhausted worker taking early retirement. From now on, he would keep away from dangerous ridges, taking care to temper his feelings with prudence and to control the intensity of his desires. He had done well, he thought, at keeping his distance from trouble and chaos, and approaching the serenity he yearned for. His relationships with people ever since that day had been non-committal and temporary, as he swam calmly towards his goal, on a course of work, study and versification – a near-perfect state of affairs.

His goal, which he had now achieved, was to be posted to the Paris Crime Squad under *Commissaire* Adamsberg. Veyrenc was satisfied with this, but it had surprised him. An unusual microclimate reigned in the squad. Under the almost imperceptible leadership of their chief, the officers allowed their potential to develop unchecked, indulging in humours and whims unrelated to precise objectives. The squad had achieved undeniable results, but Veyrenc remained highly sceptical. Was this efficiency the result of Adamsberg's strategy, or was it simply the benevolent hand of providence? Providence seemed to have turned a blind eye, for example, to the fact that Mercadet had put down cushions on the first floor and went to sleep there for several hours a day; to the abnormal office cat, which defecated on reams of paper; to *Commandant* Danglard's practice of concealing his bottles of wine in a cupboard in the basement; to the papers, quite unrelated to any investigations, that lay about on tables: estate agents' prospectuses, race cards, articles on ichthyology, private notes, international newspapers, colour spectra – to name only those he had noticed in one month. This state of affairs did not seem to trouble anyone, except perhaps *Lieutenant* Noël, a cussed character who found fault with everyone. And who, the second day he was there, had made an offensive remark about Veyrenc's hair. Twenty years earlier, it would have provoked tears, but nowadays he couldn't care less – well, not much less. Veyrenc folded his arms and leaned back against the wall. Unshakeable strength allied to a solid physique.

As for the *commissaire* himself, Veyrenc had taken some time to identify him. Seen from a distance, Adamsberg looked nondescript. Several times in the corridor, Veyrenc had passed this small man, a slow-moving bundle of tension, whose face was curiously angular and whose clothes and demeanour were dishevelled, without realising that he was one of the most famous figures, for good or ill, in the Serious Crime Squad. Even his eyes did not seem to be much use. Veyrenc had been waiting for his official interview since his first day on the job. But Adamsberg had never even noticed him, going round as he did in a daze of either profound or vacant thought. Perhaps it was possible that a whole year would go past before the *commissaire* noticed that his team had acquired a new member.

The other officers, however, had not missed the considerable opportunity offered by the arrival of a New Recruit. Which was why Veyrenc found himself stuck here in the broom cupboard on the seventh floor of a building, carrying out an excruciatingly boring surveillance duty. Normally, he should have been relieved regularly, and at first that had happened. Then the relief had become more erratic, with the excuse that X was depressive, Y might fall asleep, Z suffered from claustrophobia, or irritation or backache. As a result, he was now the only officer still mounting guard from morning to night, sitting on a wooden chair.

Veyrenc stretched out his legs as best he could. Newcomers usually get treated this way, and he was not particularly downcast. With a pile of books at his feet, a pocket ashtray in his jacket, a view of the clouds through the skylight and his pen in working order, he could almost have been happy here. His mind was at rest, his solitude was overcome, his objective reached.

V

Dr Lagarde had made life complicated by asking for a drop of barley water in her café au lait, but at last the drinks had arrived at their table.

'What's the matter with Dr Roman?' she asked as she stirred the frothy liquid.

Adamsberg made a gesture of ignorance. 'An attack of the vapours, he says. Like ladies in the nineteenth century.'

'Gracious me. What kind of a diagnosis is that?'

'His own. He's not suffering from depression, no serious symptoms. But all he can do is drag himself from one sofa to another, between a siesta and the crossword.'

'Gracious me,' said Ariane again, with a frown. 'But Roman's a tough guy, and a very competent pathologist. He loves his work.'

'Yes, but there it is, he's suffering from an attack of the vapours. We hesitated a long time before getting a replacement.'

'And why did you ask for me?'

'I didn't ask for you.'

'I was told the Serious Crime Squad of Paris was clamouring for me.'

'Well, it wasn't at my request. But I'm glad you're here now.'

'To get these two guys away from the Drug Squad.'

'According to Mortier, they aren't just two guys. They're two villains, and one of them's black. Mortier's head of the Drug Squad. We don't get on.'

'Is that why you're refusing to hand these bodies over?'

'No, I'm not chasing after bodies for the sake of it. It's just that those two should come to me.'

'As you said before. So tell me about it.'

'We don't know anything about them. They were killed some time in the night between Friday and Saturday, at the Porte de la Chapelle. To Mortier, that means only one thing: dope. According to him, blacks do nothing all day long but deal drugs, that's all their life consists of. And there was a syringe mark on the inside elbow in both cases.'

'I saw that. The routine analysis didn't turn anything up. So what do you want me to do?'

'Take a look and tell me what was in the syringe.'

'Why don't you buy the drugs hypothesis? No shortage of narcotics round La Chapelle.'

'The mother of the big black guy tells me her son never touched the stuff. Didn't use it, didn't deal it. The other one's mother doesn't know whether he did or not.'

'And you're ready to take the word of their old mothers?'

'My own mother always used to say I had a head like a sieve, the wind went in one side and came out the other. She was right. And as I told you, they had dirt under their fingernails.'

'Like a lot of no-hopers round the Flea Market.'

Ariane said 'no-hopers' in the pitying tone of the well-off and indifferent, for whom poverty is a fact of life rather than a problem.

'It's not just dirt, Ariane, it's soil. And these guys didn't go in for gardening. They lived in squalid rooms, in godawful tower blocks, without heating and lighting, the sort of place no-hopers get from the city council. With their old mothers.'

Dr Lagarde was staring at the wall. When Ariane was observing a corpse, her eyes narrowed to a fixed position, as if they were high-precision microscope lenses. Adamsberg felt sure that if he examined her pupils at that moment he would have found perfect representations of the two bodies, the white one in the left eye, the black one in the right.

'Well, I can tell you one thing that might help you, Jean-Baptiste. It was a woman that killed them.'

Adamsberg put his cup down, hesitating to contradict the doctor for the second time in his life.

'Ariane, did you see the size of them?'

'What do you think I look at in the mortuary? Old photographs? I saw your guys. Big lads, who could lift up a wardrobe with one finger, yes. Even so, they were both killed by a woman.'

'Explain.'

'Come back tonight. I've got a few more things to check.'

Ariane stood up, and put on over her suit the clinical overall she had left on the peg. The owners of cafés near the morgue did not appreciate doctors in white coats dropping in. It put off the other customers.

'I can't tonight. I'm going to a concert.'

'All right, come round after the concert. I work late – I expect you remember.'

'No, I can't, it's in Normandy.'

'Gracious me,' said Ariane, stopping still. 'What's on the programme?'

'No idea.'

'You're going all the way to Normandy to listen to it and you don't even know what they're playing? Or perhaps you're trailing after a woman?'

'I'm not trailing after her, I'm politely accompanying her.'

'Gracious me. Well, come by tomorrow. Not in the morning, though. I sleep late.'

'Yes, I remember. Not before eleven, then?'

'Not before midday. Everything gets accentuated as time goes by.'

Ariane perched back on her chair, as if in temporary hesitation.

'There's something I'd like to tell you. But I don't know if I really want to.'

Silence, however long it lasted, had never embarrassed Adamsberg. He waited, letting his thoughts run towards the evening concert. Five minutes went past, or ten, he couldn't have said.

'Seven months later,' said Ariane, having taken a sudden decision, 'the murderer made a complete confession.'

'The one in Le Havre, you mean?' said Adamsberg, looking up.

'Yes, the man with the twelve rats. He hanged himself in his cell ten days after that. You'd got it right, not me.'

'And you weren't too happy about that?'

'No, and neither were my bosses. I missed my promotion. I had to wait another five years. You'd practically given me the solution on a plate, and I hadn't wanted to hear what you were saying.'

'You didn't tell me about it.'

'I'd forgotten your name. In fact I'd deliberately wiped you out of my mind. With your glass of beer.'

'And you're still angry with me?'

'No, actually. It was thanks to the rat man that I started my research on dissociation. Have you read my book?'

'Some of it,' Adamsberg prevaricated.

'I invented the term "dissociated killers".'

'Yes, I remember – I've heard of them,' Adamsberg corrected himself. 'People who are split in two.'

The doctor pulled a face.

'Let's just say individuals who are made up of two distinct parts: one that kills, one that leads a normal life – and both halves are almost entirely unconscious of the other's existence. It's quite rare. For instance, that district nurse they arrested in Asnières, two years ago. This kind of murderer is dangerous, and recidivist, and almost impossible to spot. Nobody suspects them, not even themselves, and they go to extraordinary lengths to stop the other half of themselves from finding out.'

'I remember the nurse. So, according to you, she was a dissociated killer, was she?'

'Almost the classic case. If she hadn't crossed the path of some genius in the police force, she'd have gone on killing people until the day she died, and denied it to herself. Thirty-two victims in forty years, without turning a hair.'

'Thirty-three,' Adamsberg corrected her.

'Thirty-two. I'm well placed to tell you, I interviewed her for hours.'

'It was thirty-three, Ariane. I arrested her.'

The doctor paused, then smiled.

'Ah, did you now?'

'So when the Le Havre killer cut open those rats, he was the other part of himself. Number Two, the murderous one?' said Adamsberg.

'Are you interested in dissociation?'

'That case of the nurse still haunts me, and the Le Havre man sort of belongs to me too. What was his name?'

'Hubert Sandrin.'

'And when he confessed? Was he still the other one then?'

'No, that would be impossible, Jean-Baptiste: the other one never denounces himself.'

'But Number One couldn't confess, because he didn't know about the murder.'

'That's the point. For a few moments, the dissociation stopped working and the barrier between the two selves opened up, like a crack in a wall. And, through the crack, Hubert Number One saw the other one, Hubert Number Two, and was overcome with horror.'

'And that sometimes happens?'

'Hardly ever. But dissociation is rarely perfect. There are always a few leaks. Odd words leap from one side of the wall to the other. The murderer doesn't notice, but an analyst can surprise them. And if the jump is too abrupt, it can cause a breakdown, a personality crash. That's what happened to Hubert Sandrin.'

27

'What about the nurse?'

'Her wall has stayed intact. She has no idea what she's done.'

Adamsberg seemed to be thinking, rubbing his cheek with his finger.

'That surprises me,' he said quietly. 'It seemed to me she knew perfectly well why I was arresting her. She came along like a lamb, without a word.'

'Part of her did, which explains her consent. But she has no memory of her actions.'

'Tell me something. How did the guy in Le Havre find out about his other self?'

Ariane smiled broadly, flicking her cigarette ash to the ground.

'It was because of you and your rats. At the time, the local press made a bit of a song and dance about them.'

'Yes, I remember.'

'Well, Hubert Number Two, the murderer – let's call him Omega – had kept newspaper cuttings, out of sight of Hubert Number One – let's call him Alpha.'

'Until Alpha found the cuttings that Omega had hidden away?'

'Exactly.'

'Do you think Omega had wanted that to happen?'

'No. Alpha simply moved house. The cuttings fell out of a cupboard. And it detonated the explosion.'

'So if it hadn't been for my rats,' Adamsberg summed up quietly, 'Sandrin wouldn't have denounced himself. Without his case, you wouldn't have started working on dissociation. Every psychiatrist and detective in France knows about your studies.'

'Yes,' admitted Ariane.

'So I reckon you owe me a beer.'

'Certainly.'

'By the Seine.'

'OK, if you like.'

'And, of course, you won't hand these guys over to the Drug Squad?'

'It's the bodies that will decide that, Jean-Baptiste, not you and not me.'

'The syringe mark, Ariane, and the earth under their nails. Take a look at the earth for me. Tell me if that's what it is.'

They got up together, as if Adamsberg's words had been a signal for them to leave. The *commissaire* walked along the street as if he was strolling aimlessly, and the doctor tried to follow his slow pace, her mind already on the autopsies awaiting her. Adamsberg's preoccupation puzzled her.

'There's something about those bodies that bothers you, isn't there?'

'Yes.'

'Not just because of the Drug Squad?'

'No. It's just . . .' Adamsberg broke off. 'I'm going this way. I'll see you tomorrow, Ariane.'

'It's just . . . ?' the doctor insisted.

'Nothing that will help your analysis.'

'But tell me anyway.'

'Just a shade, Ariane, a shade hovering over them, or over me.'

Ariane watched Adamsberg walk away down the avenue, a wayward silhouette, taking no notice of anyone else. She recognised his style from twenty-three years back. The gentle voice, the slow gestures. She had not paid much attention to him when he was young, so she had understood nothing. If she was starting over again, she would listen to his story about the rats. She plunged her hands in the pockets of her overall and set off towards the two bodies waiting to take their place in history. Just a shade hovering over them. Today she could understand that kind of strange remark.

VI

LIEUTENANT VEYRENC TOOK ADVANTAGE OF HIS LONG HOURS IN THE BROOM cupboard to copy out in large handwriting one of Racine's plays for his grandmother, whose sight was going.

Nobody had ever understood the exclusive passion his grandmother had declared for this author, and no other, when she had been left a war orphan. The family knew that when there was a fire at her convent school, she had rescued a complete edition of Racine, except for the volume containing *Phèdre*, *Esther* and *Athalie*. As if the books had been granted to her by divine intervention, the little country girl had read them over and over, for eleven years. When she'd left the convent, the mother superior had given the volumes to her as a sort of vade-mecum, and his grandmother had gone on reading them, over and over, without changing the order, or ever having the curiosity to seek out *Phèdre*, *Esther* and *Athalie*. She would recite the speeches of this lifelong companion all the time, and the young Veyrenc had grown up hearing the twelve-syllable alexandrines, which had become as natural to his childish ears as if someone were singing around the house.

Unfortunately, he had picked up the habit as well, replying to his grandmother in the same mode – lines twelve syllables long. But since he had not had thousands of verses ingrained in his mind, night after night, he had to invent them. As long as he was living in the family home, it had hardly mattered. But once he was out in the world, this Racinian reflex had cost him dear. He had tried to suppress it by various methods, without success, then had given up the attempt and had gone on versifying unstoppably, muttering like his grandmother, a habit which had exasperated his superior officers. But it had also preserved him in some ways, since encapsulating life in twelve syllables had introduced an extraordinary distance – *'to no other compared'* – between himself and the hurly-burly of the world. The effort of standing back had always brought him into a calmer and more reflective state and had above all stopped him making irreparable mistakes in the heat of the moment. Racine, despite the intensity of his dramas and his incendiary language, was the best antidote to haste, cooling immediately any temptation to go over the top. Veyrenc had started deliberately using verse this way, realising that his grandmother had contrived similarly to regulate and manage her life. It was a personal medicine – *'to all others unknown'*.

At the moment, his grandmother was unable to take her regular potion, so Veyrenc was copying out *Britannicus* in big letters for her: He had reached the point when Junie was emerging from her bedchamber,

> *In the simple array*
> *Of a beauty from sleep summoned forth by the day.*

Veyrenc raised his pen from the paper. By the sound of her boots, he could hear the grain of sand coming up the stairs – for the grain of sand always wore a recognisable pair of boots, criss-crossed with leather straps. The grain of sand would stop first on the fifth floor, and ring the bell of the flat belonging to her invalid neighbour, bringing her her mail and her lunch. She would then be up on the seventh within a quarter of an hour. The grain of sand, otherwise known as the resident on his landing, was Mlle Forestier, Camille, whom he had now been guarding for nineteen days. According to the little he had been told, she

31

was to be kept under police protection for six months, shielding her from the possible vengeance of a murderous old man. Otherwise, all he knew of her was her name. And that she was bringing up a baby on her own, without any man on the horizon. He could not guess what her occupation was – he hesitated between plumber and musician. About twelve days ago, she had politely requested him to come out of the broom cupboard because she needed to solder a pipe inside it, at ceiling level. He had moved his chair out on to the landing and watched her precise and concentrated gestures, registering the metallic sound of the tools and the flame from her soldering iron. It was during this episode that he had felt himself slipping towards the forbidden and feared chaos. Since then, she had brought him a cup of hot coffee twice a day at eleven and four.

He heard her put down her bag on the fifth floor. The idea of leaving his broom cupboard that moment once and for all, so that he would never see this young woman again, made him rise from his chair. He tensed his arms, looked up at the skylight and considered his face reflected in the dusty pane. Abnormal hair, ordinary features, I'm ugly, I'm invisible. Veyrenc took a deep breath and muttered to himself:

> 'But I see that thy soul is filled with sudden fear,
> Thou, the victor of Troy, hero without a peer,
> Who gained both the city and people with great art.
> Can a woman's fair face make tremble that brave heart?'

No, no way. Veyrenc sat down again calmly, cooled by his four lines of dramatic verse. Sometimes it took six or eight, other times two were enough. He took up his copying task once more, feeling pleased with himself. Grains of sand pass, birds fly away, control remains. There was no cause for concern.

* * *

Camille stopped at the fifth floor and shifted the baby on to her other arm. The simplest thing would probably be to go downstairs and come back after eight o'clock when the duty officer would have changed. The nine conditions of the warrior are to flee, according to a Turkish friend of hers, a cellist at the church of Saint-Eustache, who was a mine of proverbs, as Byzantine as they were incomprehensible and beneficial. Apparently there was a tenth condition, but Camille didn't know what that was and preferred to make up her own version. She took the letters and the groceries out of her bag and rang the bell. The stairs had become too much for Yolande, whose legs were weak and whose bulk was great.

'Such a shame,' said Yolande, opening the door. 'Bringing up that child on your own.'

Yolande said this every day. Camille would go in, put down the provisions and the letters. Then the old lady, for some reason known only to herself, would offer her some warm milk, as if for a baby.

'It's OK, it's quite all right,' Camille would reply automatically as she took her seat.

'No, it's no good. A woman doesn't want to be on her own. Even if men are nothing but trouble.'

'Well, there you are, Yolande. Anyway, women can be nothing but trouble too.'

They had exchanged these remarks a hundred times, almost word for word, but Yolande never seemed to recollect that. At this point, Camille's comment would plunge the large old woman into meditative silence.

'In that case,' Yolande would then say, 'they'd do well to keep apart, if love just brings them both grief.'

'Could be.'

'But you know, my dear, you shouldn't keep putting them off. Because when it comes to love, you can't always do what you want.'

'But Yolande, who's going to do for us what we don't want to do?'

Camille smiled, and Yolande sniffed by way of reply, her heavy hand moving to and fro across the tablecloth in search of a non-existent crumb. Who? Why, the Powers-that-be, of course, Camille silently completed the answer. She knew that Yolande saw the signs of the Powers-that-be everywhere. This was her private pagan religion, which she didn't talk about much, for fear that it might be taken from her.

Eight stairs from her landing, Camille slowed down. The Powers-that-be, she thought. Who had parked this man with the crooked smile in the cupboard outside her apartment. He was no better-looking than average, if one didn't look too closely. But much better-looking if one had the bad idea of thinking about it afterwards. Camille had always been susceptible to elusive features and undulating voices, which was why she had spent fifteen years, on and off, in the arms of Jean-Baptiste Adamsberg, and kept promising herself not to return to them. To him or to anyone else blessed with that subtle sweetness and treacherous tenderness. There were plenty of men in the world who were less difficult to pin down, if one wanted a bit of straightforward contact that would allow you to come home relieved and peaceful, without needing to think about them any more. Camille felt no need of permanent company. Why the hell, then, had some chance dictated, thanks to the Powers-that-be, no doubt, that this guy on the landing, with his husky voice and his crooked lip, should touch her senses? She stroked the head of little Thomas, who was dribbling as he slept on her shoulder. Veyrenc. With his strange black-and-tan hair. A grain of sand in the works and an inconvenient disturbance. Distrust, vigilance and flight.

VII

No sooner had Adamsberg left Ariane than a hailstorm swept over the Boulevard Saint-Marcel, blurring its outlines and making a Parisian avenue look like any country road drenched by a sudden flood. Adamsberg walked on contentedly, since he was always happy in a downpour and was now also satisfied to be able to close the file on the killer in Le Havre after twenty-three years. He looked up at the statue of Joan of Arc, who was bearing the assault of icy hail without flinching. He felt heartily sorry for Joan of Arc; he would have hated to hear voices telling him to do this and that. He already had enough trouble obeying his own instructions, or indeed even identifying them, and would have seriously objected to orders coming from celestial voices. Voices like Joan's would have taken him into the lions' den after a brief and glorious epic struggle, since that kind of story always ended in tears. On the other hand, Adamsberg did not object to picking up the pebbles that heaven placed in his path to charm him. He needed another one for the Squad, and was searching for it.

When, after the five weeks' compulsory leave ordered by his *divisionnaire*, he had come back from the Pyrenees to the Paris Crime Squad, he had brought with him thirty or so grey pebbles, washed smooth by the river, and had placed one on each of the desks of his colleagues for them to use as paperweights or anything else they pleased. A rustic offering that no one dared refuse, even those who had no wish to keep a pebble on their desk. An offering which did not help them understand why the *commissaire* had also brought back with him a gold wedding ring now to be seen on his finger, and striking sparks of curiosity from every doorway he passed. If Adamsberg had got married, why hadn't he told the team? And above all, who had he married, and why? Had he finally and straightforwardly married the mother of his son? Or somehow forged a fraternal union with his long-lost brother? Or a mythical one with a swan? With Adamsberg, all solutions were possible, as rumours flew quietly from desk to desk and from pebble to paperweight.

It was generally expected that *Commandant* Adrien Danglard would resolve the puzzle, partly because he was Adamsberg's longest-standing colleague, having spent years alongside him in a relationship which allowed for no concealment or precautions, and partly because Danglard couldn't stand Unsolved Questions. These Unsolved Questions cropped up at every turn, like dandelions, turning into a host of uncertainties, fuelling his anxiety and making his life a misery. Danglard worked ceaselessly to eliminate the Unsolved Questions, like a maniac who keeps trying to remove non-existent specks from his coat. The gigantic task usually led him to a dead end and then to a feeling of powerlessness; the powerlessness, in turn, drove him down to the basement of the building, where the bottle of white wine was concealed, the only thing that could help him deal with any Unsolved Question that was too thorny. If Danglard took the trouble to conceal his bottle so far away, it was not for fear that Adamsberg would discover it, since the *commissaire* was, by some supernatural means, perfectly aware of his secret. It was simply that going up and down the spiral staircase to the basement was sufficient of an obstacle for Danglard to postpone calling on his heart-starter until later. So he patiently gnawed away at his doubts at the same time as he chewed incessantly at the ends of his pencils.

Adamsberg had developed a theory running exactly contrary to the pencil-chewing, which posited that the number of uncertainties a single person can support at the same time cannot multiply indefinitely, and reaches a maximum of three or four. That did not mean that there were no more, but that only three or four uncertainties could be in proper working order simultaneously inside a human brain. Danglard's mania for eradicating them was therefore futile, since no sooner would he have resolved two Unsolved Questions than another two would take their place, and he would not have had to concern himself with these if he had had the wisdom to stick with the old ones.

Danglard had no time for this hypothesis. He suspected Adamsberg of liking uncertainty to the point of inactivity. Of liking it to the point of deliberately creating it himself, to cloud the clearest perspectives, for the sheer pleasure of wandering irresponsibly through them, in the same way he liked walking in the rain. If one didn't know the answer, if one didn't know anything, why bother one's head about it at all?

The sharp conflicts between Danglard's precise 'Why?' and the *commissaire*'s nonchalant 'I don't know' punctuated the squad's investigations. None of the others tried to understand the core of this bitter struggle between accuracy and vagueness, but they all favoured one side or another. The positivists thought that Adamsberg dragged out investigations, taking them wilfully into the fog, leaving his colleagues trailing behind him without instructions or road maps. The others, the cloud shovellers – thus named after a traumatic visit by the squad to Quebec – thought that the *commissaire*'s results quite justified the vagaries of the investigation, even if the essentials of his work methods escaped them. According to mood, or to the circumstances of the moment, which might inspire either jumpiness or relaxation, someone could be a positivist one day and a cloud shoveller the next or vice versa. Only Adamsberg and Danglard, the two principal antagonists, never varied their position.

Among the more anodyne Unsolved Questions there was still that wedding ring glinting on the *commissaire*'s finger. Danglard chose the day of the hailstorm to ask Adamsberg about it, simply by looking pointedly at the ring. The *commissaire* took off his wet jacket, sat sideways and stretched out his hand. The hand, too big for the size of his body, weighed down at the wrist with two watches which rattled together, and now further embellished with the gold ring, did not match the way he dressed, which was negligent, bordering on the scruffy. It was as if the richly adorned hand of some old-fashioned aristocrat were attached to the body of a peasant, excessive elegance conjoined with the sunburnt skin of a mountain villager.

'My father died, Danglard,' Adamsberg explained calmly. 'We were both sitting under a pigeon-shooting hide, and watching a buzzard circling in the sky over our heads. The sun was very bright, and he just keeled over.'

'You never told me,' muttered Danglard, who found the *commissaire*'s secrets irritating, for no reason.

'I stayed there until evening, lying beside him, holding his head against my shoulder. We might be there yet, but some hunters came across us at nightfall. Before they closed his coffin, I took his wedding ring. Did you think I had got married? To Camille?'

'I had wondered.'

Adamsberg smiled.

'That's a Question Resolved, Danglard. You know better than I do that I've let Camille go ten times, thinking that the train would come along for the eleventh time on a day that suited me. But that's just when it stops coming along.'

'You never know, the points might change.'

'Trains are like people, they don't like going round in circles. In the end it gets on their nerves. After we buried my father, I amused myself picking up pebbles from the river bed. That's something I *can* do. Think about the infinite patience of the water, running over the stones. And the stones allow it to run, but the river is gradually wearing away all their rough edges, without seeming to. The water wins in the end.'

'If it comes to a fight, I'd prefer stones to water.'

'As you like,' Adamsberg replied with a shrug. 'But talking of stones and water, there are two things to report, Danglard. First, I've got a ghost in my new house. A bloodthirsty and avaricious nun, who was killed by a tanner in 1771. He murdered her with his bare fists. Just like that. She's taken up residence in a fluid sort of way in my attic. That's the water.'

'I see,' said Danglard, prudently. 'And the stones?'

'I've seen the new pathologist.'

'Elegant woman, bit stand-offish, but works hard at her job, they say.'

'And very talented, Danglard. Have you read her thesis about murderers who are split in two?'

A pointless question, since Danglard had read everything, even the fire-evacuation instructions in hotel bedrooms.

'On *dissociated* murderers, you mean,' Danglard corrected. '*Either Side of the Crime Wall.* Yes, the book made quite a stir.'

'Well, it turns out she and I had a major bust-up over twenty years ago, in a café in Le Havre.'

'So you're enemies?'

'No, that kind of clash can sometimes create a close friendship. But I don't advise you to go to a café with her – she mixes drinks that would knock out a Breton fisherman. She's taken charge of those two men killed at La Chapelle. She seems to think a woman killed them. She's going to refine her preliminary conclusions this evening.'

'A *woman*?'

The usually languid Danglard sat up, in shock. He hated the idea that women might be killers.

'Has she seen the size of those two guys? Is she joking?'

'Not so fast, Danglard. Dr Lagarde doesn't make mistakes, or hardly ever. Suggest her hypothesis to the Drug Squad, anyway – it'll keep them off our backs for a bit.'

'You won't be able to hold Mortier off at all. He's been getting nowhere with the dealer networks in Clignancourt-La Chapelle for months. It's not looking good and he needs results. He's called in twice already this morning. I warn you, he's screaming blue murder.'

'Let him scream. The water will win in the end.'

'So what are you going to do?'

'About my nun?'

'No, about Diala and La Paille.'

Adamsberg looked at Danglard in bewilderment.

'Those are their names,' Danglard explained. 'The two victims. Diala Toundé and Didier Paillot, known as "La Paille". So should we go to the morgue tonight?'

'No, I'm in Normandy tonight. For a concert.'

'Ah,' said Danglard, heaving himself to his feet. 'You're hoping for the points to change?'

'I'm humbler than that, *capitaine*. I'm just going to look after the baby while she plays.'

'*Commandant*, I'm a *commandant* now. Don't you remember? You were at my promotion ceremony. What concert, anyway?' asked Danglard, who always took Camille's interests to heart.

'It must be something important. It's some British orchestra with period instruments.'

'The Leeds Baroque Ensemble?'

'It's some name like that,' said Adamsberg, who had never managed to learn a word of English. 'Don't ask me what she's playing, I've no idea.'

Adamsberg stood up, and flung his damp jacket over his shoulder. 'While I'm away, can you look after the cat, and Mortier, the two bodies, and the temper of *Lieutenant* Noël, who is getting more and more difficult? I can't be everywhere, and duty calls just now.'

'Since you're being a responsible father,' muttered Danglard.

'If you say so, *capitaine*.'

Adamsberg accepted without demur Danglard's grumbling reproaches which he considered almost always to be justified. A single parent, the *commandant* was bringing up his five children like a mother hen, whereas Adamsberg had hardly registered that Camille's newborn baby was his. At least he had memorised his name: Thomas Adamsberg, known as Tom. That was at least one point in his favour, thought Danglard, who never completely despaired of the *commissaire*.

VIII

By the time he had driven the 136 kilometres to the village of Haroncourt in the *département* of the Eure, Adamsberg's clothes had dried in the car. He had only to smoothe them out by hand before putting on his jacket and finding a bar where he could wait in the warm for his prearranged rendezvous. Sitting comfortably on a battered leather banquette, with his back to the wall and a glass of beer in front of him, the *commissaire* examined the noisy group which had just taken possession of the café, rousing him from a semi-doze.

'Want me to tell you what I think?' said a big fair-haired man, pushing his cap back with his thumb.

He's going to tell them anyway, thought Adamsberg.

'Summat like that? Want me to tell you?' the man was repeating.

'We need a drink first.'

'We do at that, Robert,' said his neighbour, pouring out generous helpings of white wine into the six glasses.

So the big fair one was Robert – built like a wardrobe. And he was thirsty. It was the aperitif hour: heads sunk into shoulders, fists clenched around glasses, chins jutting at aggressive angles. The majestic hour, when the men of the village foregather and the angelus is rung, a time for sage opinions and nods of the head, a time for rural rhetoric, pompous and trivial. Adamsberg knew the score by heart. He had been born into this music, had grown up hearing its solemn developments, its rhythms and its themes, its variations and counterpoints, and he knew the players. Robert had sounded the first note on the violin, and all the other instruments would be moving into place at once, in an unvarying order.

'Tell you what, though,' said the man on Robert's left. 'It's not just a drink we need after that. Makes you sick to your stomach.'

'That it does.'

Adamsberg turned to have a better view of the last speaker, who had the humble but essential task of punctuating every turn in the conversation, as if on a double bass. He was small and thin, the least robust-looking of the group. That figured.

'Whoever did that,' said a tall stooped individual at the end of the table, 'he's no human being.'

'No, he's an animal.'

'Worse than an animal.'

'That he is.'

The first subject had been introduced. Adamsberg got out his notebook, still warped with rain, and started sketching the faces of the actors in the little drama. These were Norman heads, no mistake about it. He realised that they looked like his friend Bertin, a descendant of the god Thor, wielder of thunderbolts, who kept a café on a square in Paris. Square-jawed and high-cheekboned, fair-haired and blue-eyed, with an elusive expression in them. It was the first time Adamsberg had set foot among inland Normandy's damp woods and fields.

'What I think,' Robert was saying, 'is it's some young fellow. Some nutter.'

'Nutters aren't all young.'

This contrapuntal interjection came from the oldest speaker at the head of the table. Alerted, the other faces turned his way.

'Because when a young nutter grows up, he turns into an old one.'

'Dunno about that,' grunted Robert.

So Robert had the difficult but also essential task of contradicting the elder of the tribe.

'I'm telling you they do,' the older man said. 'But say what you like, whoever did that, crazy's the word all right.'

'A savage.'

'Stands to reason.'

Recapitulation and development of the first subject.

' 'Cos there's killing and killing,' said Robert's neighbour, a man with hair less fair than the rest.

'Dunno about that,' said Robert.

'Yes, I'm telling you there is,' said the old man. 'Whoever did that, they were just out to kill, nothing else. Two shots in the ribs, and that's it. Didn't even do anything with the remains. Know what I call that?'

'Cold-blooded murder.'

'That it is.'

Adamsberg had stopped sketching and started listening. The older man half-turned towards him, with a sideways look.

'Then again,' Robert was saying, 'where's Brétilly? Not our neck of the woods – thirty kilometres away. So why should we care?'

' 'Cos it's shameful, Robert, that's why.'

'I don't even think it was someone from Brétilly. I'll bet it was a Parisian. Anglebert, what do you think?'

So the old man who dominated the group from the top of the table was Anglebert.

'Yes, Parisians now, they can be crazy,' he said.

'The life they lead.'

Silence fell around the table and a few faces turned furtively towards Adamsberg. When men foregather for a drink in the evening, the newcomer is inevitably spotted, weighed up and rejected or accepted. In Normandy, like everywhere else, and possibly a bit more so than anywhere else.

'What makes you so sure I'm a Parisian?' Adamsberg asked calmly.

The old man jerked his chin at the book on the *commissaire*'s table, next to his glass of beer.

'The metro ticket,' he said. 'You've marked your page with a Paris metro ticket. Easy to spot.'

'But I'm not a Parisian.'

'Not from Haroncourt, though, are you?'

'No, I'm from the Pyrenees, from the mountains.'

Robert raised one hand and let it fall heavily on the table.

'A Gascon!' he concluded as if a sheet of lead had fallen on the table.

'I'm from the Béarn,' Adamsberg said pointedly.

The weighing-up process began.

'People from the mountains, they've been trouble,' said Hilaire, a balding but slightly less old elder statesman, at the other end of the table.

'When was that?' asked the not-so-fair one.

'Don't you bother asking, Oswald, it was way back.'

'Well, what about the Bretons? Man from the Pyrenees, at least he's not going to try and take the Mont Saint Michel away from us.'

'That's true enough,' said Anglebert, nodding.

'Well,' hazarded Robert, looking at the newcomer, 'you don't look to me like you're descended from the Vikings. So where do people in the Béarn come from, then?'

'Straight out of the mountain,' Adamsberg replied. 'Stream of lava came down the mountainside and when it hardened, it turned into us.'

'Stands to reason,' said the one who punctuated every stage in the conversation.

The men sat waiting, silently asking to be told what had brought this stranger to Haroncourt.

'I'm looking for the chateau.'

'That's easy. There's a concert on there tonight.'

'I'm with one of the musicians.'

Oswald brought out the local paper from his inside pocket and unfolded it carefully. 'Here's a picture of the orchestra,' he said.

That constituted an invitation to approach their table. Adamsberg crossed the room, holding his beer in his hand, and observed the page that Oswald held out to him.

'Here,' he said, pointing. 'That one, the viola player.'

'The pretty girl?'

'That's her.'

Robert served another round of drinks, as much to mark the significance of the pause as to absorb more alcohol. An archaic problem now tormented the gathering. What was this woman to the intruder? Mistress? Wife? Sister? Girlfriend? Cousin?

'And you're with her?' Hilaire asked.

Adamsberg nodded. He had been told that Normans never ask a direct question, a myth, as he had thought, but in front of him he had a clear example of their proud silence. If you ask too many questions you reveal yourself, and if you reveal yourself you're less of a man. Ill at ease, the group turned to the elder statesman. Angelbert tilted his unshaven chin, scratching it with his fingers.

'Because she's your wife,' he asserted.

'Was,' said Adamsberg.

'But you're still coming along with her.'

'A question of consideration.'

'Stands to reason,' said the punctuator.

'Women,' Anglebert said in a low voice. 'Here one day, gone the next.'

'You don't want 'em when you got 'em,' commented Robert. 'Then when they've gone, you do.'

'You lose them,' Adamsberg agreed.

'Dunno how it is,' said Oswald.

'Lack of consideration,' Adamsberg explained. 'Or at least it was that in my case.'

Here was someone who didn't make a secret of things, and who'd had woman trouble, which chalked up two good points in this male gathering. Anglebert pointed to a chair.

'You've got time to sit down, pal, haven't you?'

The familiar tone meant he had been provisionally accepted in this assembly of Normans from the flatlands. A glass of white wine was pushed towards him. This evening the assembly had a new member, and there would be plentiful comment on him next day.

'Who's been killed, then? In Brétilly?' Adamsberg asked, after drinking the requisite number of mouthfuls.

'Killed? Massacred more like! Shot down like, well, like vermin.'

Oswald brought another paper out of his pocket and handed it to Adamsberg, pointing to a photograph.

'What it is,' said Robert, who had not lost the thread of the previous conversation, 'you'd do better to be not so considerate first, and more considerate after. With women. Less trouble that way.'

'Never know where you are with 'em,' agreed the old man.

'Never do,' said the punctuator.

Adamsberg was looking at the newspaper article with a frown. A russet-coloured beast was lying in a pool of blood under the headline 'Odious massacre at Brétilly'. He turned the paper over to see that it was a monthly magazine, the *Western France Hunting Gazette*.

'You a hunter?' asked Oswald.

'No.'

'Well, you won't understand, then. Stag like that, eight points, you just don't shoot 'im like that. Diabolical.'

'Seven points,' corrected Hilaire.

''Scuse *me*,' said Oswald, an edge to his voice, 'but that one there, he's got eight points.'

'Seven.'

Quarrel imminent. Anglebert took control. 'You can't tell from the picture,' he said. 'Seven or eight.'

Everyone took a drink, feeling relieved. Not that a little discord was unwelcome and indeed necessary in the evening concert. But tonight, with an intruder present, there were other priorities.

'See that?' said Robert, pointing with his large finger at the photo. 'That's no hunter's doing. That fellow, he hasn't touched the carcass, he hasn't taken the pieces, or the honours or anything.'

'The honours?'

'The antlers and the hoof, front right. What he's done, he's slit it open, just out of cussedness. A maniac. And what have the Evreux cops done about it? Nothing, that's what. They couldn't give a toss.'

''Cos it's not a murder for them,' a voice said.

'Want me to tell you what I think? When someone kills an animal like that, he's wrong in the head. Who's to say after that he won't go off and kill a woman? Murderers, they practise on animals, then go on . . .'

'True enough,' said Adamsberg, thinking of the twelve rats in Le Havre.

'But the cops are so dumb they can't see it when it's staring them in the face. Stupid bastards.'

'It's only a stag, though,' objected the objector.

'You're stupid too, Alphonse. If I was a cop, I'd get going after this so-and-so – and quickly, too.'

'Me too,' murmured Adamsberg.

'Ah, you see, even this guy from the Pyrenees agrees with me. 'Cos a massacre like that, Alphonse, you listen to me, it means there's some maniac loose out there. And you better believe me, I know what I'm talking about – you'll be hearing more about him before long.'

'The Pyrenean agrees with that, too,' said Adamsberg, while the old man started to refill his glass for him.

'Ah, see that, and he isn't even a hunter!'

'Nope,' said Adamsberg. 'He's a cop.'

Anglebert suspended his arm, holding the bottle of white wine over the glass. Adamsberg met his gaze. The challenge began. With a slight nudge, Adamsberg indicated that he would like the glass filled up. Anglebert didn't move.

'We're not big fans of the cops round here,' said Anglebert, still not moving his arm.

'Who is?' Adamsberg rejoined.

'Ah, but here we're even less their fans than anywhere else.'

'I didn't say I was their fan, I said I was a cop.'

'You're not a fan, then?'

'Wouldn't be much point, would there?'

The old man screwed up his eyes, concentrating all his attention on this unexpected duel.

'So why are you a cop, then?'

'Because of a lack of consideration.'

The rapid reply was above the heads of everyone there, including Adamsberg, who would have been hard put to it to explain what he meant. But nobody dared to reveal his puzzlement.

'Stands to reason,' said the punctuator.

And as if a film had been paused for a moment, the movement of Anglebert's arm resumed, his elbow went up and the wine poured into Adamsberg's glass.

'Or, you might say, because of this kind of thing,' Adamsberg added, pointing to the slaughtered stag. 'When did it happen?'

'A month back now. Keep the paper if you're interested. Because the Evreux cops don't give a damn.'

'Stupid pricks,' said Robert.

'What's that?' said Adamsberg, pointing to a stain on the animal's side.

'The heart,' said Hilaire with disgust. 'He's put two bullets into the ribs, than he's took out the heart with a knife and cut it to bits.'

'Is that a tradition? To take the heart out?'

There was a fresh moment of indecision.

'You tell him, Robert,' Anglebert ordered.

'Surprises me, all the same,' said Robert, 'that you're from the mountains and you don't know anything about hunting.'

'I used to go out with the men on trips,' Adamsberg admitted. 'And I went up in the pigeon-shooting hides we have down there, like all the kids.'

'All the same.'

'But nothing else.'

'Well, now. When you make a kill,' Robert explained, 'first you take the skin off to make a cover. Then you cut off the honours and the haunches. You don't touch its innards. You turn it over and you carve the fillets to keep. Then you chop off the head, for the antlers. When you've finished, you cover the animal with its skin again.'

'That's right.'

'But bloody hell, you don't go cutting its heart out. Yeah, in the old days, some people used to. But we've moved on from then. Nowadays you leave the heart inside.'

'Who used to do it?' asked a voice.

'Never you mind – it was way back.'

'Whoever it was,' said Alphonse, 'what he was after was killing it, then ripping its heart out. He didn't even take the horns, and that's the only thing people take when they don't know nothing about it.'

Adamsberg looked up at the large antlers displayed on the wall of the café, over the door.

'No,' said Robert. 'That's crap, that lot.'

'Don't talk so loud,' said Anglebert, pointing to the counter, where the café owner was playing dominoes with a couple of youngsters too inexperienced to join in the gathering of the elders.

Robert cast a glance at the owner, then turned back to the *commissaire*.

'He's from away,' he said.

'Meaning?'

'He's from Caen, not from round here.'

'Caen's in Normandy, isn't it?'

There were a few exchanges of glances and pulled faces. Could they really trust this mountain dweller with such intimate and painful information?

'Caen's in *Lower* Normandy,' Anglebert explained. 'Here you're in Upper Normandy.'

'And that's important?'

'Let's just say you don't compare them. The real Normandy's the Upper one, here.'

Anglebert's gnarled finger pointed to the wooden table. As if Upper Normandy could be reduced to the size of the café in Haroncourt.

'But you watch out,' Robert added. 'Over there in Calvados, they'll tell you different. But don't you listen to them.'

'All right,' Adamsberg promised.

'And over there, it rains all the time, poor sods.'

Adamsberg looked up at the windows, against which the rain was beating continuously.

'There's rain and rain,' Oswald explained. 'Here, it doesn't rain, it's just a bit damp. Don't you have them where you come from? Outsiders?'

'Yes,' Adamsberg agreed. 'There's bad feeling between the people in the Gave de Pau valley and the Gave d'Ossau valley.'

'Yeah, course there is,' agreed Anglebert, as if he already knew all about that.

Although he was well used to the ponderous music of the evening male ritual, Adamsberg understood that the Normans, true to their reputation, were more difficult to get through to than other people. They didn't say much. Here their sentences came out cautiously and suspiciously, as if testing the ground with every word. They didn't speak loudly, nor did they tackle their subjects head-on. They went round them, as if putting a subject directly on the table was as indelicate as throwing down a piece of raw meat.

'So why is that crap?' Adamsberg asked, pointing to the antlers over the door.

'Because those are *cast* antlers. OK for decoration, to show off. Go and have a look if you don't believe me. You can see the bump at the base of the bone.'

'It's a bone?'

'Don't know a thing, do you?' said Alphonse sadly, sounding regretful that Angelbert had allowed this ignoramus to join them.

'Yes, it's a bone,' the old man confirmed. 'It grows out of the skull – only the deer family does that.'

'What if *we* had skulls that bulged out?' wondered Robert fancifully.

'With ideas growing on 'em,' said Oswald with a thin smile.

'Wouldn't be a big bulge in your case, Oswald.'

'Practical for the cops,' said Adamsberg. 'But risky. You'd be able to read people's thoughts.'

'Stands to reason.'

There was a pause for thought and for a third round of drinks.

'So what *do* you know about? Apart from police stuff?' asked Oswald.

'No questions,' decreed Robert. 'He knows what he knows. He's asking you what you know about.'

'Women,' said Oswald.

'So does he. Or he wouldn't have lost his.'

'Stands to reason.'

'There's knowing about women and knowing about love, and it's not the same thing. Specially with women.'

Anglebert sat up as if dispelling a memory.

'Explain it to him,' he said, gesturing towards Hilaire and tapping his finger on the photo of the stag that had been slit open.

'Right. So a red deer stag, he loses his antlers every year.'

'What for?'

''Cos they get in the way. The only reason to have antlers is for the rut, to get the hinds. So when the rutting season's over, they fall off.'

'What a pity,' said Adamsberg, 'when they're so beautiful.'

'Like everything beautiful,' said Anglebert, 'they're complicated.

They're heavy, you got to understand, and they catch on the branches. So after the fighting they fall off.'

'It's like laying down his arms, if you like. He's got his females, he drops his weapons.'

'Females, now, they're complicated,' said Robert, still pursuing his train of thought.

'But beautiful.'

'Like I said,' muttered the old man, 'more beautiful they are, more complicated. No good trying to understand everything in this world.'

'No, right,' said Adamsberg.

'Ah, well.'

Four of the men took a mouthful of wine at the same time, with no apparent coordination.

'So it falls off, and that's what we call cast antlers,' Hilaire went on. 'You can find them in the forests like mushrooms. But antlers from a kill, they've been cut off from the animal you hunted. See? *Living* bone.'

'And this killer doesn't care about living bone,' said Adamsberg, returning to the murdered stag. 'He's just interested in death. Or the heart.'

'That he is.'

IX

ADAMSBERG TRIED TO EXPEL THE STAG FROM HIS MIND. HE DIDN'T WANT TO go into the hotel room with all that blood in his head. He paused in front of the door, wiping his thoughts, clearing his brow, and forcing himself to think about clouds, marbles and blue skies. Because in the hotel room a child aged nine months was asleep. And with children you never know. They can penetrate your skull, hear the ideas moving around, feel the sweat of anguish and maybe even see a picture of a slaughtered stag in their father's head.

He pushed the door open quietly. He had not told the male assembly the truth. Accompanying, yes, out of consideration, yes, but so as to babysit the child, while Camille played her viola up at the chateau. Their last break-up – had it been the fifth or the seventh? he wasn't sure – had led to an unforeseen catastrophe. Camille had become a good friend, a comrade, something that drove him to desperation. Towards him she was absent-minded, smiling, affectionate and familiar: in short, and tragically, just a good friend. This new state of affairs disconcerted Adamsberg who was trying to find the fault line, to dislodge the feeling beating under this natural mask, like a crab under a rock. But Camille seemed really to be walking away into the distance, freed of her former stress. And as he said to himself, as he greeted her with a polite kiss, trying to bring an exhausted friend back towards a renewal of love was a near-impossible task. He was therefore concentrating, in a fatalist manner and to his own surprise, on his paternal function. He was a beginner in that domain, and was still trying to assimilate the information that the child was his son. He thought he would have put in as much effort if he had found the baby on a park bench.

'He's not asleep yet,' said Camille, putting on her formal black jacket. 'I'll read him a story. I've brought a book.'

Adamsberg pulled a large volume out of his overnight bag. The fourth of his sisters had taken it upon herself to try and cultivate his mind and complicate his life. She had packed for him a four-hundred-page book on architecture in the Pyrenees, something he had no interest in, and given him the assignment of reading it and telling her what he thought of it. His sisters were the only people Adamsberg obeyed.

'*Buildings of the Béarn,*' he read. '*Traditional techniques from the twelfth to the nineteenth century.*'

Camille shrugged and smiled, unmistakably taking on the role of a sympathetic friend. As long as the child went to sleep – and on this point she trusted Adamsberg absolutely – his oddities didn't matter. Her thoughts were entirely concentrated on the concert that evening – a heaven-sent engagement for her, and no doubt due to Yolande's regular prayers to the Powers-that-be.

'He likes this one,' Adamsberg said.

'Yes, why not?'

No criticism, no irony. The blank neutrality of authentic friendship.

Once he was alone, Adamsberg examined his son, who was looking at him with a philosophical expression – if that can be said of a nine-month-old baby. The child's concentration on something far away, his indifference to little worries, even his placid absence of desires concerned Adamsberg, since so much of that resembled him. Not to mention the dark eyebrows, the nose which looked as if it would later be dominant, and a face so unusual in every respect that he looked two years older than his age. Thomas Adamsberg was a chip off the old block, which was not what the *commissaire* would have wished on him. But through the resemblance, Adamsberg was starting to see, in fits and starts, that this child really was the fruit of his own loins.

He opened the book at the page marked by the metro ticket. He usually turned down the corner of the page, but his sister had asked him not to spoil this book.

'Tom, now listen to me, we're both going to be educated, we've got no choice. Remember what I read you last time about north-facing façades? Remember all that? Now, this is how it goes on.'

Thomas looked up calmly at his father, his expression attentive but indifferent.

'. . . *"The use of stones from the river bed to build walls, a combinatory approach indicating an organisation adapted to local resources, is a widespread, though not universal practice."* Like the sound of that, Tom? *"The introduction of the opus piscatum into many of these walls constitutes a compensatory mechanism, occasioned by the small dimensions of the materials and the weakness of the unstable mortar."'*

Adamsberg put the book down, meeting his son's gaze.

'I don't know what the hell the *"opus spicatum"* is, son, and I don't care. So we can agree about that. But I'm going to teach you how we resolve a problem like this when it crops up in our lives. How to proceed when you don't understand something. Just watch.'

Adamsberg took out his mobile and slowly tapped out a number under the child's unconcerned eyes.

'What you do is you call Danglard,' he explained. 'It's quite simple. Just remember that, always keep his phone number about you. He can fix anything in this line of country. You'll see, just pay attention now.'

'Danglard? Adamsberg. I'm sorry to disturb you, but the little one doesn't understand this word, and needs an explanation.'

'Go ahead,' said Danglard wearily. He was used to the *commissaire's* wayward habits. He had implicitly been given the mission of dealing with them.

'*Opus spicatum*. He wants to know what that means.'

'No, he doesn't – he's only nine months old, for God's sake.'

'I'm not joking, *capitaine*, he wants to know.'

'*Commandant*,' Danglard corrected.

'Danglard, are you going to harp on about your rank for ever? *Capitaine* or *commandant*, does that really matter between us? Anyway, that isn't the question. The question concerns the *opus spicatum*.'

'*Piscatum*,' Danglard corrected.

'OK. It's some sort of *opus* they put in village walls by some compensatorily occasioned mechanism. Tom and I are stuck in this place, and we can't think about anything else. Except that in Brétilly, a month ago, someone demolished a stag and didn't even take the antlers, but cut out the heart. What does that say to you?'

'Some crazy lunatic,' said Danglard, gloomily.

'Exactly. That's what Robert said too.'

'Who's Robert?'

Danglard might curse as much as he liked every time Adamsberg called him up for some inconsequential trifle, but he could never tear himself away from the conversation, assert himself, or get cross and hang up. The *commissaire*'s voice, like a slow, gentle and embracing breeze, carried his will-power along like a leaf on the ground, or one of the damned pebbles in the damned river. Danglard reproached himself for this, but in the end he always gave way. The water wins in the end.

'Robert's a new friend I've made in Haroncourt.'

There was no need to tell Danglard where the little village of Haroncourt was. With his compendious and encyclopedically organised memory, the *commandant* knew all the districts and municipalities in France, and could tell you at once who was the local police chief.

'Had a good evening, then?'

'Very.'

'Is she still just good friends?' Danglard hazarded.

'Alas, yes. The *opus spicatum*, Danglard, that's where we were.'

'*Piscatum*. If you're educating him, at least try to do it correctly.'

'That's why I'm calling you. Robert thinks it was just some young nutter who did the deed. But Angelbert, who's the elder statesman round here, isn't so sure – he thinks a young nutter can turn into an old one.'

'And this high-level conference took place where?

'In the café, at aperitif time.'

'How many glasses of wine?'

'Three. What about you?'

Danglard stiffened. The *commissaire* was keeping an eye on his drinking problem, and that rankled.

'I'm not asking you about *your* way of life, *commissaire*.'

'Yes, you are, you asked if Camille was still just a good friend.'

'OK,' said Danglard, giving in. 'The *opus piscatum* is a way of mounting flat stones – or tiles or pebbles – obliquely so that it looks like a herringbone, hence its name, which comes from the Latin for fish. It goes back to the Romans.'

'Ah. And then what?'

'Then nothing. You asked me a question, I gave you the answer.'

'But what's it *for*, Danglard?'

'Well, *commissaire*, what are *we* for? Why are we on this earth?'

When Danglard was in a bad way, the Unsolved Question of the infinite cosmos returned to plague him, as well as the fact that the sun would explode in four billion years, and that humanity was but a miserable and desperate chance occurrence on a piece of matter whirling through space.

'Is there anything precise that's depressing you?' asked Adamberg, anxiously.

'I'm just depressed, that's all.'

'The kids are asleep?'

'Yes.'

'Go out, then, Danglard, go and find an Oswald or an Anglebert. There are plenty of them in Paris as well as here.'

'Not with names like that, there aren't. And anyway, what could they tell me?'

'That cast-off antlers aren't as highly prized as antlers from a hunted stag.'

'I know that already.'

'That it's only members of the deer family that have a bone growing out of their forehead.'

'Know that, too.'

'That *Lieutenant* Retancourt is sure not to be asleep, and that it would be beneficial to go chat with her for an hour.'

'Yes, that's probably correct,' said Danglard after a silence.

Adamsberg heard a little more optimism in his deputy's voice, and hung up.

'See, Tom,' he said, cradling the baby's head in his hand, 'they put a herringbone in a wall, and don't ask me why. We don't need to know that, because Danglard knows all about it. Let's give up on this book – it's boring.'

As soon as Adamsberg put his hand round the child's head the baby went off to sleep, as indeed did any other child. Or adult. Thomas's eyes were closed within a few moments, and Adamsberg gently removed his hand, looking in mild puzzlement at his palm. Perhaps one day he would understand through which pores of his skin drowsiness seeped out. Not that it interested him overmuch.

His mobile rang. It was the pathologist, very wide awake, calling from the morgue.

'Wait a minute, Ariane, I just have to put the baby down.'

Whatever the purpose of her call, and it certainly would not be a social one, the fact that Ariane was thinking about him was a distraction in his present state of having no woman on the horizon.

'The gash on the throat – we're talking about Diala now – is horizontal.

The hand holding the blade was therefore neither high above the point of impact nor well below, or the wound would have been slanting. Like in Le Havre. You follow me?'

'Yes,' said Adamsberg, playing with the baby's toes, which were like little round peas in a pod. He lay down on the bed to listen to Ariane's voice. To tell the truth, he didn't much care about the techniques she must have used, he simply wanted to know why she was so sure it was a woman.

'Diala stood one metre eighty-six. The base of his carotid artery would be one metre fifty-four from the ground.'

'Well, what does that tell us?'

'The cut would be horizontal if the aggressor's clenched fist holding the knife was below his eyes. That would give us an aggressor of one metre sixty-six. If we do the same calculation for La Paille, where there's a slight downward trajectory, we get a killer of between one metre sixty-four and one metre sixty-five. But perhaps one metre sixty-two, if we take high heels into account.'

'A hundred and sixty-two centimetres,' said Adamsberg pointlessly.

'That's well below the average height for a man. It's got to be a woman, Jean-Baptiste. And as for the syringe marks on the arm, they both punctured the vein very precisely.'

'You're thinking it's a professional?'

'Yes, using a medical syringe. The very fine gauge and the angle of the insertion mean it wasn't just any old needle.'

'So someone injected them with something before they died?'

'No, nothing. Nothing at all was injected.'

'Nothing? Air do you mean?'

'Air would definitely be *something*. No, this person didn't inject them with anything, just made a jab.'

'Without having time to finish?'

'Or without needing to. She jabbed them after they were dead, Jean-Baptiste.'

Adamsberg hung up, thoughtfully. Thinking of old Lucio and wondering whether at this very moment Diala and La Paille were trying to scratch an unfinished injection in their dead arms.

X

ON THE MORNING OF 21 MARCH, THE *COMMISSAIRE* TOOK THE TIME TO greet every tree and little branch on his new route to work, from the house to the office. Even in the rain, which had not stopped since that hailstorm over Joan of Arc, the date deserved effort and respect. Even if, like this year, Spring was late, perhaps on account of some previous engagement. Or maybe she had slept in, as Danglard did one day in three. Spring is capricious, Adamsberg thought, you can't expect her to arrive punctually on the morning of 21 March, when you think of the astronomical quantity of buds she has to deal with, not to mention all those larvae, roots and seeds, things you can't see but that must certainly take up a huge amount of her energy. By comparison, the non-stop work of the Crime Squad was negligible, a joke really. A joke that gave Adamsberg a good conscience while he took his time walking through the streets.

As the *commissaire* strolled at a leisurely pace across the large shared hall known to the staff as the Council Chamber, to place a sprig of forsythia on the desks of the six female officers, Danglard came rushing to meet him. The *commandant*'s shambling body – which seemed to have melted like a candle, wiping out his shoulders, making his torso shapeless and his legs crooked – was not suited to rapid walking. Adamsberg always watched with interest when he tackled long distances, wondering whether one day he would lose one of his limbs in the process.

'We've been looking for you,' puffed Danglard.

'I was paying homage, *capitaine*, and just now I'm paying my respects.'

'But for heaven's sake, it's after eleven.'

'The dead aren't going to quibble over a couple of hours. My appointment with Ariane isn't until four o'clock. She sleeps in all morning. Be careful not to forget that.'

'It's nothing to do with the deaths. It's the New Recruit. He's been waiting for you for two hours. This is the third time he's made an appointment to see you. And when he turns up, he's left sitting on a chair as if you couldn't care less.'

'Sorry, Danglard, I had an important rendezvous that was fixed a year ago.'

'With?'

'With the Spring. She's touchy. If you forget her, she's liable to go off and sulk. Then it's no good trying to catch her. But the New Recruit will be back. Anyway, which New Recruit are we talking about?'

'Oh for God's sake, the one who's replacing Favre. Two hours he waited.'

'What's he like?'

'Red-haired.'

'Good, that makes a change.'

'Actually his hair's dark, but it has ginger stripes in it, sort of black-and-tan effect. Odd-looking, I've never seen anything like it before.'

'All the better,' said Adamsberg, putting his last flower on the desk belonging to Violette Retancourt. 'If we have to have New Recruits, best they should be *really* new, out of the ordinary.'

Danglard thrust his gangling arms into the pockets of his elegant jacket and watched as the massive *Lieutenant* Retancourt put the little yellow flower in her buttonhole.

'This one seems rather *too* out of the ordinary, perhaps,' he said. 'Have you read his file?'

'Dipped into it. At any rate he's here on probation for six months, whether we like it or not.'

Before Adamsberg could open his office door, Danglard held him back.

'He's not there any longer, he's gone off on duty to the broom cupboard.'

'He's guarding Camille? Why's that? I asked for experienced officers.'

'Because he's the only one who will put up with that damn cubbyhole on the landing. The others are all fed up with it.'

'And since he's new, the others have landed him with it.'

'Correct.'

'Since when?'

'Since three weeks ago.'

'Send Retancourt. To protect Camille. She can stand anything, even the broom cupboard.'

'She did offer. But there's a problem.'

'I don't see any problem that would hold Retancourt up.'

'Just the one. She can't turn round in the space.'

'Ah, too big,' said Adamsberg pensively.

'Too big,' Danglard confirmed.

'It was her magical size that saved my life, Danglard.'

'Maybe so, but she can't fit into that cupboard and that's that. So she can't take over from the New Recruit.'

'OK, *capitaine*, I get it. How old is he, this New Recruit?'

'Forty-three.'

'What's he like?'

'From what point of view?'

'Aesthetic, seductional.'

'There's no such word as "seductional".'

The *commandant* ran his hand over the back of his neck, showing his embarrassment. Sophisticated as Danglard's mental processes were, he was, like all men, reluctant to comment on the physical appearance of other men, pretending he hadn't noticed anything. Adamsberg, on the other hand, really wanted to know what the man looked like who had been allowed to sit for three weeks on Camille's landing.

'What's he look like?' Adamsberg persisted.

'Quite good-looking,' Danglard admitted reluctantly.

'Not my lucky day, then.'

'You could say that. It's not Camille that I'm worried about, though, it's Retancourt.'

'She's susceptible?'

'So they say.'

'Quite good-looking in what way?'

'Built like a tree trunk, crooked smile, melancholy expression.'

'Certainly not my lucky day,' commented Adamsberg again.

'Well, you can't go round killing all the other men in the world.'

'One could perhaps go round killing all the ones with melancholy expressions.'

'Conference time,' Danglard announced abruptly, looking at his watch.

Danglard was of course responsible for giving the name 'Council Chamber' to the large room in which they held meetings, in this case a general assembly of the twenty-seven officers in the squad. But the *commandant* had never owned up to it. Similarly he had planted the term 'conference' in the minds of his fellow officers, instead of 'meeting' which he found off-putting. Adrien Danglard's intellectual authority carried such weight that everyone accepted his dictates without questioning their appropriateness. Like a medicine taken in full confidence, the new words that the *commandant* introduced were absorbed without qualm, and were so rapidly integrated that they became irreversible.

Danglard pretended not to be involved with these small alterations to the language. To listen to him, these slightly pompous terms had risen up through the ages, impregnating the buildings like ancient moisture sweating out of the walls through the cellars. A perfectly plausible explanation, according to Adamsberg. Why not? Danglard had replied.

The conference was due to discuss the two murders at La Chapelle and the death of a sixty-year-old woman from a heart attack in a lift. Adamsberg made a quick head count. Three were missing.

'Where are Kernorkian, Mercadet and Justin?'

'In the *Brasserie des Philosophes*,' explained Estalère. 'They'll be finished in a minute.'

The number of murders with which the Serious Crime Squad had had to deal in two years had not yet extinguished the astonished cheerfulness that beamed out of Estalère's green eyes. He was the youngest member of the team. Tall and thin, Estalère had attached himself to the ample and indestructible Violette Retancourt, whom he worshipped with a near-religious passion and from whom he rarely strayed more than a few feet away.

'Well, tell them to get up here quickly,' ordered Danglard. 'I don't suppose they're finishing a philosophical debate.'

'No, *commandant*, just their cups of coffee.'

As far as Adamsberg was concerned, whether it was called a conference or a meeting mattered little. He was not suited to collective discussions and was disinclined to distribute tasks. These general briefings bored him so intensely that he could scarcely remember having followed a single one from beginning to end. Sooner or later, his thoughts would leave the table, and from far away (but where?) meaningless fragments of sentences would reach him, about taking names and addresses, questioning suspects, putting tails on people. Danglard watched the degree of absent-mindedness in the *commissaire*'s brown eyes and nudged him when it reached critical level. As he had done just now. Adamsberg recognised the signals and returned to earth, emerging from what some would term a state of blankness but which was for him a vital safety valve, allowing him to explore uncharted directions on his own. Pointless ones, Danglard opined. Yes, pointless, Adamsberg agreed. They were coming to a conclusion in the case of the sixty-year-old woman, thanks to some good detective work by *lieutenants* Voisenet and Maurel, who had smelled a rat and discovered that the lift's mechanism had been tampered with. The arrest of her husband was imminent, and the drama was reaching its conclusion, leaving in Adamsberg's mind a trail of sadness, as always when he encountered everyday brutality at a turn on the stair.

The investigation into the murders at La Chapelle was currently classified as following up a couple of routine underworld killings. It was now eleven days since the tall black man and the hefty white man had been discovered lying dead, each one in a cul-de-sac, the first in the Impasse du Gué, the second in the Impasse du Curé. It had now been established that Diala Toundé, aged twenty-four, had sold trinkets and belts under the bridge at the edge of the Clignancourt quarter, while the white man, Didier Paillot, known as La Paille, twenty-two, tried to engage passers-by with his card tricks in the main alleyway in the Flea Market. The two men did not apparently know each other, and their common denominator was that they were both massively built and had dirt under their fingernails. On account of which, Adamsberg, flying in the face of reason, had obstinately refused to pass the case over to the Drug Squad.

Questioning residents in the buildings where both men lived – labyrinths of cold rooms, and non-functioning lavatories in dark stairwells – had produced nothing, nor had visits to all the cafés in the sector from the Porte de la Chapelle to Clignancourt. Both mothers, who were devastated, had claimed that their boys were the best of sons, one showing off a nail-clipper and the other a shawl which they had been given only the month before. *Brigadier* Lamarre, overcome with timidity, had returned to base very upset.

'Their old mothers,' said Adamsberg. 'If only the real world was like the dreams of old mothers.'

A nostalgic silence hung for a moment over the conference, as if each person present was remembering what the dream of his or her old mother had been, and whether he or she had lived up to it, and if not by what margin the reality had fallen short.

Retancourt had come no nearer than anyone else to fulfilling the dreams of her old mother, who had hoped her daughter would be a blonde air hostess, calming and charming airline passengers; a hope that her daughter's height of one metre eighty and weight of a hundred and twenty kilos had ruled out after puberty, leaving only the blonde hair – and an ability to calm people which was indeed out of the ordinary. Retancourt had made a small inroad, two days earlier, into the obstructions that seemed to be blocking this inquiry.

After a week of getting nowhere, Adamsberg had taken Retancourt off the almost finished case of a family murder in an elegant dwelling in Reims and had sent her to Clignancourt, rather as one might try a magic potion as a last resort, without being sure what to expect from it. He had sent *Lieutenant* Noël with her, a hefty, broad-shouldered and leather-jacketed character with protruding ears, a man with whom he did not get on well. But Noël was, he thought, suitable for protecting Retancourt on this difficult assignment. In the end, and he really ought to have expected it, it was Retancourt who had come to Noël's rescue, after their inquiries in a café had degenerated into a brawl that spilled out into the street. Retancourt's massive intervention had calmed down the group of angry men and she'd pulled Noël free from the three individuals who seemed bent on making him eat his birth certificate. Her talent for resolving matters had impressed the bistro owner, who was getting tired of the fights that often broke out in his establishment. Forgetting the rule of silence in the Flea Market district, and possibly moved by an admiration of the same order as that felt by Estalère, he had come running after Retancourt to get something off his chest.

Before making her report, Retancourt untied and redid her short ponytail, the only trace, Adamsberg thought, of her childhood shyness.

'According to Emilio – that's the café owner – it's true that Diala and La Paille weren't normally seen together. Although they operated only about five hundred metres apart, they weren't working the same zones in the market. The geographical divisions of the *quartier* mean that various tribes who shouldn't mix are kept apart, or there might be trouble and reprisals. Emilio says that if Diala and La Paille got involved in something together, it wouldn't have been on their own initiative, it must have been through some other person, a stranger to the ways of the market.'

'An outsider,' said Lamarre, for once abandoning his usual reserved approach.

Which reminded Adamsberg that the timid Lamarre came from Granville – from Lower Normandy, therefore.

'Emilio thinks that this stranger might have chosen them because of their brute strength: for some raid, or perhaps to intimidate or beat someone up. But at any rate, whatever it was turned out well, because two days before the murders they turned up for a drink in his bistro. It was the first time he'd ever seen them together. It was nearly two in the morning, and Emilio wanted to shut up shop. But he didn't dare say no to them, because the pair of them were well launched – they were big lads and they'd already had way too much to drink.'

'We didn't find any money on them, or in their lodgings.'

'Maybe the murderer took it back from them.'

'Did Emilio hear what they said?'

'He wasn't particularly listening, he was just going to and fro, clearing up. But these two were alone in the café, they weren't taking any precautions, and were laughing and shouting at the tops of their voices. In the end, he had to tell them to shut up, they were shouting loud enough to waken the dead, never mind his mother upstairs. That just made them fall about laughing all the more, they nearly pissed themselves. Emilio gathered that they'd had some work that was very well paid, and had only taken an evening. No mention of any fight or anything. It was on the other side of Paris, in Montrouge, and their boss had just left them there once the job was done. Montrouge, Emilio's sure about that. He fixed them some sandwiches and they finally pushed off at about three o'clock in the morning.'

'Perhaps they had to deliver or collect some heavy consignment,' suggested Justin.

'It doesn't sound like drugs to me,' Adamsberg said, obstinately.

The previous night, in Normandy, he had refused to answer the *n*th call from Mortier. He could have told Mortier that one of the mothers swore blind that her son, Diala, didn't touch drugs. But for the head of the Drug Squad, the fact that someone had a black mother at all was enough to create a presumption of guilt. Adamsberg had managed to obtain from his *divisionnaire* a delay before he had to hand over the file, and the deadline was in two days.

'Retancourt,' said the *commissaire*, 'did Emilio notice anything about their hands, or their clothes? I'm thinking mud or earth.'

'Don't know.'

'Call him.'

Danglard announced a break. Estalère jumped up. The *brigadier* had a passion for things that interested nobody else, such as memorising personal preferences. He brought out twenty-eight plastic cups on three trays, putting in front of each officer his or her favourite drink – coffee, chocolate, tea, large, medium or small, with or without milk and sugar – without making a single mistake. He knew that Retancourt liked her coffee black and without sugar, but that she liked to have a spoon to stir it with. He would not have forgotten the spoon for the world. Nobody knew why this chore gave such innocent pleasure to Estalère, who had something of the medieval page-boy about him.

Retancourt came back, holding her phone, and Estalère pushed towards her a cup of sugarless coffee and a spoon. She smiled her thanks, and the young man sat down happily at her side. Of them all, Estalère still did not seem to have fully grasped that he was working on serious crimes, but went about in the team like a happy teenager, glad to be one of the gang. He would have slept there if he could.

'Yes, they had dirty hands, stained with earth,' Retancourt announced.

'Shoes as well. After they had gone, Emilio had to sweep up dried mud and bits of gravel they had left under their table.'

'What's the idea?' asked Mordent, poking his head up from his stooping shoulders, like a great grey heron sitting at the table. 'Had they been digging up a garden or something?'

'Digging in the earth, at any rate.'

'Should we start looking in all the parks and waste ground in Montrouge?'

'But what would they have been doing in a park? With something heavy?'

'Go and take a look anyway,' said Adamsberg, giving up and suddenly losing interest in the conference.

'Perhaps they had a trunk to move somewhere?' suggested Mercadet.

'What the heck would they be doing with a trunk in a garden?'

'Well, something else that's heavy,' said Justin. 'Heavy enough to need two big guys who wouldn't ask too many questions.'

'But the job must have been so important that someone wanted to shut them up afterwards,' Noël pointed out.

'Digging a hole, burying a body,' suggested Kernorkian.

'If you were going to do that,' said Mordent, 'you'd hardly hire two strangers, would you? You'd do it on your own.'

'A heavy object, then,' suggested Lamarre mildly. 'Bronze, stone, a statue, perhaps?'

'What would you bury a statue for, Lamarre?'

'I didn't say I'd bury a statue.'

'Well, what would you be doing with a statue?'

'I'd have stolen it from some public place,' said Lamarre after thinking for a moment. 'I'd get it taken somewhere to hide it, then I'd sell it. There's a market for stolen works of art. Know how much you'd get for a statue off the façade of Notre-Dame?'

'They're all nineteenth-century copies,' Danglard interjected. 'You'd do better to try Chartres.'

'OK, know how much you'd get for a statue from Chartres Cathedral?'

'No, how much?'

'How should I know? But thousands, I bet.'

Adamsberg heard only fragments of this discussion – park, statue, thousands – until Danglard nudged him.

'What we'll do is start from the other end first,' he said, sipping his coffee. 'Retancourt will go back to Emilio. She'll take Estalère who has good eyesight, and the New Recruit because he's in training.'

'The New Recruit's in the broom cupboard.'

'Well, we'll get him out of there.'

'He's been in the force for eleven years,' said Noël. 'He doesn't need lessons like a schoolkid.'

'Some training in working with all of *you*, Noël, isn't the same thing.'

'What are we supposed to be looking for at Emilio's?' asked Retancourt.

'The remains of the gravel they left on the floor.'

'But *commissaire*, it's almost a fortnight since the men were in the café.'

'What sort of floor is it? Tiled?'

'Yes, black and white.'

'Of course,' said Noël, with a shout of laughter.

'Ever tried to sweep up gravel? Without losing a single piece? Emilio's bistro won't be a palace. With a bit of luck, some of that gravel will have got into a corner and stuck there, waiting for us to find it.'

'So if I've got this right,' Retancourt said, 'we've got to go up there and look for a little bit of stone?'

Sometimes Retancourt's old hostility to Adamsberg surfaced, although their relations had been transformed, during a previous case, by an exceptional episode of close bodily contact which had welded the *lieutenant* and the *commissaire* together for life. But Retancourt was one of the positivists, and considered that Adamsberg's mysterious directives obliged members of the squad to operate too much in the dark. She reproached the *commissaire* with insulting the intelligence of his colleagues and failing to make the effort to clarify for them where he was heading, or to throw them a gangplank across the marshes of his thoughts. For the simple reason, as she well knew, that he was incapable of it. The *commissaire* smiled at her.

'You've got it, *lieutenant*. A patient little white stone waiting in the dark forest. It will take us straight to the crime scene, just like the stones in Tom Thumb.'

'That's not quite right,' pointed out Mordent, who was a specialist in myths, legends and indeed horror stories. 'The pebbles help Tom Thumb to find his way back *home*, not to the Ogre's house.'

'OK, Mordent. But what we want to find is the Ogre. So we're doing it the other way round. Didn't the six other boys end up in the Ogre's house anyway?'

'Seven,' said Mordent pedantically, raising seven fingers. 'But if they found the Ogre, it was precisely because they couldn't find the pebbles.'

'Well, we're going to look for them.'

'If these pebbles exist,' added Retancourt.

'Of course.'

'And if they don't?'

'They do, Retancourt.'

And on this firm statement from Adamsberg's private Mount Olympus, to which no other mortal had access, the conference on La Chapelle ended. There was a scraping of chairs, the plastic cups were thrown away and Adamsberg called Noël over.

'Noël, stop bellyaching,' he said gently.

'She didn't need to rescue me. I'd have got out of it by myself.'

'Three guys with iron bars? Come off it, Noël.'

'I didn't need Retancourt to go playing the US cavalry.'

'Yes, you did. There's no dishonour in it just because she's a woman.'

'I don't consider her a woman. She's the size of an ox, for God's sake – she's a freak of nature. I don't owe her.'

Adamsberg rubbed his cheek with the back of his hand, as if testing his shave, the signal of a crack in his phlegmatic façade.

'Let me remind you, *lieutenant*, why Favre had to leave this outfit, after his persistent troublemaking. Just because his place is empty, there's no need for someone else to try and fill it.'

'I'm not taking Favre's place, I've got a perfectly good one of my own, and I'll do things my way.'

'Not here, Noël. If you do things your way and they clash with ours, you'll have to do it somewhere else. With the more limited members of the force.'

'Limited? Did you hear Estalère? And Lamarre burbling about statues? And Mordent with his blessed Ogre?'

Adamsberg consulted his two watches.

'I'll give you two and a half hours to go for a walk and clear your head. Go down to the Seine, take a long look at it and come back.'

'I've got reports to finish,' said Noël, hunching his shoulders in protest.

'You didn't understand me, *lieutenant*. That's an order, and a mission. You go out, and you come back in a sane frame of mind. And you'll do it every day if necessary, for a year if necessary, until looking at the seagulls over the river tells you something. Just go now, Noël, and keep out of my sight.'

XI

BEFORE GOING INTO CAMILLE'S BLOCK OF FLATS TO EXTRACT THE NEW RECRUIT, Adamsberg peered at his own eyes in a nearby car mirror. OK, he thought, straightening up. If he looks melancholy, I look melancholy in spades.

He climbed the seven floors to Camille's studio and approached her door. There were muffled sounds of life. Camille was trying to get the child to sleep. He had explained to her how to cup the baby's head in her hand, but it didn't seem to work for her. He had an advantage on that score, if nowhere else.

On the other hand, there was no sound coming from the broom cupboard which was being used as the sentry box for the duty officer. The quite good-looking New Recruit with the melancholy air must have gone to sleep. Instead of watching over Camille's safety, as his mission demanded. Adamsberg knocked on the door, tempted to give him an unfair dressing-down – unfair since it was obvious that being cooped up in that little cubicle for hours on end would have made anyone fall asleep, especially someone given to melancholy.

But there was no need. The New Recruit opened the door at once, cigarette in hand, and nodded briefly in recognition. Neither deferential nor nervous, he was simply trying to collect his thoughts rapidly, as one herds sheep into a fold. Adamsberg shook hands with him, while observing him candidly. A mild-looking man, but not all that mild.

Energy and a certain potential for anger lay behind those eyes which were indeed melancholic. As for his features, Danglard had painted too depressing a picture, professional pessimist that he was, giving up the battle before it had started. Yes, he was *quite* good-looking, but only up to a point, and then only if you were disposed in his favour. And this man was hardly any taller than himself. He was certainly more heavily built, both his face and body carrying a certain amount of soft tissue.

'I'm sorry,' said Adamsberg, 'I missed our appointment.'

'It doesn't matter. I was told something urgent had come up.'

The voice was well pitched, light and slightly husky. Quite pleasant. The New Recruit stubbed out his cigarette in a pocket ashtray.

'Yes, it was very urgent.'

'Another murder?'

'No, the first day of spring.'

'OK,' said the New Recruit, after a slight pause.

'How's this guard duty going?'

'Long and monotonous.'

'Not interesting?'

'Not at all.'

Perfect, thought Adamsberg. He was in luck. The man was blind, unable to spot that Camille was one in a thousand.

'We'll suspend it, then. I'll get a team from the thirteenth *arrondissement* to relieve you.'

'When?'

'Right away.'

The New Recruit glanced at the broom cupboard and Adamsberg wondered whether he was regretting something. But no, it was just his generally melancholy expression that suggested he clung on to things longer than other people. He picked up his books and came out without looking back, nor did he so much as glance at Camille's door. Blind and probably insensitive too.

Adamsberg pressed the light switch and sat down on the top stair, gesturing to his colleague to join him there. His tumultuous life with Camille had given him complete familiarity with this landing and with the entire staircase, to every one of whose steps he had given a name: impatience, negligence, infidelity, pain, remorse, infidelity, reconciliation, remorse, and so on for ever in a spiral.

'How many steps do you think there are on this staircase?' Adamsberg asked. 'Ninety?'

'A hundred and eight.'

'You count stairs do you?'

'I'm methodical – it's in my file.'

'Sit down. I've hardly had time to look through your file yet. You know that you're on probation, and this conversation doesn't alter that.'

The New Recruit nodded and sat down on the wooden stairs, with no sign either of insolence or distress. Under the electric light, Adamsberg could see the ginger stripes in his otherwise dark hair, like strange flashes of light. The New Recruit's hair was so thick and curly that it looked as if it would be difficult to get a comb through it.

'There were plenty of candidates for the job,' Adamsberg began. 'What were the qualities that helped you get it?'

'Pulling strings. I know *Divisionnaire* Brézillon very well. I helped his younger son out of trouble once.'

'A police matter?'

'No, a sexual matter, in the boarding school where I was teaching.'

'So you didn't set out to be a cop?'

'No, I started off in teaching.'

'What ill wind made you change your mind?'

The New Recruit lit a cigarette. His hands were square and compact. Quite attractive.

'A love affair,' Adamsberg guessed.

'Yes, she was in the force, and I thought it would be a good thing to join her. But by trailing after her I lost her, and I got stuck with the police.'

'Pity.'

'Yes.'

'Why did you want this job? To get to Paris?'

'No.'

'To join the Serious Crime Squad?'

'Yes. I made inquiries, and it suited me.'

'What did your inquiries tell you?'

'Lots of things, some of them contradictory.'

'I haven't made any inquiries about you, though. I don't even know your name, because in the office they're still calling you "the New Recruit".'

'Veyrenc, Louis Veyrenc.'

'Veyrenc,' Adamsberg repeated thoughtfully. 'And where did you get your ginger streaks, Veyrenc? They intrigue me.'

'Me too, *commissaire*.'

The New Recruit had turned his face away quickly, shutting his eyes. The New Recruit had suffered, Adamsberg sensed. Veyrenc blew a puff of smoke up at the ceiling, wondering how to finish his reply and failing to decide. In this arrested pose, his upper lip was raised slightly to the right as if pulled by a thread, a twist which gave him a peculiar charm. That and the dark eyes, reduced to triangles with a comma of long lashes at the corners. A dangerous gift from *Divisionnaire* Brézillon.

'I'm not obliged to answer that question,' Veyrenc said at last.

'No.'

Adamsberg, who had come to fetch his new colleague with no other aim than to dislodge him from Camille's door, felt that there was something disturbing about this conversation, without being able to identify why. And yet, he thought, the reason wasn't far away, it was within thinking range. He allowed his gaze to wander over the banisters, the walls, the steps, one by one, down and up again.

He knew that face.

'What did you say your name was?'

'Veyrenc.'

'Veyrenc de Bilhc,' Adamsberg corrected him. 'Your full name's Louis Veyrenc de Bilhc.'

'Yes, it's in the file.'

'Where were you born?'

'Arras.'

'An accident of birth, I presume, during an absence from home. You're not a northerner.'

'Maybe not.'

'Definitely not. You're a Gascon, a Béarnais.'

'Yes, that's true.'

'Of course it's true. A Béarnais from the Gave d'Ossau valley.'

The New Recruit closed his eyes quickly, as if making a tiny movement of retreat.

'How do you know?'

'If you have the name of a wine, you're likely to be easy to place. The Veyrenc de Bilhc grapes grow on the slopes of the Ossau valley.'

'Is that a problem?'

'Possibly. Gascons aren't the easiest of people to deal with. Melancholy, solitary, mild, hardworking, ironic and stubborn. It's a nature which is quite interesting if you can put up with it. I know some people who can't.'

'Yourself, for instance? You've got something against the Béarnais?'

'Obviously. Think, *lieutenant*.'

The New Recruit drew back a little, as an animal withdraws better to consider the enemy.

'The Veyrenc de Bilhc vintage is not very well known,' he said.

'Not known at all.'

'Except by a few wine experts, or people who live in the Ossau valley.'

'And?'

'And possibly the people in the next valley.'

'For instance?'

'The Gave de Pau valley.'

'It wasn't exactly rocket science, was it? Can't you recognise someone else from the Pyrenees when you've got one in front of you?'

'It's a bit dark on this landing.'

'Never mind, I'm not offended.'

'It's just that I don't go round looking for them.'

'What do you think happens when someone from the Ossau valley works in the same outfit as someone from the Gave de Pau valley?'

The two men both took a little time to think, staring at the wall opposite.

'Sometimes,' Adamsberg suggested, 'it's harder to get on with your neighbour than with a perfect stranger.'

'There've been run-ins between the two valleys in the past,' agreed the New Recruit, still looking at the wall.

'Yes. They've been known to kill one another over a scrap of land.'

'Over a blade of grass.'

'Yes.'

The New Recruit got to his feet and paced the landing, with his hands in his pockets. Discussion over, thought Adamsberg. They could pick it up again later, on a different footing. He stood up in turn.

'Close the cupboard and go back to the office. *Lieutenant* Retancourt is waiting to take you to Clignancourt.'

Adamsberg made a sign of farewell and went down the first flight of stairs, feeling annoyed. Sufficiently annoyed for him to have forgotten his little sketchbook on the top stair, so that he had to go back up. On the sixth-floor landing, he heard Veyrenc's elegant voice in the semi-darkness:

> *My lord, take heed to me. Am I so little worth,*
> *That anger without cause should drive me from my place?*
> *Is this the fair welcome they told me I would face,*
> *And am I to suffer, for the land of my birth?*

Adamsberg tiptoed quietly up the last few steps, stupefied.

> '*Is't a fault, or a crime, to have first seen the light*
> *So close to your valley? Am I not then allowed*
> *To have rested my eyes on the same silver cloud?*'

Veyrenc was leaning against the side of the cupboard, head lowered, auburn tears gleaming through his hair.

> '*To have run as a child on the same mountain trails*
> *Which the gods gave to you, and the same deepest vales.*'

Adamsberg watched as his new colleague folded his arms and smiled briefly to himself.

'I see,' said the *commissaire* slowly.

The *lieutenant* gave a start.

'It's in my file,' he said, by way of excuse.

'Under what?'

Veyrenc ran his hands through his hair in embarrassment.

'The *commissaire* at Bordeaux couldn't stand it. Or the one at Tarbes, or the one at Nevers.'

'And you couldn't help it?'

> '*Alas, I cannot, sire, though if I could I would,*
> *But my ancestor's blood runs in my veins for good.*'

'How the hell do you do that? Waking? Sleeping? Hypnosis?'

'Well, it runs in the family,' said Veyrenc rather shortly. 'I just can't help it.'

'Oh, if it runs in the family, that's different.'

Veyrenc twisted his lip, and spread his hands in a fatalist gesture.

'Perhaps you'd better come back to the office with me, *lieutenant*. Maybe the broom cupboard wasn't good for you.'

'That's true,' said Veyrenc, whose heart contracted suddenly as he thought of Camille.

'You know Retancourt? She's the one who's in charge of your induction.'

'Something's cropped up in Clignancourt?'

'It soon will have, if you can find some gravel under a table. She'll tell you about it, and I warn you, she doesn't like the assignment.'

'Why not hand this one over to the Drug Squad?' asked Veyrenc, as he came downstairs alongside the *commissaire*, carrying his books.

Adamsberg lowered his head without replying.

'Perhaps you can't tell me?' the *lieutenant* persisted.

'Yes. But I'm trying to think how to tell you.'

Veyrenc waited, holding the banister. He had heard too much about Adamsberg to be surprised at his odd ways.

'Those deaths are a matter for us,' Adamsberg finally announced. 'Those two men were caught up in some web, some machination. There's a shade hovering over them – they're caught in the folds of its robe.'

Adamsberg looked in perplexity at a precise point on the wall, as if to search there for the words he needed to elaborate his idea. Then he gave up, and the two men continued down to the ground floor, where Adamsberg paused once more.

'Before we go out on to the street, and before we become colleagues, can you tell me where you got the ginger streaks?'

'I don't think you'll like the story.'

'Very few things annoy me, *lieutenant*. And relatively few things upset me. Only one or two shock me.'

'That's what I've heard.'

'It's true.'

'All right. I was attacked when I was a child, up in the vineyard. I was eight years old, and the boys who went for me were about thirteen to fifteen. Five young toughs, a little gang. They hated us.'

'Who's "us"?'

'My father owned the vineyard, the wine was getting itself a reputation, it was competing with someone else's. They pinned me down and cut my head with iron scraps. Then they gashed my belly open with a bit of broken glass.'

Adamsberg, who had started to open the door, stopped still, holding the handle.

'Shall I go on?' asked Veyrenc.

The *commissaire* encouraged him with a nod.

'They left me there, bleeding from the stomach and with fourteen wounds to the scalp. The hair grew back afterwards, but it came out ginger. No explanation. Just a souvenir.'

Adamsberg looked at the floor for a moment, then raised his eyes to meet the *lieutenant*'s.

'And what made you think I wouldn't like the story?'

The New Recruit pursed his lips and Adamsberg observed his dark eyes, which were possibly trying to make him lower his own gaze. They were melancholy, yes, but not always and not with everyone. The two mountain dwellers stood facing each other like two ibex in the Pyrenees, motionless, horns locked in a silent duel. It was the *lieutenant* who, in a movement acknowledging defeat, looked down first.

'Finish the story, Veyrenc.'

'Do I have to?'

'Yes, I think so.'

'Why?'

'Because it's our job to finish stories. If you want to start them, go back to teaching. If you want to finish them, stay being a cop.'

'I see.'

'Of course you see. That's why you're here.'

Veyrenc hesitated, then raised his lip in a false smile.

'The five boys were from the Gave de Pau valley.'

'My valley.'

'Yes.'

'Come on, Veyrenc, finish the story.'

'I have finished it.'

'No, you haven't. The five boys came from the Gave de Pau valley. And they came from the village of Caldhez.'

Adamsberg turned the door handle.

'Come along, Veyrenc,' he said softly. 'We're going to look for a little stone.'

XII

RETANCOURT SANK DOWN WITH ALL HER CONSIDERABLE WEIGHT ON AN OLD plastic chair in Emilio's café.

'Not wanting to be rude,' said Emilio, 'but if the cops turn up here too often, I might as well shut up shop.'

'Just find me a little pebble, Emilio, and we're out of here. Three beers, please.'

'No, just two,' said Estalère. 'I can't drink it,' he said looking at Retancourt and the New Recruit to excuse himself. 'I don't know why, but it goes to my head.'

'But Estalère, it goes to everyone's head,' said Retancourt, who never ceased to be surprised at the naivety of this twenty-seven-year-old boy.

'Really?' said Estalère. 'It's normal?'

'Not only is it normal, it's the whole point.'

Estalère frowned, not wishing at any price to give Retancourt any hint that he was reproaching her with anything. If Retancourt drank beer during working hours, it was not only permitted but obviously recommended.

'We're not on duty now.' Retancourt smiled at him. 'We're looking for a little pebble. Quite different.'

'You're angry with him,' observed the young man.

Retancourt waited until Emilio had brought their beer. She raised her glass to the New Recruit.

'Welcome. I still haven't got your name right.'

'Veyrenc de Bilhc, Louis,' said Estalère, pleased with himself for having remembered the whole name.

'Let's stick with Veyrenc,' proposed Retancourt.

'De Bilhc,' said the New Recruit.

'You're attached to your fancy name?'

'I'm attached to the wine. It's the name of a vintage.'

Veyrenc moved his glass closer to Retancourt's but without clinking it. He had heard a good deal about the extraordinary qualities of Violette Retancourt, but all he could see at present was a tall, very well-built blonde woman, rather down-to-earth and jolly, displaying nothing that enabled him to understand the fear, respect or devotion which she inspired in the squad.

'You're angry with him,' Estalère repeated glumly.

Retancourt shrugged her shoulders. 'Well, I've nothing against going for a beer in Clignancourt. If that amuses him.'

'You're angry with him.'

'So what?'

Estalère bowed his head unhappily. The difference and indeed frequent incompatibility of behaviour between his *commissaire* and his colleague distressed him deeply. The double veneration he felt for both Adamsberg and Retancourt, the twin compasses of his existence, allowed no compromise. He would not have deserted one for the other. The young man's organism functioned entirely on nervous energy, excluding all other forces such as reason, calculation or intellectual interest. And like an engine which can only run on purified fuel, Estalère's was a rare and fragile system. Retancourt knew this, but had neither the subtlety nor the desire to adapt to it.

'He's got some idea in his head,' the young man persisted.

'The file ought to go over to Drugs, Estalère, full stop,' said Retancourt, folding her arms.

'He says not.'

'We're not going to find any stones.'

'He says we will.'

Estalère usually called Adamsberg only by the pronoun – 'He', 'Him' – as if he were the living god of their team.

'Please yourself. Look for this stone wherever you like, but don't expect me to come crawling under the tables with you.'

Retancourt surprised an unexpected sign of revolt in the *brigadier*'s green eyes.

'Yes, I will go and look for the stone,' said the young man, standing up brusquely. 'And not because the entire squad thinks I'm an idiot, you included. But he doesn't. He looks, and he knows. He looks for things.'

Estalère drew breath.

'He's looking for a stone,' said Retancourt.

'Because there are things in stones, their colour, their shape, they tell stories. And you don't see that, Violette, you don't see anything at all.'

'For instance?' asked Retancourt, gripping her glass.

'Think, *lieutenant*.'

And Estalère left the table with a show of teenage rebellion, going to join Emilio who had taken refuge in the back room.

Retancourt swirled her beer round in her glass and looked at the New Recruit.

'He's on a knife-edge,' she said. 'He gets carried away sometimes. You have to understand that he worships Adamsberg. How did your interview with him go? Was it OK?'

'Not exactly.'

'Did he jump from one subject to another?'

'Sort of.'

'He doesn't do it on purpose. He had a very hard time recently in Quebec. What do you think of him?'

Veyrence smiled his crooked smile, and Retancourt appreciated it. She found the New Recruit very attractive, and kept looking at him, checking over his face and body, seeing through his clothes, reversing the usual gender roles by which men mentally undress a pretty girl they see in the street. At thirty-five, Retancourt behaved like an old bachelor at the theatre. Without any risk of involvement, for she had locked up her emotional space in order to avoid any disillusionment. As a girl, Retancourt had already been massively built and she had decided that defeatism was her only defence against hope. That made her the opposite of *Lieutenant* Froissy, who took it for granted that love was the sweetest thing, and that it was waiting for her round every corner – and who, as a result, had accumulated an impressive number of unhappy love affairs.

'I've got a different take on him,' said Veyrenc. 'Adamsberg grew up in the Gave de Pau valley.'

'When you talk like that, you sound like him.'

'Possibly. I'm from the next valley along.'

'Ah,' said Retancourt. 'they say you should never put two Gascons in the same field.'

Estalère walked past them without a glance and went out of the café, slamming the door.

'He's shoved off now,' said Retancourt.

'Gone back without us?'

'Apparently.'

'He's in love with you?'

'He loves me as if I were a man, as if I were what he wants to be and never will be. Big and strong, a tank, a troop carrier. In this outfit, you'd do well to take care of yourself and keep your distance. You've seen them, you've seen us all. Adamsberg and his inaccessible wanderings. Danglard, the walking encyclopedia, who has to run after the *commissaire* to stop the train going off the tracks. Noël, who's a loner and likes being as crude and narrow-minded as he can get away with. Lamarre is so shy he never looks you in the face. Kernorkian's afraid of the dark and germs. Voisenet's a heavyweight, who goes back to his zoology as soon as your back is turned. Justin's a perfectionist, meticulous to the point of paralysis. Adamsberg doesn't always remember which is Voisenet and which is Justin, he's always calling them by the wrong name, but neither one of them minds. Froissy is always unhappy about something or other, and eats to make up for it. Estalère, whom you've met now, is a worshipper. Mercadet's a genius with figures, but he can't keep his eyes open in the afternoon. Mordent's inclined to take a tragic view, and has hundreds of books on stories and legends. I'm the big fat all-purpose cow of the team, according to Noël. So what the heck are you doing in this outfit?'

'It's a project,' said Veyrenc, vaguely. 'You don't like your colleagues, then?'

'Oh yes, of course I do.'

> *'But Madame,*
> *Your words are so bitter, with scorn for all the crew,*
> *Does each one have some fault, or does blame lie with you?'*

Retancourt smiled, then looked sternly at Veyrenc.
'What did you just say?'

> *'You turn on your fellows so pitiless a gaze.*
> *However can they hope one day to win your praise?'*

'Why do you talk like that?'
'It's a habit,' said Veyrenc, smiling in turn.
'What happened to your hair?'
'A car crash – I went head first though the windscreen.'
'Ah,' said Retancourt. 'You tell lies too.'
Estalère came back into the café and strode up to their table on his long thin legs. He pushed back the empty beer glasses, felt in his pocket and put three small grey stones on the table. Retancourt examined them without changing position.

'He said "white", and he said "one",' she said.

'There are three of them and they're grey.'

Retancourt picked up the stones and rolled them around in the palm of her hand.

'Give those back to me, Violette. You're quite capable of keeping them from him.'

Retancourt jerked her head upright, clenching the stones firmly.

'Don't push me too far, Estalère.'

'Why not?'

'Because if it wasn't for me, Adamsberg wouldn't be with us at all. I rescued him from the clutches of the Canadian police. And you don't know, and never will know, what I had to do to get him out of there. So, *brigadier*, when you have proved yourself worthy of Him with some similar act of devotion, you'll have the right to shout at me. Not before.'

Retancourt put the stones rather roughly into Estalère's outstretched hand. Veyrenc saw the young man's lip start to tremble, and made a sign to Retancourt to go easy on him.

'OK, let's call a truce,' she said, lightly tapping the *brigadier*'s shoulder.

'I'm sorry,' muttered Estalère. 'I wanted those stones.'

'Are you sure they're the right ones?'

'Yes.'

'But for the last thirteen days, Emilio has been sweeping out the café at night, and the dustbins are emptied every morning.'

'That night, it was very late. Emilio just swept the floor very quickly to get the mud and gravel up, and brushed it all outside into the street. I went looking where any stones would have ended up, by the wall, against the next-door step, where no one ever goes.'

'Back to base,' said Retancourt, putting her jacket back on. 'Only another day and a half before the drugs people grab the case from us.'

XIII

IN THE LITTLE ROOM WITH THE DRINKS MACHINE, ADAMSBERG HAD FOUND on the floor two big foam cushions covered with an old blanket, creating a makeshift bed and transforming the area into a refuge for the homeless. It was no doubt the work of Mercadet, who was bordering on the narcoleptic, and whose need for sleep was agonising to his professional conscience.

Adamsberg served himself a coffee from the kindly machine and decided to try out the bed. He sat down, pushed a cushion behind his back and stretched out his legs.

Yes, one could have a nap there, no doubt about it. The warm foam wrapped itself round one's body insidiously, almost giving the feeling of having company in bed. Perhaps one could do some thinking there, but Adamsberg was only capable of thinking when he was out for a stroll. If you could call it thinking. He had long ago been forced to the conclusion that in his case it did not correspond to the normal definition of thought: to shape and combine ideas and judgements. It was not for want of trying: sitting on a proper chair, elbows leaning on a table, without distractions, pen and paper to hand, pressing his fingers to his forehead. An approach which merely succeeded in disconnecting his logical circuits. His unstructured mind was like an unreadable map, a magma in which nothing clear emerged to be identified as an Idea. Everything always seemed to be linked to everything else, in a network of little pathways where sounds, smells, flashes of light, memories, images, echoes and grains of dust mingled together. And that was all he had at his disposal to act as *Commissaire* Adamsberg, running the twenty-seven officers in his outfit and obtaining, as his *divisionnaire* was always reminding him, Results. He ought to have been anxious. But that day, other floating bodies were taking up all the space in his mind.

He stretched out his arms, then folded them behind his head, appreciating the initiative of his drowsy colleague. Outside, rain and shadows. Which had nothing to do with each other.

Danglard stopped short before operating the machine when he found the *commissaire* asleep, and tiptoed backwards out of the room.

'I'm not asleep, Danglard,' Adamsberg said, without opening his eyes. 'Go ahead and get your coffee.'

'This bedding's Mercadet's is it?'

'I imagine so, *capitaine*. I'm trying it out.'

'You may have some competition there.'

'Or multiplication. Another six couches in the corners if we don't watch out.'

'There are only four corners,' objected Danglard, hoisting himself on to one of the high bar stools and swinging his legs.

'Well, it's more comfortable than those damn bar stools. I don't know who produces them but they're too tall. I can't even reach the foot rest. We look like a lot of storks on chimney pots.'

'They're Swedish.'

'The Swedes must be taller than us. Do you think that makes a difference?'

'What?'

'Size. Do you think it makes a difference if your head is nearly two metres above your feet? If the blood has such a long way to go up and down all the time? Do you think it makes the thought process purer if the feet are too far away to matter? Or would a little man think better, because the circulation would be more rapid and concentrated?'

'Immanuel Kant,' said Danglard without enthusiasm, 'was only one metre fifty tall. He was all thought, impeccably constructed.'

'What about his body?'

'He never bothered to use it.'

'But that's no good either,' murmured Adamsberg, closing his eyes again.

Danglard considered it more prudent and useful to head back to his office.

'Danglard. Can you see it?' said Adamsberg in a level tone of voice. 'The Shade?'

The *commandant* turned back, and looked towards the rain which darkened the window. But he was too much of a connoisseur of Adamsberg to think the *commissaire* was talking about the weather.

'It's there, Danglard. It's hiding the light. Feel it? It's surrounding us, looking at us.'

'A dark presence?' he suggested.

'Something like that. All round us.'

Danglard took time to think, rubbing the back of his neck. What Shade could this be? When and how had 'it' appeared? Since the traumatic events which had befallen Adamsberg in Quebec and had forced him to take more than a month's leave to recover, Danglard had been watching him closely. He had been following his quick return to form after the shocks which had almost stripped him of his reason. And it seemed to Danglard that everything had gone back to normal fairly quickly, or at any rate to what passed for normal in Adamsberg's case. He felt his fears creeping up again. Perhaps Adamsberg wasn't so far away from the abyss into which he had almost fallen.

'Since when?' he asked.

'A few days after I got back,' replied Adamsberg, suddenly opening his eyes and sitting up straight. 'Perhaps it was waiting, prowling around us.'

'Us?'

'The Squad. Our base. That's the Shade's territory too. When I go away – when I went to Normandy, for instance – I don't sense it any more. When I get back, there it is again, quiet and grey. Perhaps it's the Silent Sister.'

'And who might that be?'

'Sister Clarisse, the nun who was killed by the tanner.'

'You believe in her?'

Adamsberg smiled.

'I heard her the other night,' he said, quite cheerfully. 'She was walking about in the attic, with a sound like a robe sweeping the ground. I got up and went to have a look.'

'And there was nothing there?'

'No, stands to reason,' said Adamsberg, with a fleeting memory of the punctuator of Haroncourt.

The *commissaire* looked all round the little room.

'And does she bother you?' asked Danglard carefully, feeling he was stepping into a minefield.

'No, but this isn't a friendly ghost, Danglard, bear that in mind. Not there to help us.'

'Since you got back, nothing special's happened, except we've got this New Recruit.'

'Veyrenc de Bilhc.'

'Does he bother you? Did he bring the Shade with him?'

Adamsberg thought over Danglard's suggestion.

'Well, he does bother me a bit. He comes from the valley next to mine. Did he tell you about it? The Ossau valley? And about his hair?'

'No. Why should he?'

'When he was a little kid, five other boys attacked him. They slashed his stomach and cut up his scalp.'

'And?'

'And these boys came from my village, and he knows that. He

pretended he was only just discovering it, but he was perfectly aware of it before he got here. And if you ask me, that's why he's here at all.'

'But why?'

'Chasing memories, Danglard.'

Adamsberg lay back again on the cushions.

'Remember that woman we arrested a couple of years ago? The district nurse? I'd never had to arrest an old woman before. I hated that case.'

'She was a monster,' said Danglard in a shocked voice.

'According to our pathologist, she was a dissociated killer. With her Alpha self, which went about its everyday business, and her Omega self, which was an angel of death. What are Alpha and Omega, anyway?'

'Letters from the Greek alphabet.'

'If you say so. She was seventy-three years old. Remember what she looked like when we arrested her?'

'Yes.'

'Not a happy memory was it, *capitaine*? Do you think she's still spying on us? Do you think she could be the Shade? Cast your mind back to the case.'

Yes, Danglard could perfectly well cast his mind back. It had begun at the home of an elderly woman who had apparently died of natural causes, and there was a routine procedure to determine the cause of death. The local GP and the police pathologist, Dr Roman, at that stage not having a fit of the vapours, had reached agreement in fifteen minutes. A cardiac arrest. The television was still on. Two months later, Lamarre and Danglard had been in attendance for another routine formality, this time concerning a man of ninety-one who had died sitting in his armchair, his hand still holding a book, curiously enough entitled *The Art of Being a Grandmother*. Adamsberg had arrived just as the two doctors were agreeing the certificate.

'An aneurysm, I'd say,' said the man's own physician. 'You can never predict them, but when they strike, they strike. Any objection, doctor?'

'None at all,' Roman had replied.

'OK, let's do the paperwork.'

The GP had already pulled out his pen and was about to sign the certificate.

'Stop,' said Adamsberg.

They both looked at the *commissaire*, who was standing against the wall, arms folded, looking at them.

'Anything wrong?' Roman had asked.

'Can't you smell anything?'

Adamsberg moved away from the wall and approached the body. He sniffed close to the old man's face and vaguely patted his sparse hair. Then he walked around the small two-room flat, his nose in the air.

'It's in the air, Roman. Look around, instead of at the body.'

'Around where?' asked Roman looking up through his glasses at the ceiling.

'Roman, this old man was murdered.'

The GP looked impatient as he pocketed his fat fountain pen. This little man with vague eyes who had just turned up, hands thrust in the pockets of a scruffy pair of trousers, and whose arms were as brown as if he spent his life out of doors, did not inspire him with confidence.

'My patient was worn out, like an old workhorse. Like I said, when it strikes, it strikes.'

'It strikes all right, but not necessarily from heaven. Can you smell it, doctor? It's not a perfume, not a medicine. It's something like camphor, camomile, pepper, orange blossom.'

'We've made our diagnosis, and you're not a doctor as far as I know.'

'No, I'm a policeman.'

'I dare say. But if you're not satisfied, go and tell your *commissaire*.'

'I am the *commissaire*.'

'He is the *commissaire*,' Roman confirmed.

'Oh, bloody hell,' said the doctor.

Danglard, who had been there before, had watched as the GP gradually responded to Adamsberg's voice and manner, yielding to the persuasiveness that seemed to flow out of him like an insidious breath. He had seen the doctor bend and submit, like a tree in the wind, as so many others had before him, men of bronze and women of steel, seduced by a charm that was neither brilliant nor showy, but which obeyed no rhyme or reason. It was an arrogant phenomenon, which always left Danglard both satisfied and irritated, divided between his affection for Adamsberg and his pity for himself.

'Yes,' said Danglard sniffing the air. 'I know this smell. It's some expensive sort of oil, they sell it in little capsules at aromatherapists. It's supposed to settle the nerves. You put a drop on each temple and one at the back of the neck, and it works wonders. Kernorkian in our office uses it.'

'That's what it is, Danglard, you're right. That must be why I recognised it. And I don't suppose your patient was in the habit of buying it.'

The doctor looked round the two poor little rooms, which indicated near-abject poverty rather than the means to buy expensive aromatherapy products.

'But it doesn't *mean* anything,' he said tentatively.

'That's because you weren't attending a woman who died a month or two back. Same smell there. Do you remember it, Danglard? You were there.'

'I didn't notice anything.'

'Roman, what about you?'

'Sorry, nothing.'

'It was the same smell. So the same person could have been here and in the other case, just before they died. Who was the district nurse, doctor?'

'A very competent woman. I'd recommended her to him.'

The doctor rubbed his shoulder, looking embarrassed.

'She's past retiring age. She has been, well, I have to say, working unofficially. So she could visit my patients every day without them having to pay too much. When there's no money left, you have to turn a blind eye to the rules.'

'What's her name?'

'Claire Langevin. She's very competent, forty years' experience in hospital nursing and a specialist in geriatrics.'

'Danglard, call the office. Get them to check with the old lady's GP – call him and ask what was the name of the nurse who visited her.'

They stood talking shop for about twenty minutes while Danglard went back to the patrol car. The doctor had pulled out from under the patient's bed a bottle of home-made fortified wine.

'He always offered me a little glass of this stuff – real rot-gut.'

Then he had put it back under the bed, looking sad. Danglard returned.

'Claire Langevin,' he announced.

Silence. All eyes were on the *commissaire*.

'A killer nurse,' said Adamsberg. 'One of the sort they call angels of death. When they come down to earth, they kill. And when they fall, they really fall.'

'Oh my God,' whispered the doctor.

'How many other patients have you recommended her to, doctor?'

'Oh my God.'

In under a month, the macabre list of the thirty-three victims of the death-dealing angel had been established: in hospitals, private nursing homes, clinics and in their own houses. She had spent the last half-century working in France, Germany and Poland, distributing death by injecting air bubbles into arm after arm.

One February morning, Adamsberg and four of his men had surrounded her suburban villa, with its gravel paths and neat little flower beds. Four experienced men, used to dealing with tough male killers, but that day reduced to a state of impotence, sweating with unease. When women went off the rails, Adamsberg said, the world seemed to teeter on its axis. In fact, he had confided to Danglard as they walked up the path, men only allow themselves to kill each other because women don't, but when women cross the red line, the universe tilts.

'Maybe,' Danglard had said, feeling as upset as the others.

The door had opened on a very wrinkled old woman, neat and poised, who had asked the police to please be very careful of her flowers, her paintwork and her borders. Adamsberg had considered her carefully, but could find nothing in her face, neither the flame of hatred nor the fury of killing he had sometimes detected in others. Nothing but a blank-faced and unnaturally thin old woman. The men had handcuffed her almost in silence, reciting their usual formulae, to which Danglard had added under his breath: '*Do not condemn woman if she stoops to such crime/Who knows with what torments she has fought all this time.*' Adamsberg had assented, without knowing who Danglard was suppli-cating with this evening prayer in broad daylight.

'Yes, of course I remember the case,' said Danglard with a shudder. 'But she's nowhere near here. They've got her under lock and key in Freiburg. She can't be sending a shade over you from there.'

Adamsberg had stood up. Pressing his hands against the wall, he was watching the rain still falling.

'No. Ten months and five days ago, Danglard, she somehow managed to kill a prison guard. And got herself out of the prison.'

'Good God,' said Danglard, crushing his plastic cup. 'Why weren't we told?'

'The Baden Land authorities neglected to send us a message.

Administrative slip-up. I only heard about it when I got back from leave.'

'Have they found her?'

Adamsberg made a vague sign towards the street.

'No, *capitaine*. She's still out there somewhere.'

XIV

ESTALÈRE HELD OUT HIS HAND, DISPLAYING THE THREE PIECES OF GRAVEL from Clignancourt as if they were diamonds.

'What is it, *brigadier*?' asked Danglard, hardly taking his eyes off his computer screen.

'It's for him, *commandant*. What he asked me to find.'

Him. Adamsberg.

Danglard looked at Estalère without seeking to understand, and hurriedly pressed the button on the intercom. It was after nightfall, and his children were waiting for him to come home for supper.

'*Commissaire*? Estalère's got something for you. He's on his way,' he added for the young man's benefit.

Estalère didn't budge, still holding out his hand.

'Take it easy, Estalère. He'll be along in a minute. He never rushes.'

When Adamsberg came in five minutes later, the young officer had still hardly changed position. He was waiting, transformed into a statue by hope. He kept repeating to himself the *commissaire*'s words at the conference: 'Take Estalère, he's got good eyesight.'

Adamsberg examined the trophy the young man offered him.

'So they were waiting there, after all?' he said with a smile.

'Outside, by the door, up against the step.'

'I knew you'd find them for me.'

Estalère stood upright, as pleased as a baby bird returning home from its first flight.

'Right. Off to Montrouge,' said Adamsberg. 'We've only got one day left, so it will have to be a night-time job. Better be four people, six if possible. Justin, Mercadet and Gardon are on duty. They can go with you.'

'Mercadet's on night shift, but he's asleep,' pointed out Danglard.

'Well, take Voisenet then. And Retancourt, if she agrees to put in some overtime. When she wants to, Retancourt can go without sleep, drive for ten nights in a row, cross Africa on foot and catch up with a plane in Vancouver. She channels her energy, it's magic.'

'I know, *commissaire*.'

'You'll have to check out all the parks, gardens, waste patches and so on. Don't forget building sites. Take samples everywhere.'

Estalère went off practically at a run, clutching his treasure.

'Do you want me to go too?' asked Danglard, switching off his computer.

'No, go home and have supper with the kids. I'll do the same, because Camille is playing in a concert at Saint-Eustache.'

'I can ask the neighbour to come in and give them their supper, if you want. We've only got twenty-four hours.'

'Big Eyes will manage all right. He won't be on his own.'

'Why do you think he opens his eyes so wide?'

'He must have seen something when he was a child. We all saw something when we were children. Some of us stayed with our eyes too wide open, or our body too big or our head too vague or . . .' Adamsberg stopped himself and forced the thought of the New Recruit's ginger streaks out of his mind. 'I think Estalère found the gravel all on his own. I think Retancourt didn't want to know, and just sat having a drink with the New Recruit. A beer, probably.'

'Could be.'

'Retancourt can still get mad at me.'

'You drive everyone mad, *commissaire*. Why not her?'

'Everyone, but not her. That's what I'd like. See you tomorrow, Danglard.'

Adamsberg was lying on on his back on the new bed, with the child lying on his stomach like a little monkey clinging to its father's fur. Both of them had had their supper, both of them were quiet and peaceful. They were snuggled up in the big red eiderdown that Adamsberg's second sister had given him. No sign of the nun in the attic. Lucio Velasco had enquired discreetly about the presence there of Clarisse, and Adamsberg had reassured him.

'Now I'm going to tell you a story, son,' said Adamsberg in the dark. 'A story from the mountains but not that *opus spicatum*. We've had enough of those walls. I'm going to tell you about an ibex, that's a kind of mountain goat, in the Pyrenees, that met this other ibex. You need to know that an ibex doesn't like it if another one comes on to his territory. He likes all the other animals – rabbits, bears, marmots, wild boar, all the birds, anything you like. But not another ibex. Because the other one wants to take over his territory and his wife. And he goes for him with his big horns.'

Thomas stirred, as if he recognised the seriousness of the situation, and Adamsberg caught his little fists in his hands.

'Don't worry, there'll be a happy ending. But today, I nearly got hit by the horns. Only I hit back and the ginger ibex ran away. One day you'll have horns too. The mountain will give them to you. And I don't know whether that's a good thing or not. But it's your mountain, so you'll have to put up with it. Tomorrow or the next day, the ginger ibex will be back for another try. I think he's angry.'

The story sent Adamsberg to sleep before his son. In the middle of the night, when neither of them had moved an inch, Adamsberg suddenly opened his eyes and reached for the telephone. He knew her number by heart.

'Retancourt? Are you in bed or in Montrouge?'

'What do you think?'

'Montrouge, on some muddy building site.'

'Bit of waste land.'

'And the others?'

'Scattered around. We're looking everywhere, picking stuff up.'

'Call them all in, *lieutenant*. Where are you exactly?'

'Opposite 123 Avenue Jean-Jaurès.'

'Stay where you are. I'm on my way.'

Adamsberg got up with care, put on his trousers and jacket, and attached the baby in a sling across his stomach. If he kept one hand over Tom's head and another under his bottom, there was no risk that he would wake up. And so long as Camille did not find out that he had taken his son out on a cold night to Montrouge with a lot of bad company, namely the police, all would be well.

'You won't tell on me, will you, Tom?' he whispered, wrapping the baby in a blanket. 'You won't tell her where we've been tonight? Don't have any choice – we've only got one day left. Come along, little one, and stay asleep.'

A taxi put him down on the Avenue Jean-Jaurès twenty minutes later. The group was waiting for him, huddled together on the pavement.

'Jean-Baptiste, you're crazy to bring the baby out,' said Retancourt, coming up to the car.

Occasionally, as a consequence of the close contact which had saved their lives, the *commissaire* and *lieutenant* moved on to first-name terms, as a train switches points, passing into the '*tu*' of intimate complicity. They knew that their union was indestructible. An unswerving love, like all those that are never consummated.

'Don't worry, Violette, he's sleeping like an angel. As long as you don't give me away to Danglard, who would give me away to Camille, it'll be all right. Why's the New Recruit here?'

'He's replacing Justin.'

'How many cars have you got?'

'Two.'

'You take one, I'll go in the other. Meet up at the main gate to the cemetery.'

'Why?' asked Estalère.

Adamsberg rubbed his cheek.

'Your gravel, *brigadier*. Do you remember what made Diala and Paille kill themselves laughing?'

'They laughed at something?'

'Yes,' said Voisenet. 'When Emilio told them to keep their voices down.'

'That's right, when Emilio said they were shouting loud enough to *waken the dead*. That could be because they had just *been* waking the dead. It was the job they'd been hired to do. Dig up someone's grave.'

'Oh, the big cemetery, here, in Montrouge,' said Gardon suddenly. 'That must be it.'

'They must have had to open a grave. Come on. Bring all your torches.'

The cemetery attendant proved hard to wake but easy to question. In the endless nights here, a diversion, even one caused by the police, made a welcome change. Yes, a grave had been disturbed. Someone had lifted a tombstone. In fact, they'd broken it by turning it over. It had been found in two pieces alongside the tomb. The family had had a new slab put in its place.

'And the grave?' asked Adamsberg.

'What about the grave?'

'After the stone was taken off, what happened? Did they dig it up?'

'No, they didn't even do that. Just vandals.'

'When was this?'

'About a fortnight ago. It was a night between Wednesday and Thursday. I'll look it up.'

The man pulled out of a bookcase a large register with grubby pages.

'The night of the sixth to the seventh of March,' he said. 'I have to put everything down in here. Do you want the location of the grave?'

'Later. For now, just take us there.'

'Oh, no, no,' said the attendant, retreating into his little cubbyhole.

'Just take us to the grave, for Christ's sake. How do you think we're going to find it without you? The cemetery's huge.'

'No,' said the man. 'No way.'

'Are you on duty here, yes or no?'

'There are two of us now. So I'm not setting foot in there.'

'Two? There's another attendant?'

'No, someone else comes at night.'

'Who?'

'I don't know and I don't want to know. A shape. So I'm not going in there.'

'Have you seen it?'

'Like I'm seeing you. Not a man, not a woman, a shape, grey, moving slowly. It slides along as if it was going to fall. But it doesn't fall.'

'When did you see this?'

'Two or three nights before the stone was broken. So I've stopped going in.'

'Well, we have to go in, and you're coming with us. We won't leave you on your own. I've got a *lieutenant* here who'll protect you.'

'You're not giving me any choice, is that it? Cops, always the same. And you've brought a baby along? And you're not scared?'

'The baby's asleep. The baby isn't scared of anything. If he's going in, you can, can't you?'

Flanked by Retancourt and Voisenet, the attendant led them quickly towards the grave, still extremely anxious to get back to the safety of his hut.

'There you are,' he said. 'It was there.'

Adamsberg pointed a torch at the tombstone, a horizontal slab.

'A young woman,' he said. 'Who died aged thirty-six, over three months ago. Do you know how?'

'A car crash, that's all they told me. Sad.'

'Yes.'

Estalère was looking at the alley between the graves.

'The gravel, sir,' he said. 'It's the same.'

'Yes, *brigadier*. Take a sample, though.'

Adamsberg turned the beam of his torch on to his two watches.

'Almost half past five. In another half an hour, we can wake the family. We'll need their permission.'

'To do what?' asked the guardian, now somewhat reassured by his group escort.

'To take the slab off.'

'How many times is this blessed slab going to be moved?'

'If we can't take it up, how are we going to find out why they did it?'

'Logical,' murmured Voisenet.

'But they didn't dig anything up,' protested the attendant. 'I've already told you. There wasn't anything out of place, not a scratch. And on the earth there were still faded rosebuds from the funeral. That proves they didn't touch it, doesn't it?'

'Possibly, but we need to make sure.'

'Don't you believe me?'

'Listen, two men were killed two days later because of this. They got their throats cut. High price to pay, isn't it, for turning over a tomb-stone? Just out of vandalism.'

The attendant scratched his stomach in puzzlement.

'So they must have done something else,' Adamsberg continued.

'Well, I don't see what.'

'That's what *we*'re going to see.'

'OK.'

'And to do that we need to take the stone off again.'

'Yes, sir.'

Veyrenc pulled Retancourt to one side.

'Why does the *commissaire* wear two watches?' he asked. 'Is he on US time or something?'

'No, he's not on any time in particular. I think he already had one, then his girlfriend gave him one, so he put that one on as well. And since then he's had two watches.'

'Because he can't decide between them?'

'No, I think it's simpler than that. He's got two watches, so he wears two watches.'

'I see.'

'You'll soon learn.'

'I can't work out why he thought of checking the cemetery. Given that he was asleep.'

'Retancourt,' Adamsberg called. 'The men can go and rest. I'll come back with another team when I've taken Tom back to his mother. Can you hold the fort until then, and take care of the permissions?'

'I'll stay with her,' proposed the New Recruit.

'Oh yes, Veyrenc?' asked Adamsberg sharply. 'You think you can stay awake long enough?'

'And you don't think I can?'

The *lieutenant* had briefly closed his eyes, and Adamsberg was cross with himself for alluding to it. Ibex bucks in the mountains. The *lieutenant* ran his hand through his strange hair. Even at night the auburn streaks showed up.

'We've got work to do, Veyrenc, nasty work,' said Adamsberg in a gentler tone. 'If it's waited thirty-four years, it can wait a few more days. I propose we have a truce.'

Veyrenc seemed to hesitate. Then he nodded silently.

'OK,' said Adamsberg, walking away. 'I'll be back in about an hour.'

'What was all that about?' asked Retancourt as she walked after the *commissaire*.

'A war,' replied Adamsberg shortly. 'The war of the two valleys. Don't get involved.'

Retancourt stopped, looking annoyed and scuffing the gravel with her shoe.

'Serious war?' she asked.

'Pretty serious.'

'What did he do?'

'Or what *will* he do? You like him a lot, don't you, Violette? Well, don't get between the tree and the bark. Because one day you may have to choose. Between him and me.'

XV

By ten o'clock in the morning the tombstone had been raised, revealing a surface of smooth compacted earth. The attendant had been quite right: the soil was intact, and covered with the blackened remains of roses. The team of police, tired and disappointed, wandered around it in perplexity. What would old Anglebert have said if he had seen their demoralised state, Adamsberg wondered.

'Take a few photographs anyway,' he said to the freckled photographer, a talented and friendly lad whose name he regularly forgot.

'Barteneau,' whispered Danglard, one of whose self-imposed jobs was to remedy the social deficiencies of the *commissaire*.

'Barteneau, take some photos. Close-ups as well.'

'I told you,' the attendant was muttering. 'They didn't do anything else. Not a scratch on the earth.'

'There's got to be something,' Adamsberg replied. The *commissaire* was sitting cross-legged on the tombstone, chin on his hands. Retancourt moved away, leaned up against a nearby memorial statue and closed her eyes.

'She's taking a little nap,' the *commissaire* explained to the New Recruit. 'She's the only one in our squad who's capable of doing this, sleeping standing up. She explained to us once how she does it, and they all had a go. Mercadet almost managed it. But as soon as he dropped off, he fell over.'

'Anyone would, wouldn't they?' whispered Veyrenc. 'So she doesn't fall over?'

'No, that's just it. Take a look – she really is asleep. You can talk in a normal voice. Nothing will wake her if she's made up her mind.'

'It's a question of concentration,' said Danglard. 'She can channel her energy in any direction she likes.'

'Still doesn't work for the rest of us, though,' remarked Adamsberg.

'Maybe all they did was piss on the grave,' suggested Justin, who was sitting near the *commissaire*.

'That's a lot of trouble and a lot of money, just to piss on someone's grave.'

'Sorry, I was just trying to relieve the tension.'

'I'm not criticising you, Voisenet.'

'Justin.'

'I'm not criticising you, Justin.'

'But it didn't relieve the tension anyway.'

'Only two things really relieve tension, laughing or making love. We're not doing either at the moment.'

'So I see.'

'What about sleeping?' asked Veyrenc. 'Doesn't that relieve the tension?'

'No, *lieutenant*, that just allows you to rest. There's a difference.'

The team fell silent and the attendant asked if it was finally all right for him to leave them. Yes, it was.

'We ought to take advantage of the lifting equipment to put the stone back,' Danglard proposed.

'Not straight away,' said Adamsberg, his chin still on his hands. 'We keep looking. If we don't find anything, the sodding Drug Squad will have the bodies from us by tonight.'

'We're not going to stay here for days just to stop Drugs getting them, are we?'

'His mother said he didn't touch drugs.'

'Oh, mothers,' said Justin, with a shrug.

'You're relieving the tension too much there, *lieutenant*. One should believe mothers when they say something.'

Veyrenc was coming and going off to one side, occasionally throwing an intrigued glance at Retancourt who was indeed fast asleep. From time to time, he spoke to himself.

'Danglard, try and hear what the New Recruit is saying.'

The *commandant* took a casual stroll in the alleyways and came back.

'Do you really want to know?'

'I'm sure that *will* relieve the tension.'

'Well, he's muttering some lines of poetry, beginning with "O Earth".'

'What comes next?' asked Adamsberg, feeling discouraged.

> '*O Earth, when I query, why disdain to reply?*
> *And of this night's foul work all knowledge now deny?*
> *Has the key been withheld, or are my ears too weak*
> *To hear of thy suff'ring, a sin too great to speak?*

And so on. I can't remember it all. I don't know who it's by.'

'That's because it's by him. He speaks in verse as easily as other people blow their noses.'

'Odd,' said Danglard, with a perplexed frown.

'It runs in the family, like all odd things. Tell me the lines again, *capitaine*.'

'They're not very good.'

'At least they rhyme. And they're saying something. Tell me again.'

Adamsberg listened attentively, then stood up.

'He's right, the earth does know and we don't. Our ears are too weak to hear what it's telling us, and that's the problem.'

The *commissaire* returned to the graveside, with Danglard and Justin at his sides.

'If there's a sound to be heard, and we're not hearing it, it means we're deaf. The earth isn't dumb, but we're not skilled enough. We need a specialist, an interpreter, someone who can hear the sound of the earth.'

'What do you call one of those?' asked Justin, anxiously.

'An archaeologist,' said Adamsberg, taking out his telephone. 'Or a shit-stirrer, if you prefer.'

'You've got one in the team?'

'I have,' Adamsberg started to say, as he tapped in the number, 'a specialist who's excellent at discovering . . .' The *commissaire* paused, looking for the right word.

'Fleeting traces of the past,' suggested Danglard.

'Exactly. You couldn't put it better.'

It was Vandoosler Senior, a cynical retired detective, who picked up the phone. Adamsberg quickly explained the situation.

'Stymied and snookered, are you?' asked Vandoosler, with his cackling laugh. 'Out for the count?'

'No, Vandoosler, since I'm calling you. Don't play games with me, I'm short of time today.'

'OK. Which one do you want this time? Marc?'

'No, I need the prehistoric expert.'

'He's in the cellar, working on arrowheads.'

'Tell him to get up here as fast as he can, the cemetery in Montrouge. It's urgent.'

'Given that he's working on something from 12,000 BC, he'll tell you nothing's urgent. It's very hard to tear Mathias away from his flints.'

'Look, it's me, Adamsberg, Vandoosler. Don't give me grief like this. If you don't help me, the case is going over to Drugs.'

'Oh, that's different. I'll send him right away.'

XVI

'WHAT DO WE EXPECT HIM TO DO? ASKED JUSTIN, WARMING HIS HANDS ON a cup of coffee in the keeper's lodge.

'What the New Recruit said. We want him to find out the secret of the earth. Your twelve-syllable verses sometimes make sense, Veyrenc.'

The daytime attendant looked at Veyrenc with curiosity.

'He makes up poetry,' Adamsberg explained.

'On a day like this?'

'Especially on a day like this.'

'Right,' said the keeper, accepting it. 'Poetry – that complicates things, doesn't it? But perhaps if you complicate things, you understand them better. And if you understand, you simplify. In the end.'

'Yes,' said Veyrenc, surprised.

Retancourt was back with them, looking rested. The *commissaire* had woken her simply by touching her shoulder, as if he was pressing a button. Through the window of the lodge, she watched as a blond giant crossed the street: he had shoulder-length hair, was wearing very few clothes, and his trousers were held up with string.

'Here comes our interpreter,' said Adamsberg. 'He smiles a lot, but it's not always easy to say why.'

*   *   *

Five minutes later, Mathias was kneeling alongside the grave, looking at the earth. Adamsberg signalled to his team to keep quiet. The earth doesn't speak loudly, so you have to listen very carefully.

'You haven't touched anything?' Mathias asked. 'Nobody has moved the rose stems?'

'No,' said Danglard, 'and that's what's so mysterious. The family scattered roses all over the grave, and the tombstone was placed on top. That proves the soil hasn't been disturbed.'

'There are stems and stems,' said Mathias.

He moved his hand quickly from rose to rose, going round the grave on his knees and feeling the soil in various places, like a weaver testing the quality of silk. Then he raised his head and smiled at Adamsberg.

'See it?' he asked.

Adamsberg shook his head.

'Some of the rose stems move if you just touch them lightly, but others are embedded well in. All the ones here are still where they were left,' he said, pointing to the flowers at the bottom end of the grave. 'But these ones are just loose on the surface – they've been moved. See?'

'I'm listening,' said Adamsberg, with a frown.

'What it means is that someone has dug into the grave,' said Mathias, carefully removing the flowers from the head of the grave, 'but only part of it. Then the withered flowers were put back over the top, to make it look as if the earth hadn't been disturbed. But, you know,' he went on, standing up in a single movement, 'it still shows. A man can move a rose stem and a thousand years later you can still tell he did it.'

Adamsberg nodded, impressed. So if he touched the petal of a flower tonight, in the dark, without telling anyone, a thousand years in the future some guy like Mathias would know all about it. The idea that all his actions might leave their ineradicable traces behind seemed a little alarming. But he was reassured by looking at the prehistorian, who was taking a trowel out of his back pocket and cleaning it with his fingers. Experts like Mathias didn't grow on trees.

'It's very difficult,' said Mathias, pursing his lips. 'It's a hole that's been filled in again with exactly the same earth. It's invisible. So someone dug a hole, but where?'

'You can't find it?' asked Adamsberg, suddenly anxious.

'Not by looking.'

'How, then?'

'With my fingers. When you can't see anything, you can always feel. But it takes longer.'

'Feel what?' asked Justin.

'The edges of the trench, the gap between its edge and the surrounding area. Where one bit of earth meets another. There's got to be a line, and it's just a matter of finding it.'

Mathias ran his fingers over the apparently uniform surface of the soil. Then he seemed to dig his fingertips into a phantom crack, which he slowly followed. Like a blind man, Mathias was not actually looking at the ground, as if the illusion provided by his eyes might have spoiled the search; he was concentrating entirely on his sense of touch. Gradually he traced the outline of a rough circle about one metre fifty across, which he then redrew with the tip of the trowel.

'I've got it now, Adamsberg. I'm going to dig it out myself, so that I can follow the sides of the hole, if you can get your men to take the earth away. That'd be quicker.'

Eighty centimetres down, Mathias looked up, pulled off his shirt, and put his hands over the sides of the hole.

'I don't think whoever it was was burying anything. We're too deep now. He was trying to reach the coffin. There were two people.'

'Correct.'

'One was digging and the other was emptying the bucket. At this point, they swapped over. No two people handle a pickaxe the same way.'

Mathias took up the trowel again and plunged into the hole. They had borrowed spades and buckets from the keeper, and Justin and Veyrenc were emptying the soil out. Mathias held out some gravel to Adamsberg.

'When they filled it in, they picked up a bit of gravel from the alleyway. The one with the pickaxe was getting tired, his strokes are less straight. They haven't buried anything in here – the hole's quite empty.'

The young man continued to dig for an hour in silence, breaking it only to say: 'They've swapped over again' and 'They've changed the pickaxe for something smaller.' Finally, Mathias stood up and leaned his elbows on the edge of the hole, which was now more than waist-deep.

'By the state of the roses,' he said, 'I suppose the man in the grave hasn't been there long.'

'Three and a half months. And it's a woman.'

'Well, this is the parting of the ways, Adamsberg. I'll leave the rest to you.'

Mathias pressed his hands on the edges of the hole and jumped out. Adamsberg looked in.

'You haven't reached the coffin. They stopped before it?'

'I've reached the coffin. But it's open.'

The men of the squad exchanged glances. Retancourt moved forward. Justin and Danglard stepped back.

'The wood of the lid has been forced in with a pick and pulled off. More earth has fallen inside. You called me to explore the earth, not the corpse. I don't want to see it.'

Mathias put his trowel back in his pocket and rubbed his large hands on his trousers.

'Marc's uncle's expecting you for supper some day, you know,' he said to Adamsberg.

'Yes.'

'We don't have much money these days. Let us know ahead of time, so Marc can pinch a bottle and something to eat. Rabbit, shellfish? Would that do you?'

'That would be perfect.'

Mathias shook hands with the *commissaire*, smiled briefly at the others, and loped off, carrying his shirt over his arm.

XVII

DANGLARD WAS EXAMINING HIS DESSERT, AN EXPRESSION OF SHOCK ON HIS pale face. He had a horror of exhumations and other atrocious aspects of the profession. The idea that some diabolical grave-robber should be forcing him to look into an open coffin was driving him to the edge of psychic collapse.

'Eat up, Danglard,' Adamsberg insisted. 'You need some sugar. And drink your wine.'

'Hell's bells, they must be seriously sick to want to put something in a coffin,' Danglard muttered.

'To put something in, or perhaps to take something out.'

'Whatever. Surely there are enough hiding places in the world not to go poking about there.'

'Maybe this person was in a hurry. Or perhaps they'd put something into the coffin before they screwed it down.'

'Must be something very precious if he had the stomach to go and fetch it three months later,' commented Retancourt. 'Money or drugs, perhaps – it always comes back to that.'

'What doesn't fit,' Adamsberg said, 'is not so much whether this individual is sick. It's that he chose the head of the coffin and not the foot. After all, there's less room at the head, and it's much more distressing.'

Danglard nodded silently, still contemplating his dessert.

'Unless whatever it was was *already* in the coffin,' said Veyrenc. 'If he didn't put it there himself, he didn't have any choice.'

'For instance?'

'Earrings, maybe, or a necklace belonging to the dead woman.'

'Jewel robberies are deeply uninteresting,' muttered Danglard.

'People have been robbing tombs since the beginning of time, *capitaine*, and precisely for stuff like that. We're going to have to find out if this woman was rich. Anything on the register?'

'Elisabeth Châtel, unmarried, no children, born at Villebosc-sur-Risle, near Rouen,' Danglard reeled off.

'What is it with these people from Normandy? I can't seem to get away from them. What time are we expecting Ariane?'

'Who's Ariane?'

'The pathologist.'

'Six o'clock.'

Adamsberg pushed his finger round the rim of his wineglass, producing a painful whine. 'Eat the damn pudding, *capitaine*. You don't have to stick around for the rest of this.'

'If you're staying, I'm staying.'

'Sometimes, Danglard, you have a medieval way of carrying on. Hear that, Retancourt? I stay, he stays.'

Retancourt shrugged, and Adamsberg once more made a strident noise with his wineglass. The television set in the café was transmitting a rowdy football match. The *commissaire* stared for a while at the figures running all over the pitch, their movements followed with fascination by the dining customers, whose heads were all turned towards the screen. Adamsberg had never been able to understand this passion for football matches. If some fellows liked kicking a ball into a goal mouth, which he could well understand, why give yourself the bother of having to do it against another lot of characters who were determined to stop you? As if the world wasn't full enough already of people who stopped you kicking the ball where you wanted it to go.

'What about you, Retancourt?' Adamsberg asked. 'Are you staying? Veyrenc can go home, he's exhausted.'

'I'll stay,' said Retancourt rather sulkily.

'How long for, Violette?'

Adamsberg smiled. Retancourt untied and redid her ponytail, then got up to go to the washroom.

'Why are you bugging her?' Danglard asked when the other two were out of earshot.

'Because she's getting away from me.'

'Where to?'

'To the New Recruit. He's powerful – he's going to drag her off.'

'If he wants to.'

'That's just it, we don't know what he wants. It's going to be a worry. He's trying to place his kick somewhere, but what kind of a kick and where? This isn't the kind of game where we can afford to be caught off guard.'

Adamsberg took out his notebook, its pages now sticking together, wrote four names on it and tore out the sheet.

'When you've got a moment, Danglard, can you get me some info on these four names?'

'Who are they?'

'They're the ones who cut up his scalp when he was a kid. It's left visible traces on the outside, but much worse ones on the inside.'

'What am I looking for?'

'I just want to know if they're alive and well.'

'Is this serious?'

'Shouldn't be. I hope not.'

'You said there were five of them.'

'Yes, there were.'

'So what about the fifth one?'

'Well?'

'Well, what do we do about him?'

'The fifth one, Danglard, I'll take care of personally.'

XVIII

MORDENT AND LAMARRE, WHO WERE PART OF THE DAY SHIFT, WERE BOTH
wearing breathing masks as they finished extracting the sediments
that had fallen into the coffin. Adamsberg was kneeling at the edge
of the pit and passing buckets to Justin. Danglard was sitting on a
tombstone about fifty metres away, with his legs crossed and the air
of an other-worldly English aristocrat. He was staying at the scene as
promised, but keeping his distance. The more oppressive reality
became, the more Danglard cultivated an elegant stance, self-control
combined with a kind of cult of nonchalance. The *commandant* had
always counted on the cut of his British-style suits to compensate for
his unprepossessing appearance. His father – not to mention his
grandfather, a coal miner in Le Creusot – would have detested this
kind of attitude. But then his father should have made more of an
effort to have a better-looking son; he was simply reaping what he
had, literally, sown. Danglard dusted off his lapels. If only he had had
a crooked smile and a tender cheek, like the New Recruit, he would
have tried to lure Retancourt away from Adamsberg. The others in
the squad dismissed her as 'too fat' or 'too big to handle', the cruel
judgement bandied about in the *Brasserie des Philosophes*. But
Danglard considered her perfect.

From his observation post, he watched the pathologist in turn go down into the pit, using a ladder. She had put a set of green overalls on top of her clothes, but had not bothered to put on a mask, any more than Roman would have. These pathologists had always amazed Danglard. They were so unconcerned, tapping corpses casually on the shoulder, sometimes making childish jokes, and yet they had to spend their days in abominable surroundings. But the truth was, Danglard reflected, that they were professionals, relieved not to have to deal with the anguish of the living. Perhaps in this branch of post-mortem medicine there was a measure of tranquillity.

Night had fallen, and Dr Lagarde was completing her work under the light of arc lamps. Danglard watched her climb easily back up the ladder, pull off her gloves and toss them casually on to the heap of soil before going over to Adamsberg. From a distance, it seemed to him that Retancourt was sulking. The familiarity that linked the *commissaire* and the pathologist visibly irritated her. All the more since Ariane Lagarde had a formidable reputation, and even in her earth-stained overalls she was still a very beautiful woman. Adamsberg took off his mask and led the doctor away from the pit.

'Jean-Baptiste, there's nothing to be seen but the head of a woman who's been dead three or four months. No mutilation, no violence. Everything's there, and all present and correct. No more, no less. I wouldn't suggest you bother to bring the whole coffin up, you'll just find the cadaver inside.'

'Ariane, I'm trying to understand what's gone on. The grave-robbers were paid handsomely to open up this tomb. Then they were killed to shut them up. Why?'

'You're tilting at windmills. We can't always tell what lunatics are after. I'll compare the earth here with the earth that was under Diala and La Paille's fingernails. Did you get me some samples?'

'Every thirty centimetres.'

'Perfect. You should eat something, then go home and get some sleep. I'll come with you.'

'He must have wanted something from the body, Ariane, this killer.'

'*She* wanted, you mean. I told you it was a woman, for heaven's sake.'

'OK, for the sake of argument.'

'I'm certain about that, Jean-Baptiste.'

'If it's just a question of height, that isn't enough.'

'I've got other indications.'

'All right. So the *female* killer wanted to collect something from the body in the grave.'

'Well, she must have taken it. The trail stops there.'

'If the dead woman had been wearing earrings, you'd be able to tell that, would you, from her pierced ears?'

'Jean-Baptiste, her ears aren't there any more.'

One of the arc lamps suddenly blew, with a puff of smoke in the night, and seemed to notify everyone that the macabre spectacle was drawing to a close.

'We put it all back?' asked Voisenet.

XIX

ARIANE DROVE RATHER TOO ERRATICALLY FOR ADAMSBERG'S TASTE. HE LIKED, when he was a passenger, to lean his head against the window and be wafted smoothly along. She was looking out for a restaurant to eat at, as they drove through the wide streets.

'Do you get on well with the fat *lieutenant*?'

'She's not a fat *lieutenant*, she's a divinity with sixteen arms and twelve heads.'

'Gracious. I hadn't noticed.'

'Well, it's true. She uses them as she pleases. Speed, mass, invisibility, serial analysis, transport, physical transformation, depending on what's called for.'

'Sulking as well.'

'It happens. I often get on her nerves.'

'She's working with the man with stripy hair?'

'She's training him. He's a New Recruit.'

'She's not just training him, she likes him a lot. Well, he is quite dishy.'

'Yes, quite.'

Ariane braked suddenly at a red light.

'But since life isn't fair,' she went on, 'it's your elegant but ugly *commandant* who's interested in the *lieutenant*.'

'Danglard? Really? Interested in Retancourt?'

'If Danglard's the tall sophisticated guy who was sitting way over there. Looking like a disgusted academician, who'd have liked to have a drink to stop himself feeling sick.'

'That's him,' Adamsberg confirmed.

'Well, he's attracted to the blonde *lieutenant*. He won't get anywhere with her by keeping his distance.'

'Love is the only battle that is won by retreating, Ariane.'

'What cretin made that up? You?'

'Bonaparte. Not a bad strategist, by all accounts.'

'What about you?'

'I'm retreating at the moment. I don't have any choice.'

'You're unhappy?'

'Yes.'

'All the better. I love hearing other people's stories and the unhappier the better.'

'There's a space,' said Adamsberg, pointing out a gap. 'Let's eat here. What kind of unhappy stories?'

'A long time ago, my husband ran off with a sporty paramedic, thirty years younger than him,' said Ariane as she backed into the space. 'Always the way, isn't it? Glamorous paramedics.'

She wrenched on the handbrake with a squeal, as the only conclusion to her story.

Ariane was not the kind of doctor who waits for the end of the meal before talking about the job, so as to keep the grisly details of the morgue separate from the pleasures of the table. As she ate, she drew on the paper tablecloth a sketch of the wounds suffered by Diala and La Paille, with angles and arrows to explain the nature of the injuries, so that the *commissaire* should understand the technology.

'Remember how tall we said the killer was?'

'A hundred and sixty-two centimetres.'

'So there's a ninety per cent chance it was a woman. There are two other arguments: the first is psychological, the second mental. Are you listening?' she added doubtfully.

Adamsberg nodded his head several times, while removing the meat from his kebab and wondering whether he might or might not try to sleep with Ariane that night. By some miracle, due no doubt to her mixtures of improbable liquids, Ariane's body was not that of a sixty-year-old. Such thoughts propelled him back over twenty years earlier, when he had already cast longing glances at her shoulders and breasts from across a table. But Ariane was thinking of nothing but her corpses. Or so it seemed, since women with her degree of poise know how to conceal their desires under an impeccable appearance, almost to the point of forgetting about them and coming close to being surprised by them. Camille, by contrast, with her irrepressible love of the natural, was not gifted at such concealment. It was easy to make Camille tremble, or blush, but Adamsberg did not expect to see such tell-tale signs from the pathologist.

'Do you make a distinction between the psychological and the mental?' he asked.

'The mental is what I would describe as a compression of psychological phenomena over the longer timescale of history, in such a way that the effects are so deeply buried that they are mistakenly confused with the innate.'

'Ah', said Adamsberg, pushing back his plate.

'You *are* listening, aren't you?'

'Yes, of course I am, Ariane.'

'Well, it's obvious that a man who was no more than one metre sixty-two tall – and there are very few men in that category – would never be tempted to attack someone the size of Diala and La Paille. But if they were facing a woman, those lads would have no reason to fear anything. And I can tell you quite categorically that when they were killed they were standing up, and they were quite relaxed. The second argument is both mental and more interesting: in both cases just the one wound, the first cut, would have been enough to floor these men and kill them.

It's what I call the first incision. Here,' said Ariane, pointing to a mark on the tablecloth. 'The weapon was a sharpened scalpel and the attack was lethal.'

'A scalpel? Are you sure about that?'

Adamsberg refilled the glasses with a frown, tearing himself away from his irrelevant erotic musings.

'Absolutely. And when someone uses a scalpel instead of an ordinary knife, say, or a razor, it's because the attacker knows how to use it and what result it will produce. Nevertheless, Diala received two further cuts, and La Paille three. I call those the secondary incisions, made once the victim was on the ground, and those are not horizontal.'

'I'm listening,' Adamsberg assured her, before Ariane could ask him again.

The pathologist raised her hand to mark a pause, drank a mouthful of water, then some wine, then more water, before picking up her pen once more.

'These secondary incisions point to a wealth of precautions being taken, a concern to see that the job was completely finished and, if possible, impeccably performed. Going to these excessive lengths betrays surviving traces of school discipline, possibly associated with neurotic perfectionism.'

'Hmm, yes,' said Adamsberg, who was reflecting that Ariane could very well have written the book on the compensatory stones in Pyrenean architecture.

'This striving for excellence is always a form of defence against a threatening external world. And it's essentially a feminine trait.'

'Threatening?'

'A desire for perfection, a wish to check everything in the world. The percentage of men displaying these symptoms is negligible. See, tonight I checked that my car door was properly shut. You didn't. And I also checked that I had the keys in my bag. Do you know where your car keys are?'

'Hanging on the nail in the kitchen, as usual, I suppose.'

'You just suppose?'

'Yes.'

'But you're not sure?'

'Christ almighty, Ariane, I can't swear to it.'

'Just from that, without needing to look at you, I can tell that you're a man, and I'm a woman, living in a Western country, with a margin of error of no more than twelve per cent.'

'It would be simpler just to look at me, wouldn't it?'

'But remember that I haven't been able to look at the killer of Diala and La Paille. Who is a woman, about one metre sixty-two tall, with a ninety-six per cent chance of probability, given the intersections of our three parameters, and making an allowance for high heels of an average three centimetres.'

Ariane put down her pen and took another sip of wine in between two sips of water.

'OK, what about the injections in the arm?' asked Adamsberg, picking up her expensive pen and twisting its cap on and off.

'The injections are to throw us off the track. One might hypothesise that the murderer wanted to nudge the police towards a drugs scenario.'

'Well, not very successfully, especially since there was only one puncture mark.'

'Still, Mortier fell for it.'

'In that case, why didn't the murderer simply give them both a shot of heroin and have done with it?'

'Perhaps she didn't have any? Please give me back my pen – you're going to ruin it and I'm fond of it.'

'A souvenir from your ex-husband?'

'Precisely.'

Adamsberg rolled the pen towards Ariane, who caught it three centimetres from the edge of the table and put it in her handbag along with her keys.

'Coffee?'

'Yes, please, and ask them for some crème de menthe and milk.'

'Of course,' said Adamsberg, making a sign to the waiter.

'The rest is just supplementary detail,' Ariane went on. 'I'd say the murderess is quite elderly. A young woman would hardly have taken the risk of being alone at night with characters like Diala and La Paille in a deserted cemetery.'

'Very true,' said Adamsberg, who was immediately reminded of his idea of going to bed with Ariane later on.

'Finally, I suppose, as you do, that she must have medical connections. The choice of the scalpel, of course, the precise nature of the incision which severed the carotid artery, and the presence of a syringe, very accurately inserted into the vein. Virtually a triple signature.'

The waiter brought their coffee over and Adamsberg watched as Ariane composed her mixture.

'You haven't finished yet.'

'No. I've got a bit of a puzzle for you.'

Ariane thought for a moment, tapping her fingers on the tablecloth.

'I don't like to make a statement when I'm not quite sure about something.'

'In my case that's just what I do like to do.'

'Well, it's possible that I have a clue about her madness and possibly the nature of her psychosis. She seems to me in any case to be sufficiently insane to keep her two worlds separate.'

'Does that leave traces?

'She put her foot on La Paille's torso to make the final incisions. From which we can tell that she polishes the soles of her shoes.'

Adamsberg gave Ariane a blank look.

'She *polishes the soles* of her shoes,' the pathologist insisted, more loudly, as if to wake him up. 'There were traces of shoe polish on La Paille's T-shirt.'

'I heard you, Ariane. I'm just trying to work out the connection between the two worlds.'

'I've seen two cases like this, one in Bristol, one in Berne. Men who polished the soles of their shoes, several times a day, to preserve theselves from the filth of everyday life. Their way of isolating themselves, protecting themselves.'

'Dissociating themselves?'

'I don't think about dissociation every minute of the day. But you're right, the man in Bristol was pretty much a case. The barrier between oneself and the ground, a way of preserving one's body from contact with the rest of the world, yes, it does remind one of the walls that dissociators build up. Particularly when it's the ground on which crime is committed, or the ground of the dead, like the cemetery. That doesn't mean to say that this murderer polishes the soles of her shoes every day.'

'Just the Omega part of her, if she's a dissociator?'

'No, no, you're wrong. It's the Alpha one who wants to keep herself clear of the crimes. Omega commits them.'

'Using shoe polish,' said Adamsberg with a doubtful grimace.

'Shoe polish is perceived as a waterproof material, a protective film.'

'What colour?'

'Navy blue. And that's another thing that makes me think it's a woman. Blue shoes are generally worn with navy suits, a conventional, rather austere way of dressing that one finds specifically in certain uniforms or professions: aviation, administration, hospitals, religious bodies – the list could be a long one.'

Faced with the mass of information which the pathologist was piling on the table, Adamsberg's expression darkened. Ariane had the impression that his face was changing before her eyes, the nose becoming more hooked, the cheeks more hollow, the bone structure more evident. She had neither seen nor understood anything twenty-three years earlier. She had not noticed this man who crossed her path, had not seen that he was attractive, and that she could have taken him in her arms on the quayside at Le Havre. Now the quayside was far away and it was too late.

'You don't look pleased,' she said, dropping her professional tone. 'Do you want a dessert?'

'Why not?' he said. 'Pick something for me.'

Adamsberg ate a slice of tart without noticing whether it was apple or plum, without knowing whether he might sleep with Ariane, or where he could have put his car keys since his return from Normandy.

'I don't think they are hanging up in the kitchen,' he said finally, spitting out a stone.

Must be plum, he calculated.

'Was that what was preoccupying you?'

'No, Ariane, it was the Shade. Remember that old district nurse, and her thirty-three victims?'

'The one with dissociation?'

'Yes. Do you know what happened to her?'

'Yes, naturally, because I interviewed her several times. She was sent to prison in Freiburg. She's been as good as gold there, back in one hundred per cent Alpha mode.'

'No, Omega, Ariane. She killed one of the guards.'

'Good Lord. When?'

'Ten months ago. Disjunction – followed by escape.'

The doctor poured herself half a glass of wine and swallowed it without water.

'Tell me something,' she said. 'Was it really you that identified her? Just you?'

'Yes.'

'If it hadn't been for you, she'd still be free.'

'Yes.'

'And she knows that? She understood that?'

'I think so.'

'How did you get on to her?'

'By her scent. She used some stuff called Relaxol, a sort of camphor-and-orange aromatherapy oil that she dabbed on herself.'

'Well, watch out, Jean-Baptiste. Because, for her, you're the one who broke down the wall that Alpha mustn't know about, at all costs. You're the one who knows, so you need to disappear.'

'Why?' asked Adamsberg, drinking a mouthful from Ariane's glass.

'So that she can become a peaceful Alpha again, somewhere else, in another life. You're a threat to everything she's built up. Perhaps she's looking for you.'

'The Shade.'

'I think the shade must come from something inside you, some unfinished business.'

Adamsberg's eyes met the intelligent gaze of the doctor, and he saw once again a path in Quebec at night-time. He moistened his finger and rubbed it round the edge of his wineglass.

'The watchman at the Montrouge cemetery saw her too. The Shade was walking in the cemetery a few nights before the tombstone was smashed. It wasn't walking normally.'

'Why do you make that noise with your glass?'

'So as not to scream myself.'

'Go ahead and scream, I'd rather that. Are you thinking of the nurse? As a possibility for the Diala and La Paille murders?'

'Well, you described an elderly female murderer, armed with a syringe, possibly dissociated, and with a medical background. It tends to add up.'

'Or not. Do you remember how tall she was, the nurse?'

'No, not very clearly.'

'Or what kind of shoes she wore?'

'No, not that either.'

'Well, try checking that out before you make your wineglass scream. Just because she's out of jail doesn't mean she can get about everywhere.

Don't forget that her speciality is killing old people in their beds. She hasn't been known to rob tombs or go round cutting the throats of hefty young men in La Chapelle. It doesn't fit anything we know about her.'

Adamsberg agreed. The solid reasoning put forward by the pathologist took him away from his nightmares. The Shade couldn't be everywhere – Freiburg, La Chapelle, Montrouge. She was above all inside his head.

'You're right,' he said.

'If I were you I'd just go on investigating carefully, routine stuff, step by step. Shoe polish, shoes, the portrait of the killer I've worked out, any witnesses who might have seen her with Diala or La Paille.'

'You're advising me to proceed logically, basically.'

'Yes. Do you know any other way?'

'The other way is the only one I know.'

Ariane offered to drop Adamsberg off at his home, and he accepted. The drive would enable him to resolve the erotic question still in suspense. But by the time they arrived, he was fast asleep, having forgotten about the Shade, the pathologist and the tomb of the unknown Elisabeth. Ariane was standing on the pavement, holding the car door open and gently shaking his shoulder. She had left the engine running, a sign that there was strictly nothing to be attempted, therefore no problem to resolve. As he went into the house, he checked the kitchen to see if his car keys were on the hook. They weren't.

I'm a man, he concluded. At least, allowing for a margin of error of twelve per cent, as Ariane would say.

XX

VEYRENC HAD LEFT THE TEAM IN MONTROUGE AT THREE P.M. AND GONE
straight to bed, where he had slept like a log. So by nine in the evening
he was up again, refreshed but full of detestable nocturnal thoughts
which he would have liked to escape. But how and where? Veyrenc knew
there was no way out until the tragedy of the two valleys had reached
its resolution. Only then would a space open up in front of him.

> *I shall move more surely if I move without speed.*
> *Desp'rate conflicts are lost if one does not take heed.*

Very true, Veyrenc said to himself, relaxing a little. He had rented a
furnished room for six months, and there was no hurry. He switched
on his small television set and sat down quietly. A natural-history docu-
mentary. Perfect, that would do very well. Veyrenc saw once more
Adamsberg's fingers clenched on the door handle. 'They came from the
Gave de Pau valley.' Veyrenc smiled.

> *And at these words, my lord, I saw your face turn pale,*
> *You who until today could make vast empires quail,*
> *Striding proud and careless across the conquered plain,*
> *Without a backward glance for the soldier in pain.*

Veyrenc lit a cigarette and put his ashtray on the arm of his chair. A herd of rhinoceroses was charging rowdily across the television screen.

> *Too late now, when your throne is shak'n with sudden dread*
> *To seek the forgiveness of a child who has fled,*
> *For the child is a man, whose face is like your own.*

Veyrenc jumped up, suddenly irritated. What throne, what lord, what soldier, what forgiveness? Who precisely is shaken with sudden dread? He paced up and down for an hour in his room before making up his mind.

He had made no preparations, thought of no words to say or reasons to give. So when Camille opened the door he stood there without speaking. He seemed to recall afterwards that she was aware that he was no longer on duty, that she had not been surprised to see him – perhaps even relieved, as if she'd known that the inevitable would happen, and welcomed it with both embarrassment and naturalness. Later, he remembered things more clearly. He had stepped inside and stood looking at her. He had touched her face with his hands. He had said – probably it was the first thing he had said – that he could leave at once. Then they both knew that he could not possibly leave and that what happened was inevitable. That it had been laid down and agreed from his very first day on the landing. That there was no way of avoiding it. Who had kissed the other first? He had, perhaps, since Camille was as anxious as she was adventurous. He was unable to reconstruct that first moment, except that he was still aware of the simple fact that he had reached his goal. He it was, again, who had taken the dozen steps towards the bed, leading her by the hand. He had left her at four in the morning with a gentle embrace, for neither of them wanted to

137

speak next day of this predictable, fore-ordained and almost silent coming together.

When he arrived home, the television was still on. He switched it off and the grey screen swallowed up both his complaint and his resentment.

> *Ah, soldier, what is this?*
> *If a woman should yield to your ardent embrace*
> *Will that make you forget why you came to this place?*

And Veyrenc fell asleep.

Camille had left the lamp on and was wondering whether giving in to the inevitable was a mistake or a good idea. 'In affairs of the heart, it is better to regret things done than to regret things left undone.' A Byzantine proverb is sometimes the only thing that can help you organise your life – almost – to perfection.

XXI

THE DRUG SQUAD HAD BEEN OBLIGED TO GIVE UP ITS CLAIM, BUT Adamsberg was not far off doing the same. His road was blocked: doors seemed to be closing on the investigation whichever way he looked.

Perhaps the Swedish stools weren't so bad after all, because you couldn't really sit on them, only perch there as if on horseback, with your legs dangling. Adamsberg had settled on one, quite comfortably, and was looking out of the window at the cloudy spring sky, which seemed as sunk in gloom as his inquiries. The *commissaire* did not enjoy sitting at his desk. After an hour sitting still, he felt the itch to get up and walk around, even if it was only round his office. This high bar stool gave him a new possibility, a sort of halfway house between standing and sitting, allowing his legs to swing gently as if he were suspended in the void, or flying through the air – something that suited the shoveller of clouds. Behind him, on the foam cushions, Mercadet was dozing.

The soil under the fingernails of the two men did, of course, come from the grave. It had been confirmed. But where did that lead? It said nothing about whoever had sent them to Montrouge, nor about what they had come to dig for underground, something sufficiently terrible to have cost them their lives two days later. Adamsberg had checked the recorded height of the nurse at his first opportunity: one metre sixty-five – neither too tall nor too short to be ruled out of the picture.

The information about the dead woman threw his thoughts into even greater confusion. Elisabeth Châtel, from the village of Villebosc sur Risle, in Upper Normandy, had been employed by a travel agent in Evreux. She hadn't been handling dodgy sex tourism or adventurous safaris, just coach trips for elderly tourists. She had not been wearing any jewellery when she was buried. A search of her home had revealed no hidden wealth, nor any passion for valuables. Elisabeth had been austere in her tastes, never wearing make-up, and dressing plainly. Her relatives described her as religious and, from what one gathered, under-lying their words was the assumption that she had never had any relationship with a man. She had paid no more attention to her car than to her person, and that was what had caused her death on the dangerous three-lane road between Evreux and Villebosc. The brake fluid had leaked and her car had been crushed by a truck. The previous most significant event in the Châtel family had been in 1789, when the family had been split between those who favoured the Revolution and those who opposed it. There had been a death as a result, and since then the two feuding branches of the clan had not spoken to each other. Even in death they were divided, with one branch being buried in the village graveyard at Villebosc, the other in a concession in the cemetery at Montrouge.

This cheerless summary seemed to contain the entire life of Elisabeth, a life apparently devoid of either friends or secrets. The only remark-able thing that had happened to her was the interference with her grave. None of that made sense, thought Adamsberg, swinging his legs. For the sake of this woman, who had apparently attracted no desire during her lifetime, two men had died after trying to reach her head in the coffin. Elisabeth had been placed in the coffin at the hospital in Evreux, and nobody could have had the opportunity to slip anything inside it.

At two o'clock there was to be a hasty conference at the *Brasserie des Philosophes*, where half the staff was still eating lunch. Adamsberg was not one to fuss about the conferences, either their regularity or the venue. He walked the hundred metres across to the brasserie, trying to find, on the map which kept flapping in the wind, the location of Villebosc-sur-Risle. Danglard pointed it out to him.

'Villebosc comes under the Evreux gendarmerie,' he said. 'It's one of those villages with half timbering and thatched roofs, and you should know it, because it's only fifteen kilometres from your Haroncourt.'

'What Haroncourt?'Adamsberg asked, trying to control the map which was flapping about like a sail.

'You know – Haroncourt, where you went for that concert, when you were being the gallant escort and babysitter.'

'Of course. I'd forgotten the name of the village. Have you noticed that maps are like newspapers, shirts and obsessions? Once you've unfolded them, there's no way you can get them folded up again.'

'Where did you get that map?'

'From your office.'

'Give it here, I'll fold it,' said Danglard, extending an impatient hand.

Danglard, unlike Adamsberg, appreciated those objects – and ideas – which imposed a discipline on him. Every other morning, he would find that his newspaper had already been consulted by Adamsberg and as a result was lying crumpled on the desk. For lack of any more serious matter, it bothered him. But he could hardly complain about this disorder, since the *commissaire* regularly arrived in the office before it was light – and looked at the newspaper – while never complaining about Danglard's habitually poor timekeeping.

The officers were huddled in their usual spot in the brasserie, a long alcove lit by two large stained-glass windows that threw blue, green or red reflections on their faces, according to where they sat. Danglard, who considered the windows ugly and refused to have a blue face, always sat with his back to them.

'Where's Noël?' asked Mordent.

'On work experience by the Seine,' explained the *commissaire* as he sat down.

'Doing what?'

'Inspecting the seagulls.'

'Anything's possible,' said Voisenet peaceably, speaking as an indulgent positivist and zoologist.

'Anything's possible,' Adamsberg agreed, putting a packet of photocopies on the table. 'So now we're going to work logically. I've prepared your marching orders, with a new description of the killer. For the moment, we're looking for an older woman, height about one metre sixty-two, conventional in appearance, who may wear navy-blue shoes, and who has some kind of medical knowledge. We're starting the inquiry at the Flea Market on this basis, in four teams. You'll each have photos of the nurse Claire Langevin, the serial killer with the thirty-three victims.'

'The angel of death?' asked Mercadet, sipping his third cup of coffee ahead of the others, in order to stay awake. 'Isn't she in prison?'

'Not any more. She killed a guard and escaped, ten months ago. She may have arrived via the Channel coast, and she's probably back in France. Don't show the photographs till the end of your inquiries, don't influence the witnesses. It's just a possibility, no more than a shadow of a chance.'

Just then Noël came into the cafe and found a place, in a green light, between two colleagues. Adamsberg glanced at his wristwatches. At this time, Noël should have still been going towards the river and have got as far as Saint-Michel. The *commissaire* hesitated, then said nothing. From his stubborn expression and insomnia-darkened eyes, it was clear that Noël was looking for an excuse to do something – lob a ball into play, for instance – either to pacify or to provoke. Better to bide one's time.

'As for this Shade,' he went on, 'approach her with the utmost caution, it's dangerous territory. We need to find out whether Claire Langevin wore navy leather shoes, if possible whether they were polished, and in particular polished underneath.'

'*Underneath?*'

'You heard, Lamarre, polished on the soles. Like you put wax on the underneath of skis.'

'What for?'

'It insulates the wearer from the ground, so that they glide across it without touching it.'

'Ah, I didn't know that,' said Estalère.

'Retancourt, will you go to the last address we had for the nurse, that house? Try to find out from the estate agent where her belongings are. They might have been thrown out, or they may have been kept. And go and see the last patients she had dealings with.'

'The ones she didn't kill,' pointed out Estalère.

There was a short silence, as so often after the naïve remarks of the young officer. Adamsberg had explained to everyone that Estalère would settle down with time and that one had to be patient. So everyone tended to protect him, even Noël, since Estalère was not a sufficiently credible rival to pose any threat.

'Go via the lab, Retancourt, and take a technical team with you. We need to look closely at the floors of the house. If she really did polish the underside of her shoes, there might be some traces on the floor-boards or tiles.'

'Unless the agency has had the whole place cleaned.'

'True. But as I said, we're proceeding logically for the time being.'

'So we check for marks.'

'And above all, Retancourt, you have to protect me. That's your mission.'

'Protect you? From . . . ?'

'Her. It's possible that she's after me. Apparently, according to the expert, she may want to eliminate me, so that she can carry on and rebuild the wall I tore down when we caught her.'

'What wall?' asked Estalère.

'The wall inside her,' said Adamsberg, tracing a line with his finger from his forehead to his navel.

Estalère leaned forward in concentration.

'Is she a dissociator?' he asked.

'How did you know?' asked Adamsberg, who was always astonished at the sudden flashes of intuition from the young *brigadier*.

'I read Lagarde's book. She talks about "inner walls". I remember it perfectly. I remember everything.'

'Well, you're quite right. she's a dissociator. You could all reread the book, in fact,' said Adamsberg who had still not done so himself. 'I can't remember the exact title.'

'*Either Side of the Crime Wall*,' said Danglard.

Adamsberg looked at Retancourt, who was flipping through the photographs of the elderly nurse and registering the details.

'I don't have time to protect myself from her,' he said. 'And I'm not really convinced enough to take steps. I've no idea what kind of danger it might be, from what direction it might come, or what precautions to take.'

'How did she kill the prison guard?'

'Stabbed him in the eyes with a fork, among other things. She would kill with her fingernails if she could, Retancourt. According to Lagarde, who's familiar with her, she's incredibly dangerous.'

'Well, get a bodyguard, *commissaire*. That would be the most reasonable thing to do.'

'I'd rather it was you – I'd have more confidence.'

Retancourt shook her head, weighing up the gravity of the mission and the irresponsibility of the *commissaire*.

'I can't help you at night,' she said. 'I'm not going to sleep standing up outside your door.'

'Oh, night-time's not a problem,' said Adamsberg with an airy wave of the hand. 'I've already got a bloodthirsty ghost keeping me company in the house.'

'Really?' asked Estalère.

'A certain Saint Clarisse, who was killed by a heavy-fisted tanner in 1771,' said Adamsberg, with a touch of pride. 'She's called "the Silent Sister". She used to rob old folk and cut their throats. A direct rival for our nurse, if you like. If Claire Langevin tried to get into my house at night, she'd have a job to get near me. Because Saint Clarisse has a penchant for killing women, especially old ones. So you see, I'm not afraid.'

'Who told you all that stuff?'

'My neighbour, an ancient Spaniard with one hand. He lost the other in the civil war. He says the nun's face is like a wrinkled walnut.'

'How many did your one kill?' asked Mordent, who seemed amused by the story. 'Seven, like in fairy tales?'

'Spot on.'

'And you've seen her?' asked Estalère, disconcerted by the smiles all round.

'Just a legend,' said Mordent, separating the syllables as was his habit. 'Clarisse doesn't exist.'

'Just as well,' said the *brigadier*. 'But is your Spaniard crazy or what?'

'Not at all. He was bitten by a spider on the arm he's lost, and it still itches sixty-nine years later. He scratches a point in the air.'

The arrival of the waiter distracted Estalère from his perplexity. He jumped up to place a collective coffee order. Retancourt, taking no notice of the clatter of crockery, was still looking at the photos of the nurse, while Veyrenc was talking to her. The New Recruit had not shaved and he had that soft indulgent look of a man who has been up all night making love. That reminded Adamsberg that he had let Ariane get away while he had been sleeping like a log in her car. The reflections from the windows lit up the strange colours of the *lieutenant*'s striped hair.

'Why is it your job to protect Adamsberg?' Veyrenc was asking Retancourt. 'Just you, on your own?'

'It's become a habit.'

'I see:

> "*So 'tis you, dear Madame, who the buckler must wield,*
> *To act 'gainst the killer, as armour and shield.*
> *I give you my valour, to the very last breath,*
> *Beside you for vict'ry, or beside you for death.*"'

Retancourt smiled, distracted for a moment from her preoccupations.

'Is that really what you want, Veyrenc?' asked Adamsberg, trying not to sound too cold. 'Or is that just poetic licence? Do you really want to help Retancourt protect me? Think before you answer, and estimate the danger. Making up verse won't help.'

'Retancourt's perfectly capable of handling it,' interrupted Noël.

'Shut up,' said Voisenet.

'Yeah, just shut up,' said Justin.

Adamsberg realised that on the staff Justin sometimes played exactly the same role as the punctuator at Haroncourt, while Noël was the most aggressive of the contradictors.

The waiter brought the coffees, which provided a brief interlude. Estalère passed them round with scrupulous attention, making sure that everyone had the right one. The others let him do it: they were used to it.

'I accept,' said Veyrenc, somewhat tight-lipped.

'What about you, Retancourt?' Adamsberg asked. 'Do you accept him?'

Retancourt looked at Veyrenc in a clear-eyed and neutral way, appearing to weigh up his capacity to help her, visibly assessing him by some standard of her own making. She looked almost like a horse-dealer appraising her animal, and the examination was sufficiently unsettling to cause a silence round the table. But Veyrenc took no offence at the process. He was the New Recruit, it was his job. And he had himself provoked this irony of fate. He was to protect Adamsberg.

'OK, I accept,' Retancourt concluded.

'Very well,' said Adamsberg.

'Him?' said Noël, between gritted teeth. 'But he's new round here, for fuck's sake.'

'He's got eleven years' service,' retorted Retancourt.

'Well, I'm against,' said Noël, raising his voice. 'This guy won't protect you, *commissaire*, he hasn't the slightest wish to.'

Well spotted, thought Adamsberg.

'Too late, it's been decided,' he decreed.

Danglard was observing the scene anxiously, while filing his nails and weighing up Noël's obvious jealousy. The *lieutenant* zipped up his leather jacket, as he did whenever he was about to overstep the line.

'It's up to you, *commissaire*,' he said with a harsh laugh, as the green light flickered across his face. 'But to fight a monster like that you need a tiger. And far as I know,' he said, jerking his chin towards the New Recruit's hair, 'there's more to a tiger than stripes.'

He's hit the spot, Danglard had time to think, before Veyrenc turned deathly pale and got to his feet opposite Noël. Then he sat down again, as if all the strength had gone out of him. Adamsberg read on the New Recruit's face such suffering that a knot of pure rage formed in his stomach, relegating the war of the two valleys into the far distance. Angry outbursts were so rare with Adamsberg that they were dangerous, as Danglard well knew. He stood up in turn, and moved round the table quickly, seeking to fend off a scene. Adamsberg had hauled Noël to his feet and, pressing his hand hard against his chest, was pushing him step by step towards the street. Veyrenc sat motionless, one hand involuntarily on his cursed hair, without even looking at them. He was simply aware that two women, Retancourt and Hélène Froissy, were sitting silently beside him. As long as he could remember, apart from his chaotic love life, women hadn't hurt him: they had never made insults or flippant remarks about his hair. Since the age of eight, he had always had girls as friends, never a single male companion. He had no idea how to talk to men and didn't want to.

Adamsberg returned to the brasserie six minutes later, alone. The tension within him had not yet dissipated, leaving his face as if illumined with a pale glow, not unlike the strange luminescence of the windows.

'Where's he gone?' asked Mordent cautiously.

'Off with the seagulls, and still flying. And if I have my way, he'll stay in the air for some time.'

'But he's already had his leave,' Estalère remarked.

This conscientious interruption had a calming effect, as if someone had opened a little window painted yellow in a room full of smoke.

'Well, he can take a bit more,' said Adamsberg, more mildly. 'Now, into your teams,' he said, glancing at his watches. 'You can pick up the photographs of the nurse from the office. Danglard will coordinate.'

'Not you?' asked Lamarre.

'No, I'm going on ahead. With Veyrenc.'

The paradoxical situation was in part beyond the control of either Adamsberg or Veyrenc, who found no verses to declaim to restore his equilibrium. He now found himself assigned to protect the *commissaire*, while Adamsberg was now Veyrenc's defender, responsibilities neither of them had wished for. Provocation can lead to undesirable consequences, Adamsberg reflected.

The two men spent a couple of hours combing the market, arranging things so that they did not have to speak directly to each other. Veyrenc did most of the questioning, while the *commissaire* appeared to be vaguely looking for some unspecified object to buy. As daylight faded, Adamsberg pointed to an abandoned wooden chest and called a pause. They sat at opposite ends of the chest, leaving maximum space between them. Veyrenc lit a cigarette, which removed the need to say anything.

'Awkward business, working together,' said Adamsberg, chin in hand.

'Yes,' agreed Veyrenc.

> '*The mysterious gods play their games with our fate,*
> *Ignoring our desires until it is too late.*'

'You're right, *lieutenant*, the gods are to blame. They get bored, so they drink and play games, and we find ourselves trampled underfoot. Both of us. Our own plans are thrown off course, and all for the gods' amusement.'

'You don't have to do this legwork. Why didn't you stay back at the office?'

'Because I'm looking for a fireguard.'

'Ah. You have an open fire?'

'Yes. When Tom starts walking it'll be dangerous. So I'm looking for a fireguard.'

'There was one back in the middle aisle. With a bit of luck, the stall might still be open.'

'You might have said earlier.'

Half an hour later, by which time it was dark, the two men were trudging back up the aisle, carrying an ancient and heavy fireguard; Veyrenc had spent a long time beating down the price, while Adamsberg had been testing its stability.

'It's fine,' Veyrenc said as they put it down beside the car. 'Good-looking, solid, and not too dear.'

'Yes, it's fine,' Adamsberg agreed. 'If you can push it on to the back seat I'll pull it from the other side.'

Adamsberg took the wheel and Veyrenc did up his seat belt. 'OK if I smoke?'

'Go ahead,' said Adamsberg, starting the engine. 'I used to smoke for years. All the kids used to smoke secretly in Caldhez. I guess it was the same with you in Laubazac.'

Veyrenc opened the car window.

'Why did you say "in Laubazac"?'

'Because that's where you lived, two kilometres from the Veyrenc de Bilhc vineyard.'

Adamsberg drove slowly, taking the bends without haste.

'Well, what of it?'

'Because it was there, in Laubazac, that you were attacked. Not in the vineyard. Why did you lie, Veyrenc?'

'I don't tell lies, *commissaire*. It was in the vineyard.'

'It was at Laubazac, on the High Meadow, behind the chapel.'

'Who was attacked, you or me?'

'You.'

'So I know what I'm talking about. If I say it was in the vineyard, it was in the vineyard.'

Adamsberg stopped at a traffic light and glanced across at his colleague. Veyrenc was obviously sincere.

'No, Veyrenc,' Adamsberg went on as he drove off again. 'It was in Laubazac, on the High Meadow. That's where the five boys came to, from the Gave de Pau valley.'

'The five louts who came from Caldhez.'

'Precisely. But they never set foot among the vines. They came to the High Meadow and they came over the path through the rocks.'

'No.'

'Yes. They had a rendezvous fixed at the chapel. That's where they attacked you.'

'I don't know what you're trying to do,' protested Veyrenc. 'But it was in the vineyard that I passed out, and my father came and fetched me and took me to hospital in Pau.'

'That was three months earlier. The day you let go of the mare, and she trampled you. You had a broken tibia, and your father picked you up in the vineyard and took you to Pau. The mare was sold after that.'

'Oh, come on,' said Veyrenc. 'How could you know that?'

'Didn't you hear about every little thing that happened in Caldhez? When René fell off the roof, but by some miracle wasn't hurt, didn't you hear about that in Laubazac? And when the grocer's shop burned down, you heard about that, didn't you?'

'Yes, of course.'

'You see.'

'But, shit, it *was* in the vineyard.'

'No, Veyrenc. The business with the mare and the attack by the boys from Caldhez were two separate incidents, one after another, and you were knocked out both times, but three months apart, with two trips to the hospital in Pau. You've mixed them up. Post-traumatic confusion, that's what the police doctor would say.'

Veyrenc undid his seat belt and leaned forward, elbows on his knees. The car was stuck in a traffic jam.

'I can't see what you're getting at, I can't at all.'

'What had you gone to do in the vineyard, when the boys appeared?'

'I'd gone to see what the grapes were like, because there'd been a storm the night before.'

'See? It's impossible. Because the attack was in February, and the grape harvest was over by then. The time with the mare, yes, that was in November, you'd gone to check the grapes for the Christmas harvest.'

'No,' repeated Veyrenc. 'And anyway, what does it matter? What the *fuck* does it matter, whether it was in the vines or in the high meadow at Laubazac? They attacked me all right, didn't they?'

'Yes.'

'Bashed my head with metal bars and slashed my stomach with a bit of glass?'

'Yes.'

'So what does it matter?'

'So it shows that you don't remember quite everything.'

'Well, I can remember their faces very well, nothing you can do about that.'

'I'm not disputing that, Veyrenc. You remember their faces, but you don't remember everything. Think about it, we'll talk about it another day.'

'Just let me off here,' said Veyrenc in a dejected voice. 'I'll walk the rest of the way.'

'What would be the point? We've got to work together for the next six months, and you wanted it that way. Don't worry, there's a fireguard poking through here between us. That will protect us.'

Adamsberg smiled briefly. His mobile rang, interrupting the valley warfare, and he passed it to Veyrenc.

'It's Danglard. Can you switch it on and hold it to my ear?'

Danglard briefly told Adamsberg that the three other teams had come back empty-handed. No woman, old or young, had been seen talking to Diala and La Paille.

'Retancourt found anything?'

'No, not much. The house is abandoned. There was a burst pipe last month, and there's ten centimetres of water on the floors.'

'She didn't find any clothes?'

'Nothing so far.'

'So all that could have waited till tomorrow, *capitaine*.'

'It's this guy, Binet. He's called you three times urgently this afternoon, according to the switchboard.'

'Who's Binet?'

'Don't you know him?'

'No, not at all.'

'Well, he knows you quite well, it seems. He's asking for you in person, urgently. He says he's got something very important to tell you. From the tone of the messages, it sounds serious.'

Adamsberg gave a puzzled glance at Veyrenc, and signed to him to take down the number.

'Can you call this Binet's number, Veyrenc, and pass it to me?'

Veyrenc punched in the number and held the phone to the *commissaire*'s ear. The traffic jam was clearing.

'Binet?'

'Hard to get hold of you, man from the Béarn!'

The man's booming voice echoed inside the car and Veyrenc raised his eyebrows.

'Not for you by any chance, is it, Veyrenc?' Adamsberg said in a whisper.

'No, don't know him,' Veyrenc whispered back, shaking his head.

The *commissaire* frowned.

'Binet, who are you?'

'Binet, Robert Binet. Oh, for . . . don't you remember me?'

'Sorry, no.'

'The café in Haroncourt, for Chrissake.'

'OK, Robert. I've got you now. How did you find out my name?'

'The Hotel du Coq, it was Anglebert's idea. He thought we should tell you right away. And we thought so, too. Of course,' said Robert, with a touch of pique, 'if you're not interested . . .'

The Norman is quick to recoil, like a snail whose horns are touched.

'No, no, Robert, of course I'm interested. What is it?'

'There's been another one. And you thought it was serious that other time, so we thought you ought to know now.'

'Another what, Robert?'

'Another one, just the same, massacred in the woods of Champ de Vigorne, near the old railway track.'

A stag, for crying out loud. Robert had been putting through urgent phone calls to Paris on account of a stag. Adamsberg sighed, feeling tired, dealing with the thick traffic and the headlights in the rain. He didn't want to upset Robert or the others in the group who had made him welcome that evening, when he had been somewhat sadly accompanying Camille to the concert. But he had had very little sleep these last nights, and simply wanted to eat and get to bed. He drove in under the entrance to the Crime Squad headquarters, and indicated by a shrug to his colleague that it wasn't anything important and he could go off home now. But Veyrenc, who seemed sunk in his own disturbed thoughts, did not move.

'Give me the details, Robert,' said Adamsberg in a resigned voice, as he parked the car. 'I'm taking notes,' he said, but without taking out a pen.

'Like I said. Massacred. Demolished.'

'What does Anglebert say?'

'You know Anglebert, he's got his own ideas about it. He thinks it's some young nutter who's got a bit older but no wiser. The thing is, he's moved from Brétilly, he's over our way now. Anglebert's not sure it's a weirdo from Paris any more. He said it could be some local weirdo.'

'And the heart?' Adamsberg asked. Veyrenc frowned.

'Cut out, thrown away, all chopped up. Same thing all over again, listen what I'm telling you. Except it's a ten-pointer. Oswald, of course, he thinks it's a niner, not that he can't count, but he always has to be different. So are you going to do something about it?'

'I guess so, Robert,' Adamsberg lied.

'Can you get over here? We'll buy your supper, we're waiting for you. What'll it take you? Hour and a half?'

'I can't come just now, I'm dealing with a double murder.'

'Ha, so are we. If you don't call this a double murder, then I don't know what is.'

'Have you told the gendarmes?'

'They couldn't give a shit. Thick as two short planks. They didn't even stir themselves to take a look.'

'And you did?'

'Yeah, this time we did. The Champ de Vigorne, that's close to us, understand?'

'So is it a tenner or a niner?'

'A tenner, of course. Oswald, he just talks a lot of rubbish to annoy. His mother was from Opportune, just by where they found the stag. So, of course, he's showing off about it. But come on, dammit, are you coming up here for a drink or not? We can't wait for ever.'

Adamsberg was trying to think of the best way to wriggle out of the situation, which was difficult, since Robert considered the slaughter of the stags as weighing the same in the balance as two men who'd had their throats cut. In the obstinacy stakes, it seemed that Normans – these ones, at any rate – were as bad as the Béarnais, at least the ones from the Gave de Pau and Ossau valleys.

'I can't, Robert, I've got a ghost on my hands.'

'Well, Oswald's got one too, and that doesn't stop him coming out for a drink.'

'He's what? Oswald?'

'He's got a ghost on his hands, like I said. In the graveyard at Opportune-la-Haute. Well, it was his nephew that saw it. He's been going on about it for a month now.'

'Put Oswald on the line.'

'Can't, he's gone out. But if you come, he'll be back here. He wants to see you too.'

'Why?'

'Because his sister's asked him to see you, about the thing in the graveyard. Maybe she's right, 'cos the police in Evreux, they don't want to know.'

'But what was it, this thing, Robert?'

'Don't ask me, I don't know.'

Adamsberg consulted his watches. Almost seven o'clock.

'I'll see what I can do, Robert.'

The *commissaire* put the mobile back in his pocket, and gazed ahead of him. Veyrenc was still sitting in the car.

'Something urgent?'

Adamsberg leaned his head against the glass of the window.

'No, it's nothing.'

'But he was talking about a *heart* being torn out.'

'It's a stag, *lieutenant*. Up there, they've got someone who gets his kicks cutting up stags, and that's got them all in a sweat.'

'A poacher?'

'No, not at all, someone who just likes killing stags. And they've got a ghost too, a Shade, up there in Normandy.'

'Nothing to do with us, though, is it?'

'Nope, not at all.'

'So why are you going?'

'I'm not going, Veyrenc. I can't do anything about it.'

'I thought you seemed like you wanted to go.'

'Too tired and it's of no importance,' said Adamsberg, opening his door. 'I'd end up smashing the car and me with it. I'll call Robert later.'

The car's doors slammed. Adamsberg locked it. The two men prepared to separate a few yards further on, in front of the *Brasserie des Philosophes*.

'If you want,' Veyrenc said, 'I could drive and you could sleep. We could get up there and back in the evening.'

Adamsberg, his mind a blank, stared at the car keys he was still holding.

XXII

COMING IN THROUGH THE RAIN, ADAMSBERG PUSHED OPEN THE DOOR of the café in Haroncourt. Anglebert had risen to greet him, standing stiffly, a posture immediately adopted by the rest of the tribe.

'Sit down, man from the Béarn,' said the old man, shaking his hand. 'We kept some food warm for you.'

'Two of you?' asked Robert.

Adamsberg introduced Veyrenc as a colleague, an event which occasioned another round of handshakes, with a little more suspicion, and the arrival of an extra chair. All of them cast quick glances at the striking hair of the newcomer. But there was no risk here of questions about this phenomenon, however unusual. That did not prevent the men from pondering the strange apparition, and working out ways to find out more about the disciple whom the *commissaire* had brought along. Anglebert was examining the similarities in appearance of the two policemen, and drawing his own conclusions.

'A cousin a few times removed,' he said, filling up the glasses.

Adamsberg was beginning to understand the way the Norman mind worked: in a sly and crafty fashion, contriving to put a question without ever asking directly. The intonation would drop at the end of the sentence, as if for a false statement.

'Removed?' asked Adamsberg, since, being from the Pyrenees, he was entitled to ask questions.

'Further off than a first cousin,' explained Hilaire. 'Anglebert's my cousin four times removed. As for this one,' he said, pointing to Veyrenc, 'you're about six or seven times removed.'

'Could be,' Adamsberg conceded.

'Anyway, he's from your part of the country.'

'Not far off, true.'

'Police is full of guys from the south-west, then,' Alphonse asked, without seeming to ask.

'Before him, I was the only one.'

'Veyrenc de Bilhc', the New Recruit said, presenting himself.

'Veyrenc will do,' said Robert, simplifying.

There were several nods to signify that this proposal was accepted. It still didn't enlighten anyone about Veyrenc's hair. That enigma would clearly take years to solve and they would have to be patient. A second plate was brought for the New Recruit, and Anglebert waited until both men had finished eating before making a sign to Robert to get down to business. Robert solemnly set out photographs of the stag on the table.

'It's not in the same position,' said Adamsberg, to try and stimulate in himself an interest he did not feel.

He was not even capable of saying why he had come at all, or how Veyrenc had understood that he wanted to come.

'Two shots hit him full on, in the chest, he collapsed on his side and the heart's down on the right.'

'So the killer doesn't have a standard approach.'

'Just wants to kill the animal, full stop.'

'Or get at its heart,' put in Oswald.

'What are you going to do about it, man from the Béarn?'

'Go and take a look.'

'What, now?'

'If one of you can take me there. I've brought some torches.'

The abruptness of this proposal took them aback.

'Well, I suppose so,' said the old man.

'Oswald could go with you. He could go and see his sister.'

'Could do,' said Oswald.

'You'll have to give them a bed for the night. Or bring them back here. No hotel up in Opportune.'

'We have to get back to Paris tonight,' said Veyrenc.

'Unless we stay here,' said Adamsberg.

An hour later they were examining the scene of the murder. Once he had viewed the animal, lying in the path, Adamsberg understood at last the genuine pain felt by the men of the village. Oswald and Robert both lowered their heads in distress. It was an animal, a stag, yes, but it was also a scene of pure savagery, a massacre of beauty.

'A cracking male,' said Robert with an effort. 'Still had plenty of life in him.'

'He had his herd,' Oswald explained. 'Five hinds. Six fights last year. I tell you, a stag like that, he'd fight like a hero, he'd have kept his hinds another four or five years before another male could beat him. Nobody from round here would have shot this one. Used to call him the Red Giant. His fawns are sturdy little things, you could see that right off.'

'See, he had these three red patches on the right, and two on the left. That's why they called him the Red Giant.'

A brother, or at least a cousin a few times removed, thought Veyrenc, folding his arms. Robert knelt down by the huge carcass and stroked its hide. In this wood, in the middle of the night, under the pouring rain, with these unshaven men standing round him, Adamsberg had to make an effort to remember that somewhere else, at the same time, cars were moving through streets and television sets were working. Mathias's prehistoric times seemed to be appearing in front of him, intact. He was no longer quite sure whether the Red Giant was an ordinary stag, or perhaps a man, or even some divine being who had been slaughtered, robbed and despoiled. The kind of stag that prehistoric men painted on the walls of a cave, in order to honour its memory.

'We'll bury him tomorrow,' said Robert, rising heavily to his feet. 'We were waiting for you, see. We wanted you to see it with your own eyes. Oswald, pass me the axe.'

Oswald felt in his big leather pouch and brought the axe out without a word. Robert felt the edge with his fingers, knelt again alongside the stag's head, then hesitated. He turned to Adamsberg.

'You do the honours, man from the Béarn,' he said. 'Cut off the antlers.'

'Robert . . .' said Oswald, uncertainly.

'No, I've thought about it, Oswald, he deserves them. He was tired, he was back in Paris, but he came all this way for the Red Giant. He gets the honour, he gets the antlers.'

'But Robert,' Oswald insisted. 'He's not from round here.'

'Well, he is now,' said Robert, putting the axe in Adamsberg's hands.

Adamsberg found himself holding a sharp weapon, and being pulled towards the stag's head.

'You cut them for me,' he said to Robert. 'I don't want to make a mess of it.'

'Can't do that. You want 'em, you have to cut 'em off yourself.'

Guided by Robert, who held the beast's head down on the ground, Adamsberg gripped the axe and struck six blows close to the skull, in the places indicated by the Norman's finger. Robert took back the axe, lifted the antlers and put them in the *commissaire*'s arms. About four kilos each, Adamsberg estimated, feeling their weight.

'Don't lose them now,' said Robert. 'They bring long life.'

'Well,' put in Oswald, 'that's not for sure, but they won't hurt.'

'And never separate them,' Robert went on. 'Hear what I'm saying? Never put one somewhere without the other.'

Adamsberg nodded in the dark, gripping the ridged antlers in his hands. It was certainly not the moment to drop them. Veyrenc shot him an ironic glance.

'*Do not stumble, my lord, 'neath the trophies of life,*' he murmured.

'I didn't ask for this, Veyrenc.'

> '*They were offered to you, you yourself gripped the knife,*
> *Do not seek to escape the strange chance of this night*
> *Which makes you the bearer of hope and new light.*'

'That'll do, Veyrenc. Carry them yourself, or shut up.'

'No, my lord, neither one nor the other.'

XXIII

Oswald's sister, Hermance, observed two rituals which were supposed to protect her from the dangers of the world: not to stay awake after ten at night, and not to allow anyone into the house wearing shoes. Oswald and the two policemen went up the stairs silently, holding their muddy shoes in their hands.

'There's only one spare bedroom,' Oswald whispered, 'but it's a big one. Is that all right?'

Adamsberg nodded, though he was far from eager to spend the night with the *lieutenant*. Similarly, Veyrenc was relieved to note that the room contained two high wooden bedsteads, about two metres apart.

> '*Between the two couches, the valley must be deep,*
> *So that bodies and souls are separate in sleep.*'

'The bathroom's next door,' Oswald added. 'Don't forget to stay barefoot. You put your shoes on, you could be the death of her.'

'Even if she doesn't find out?'

'Everything gets found out here, especially things that didn't ought to be. I'll be downstairs, man from the Béarn. We should have a word.'

Adamsberg threw his damp jacket over the rail of the left-hand bed and gently laid the antlers on the floor. Veyrenc had already lain down fully dressed, facing the wall. The *commissaire* joined Oswald in the little kitchen.

'You cousin's asleep already?'

'He's not my cousin, Oswald.'

'The hair, I suppose that's something personal?'

'Very,' said Adamsberg. 'Now, what have you got to tell me?'

'It's not me wants to tell you, it's Hermance.'

'But she doesn't know me, Oswald.'

'Maybe someone told her about you.'

'Who?'

'Parish priest, perhaps. Don't ask. Hermance, she's not what you might call reasonable. She's got her own ideas all right, but we don't always know where they come from.'

Oswald's voice had trailed off sadly, and Adamsberg changed the subject.

'Never mind, Oswald. Tell me about the ghost.'

'Wasn't me that saw it, it was my nephew. Gratien.'

'How long ago?'

'Over five weeks ago, one Tuesday night.'

'And where?'

'In the graveyard, of course. Where do you think?'

'What was your nephew doing in the graveyard?'

'He wasn't in there, he was in the lane that goes up the top of it. Well, goes up or down, depending which way you're facing. Tuesdays and Friday nights, he meets his girlfriend up there when she's worked her shift. Whole village knows about it, except his mother.'

'How old is he?'

'Seventeen. With Hermance going off to sleep at ten, like clockwork, it's easy for him to slip out. Mind now, don't give him away.'

'So what next, Oswald?'

Oswald filled two small glasses with calvados and sat down with a sigh. He raised his pale eyes towards Adamsberg and drank it off.

'Good health.'

'Thanks.'

'Want me to tell you something?'

He's going to tell me anyway, thought Adamsberg.

'This is the first time an outsider's been let take the antlers out of the district. I've seen it all now.'

'Seen it all' is a bit much, thought Adamsberg. But obviously this business with the stag was serious. '*They were offered to you, you yourself gripped the knife.*' The *commissaire* was both surprised and annoyed at himself for having memorised one of Veyrenc's lines of verse.

'Does it bother you if I take them?' he asked.

Faced with a direct and intimate question, Oswald gave an oblique anwer.

'It's like this. Robert, he must have a deal of respect for you, do a thing like that. Then again, I suppose he knows what he's doing. He doesn't make mistakes, as a rule.'

'So it's not so bad, then?' said Adamsberg, with a smile.

'No, I suppose not. When all's said and done.'

'Well, what next, Oswald?'

'Like I said. Then he saw this ghost.'

'Tell me about it.'

'This shape, like a tall woman, if you could call it a woman, all grey, all muffled up, no face. Figure of death, sort of. I wouldn't say that if my sister was here, but man to man we can say that kind of thing, can't we?'

'Yes.'

'So I'll say it. Death. Didn't walk like ordinary people. Kind of gliding along in the cemetery, very stiff and slow. Not in a hurry, going step by step.'

'Does your nephew like a drink?'

'No, not yet. Just because he's sleeping with his girlfriend doesn't mean he's a man yet. As for this ghost, what it did I can't say. Or what it was looking for. Afterwards we watched to see if anyone died in the village. No, nothing like that.'

'And that's all he saw?'

'Well, he ran straight home without waiting to find out. What would you do? So why did she come? Why here?'

'I have no idea, Oswald.'

'The priest says she appeared before, in 1809, and that was the year the apple harvest failed. The branches were bare as my arm.'

'No other consequences? Besides the apples?'

Oswald stole a glance at Adamsberg. 'Robert says you've seen a ghost too.'

'I haven't seen mine, I've just thought about it. It's a sort of dark cloud, a Shade, a veil that falls over me when I'm in the office. A doctor would say I'm imagining things. Or perhaps reviving some bad memory.'

'Doctors don't reckon much to this sort of thing.'

'Well, maybe they're right. It's probably just a dark thought. Not yet out of my head, roaming about inside.'

'Like the deer's antlers before they grow.'

'*Exactly*,' said Adamsberg, with a sudden smile.

This idea greatly pleased him, since it almost resolved the matter of his own dark Shade. The weight of a dark idea, formed inside the mind but not yet making its way to the outside. Like a child struggling to be born.

'This idea, you just get it at work?' asked Oswald, thoughtfully. 'You don't get it here?'

'No.'

'Well, something must have come into your squad,' explained Oswald, gesturing. 'Then the thing got in your head, because you're the boss. That's logical, isn't it?'

Oswald emptied the last drop of calvados into the glasses.

'Or maybe it's something personal to you,' he added. 'Anyway, I got the boy here. He's waiting outside.'

No choice. Adamsberg followed Oswald outside.

'You haven't put your shoes back on,' Oswald pointed out.

'It's fine like this. Ideas can circulate through the soles of your feet.'

'Well, if that were true,' said Oswald with a half-smile, 'my sister'd have plenty of ideas.'

'And she doesn't?'

'Tell you God's truth, she's kind enough to melt a heart of stone, but there's nothing between her ears. But there it is. She's my sister.'

'What about Gratien?'

'No comparison. Takes after his father, sharp as a needle.'

'And his father is . . . ?'

Oswald clammed up immediately, drawing in his horns like a snail.

'Amédée left your sister, then?'Adamsberg insisted.

'How do you know his name?'

'It was written on a photo in the kitchen.'

'No, Amédée's dead. Long time ago. We don't talk about it.'

'Why not?' asked Adamsberg, ignoring the warning signs.

'What's it to you?'

'You never know. With a ghost about, understand? You have to think of everything.'

'Well, perhaps so,' Oswald conceded.

'My neighbour says that the dead don't leave us if they haven't finished their lives. They come back to worry the living for centuries.'

'You mean Amédée hadn't finished living?'

'You tell me.'

'He was coming back home from another woman, one night,' Oswald said, with some reticence. 'He had a bath, so my sister wouldn't guess. And he drowned.'

'In the *bathtub*?'

'Like I said. He must have taken a queer turn or a stroke. And in the bath, there was water, right? And if your head goes under water, you can drown, just like in a pond. That was what finished my sister's mind off.'

'Was there an inquest?'

'Of course. They got everyone sweating with panic for weeks. You know what the cops are.'

'They suspected your sister?'

'They drove her crazy, yes. Poor woman. She hasn't the strength to lift a sack of potatoes. So how she could have drowned a big lad like Amédée in his bath, I don't know. Especially since she was barmy about him, stupid bugger that he was.'

'Wait a minute. You said he was as sharp as a needle.'

'You catch on quickly too, don't you?'

'What do you mean, then?'

'He's not the boy's father. Gratien's from her first marriage, her first husband. He died and all, if you want to know, two years after they married.'

'What was his name?'

'He was from Lorraine. Not from round here. Cut his legs with a scythe when he was mowing a meadow.'

'Your sister doesn't seem to have much luck.'

'You can say that again. That's why, round here, they don't make fun of her little ways. She's entitled, if it comforts her.'

Oswald jerked his head, as if relieved to have finished with the subject.

'Now what I've told you, please don't go shouting it from the rooftops. This is a family story, and it stays in the village. We've forgotten it, and that's that.'

'I never repeat things, Oswald.'

'Don't you have stories like this as well, kept in your village?'

'I've got one, yes. But at the moment it's getting out of the village.'

'Not a good idea,' said Oswald, shaking his head. 'It might seem a little thing but it's like a monster getting loose.'

* * *

Oswald's nephew, a lad with freckled cheeks like his uncle's, was standing in front of Adamsberg, his shoulders drooping. He didn't dare refuse to speak to the senior policeman from Paris, but it put him severely to the test. Stare fixed on the ground, he described the night he had seen the ghost; the story echoed what Oswald had said.

'Did you tell your mother?'

'Course I did.'

'And she wanted you to tell me about it?'

'Yes. After you came here for the concert.'

'Do you know why?'

The boy suddenly hunched his shoulders.

'People say all kinds of rubbish,' he said. 'My mother's got her own ideas, you got to understand her, that's all. Anyway, she must be right, 'cos here you are asking about it.'

'Your mother's quite right,' said Adamsberg, to calm the lad.

'People say things their own way,' Gratien insisted. 'Ain't any one way better than another, though.'

'No, no,' Adamsberg agreed. 'Just one more thing and I'll let you go. Shut your eyes. Now tell me what I look like and what clothes I'm wearing.'

'Really?'

'If the *commissaire* says so,' Oswald intervened.

'OK, you're not so tall,' Gratien began, timidly. ''Bout the same as my uncle. Brown hair . . . is it OK to say anything?'

'Everything you can think of.'

'Hair's bit of a mess, then, some of it's hanging in your eyes, the rest pushed back. Big nose, brown eyes, black jacket, canvas, lot of pockets, sleeves pushed up. Trousers . . . black as well, I think, a bit worn, and you're not wearing shoes.'

'Shirt, sweater, tie? Concentrate.'

Gratien shook his head, his eyes squeezed tight shut.

'No,' he said firmly.

'What, then?'

'Grey T-shirt.'

'Open your eyes. You're a perfect witness, very rare.' The teenager smiled, reassured by having passed this test.

'It's dark as well,' he said proudly.

'Yes, indeed.'

'You didn't trust what I said before? About the ghost?'

'Anyone's memories can change a bit, over time. What do you think the ghost was doing? Just walking about? Drifting here and there.'

'No.'

'Looking in the air? Pacing up and down, waiting? Do you think it was expecting someone?'

'No, what I think it was doing, it was looking for something, a grave maybe, but it wasn't in no hurry. It wasn't going quickly.'

'So what scared you about it?'

'It was the way it walked. And all that grey floaty stuff wrapped round it. I'm still scared.'

'Try and forget it – I'll take care of it now.'

'But what can you do about it, if it was the figure of Death?'

'We'll see,' said Adamsberg. 'We'll think of something.'

XXIV

On waking, Veyrenc found the *commissaire* already up and doing. Veyrenc, having lain down fully dressed, had slept badly: now and then a picture of either the vineyard or the High Meadow would flash before his eyes. One or the other. His father was lifting him up off the ground, he was in pain. Was it November or February? Before the late grape harvest, or after? He could no longer see the scene clearly, a headache was pulsing at his temples. Caused either by the rough wine served in the café in Haroncourt, or by the painful confusion of his memories.

'We're going back to Paris, Veyrenc. Don't forget, no shoes in the bathroom. She's had a tough life.'

Oswald's sister served them a huge breakfast, the kind that kept ploughmen going until midday. Contrary to the tragic person whom Adamsberg had been expecting, Hermance was cheerful and talkative, and indeed kind-hearted enough to melt a hundred hearts of stone. She was a tall, rather angular woman who moved around cautiously, as if she was surprised to find herself alive. Her chatter was composed of the most trivial non sequiturs, some pointless, some completely odd, and she could evidently keep it up for hours. In a sense, it was a work of great artistry, a lacy network of words, woven so fine that it contained only holes.

'. . . eat something before going to work, that's what I say every day,'

Adamsberg heard. 'Work makes you tired, yes, when I think of all that work. Yes, indeed, that's it, isn't it? You must have some work to do, I expect, I saw you came in a car. Oswald has two cars, one for work, he ought to wash that van. It carries mud everywhere, and that just makes more work, well, there you are. I didn't make your eggs too hard. Gratien, now, he won't eat eggs, of course. That's how he is, other people are different, aren't they? One thing and another, that's what makes it all so difficult, so there you are.'

'Hermance, said Adamsberg cautiously. 'Who suggested you talk to me? About the thing in the graveyard, I mean.'

'Oh yes, that's what I said to Oswald. Yes, better do that, it can't do any harm, but if it doesn't do any good, come to that, well, there you are, aren't you?'

'Yes, er, there you are,' said Adamsberg, trying to communicate on the same wavelength as Hermance. 'So someone advised you to talk to me about it? Hilaire, perhaps, or Anglebert? Or Achille? Or the priest?'

'Well, it stands to reason, doesn't it? We can't have disgusting things like that in the graveyard, and afterwards you just wonder, don't you, and that's what I said to Oswald, it wouldn't hurt to ask you. Yes, indeed.'

'We're on our way now, Hermance,' said Adamsberg, intercepting a glance from Veyrenc who was signalling to him to give up.

The two men put their shoes on outside the house, after taking care to leave their room as tidy as a stage set. From behind the door, Adamsberg could hear Hermance continuing to talk to herself.

'Ah yes, that's work isn't it? Mustn't let things get on top of you.'

'A bit missing there,' said Veyrenc sadly, as he tied his laces. 'Either she was born like that or she lost it somewhere.'

'Lost it somewhere, I think. Both her husbands died young and suddenly, one after the other. We can mention that here, but we're not allowed to repeat anything about it outside Opportune-la-Haute.'

'That's why Hilaire hinted that Hermance brought bad luck. Men would be afraid to marry her, it could be the death of them.'

'Once you get a reputation like that, you can never get rid of it. It sticks to you like a tick in your flesh. You can pull the tick off, but the jaws stay in there, still working away.'

A bit like Lucio's spider, Adamsberg thought to himself.

'Since you seem to know a few of the people round here, who do you think advised her to see you?'

'I don't know, Veyrenc. Maybe nobody at all. She was probably worried about the ghost for her son's sake. I think she's scared stiff of the gendarmes, after the inquest on Amédée. And she had must have heard Oswald mention me.'

'Do people really think she killed both her husbands?'

'They don't really think that, but they wonder about it. Whether she could have killed them in person, or maybe just by willing it. We'll take a look at the graveyard before we go back.'

'What are we looking for?'

'Whatever the ghost was up to. I promised the young man I'd sort it out. But Robert didn't talk about a ghost, he talked about a "thing", and Hermance talked about "disgusting things" in the graveyard. Or perhaps we should try another tack.'

'What?'

'To try and understand why they dragged me all the way out here.'

'If I hadn't driven you,' Veyrenc objected, 'you wouldn't be here at all.'

'Yes, *lieutenant*, I know. But it's just a feeling.'

A shade passing, thought Veyrenc.

'Apparently Oswald gave his sister a puppy,' he remarked. 'But it died.'

Adamsberg was walking up and down the grassy alleyways of the little graveyard, holding an antler in each hand. Veyrenc had offered to take one of them for him, but Robert had made it very clear that they were not to be separated. Adamsberg paced round the site, taking care not to knock the great horns against the monuments on the tombs. It was a modest graveyard, and only minimally maintained. Grass was growing up through the gravel in the walks. Most people here could not afford large funeral vaults and many graves were simply grassy mounds, some marked with a wooden cross bearing a name painted on it in white. The tombs of Hermance's two husbands had been covered by thin limestone slabs, plain grey and without flowers. Adamsberg was anxious to leave, yet he lingered, enjoying the obstinate ray of spring sunshine as it warmed the back of his neck.

'Where did this lad Gratien see the figure?' asked Veyrenc.

'Over there,' said Adamsberg, pointing.

'And what should we be looking for?'

'Dunno.'

Veyrenc nodded, without showing annnoyance. Except when it came to Pyrenean valleys, the *lieutenant* was not the kind of man to be impatient or short-tempered. This near-cousin did resemble Adamsberg in a way, as he calmly accepted the improbable or the difficult. He too was enjoying the sunshine on his back, and was tempted to stay as long as possible, walking through the wet grass. Adamsberg strolled round the little church, noticing the spring brightness which announced its presence by making the slate roof and the marble stones shine.

'*Commissaire*,' Veyrenc called.

Adamsberg walked over to him, taking his time. The sunlight was playing on the red streaks in Veyrenc's hair. If the stripes had not been the result of torture, Adamsberg would have found them quite attractive. Out of evil came forth sweetness.

'I know we don't know what to look for,' said Veyrenc, pointing to a grave. 'But this is another woman who had bad luck. Dead at thirty-eight, a bit like Elisabeth Châtel.'

Adamsberg considered the grave, a mound of earth, waiting for a headstone. He was beginning to understand the *lieutenant* a little, and knew that he would certainly not have called him over for nothing,

'The song of the earth, can you hear it?' said Veyrenc. 'Can you decipher what it's telling us?'

'If you're talking about the grass growing on the grave, I can see some blades that are short and some that are long.'

'One might think – but only if one was *looking* for something to think – that the short blades have grown later than the others.'

The two men fell silent, each asking himself at the same moment whether he was really looking for something to think.

'They'll be waiting for us in Paris,' Veyrenc objected to himself.

'One might think,' said Adamsberg, 'that the grass at the head of the grave is shorter, and therefore a later growth than the rest. It makes a sort of circle. And this woman is from Normandy, like Elisabeth.'

'But if we spent all the time visiting graveyards, we'd probably find thousands of blades of grass all different lengths.'

'Yes, that's right. But there's no reason not to check whether there's a hole under the short grass, is there?'

> *'It's for you to judge, my lord, if the signs we see here*
> *Are the products of chance, or are something to fear.*
> *And if the dark pathway you now desire to trace*
> *Will lead us to success or else into disgrace.'*

'Better find out right away,' said Adamsberg, placing the antlers on the ground. 'I'll tell Danglard we're extending our stay in the country.'

XXV

THE CAT TIPTOED ROUND THE OFFICES OF THE SERIOUS CRIME SQUAD, FROM one secure perch to another, from one knee to the next, from a *brigadier*'s desk to a *lieutenant*'s chair, as if crossing a stream on stepping stones without wetting its feet. It had started life as a little ball of fluff following Camille in the street, and had continued under the protection of Adrien Danglard, who had been obliged to give it lodging at the office. All because this cat was incapable of looking after itself, being completely without that rather disdainful independence which most cats so grandly display. Although it was an uncastrated male, it was the embodiment of dependence on others and inclined to non-stop sleep. The Snowball, as Danglard had baptised it when he took it in, was quite unlike the sort of cat a squad of police officers might have adopted as a mascot. The team took it in turns to look after the big, soft, furry creature, scared of its own shadow, which needed to be accompanied when it went anywhere, whether to eat, drink or relieve itself. But it had its favourites. Retancourt was the leader by far in this respect. The Snowball spent most of its days close to her desk, snoozing on the warm lid of one of the photocopy machines. The machine in question could not be used without giving the cat a fatal shock. In the absence of the woman he loved, the Snowball trailed back to Danglard or, in unvarying order of preference, to Justin, Froissy and, oddly enough, Noël.

Danglard considered himself lucky when the creature deigned to walk the twenty metres to its feeding bowl. One time in three, it would give up and roll on to its back, obliging someone to take it to the food or to its litter tray in the drinks room. That Thursday, Danglard was holding the cat under his arm, like a floorcloth hanging down on both sides, when Brézillon telephoned, wanting Adamsberg.

'Where the devil is he? His mobile's not on. Or perhaps he's refusing to answer it.'

'I don't know, *Monsieur le divisionnaire*. But I expect he's dealing with some pressing matter.'

'Oh, bound to be,' said Brézillon with a harsh laugh.

Danglard put the cat down, so that the *divisionnaire*'s anger should not frighten it. The consequences of the expedition to Montrouge had exasperated Brézillon. He had already told the *commissaire* to stop following up that particular lead, since tomb-robbers were never murderers, according to all the psychiatric records.

'You're not very good at lying, *Commandant* Danglard. Please inform him that I expect him to be back at his desk by five this afternoon. And what about the death in Reims? Still working on it?'

'Sorted, *Monsieur le divisionnaire*.'

'And this nurse who's on the run? What the devil are you doing about her?'

'We've put out her description. She's been reported in twenty different places already this week. We're following them up and checking.'

'And Adamsberg's in charge of that?'

'Yes, of course, sir.'

'From a country graveyard in Opportune-la-Haute?'

Danglard swallowed a couple of mouthfuls of white wine and shook his head at the cat. It was clear that the Snowball was on the verge of becoming an alcoholic and needed watching. His only independent forays were to find the personal caches used by Danglard. He had recently discovered the one underneath the boiler in the basement.

This was proof positive that the Snowball was not the imbecile everyone took him for, that he was in fact a cat of exceptional flair. But, alas, Danglard could hardly inform anyone else of this prowess.

'As you see, it's pointless trying to put one across me,' Brézillon went on.

'Not trying to, sir,' said Danglard, sincerely.

'The Squad is on a hiding to nothing. Adamsberg's leading it astray, and you're all following him. If you don't already know what he's up to, which frankly would surprise me, I'll tell you what your boss is doing right now. He's exploring an inoffensive grave in some godforsaken village out in the sticks.'

Well, why not? Danglard thought to himself. The *commandant* was usually the first to criticise Adamsberg's fantastic escapades, but he always put up the sturdiest of defences against any external attack.

'And what's that all about?' Brézillon was going on. 'I'll tell you that, too. Because some village idiot saw a ghost in a field.'

Why not? thought Danglard again, swallowing another mouthful.

'That's what Adamsberg's up to, that's what he's "checking" right now.'

'Did the Evreux gendarmes report that to you?'

'That, Danglard, is their job: to report when a *commissaire* goes off-mission. And they get on to it, fast and efficiently. I want him back here at five this evening, checking out sightings of that nurse.'

'I don't think that will attract him,' Danglard murmured softly.

'And as for the two stiffs in La Chapelle, I'm taking you off them as of now. Drugs can have them. You can tell him that, *commandant*. I presume that when *you* call him, he deigns to answer his phone.'

Danglard emptied his glass and picked up the cat, but before doing anything else, he called the number of the *gendarmerie* at Evreux.

'Get me the *commandant* – tell him it's an urgent call from Paris.'

Clenching his fingers in the cat's furry pelt, Danglard waited impatiently.

'*Commandant* Devalon? Was it you told Brézillon that Adamsberg was in your sector?'

'Listen, when Adamsberg's on the loose round here, prevention's better than cure. Who am I talking to?'

'*Commandant* Danglard. Go to hell, Devalon.'

'Don't waste your breath, Danglard. You'd do better to get your boss back home, pronto.'

Danglard banged down the receiver, and the cat stretched out its paws in fright.

XXVI

'FIVE O'CLOCK? OH, THE HELL WITH HIM, DANGLARD.'

'He knows you'll say that. Come back, *commissaire* – things will be hotting up otherwise. What are you doing, anyway?'

'We're looking for a hole under some blades of grass.'

'Who's "we"?'

'Veyrenc and me.'

'Well, get back here. Evreux's been told you're poking about in one of their cemeteries.'

'But the dead men in La Chapelle are ours.'

'Not any more. We've been taken off the case, *commissaire*.'

'OK, Danglard,' said Adamsberg after a silence. 'I get the picture.'

Adamsberg snapped his phone shut.

'We're going to have to change tactics, Veyrenc. It's going to be a bit tight for time.'

'We're giving up?'

'No, I'm calling in the expert.'

Adamsberg and Veyrenc had been feeling the surface of the earth over the grave for half an hour without finding any sign of a crack indicating a hole underneath it. Vandoosler Senior answered the phone again, which suggested that he had the job of filtering the calls to the household.

'Given up, finished, kaput?' he said.

'No, Vandoosler, since I'm calling you.'

'Which one do you want this time?'

'Same one again.'

'Bad call, he's out of town. He's off on a dig in the Essonne.'

'Well, give me his number.'

'Look, when Mathias is on a dig, nothing will make him leave it.'

'Oh for God's sake, Vandoosler, just give me the number!'

Vandoosler Senior was not mistaken, and Adamsberg gathered that he was disturbing the prehistoric expert when he eventually got through. No, Mathias couldn't come, he was uncovering a Magdalenian household with scorched hearthstones, flint chippings, reindeer antlers and other objects which he listed, in order to try and convey the situation to Adamsberg.

'This household circle is complete, it's from 12,000 BC. What are you offering me instead?'

'Another circle. Some of the grass is shorter, making a sort of ring in the middle of some longer grass, on top of a grave. If we don't find anything, our two corpses will be sent over to Drugs. Mathias, look, I'm telling you there's something important here. Your circle's already been opened up – it can wait. Mine can't.'

Mathias was no more interested in Adamsberg's investigations than the policeman was concerned with palaeolithic remains. But the two men agreed when it came to emergencies.

'What took you to this grave?' Mathias asked.

'It's the grave of a young woman from Normandy, like the one in Montrouge, and a ghost has been seen recently, prowling in the grave-yard.'

'You're in Normandy?'

'Opportune-la-Haute in the Eure *département*.'

'Clay and flint,' Mathias pronounced. 'You just need a layer of flint underneath to make the grass grow shorter and less thickly. Is there some flint around there – a wall with foundations for instance?'

'Yes,' said Adamsberg, walking towards the church.

'Look at its base and tell me what kind of vegetation there is.'

'The grass is thicker than on the grave,' said Adamsberg.

'Anything else?'

'Thistles, nettles, plantains, and some other plants I don't know the names of.'

'OK, now go back to the grave. What can you see in the short grass?'

'Some daisies,'

'Nothing else?'

'Bit of clover, couple of dandelions.'

'OK,' said Mathias after a pause. 'Did you look for the edge of a hole?'

'Yes.'

'And?'

'Why do you think I'm calling you?'

Mathias looked down at the Magdalenian household remains at his feet.

'I'm on my way,' he said.

At the café in Opportune, which was also the local grocery store and cider depot, Adamsberg was allowed to put the antlers down in the entry. Everyone knew already that he was a Pyrenean cop from Paris, who had been given Anglebert's blessing in Haroncourt, but the noble trophies he was carrying opened doors for him more effectively than any references. The café owner, a cousin of Oswald's five times removed, served the two policemen diligently, rendering honour where it was due.

'Mathias is getting a train out of Saint-Lazare in three hours,' Adamsberg reported. 'He'll be in Evreux at 14.34.'

'We'll need authorisation to exhume before he gets here,' said Veyrenc. 'But you won't get that without the *divisionnaire*'s consent. And Brézillon doesn't want you to handle this. He doesn't like you, does he?'

'Brézillon doesn't like anyone much, he just likes shouting down the phone. He gets on fine with people like Mortier.'

'Without his permission, though, we won't get a permit. So there's no point in Mathias coming.'

'Well, we'd find out whether someone had dug a hole on top of the grave.'

'Yes, but we'd still be blocked in a few hours, unless we do it unofficially. Which will be impossible, because the Evreux cops are watching us. Moment anyone lifts a pickaxe, they'll be down on us like a ton of bricks.'

'Your summary does you credit, Veyrenc.'

The lieutenant dropped a lump of sugar in his coffee and gave a broad grin, which raised his upper lip on the right.

'There is something we could try,' he said. 'But it's pretty mean.'

'Go on.'

'Threaten Brézillon, if he won't lift the ban on us, to spill the beans on something his son did fourteen years ago. I'm the only one who knows about it.'

'Yeah, that *is* pretty mean.'

'It is, isn't it?'

'How do you propose to do that?'

'I'd never carry out the threat. I've stayed on good terms with Guy, the son – I wouldn't want to hurt him, after getting him out of that mess when he was a boy.'

'Well, it could work,' said Adamsberg, resting his cheek on his hand. 'Brézillon would crack at once. Like all tough guys, he's soft underneath. Same principle as the walnut. Put pressure on it and it breaks. But you try breaking honey.'

'That makes me feel hungry,' said Veyrenc suddenly.

He went up to the counter, ordered some bread with local honey, and sat down again.

'I've thought of another possibility,' he said. 'I could call Guy direct.

I tell him the situation, and ask him to beg his father to let us go ahead.'

'Would that work?'

'I think so.

> *The child of the father has powers at his command*
> *To oblige the elder to grant a strange demand.'*

'And the son in question owes you a favour, if I've got this right?'

'If it wasn't for me, he wouldn't be a graduate of the top college in France now.'

'But he'd be doing *me* a good turn. Not you.'

'I'll tell him that I'm in on this investigation. That it's a chance to win my spurs, get promotion. Guy will play ball:

> *Happy the man who can, when the time is well set,*
> *Throw off from his shoulders the burden of his debt.'*

'That's not what I meant. You'd be doing *me* a good turn, not yourself.'

Veyrenc dipped his bread in his coffee with a graceful gesture. The *lieutenant* had hands as shapely as those on old paintings, which made them look strangely old-fashioned.

'I'm supposed to be protecting you, along with Retancourt, aren't I?' he said.

'Nothing to do with it.'

'Yes, it is, a bit. If the angel of death *is* involved in this case, we can't hand it over to Mortier.'

'Well, apart from the syringe marks, we don't have any really conclusive evidence.'

'You did something for me yesterday. About the High Meadow.'

'Memory come back now?'

'No, it's more confused, if anything. But even if the place changes, the five boys are still in the picture. Aren't they?'

'Yes, agreed. They're still the same.'

Veyrenc nodded and finished his sandwich.

'I'll call Guy, shall I?'

'Go ahead.'

Five hours later, in the centre of an area which Adamsberg had temporarily cordoned off with some stakes and string lent by the owner of the café, Mathias, stripped to the waist, was prowling round the grave like a bear who had been hauled out of his sleep to help two cubs corner their prey. The difference was that the fair-haired giant was twenty years younger than the two policemen, who stood waiting, placing their trust in the expertise of the man who could hear the song of the earth. Brézillon had given in without a word. The Opportune graveyard had been handed over to them, along with Diala, La Paille and Montrouge. A huge territory which Veyrenc had secured in a few minutes. Immediately afterwards, Adamsberg had put in a request to Danglard to send down a team equipped with digging tools, sampling materials, and two overnight bags with clean clothes and shaving kit. The Squad always had sets of equipment in store as survival packs for emergencies. It was practical, but you never knew what the clothes would be like.

Danglard should have been pleased at Brézillon's defeat, but such was not the case. The importance that the New Recruit appeared to be taking at Adamsberg's side had sparked off painful pangs of jealousy in him. In his own eyes, this represented a serious lack of poise on his part, since Danglard always hoped to rise above any petty reflexes. But he was now feeling thwarted and irritated at being left out. Accustomed to his situation of unrivalled priority with Adamsberg, Danglard could no more envisage his role and position being challenged than he could the demolition of a stone buttress built to last centuries. The New

Recruit's arrival had made his world tremble. In Danglard's anxious path through life, two things were his guiding stars, his comfort and his protection: his five children, and the esteem shown him by Adamsberg. In addition to which, some of the *commissaire*'s serenity had trickled into his own life by capillary action. Danglard did not intend to lose his privileged position, and was alarmed at the advantages the New Recruit seemed to have acquired. Veyrenc's intelligence, which was wide-ranging and subtle, conveyed by his melodious voice and linked to his pleasant face with its crooked smile, might tempt Adamsberg into his web. And what was more, this man had removed the Brézillon road-block. The day before, Danglard had acted with circumspection and chosen to say nothing about information he had received two days earlier. Now, wounded to the quick, he brought it out of his armoury and shot it off like a dart.

'Danglard,' Adamsberg had said, 'can you send the team within the hour? I can't hang on to our prehistoric man for long. He's supposed to be on another dig with flint arrowheads.'

'The prehistorian, you mean,' Danglard had corrected.

'Call the police doctor too, but not before midday. We need her here when we reach the coffin. She should reckon two and a half hours for us to do the digging.'

'I'll bring Lamarre and Estalère with me. We'll be at Opportune in an hour and forty minutes.'

'No, you stay in the office, *capitaine*. We're going to open another sodding grave, and you won't be any use sitting fifty metres away. I just need some hewers of earth and carriers of buckets.'

'I'll be there,' said Danglard without further explanation. 'And I have some news for you. You asked me to find out about four men.'

'It can wait, *capitaine*.'

'*Commandant*.'

Adamsberg sighed. Danglard often beat about the bush out of deli-cacy, but some times he beat about it even more out of anxiety, and the sophisticated process annoyed Adamsberg.

'I've got a cemetery to cordon off, Danglard,' he said more urgently. 'We've got to find some stakes and string and so on. Anything else can wait for now.'

Adamsberg switched off his phone and spun it round on the table top.

'What am I doing,' he commented, more for himself than for Veyrenc, 'in charge of twenty-seven human beings, when I could be just as happy, in fact a thousand times better off, on my own in the mountains, sitting on a stone with my feet in a stream?'

> *'The movement of beings, the disorder of souls*
> *Bring troubles in hundreds, and vexations in shoals,*
> *But we cannot escape these currents of strife*
> *For the flow is our fate: it is all human life.'*

'Yes, I know, Veyrenc. But I wish people wouldn't get so worked up. Twenty-seven different people with their worries, all bumping into each other and getting across each other, like boats in a tiny harbour. There ought to be a way to move over the waves.'

> *'Alas, my lord,*
> *One cannot be human and remain on the shore*
> *And he who would do so plunges in even more.'*

'Let's see which way the aerial points,' said Adamsberg, spinning his phone. 'Towards people or towards empty space,' he said, pointing first to the street door, then to the window, which looked out on open countryside.

'People,' said Veyrenc before it had stopped spinning. 'People,' Adamsberg confirmed, as he watched the phone come to a halt pointing to the door.

186

'Anyway, the view wasn't empty. There are six cows in that field and a bull in the next one. That's already enough to start something, isn't it?'

As in Montrouge, Mathias had taken up his position near the grave and was moving his large hands over the surface, his fingers stopping every now and then, as he followed the scars imprinted in the earth. Twenty minutes later he was using a trowel to dig up the trace of a hole 1.60 metres across, at the head of the grave. Adamsberg, Veyrenc and Danglard were standing round, watching him work, while Lamarre and Estalère were fencing off the area with yellow plastic tape.

'Same thing,' Mathias said, getting to his feet and addressing Adamsberg. 'I'll leave you to it, you know the rest.'

'But only you can tell us if it was the same people digging. If we go in, we could destroy the edges of the hole.'

'Yes, I suppose you would,' Mathias agreed, 'especially in clay. The loose earth will stick to the walls.'

It was half past five by the time Mathias had finished emptying the hole and the light had begun to fail. According to him, and following the traces left by the tools, two men had been taking it in turns to dig, probably the same ones as in Montrouge.

'One of them lifts the pick very high and strikes almost vertically, the other doesn't take it back so far and the marks left by his blows are shorter.'

'Were,' said the pathologist, who had joined the group twenty minutes earlier.

'From the settlement of the mound and the height of the grass, I'd say this was done about a month ago,' Mathias continued.

'A bit before the Montrouge job, probably.'

'When was this woman buried?'

'Four months ago,' said Adamsberg.

'In that case, I'll leave you to it,' said Mathias, with a grimace.

'What's the state of the coffin?' asked Lamarre.

'The lid's been smashed in. I didn't look beyond that.'

A curious contrast, thought Adamsberg, watching the blond giant withdraw to the car which was to take him back to Evreux, while Ariane came forward to take over, putting on her protective clothing without any apparent apprehension. They didn't have a ladder, so Lamarre and Estalère helped the doctor down into the hole. The wood on the coffin had cracked open in several places, and the two policemen stood back in reaction to the nauseating smell that arose from it.

'I told you to put masks on first,' said Adamsberg.

'Light the projectors, please, Jean-Baptiste,' came the doctor's calm voice, 'and pass me a torch. It looks as if everything's still here, like in the case of Elisabeth Châtel. As if someone had opened both these coffins just to take a look.'

'Maybe a reader of Maupassant,' muttered Danglard, who had a mask wedged firmly on his face and was trying not to stand too far from the others.

'Meaning what, *capitaine*?' asked Adamsberg.

'There's a Maupassant story about a man who's haunted by the death of his sweetheart, and he's in despair that he'll never see her face again. So, since he's determined to look at her one last time, he digs up her grave till he reaches his beloved's face. Which doesn't look anything like the face he adored. All the same, he embraces her in her decayed state, and after that, instead of the perfume of his mistress, it's the odour of her death that he carries round with him.'

'Oh yes?' said Adamsberg. 'Charming.'

'That's Maupassant for you.'

'Just a story, all the same. And the point of stories is to stop them happening in real life.'

'Well, you never know.'

'Jean-Baptiste,' called the doctor. 'Do you know how this woman died?'

'Not yet.'

'Well, I'm going to tell you. She had the back of her skull smashed in. Either she was hit with a heavy weapon, or perhaps something fell on her.'

Adamsberg moved away, lost in thought. An accident in the case of Elisabeth Châtel, and an accident in this case too – unless they were looking at two murders. Suddenly he felt disorientated. To kill two women, in order to open their graves three months later, seemed beyond all understanding. He waited in the damp grass for Ariane to finish her inspection.

'Nothing else,' said the doctor as she was hauled up out of the grave. 'They haven't taken so much as a tooth. I got the impression that the digging was aimed at the upper part of the head. Possibly whoever it was wanted some hair from the corpse. Or an eye,' she added calmly. 'But of course by now . . .'

'I know what you're going to say, Ariane,' Adamsberg interrupted. 'No eyes left.'

Danglard took refuge by the church, feeling thoroughly sick. He sheltered between two buttresses, forcing himself to study the typical construction of the little church, which had a chequerboard pattern of black flint and red brick. But the voices still reached him, despite the distance.

'Well, if someone wanted a lock of hair,' Adamsberg was saying, 'why couldn't they have cut it off the body earlier?'

'If they had access to it.'

'Look, I can imagine a sort of passion after death, like this Maupassant story, if you like, for *one* woman, Ariane, but hardly for two. Is it possible to see if the hair has been disturbed?'

'No,' said the doctor, taking off her gloves. 'She had short hair and there's no sign of it being tampered with. It's possible that you're dealing with some kind of fetishist tomb-disturber, with such a crazy obsession that she has two strong men digging up graves to satisfy it. You can seal it up again whenever you like, Jean-Baptiste, we've seen all there is to see.'

Adamsberg approached the grave and read once more the name of the dead woman: Pascaline Villemot. He had already asked for information on the cause of death. He would probably gather something about it from village gossip before the official data reached him. He picked up the two large antlers which had remained on the ground and gave the men orders to fill the hole in again.

'What are you doing with those?' asked Ariane in surprise, as she climbed out of the overalls.

'Stag's antlers.'

'I can see that, but why are you carrying them?'

'Because I can't leave them them here, Ariane, or in the café.'

'As you like,' said the doctor without insisting. She could see from Adamsberg's eyes that his mood had taken him off into the unknown and that it was no use asking him questions.

XXVII

RUMOUR HAD GOT TO WORK, RUNNING FROM TREE TO TREE ALONG THE roads between Opportune-la-Haute and Haroncourt. Robert, Oswald and the punctuator walked into the little café where the police team was eating dinner. As Adamsberg had more or less expected.

'God's sakes, this grisly stuff's following us round,' said Robert.

'Going ahead of you, to be more precise,' said Adamsberg. 'Have a seat,' he went on, moving up to make room.

This time, Adamsberg was in charge of the group of men and the roles were subtly reversed. The three Normans looked discreetly at the strikingly beautiful woman who was eating with relish at the other end of the table, taking alternate sips of wine and water.

'She's a doctor, the police pathologist,' Adamsberg explained, to help them cut short their usual circumlocutions.

'And she's working with you?' said Robert.

'She's just examined the corpse of Pascaline Villemot.'

Robert indicated with a tilt of his chin that he had understood, and that he disapproved of such activity.

'Did you know that someone had disturbed her grave?' Adamsberg asked him.

'I just knew Gratien had seen a ghost. You said it was going ahead of us.'

'Ahead in time, Robert. We're some months too late. We're way behind the events.'

'You don't seem to be in much of a hurry,' observed Oswald.

Veyrenc, whose nose was in his plate at the other end of the table, confirmed that with a nod of his head.

> *'But beware the river that runs so deep and slow,*
> *Meandering quietly as the winds start to blow,*
> *And fear its coiled strength in the coming ordeal*
> *For water relentless will always conquer steel.'*

'What's he muttering about, that skewbald cop?' asked Robert in a low voice.

'Careful, Robert, don't ever call him that. It's personal.'

'OK,' Robert agreed. 'But I can't understand what he's saying.'

'He's saying there's no hurry.'

'He doesn't talk like ordinary folk, your cousin.'

'No, it runs in the family.'

'Oh, if it runs in the family, that's different,' said Robert with respect.

'Stands to reason,' murmured the punctuator.

'And he's not my cousin,' added Adamsberg.

Robert was nursing a grudge. Adamsberg could work that out easily, from the way he was gripping his glass in his fist and grinding his teeth, as if he were chewing a piece of straw.

'What's up, Robert?'

'You came because of Oswald's ghost, not because of the stag.'

'How do you know that? The two things happened at the same time.'

'Don't try to fool me, man from the Béarn.'

'Do you want to take the antlers back?'

Robert hesitated.

'No, now you've got 'em, they're yours. But don't separate them. And don't go forgetting them.'

'I haven't let them out of my sight all day.'

'Good,' said Robert, reassured. 'And what is this ghost, anyway? Oswald said it was the figure of Death.'

'Yes, he's right in one way.'

'And in another way?'

'Let's say it's someone or something that doesn't bode any good, far as I can see.'

'And you come running,' Robert whispered, 'as soon as an idiot like Oswald tells you someone's seen a ghost. Or when a poor woman like Hermance, who's lost her wits, asks to see you.'

'Someone else who's not too bright, the caretaker in the cemetery at Montrouge, saw one as well. And in that cemetery too someone had had a grave dug up, and the coffin opened.'

'Why did you say they'd "*had*" it dug up?'

'Because two big lads were paid to do the work, and now they're both dead.'

'Couldn't this person do it himself?'

'It was a woman, Robert.'

Robert's mouth fell open and he swallowed a large gulp of wine.

'I can't believe that,' said Oswald. 'It's not human.'

'But that's what happens, Oswald.'

'And the one who goes around ripping out stag's hearts. That's a woman, too?'

'What's that got to do with it?' asked Adamsberg.

Oswald thought for a moment, looking into his glass.

'Too many things going on round here all at once,' he said at last. 'Maybe they're connected.'

'Criminals have their preferences, Oswald. The kind of people who rob tombs aren't the same kind of people who kill stags.'

'Takes all sorts,' said the punctuator.

'This here ghost,' said Oswald, hazarding a direct question, 'are we talking about the same one? The one who floats about and then digs up graves?'

'I think so.'

'Are you going to do something about it, then?'

'If you can tell me anything about Pascaline Villemot, I'm listening.'

'We only saw her on market days, but I can tell you now that she was as innocent as the Virgin Mary, and she didn't have much of a life.'

'It's one thing to die,' said Robert, 'but it's worse if you haven't lived.'

And it still itches, sixty-nine years later, Adamsberg thought.

'Do you know how she died?'

'Maybe it's tempting providence to talk about it. But she was knocked on the head by a stone, must have fallen out of the church wall, when she was weeding the bed underneath. They found her stretched out on her face, and the stone right beside her.'

'Was there an inquest?'

'The Evreux gendarmes came, and they said it was an accident.'

'Was it, though?' said the punctuator.

'Was it what?'

'Maybe it was an act of God.'

'Don't be bloody stupid, Achille. The whole world's in chaos, God's got better things to do than chuck stones at Pascaline.'

'Did she work round here?' Adamsberg asked.

'She helped out at the shoe shop in Caudebec. But the one who knew her best is the priest. She was always going to confession. He's got fourteen parishes, so he only comes here every other Friday. At seven sharp, those days, Pascaline was always down in the church. And she was probably the only woman in Opportune who'd never been with a man, so you wonder what she found to confess.'

'Where's he saying mass tomorrow?'

'He's not doing it any more. Finished.'

'What do you mean? Is he dead?'

'You've got death on the brain,' commented Robert. 'No, he's not dead, but as good as. He's depressed. It happened to the butcher in Arbec, and he was like it for two years. You're not ill, but you go to bed and don't want to get up. And you càn't say why.'

'Sad,' punctuated Achille.

'My grandmother would've called it melancholy,' said Robert. 'Sometimes it would end up in the village pond.'

'And the priest doesn't want to get up?'

'Seemingly he's up and about, but he's a changed man. Only with him, we can guess why. It's because someone stole his relics. Knocked him sideways, they say.'

'His pride and joy, they were,' remarked Achille.

'These relics, they're supposed to be Saint Jerome's bones, they were in the church in Le Mesnil. He was proud of them, all right. Mind you, three chicken bones rattling round in a glass case, that's all they were.'

'Oswald, don't insult the Lord, we're at table!'

'I'm not insulting anyone, Robert. All I said was, Saint Jerome relics? Pull the other one, they're fakes. Well, some people'll believe anything. Still, for our priest it was like he'd had his guts pulled out.'

'But can we go and visit?'

'I just told you, the relics are gone.'

'No, I mean call on the priest.'

'Oh, that I don't know. Me and Robert, we don't have anything to do with priests, it's like the cops. Can't do this, can't do that, always on at you about something.'

Oswald poured generous helpings of wine all round, as if to demonstrate his independence of the priest's exhortations.

'Some people,' said Robert, dropping his voice, 'say the priest slept around. They say, well, he's a man like anyone else.'

'So they say,' said the punctuator darkly.

'Just gossip? Or is there any evidence of that?'

'That he's a man?'

'That he slept around,' said Adamsberg patiently.

'It's because of his depression. When someone just collapses like that, and won't say why, people generally say it's because of a woman.'

'That they do,' said Achille.

'And do they whisper any woman's name?' asked Adamsberg.

'No idea,' said Robert, clamming up. He threw a rapid glance at Adamsberg, then at Oswald, which might indicate, Adamsberg thought, that Hermance was somehow involved. During this brief exchange, Veyrenc was muttering as he attacked his apple tart:

> *'The gods are my witness, I struggled without cease,*
> *To conquer my poor heart, and find a time of peace.*
> *But my mistress's grace and the warmth of her heart*
> *Pierced my soul with the force of a dagger's sharp dart.'*

The members of the Crime Squad stood up, preparing to return to Paris. Adamsberg, Veyrenc and Danglard were to stay on at the small hotel in Haroncourt. Back in its entrance hall, Danglard tugged Adamsberg's sleeve.

'Have you made your peace with Veyrenc?'

'We've declared a truce. Because we've got work to do.'

'You don't want to hear about the four names you gave me?'

'Tomorrow, Danglard,' said Adamsberg, taking his room key off the hook. 'I can hardly stand upright now.'

'OK', said the *commandant*, walking towards the wooden staircase. 'But just in case you're interested, two of them are already dead. That leaves three.'

Adamsberg froze, then put the key back on the hook.

'*Capitaine*,' he called.

'I'll get a bottle and a couple of glasses,' said Danglard, wheeling round.

XXVIII

THREE CANE ARMCHAIRS AND A SMALL WOODEN TABLE ARRANGED IN A corner formed the reception area of the hotel. Danglard put down the glasses, lit the two candles on a brass candlestick and opened the bottle.

'Just a token amount for me,' said Adamsberg, pulling away his glass. 'It's only cider.'

Danglard poured himself a realistic helping and sat down facing the *commissaire*.

'Sit on this side of me, Danglard,' said Adamsberg, pointing to the left-hand chair. 'And keep your voice down. Veyrenc doesn't need to hear this from the room upstairs. Which ones have died?'

'Fernand Gascaud and Georges Tressin.'

'The little so-and-so and Big Georges,' Adamsberg commented to himself, pulling at his cheek. 'So when was this?'

'Seven years ago and three years ago. Gascaud drowned in the swimming pool of a luxury hotel near Antibes. Tressin hadn't done so well in the world. He lived in a shack. His Calor gas bottle exploded, set the whole place on fire.'

Adamsberg pulled his feet up on to the seat of the chair and put his arms round his knees.

'Why did you say: "That leaves three"?'

'Just counting.'

'Danglard, were you seriously thinking that Veyrenc got rid of little Fernand and Big Georges?'

'I'm merely pointing out that if there were another three unfortunate accidents, the Caldhez gang would have ceased to exist.'

'Two accidental deaths are quite possible, aren't they?'

'You don't believe that about Elisabeth and Pascaline. So why would you believe it about those other ones?'

'In the case of the two women, there's a ghost been seen prowling round, and there are a lot of common elements. Both from the same area, both religious, both virgins, both desecrated after death.'

'And in the case of Fernand and Georges, both from the same village, both in the same boyhood gang, both cases of sudden death.'

'What about the other two, Roland and Pierrot?'

'Roland Seyre runs a hardware shop in Pau, Pierre Ancenot is a gamekeeper. The four of them were regularly in touch with each other.'

'It was a very close-knit gang.'

'So Roland and Pierre presumably know that both Fernand and Georges have come to tragic ends. They might smell a rat, if they've got any intelligence.'

'Intelligence wasn't their strong point.'

'In that case, they ought to be warned. To be on their guard.'

'That would be slandering Veyrenc without any proof, Danglard.'

'Or else risking the lives of the other two without lifting a finger. When the next one's killed by a stray bullet during a hunting expedition, or has a rock fall on his head, you might regret not having slandered him a bit earlier.'

'Why are you so sure of yourself, *capitaine*?'

'The New Recruit didn't come here for nothing.'

'Obviously.'

'He came for you.'

'Yes.'

'We're agreed, then. It was you that asked me to find out about these characters – you were the first to suspect Veyrenc.'

'Suspect him of what, Danglard?'

'Of being after your hide.'

'Or perhaps of coming to check something out?'

'What would that be?'

'The identity of the fifth boy.'

'The one you're taking care of personally.'

'Exactly.'

Adamsberg interrupted himself and held out his glass.

'Another symbolic dash,' he said.

'Of course,' said Danglard, pouring in a couple of centimetres.

'The fifth boy was older than the others. He didn't take part in the attack. During the fight he was several metres away, under the walnut tree, seemed to be the leader, giving orders. The one who tells people what to do without getting his hands dirty, get the idea?'

'Yes.'

'From where he was, on the ground, little Veyrenc couldn't see his face clearly.'

'How do you know?'

'Because Veyrenc was able to name four of the attackers, but not the fifth. He suspected someone but he wasn't sure. The others got four years of approved school, but the fifth got away.'

'And you think Veyrenc has just come along to find out for sure. To see if you knew him.'

'Yes, I think so.'

'No. When you asked me to check the names, you were suspicious about something. What's made you change your mind?'

Adamsberg didn't reply, just dipped a lump of sugar the dregs of his cider.

'His charm?' asked Danglard acidly. 'His verse? It's quite easy to make up verses.'

'It's not that easy. Seems quite good to me.'

'Not to me.'

'I was talking about the cider. You're touchy, *capitaine*. Touchy and jealous,' said Adamsberg wearily, crushing his sugar into the bottom of the glass with his finger.

'Oh, for God's sake. What made you change your mind?' said Danglard, losing patience.

'Keep your voice down. When Noël insulted him in the bar, Veyrenc wanted to react, but he couldn't. He couldn't even throw a punch, which would have been the easiest thing to do in the circumstances.'

'So what? He was in shock. You saw his face, he went white as a sheet.'

'Yes, because it brought back all the insults he'd had to put up with as a child, and later when he was a young man. Veyrenc didn't only have peculiar hair, he also used to limp because of the horse that had trampled him. He was scared of his shadow after that attack in the meadow.'

'I thought it was in the vineyard.'

'No, he mixed up two separate occasions when he was knocked unconscious.'

'Well that proves he's crazy,' concluded Danglard. 'A man who speaks in twelve-syllable alexandrines has got to be crazy anyway.'

'You're not usually so intolerant, *capitaine*.'

'You think it's normal, to speak in verse like he does?'

'It's not his fault. It runs in the family.'

Adamsberg wiped up the melted sugar from the cider with a finger. 'Think, Danglard. Why didn't Veyrenc punch Noël? He's quite big enough to have knocked him down.'

'Because he's new round here, because he didn't know how to respond, because the table was between them.'

'Because he's mild by nature. He's never used his fists. It doesn't interest him. He lets other people do that. He hasn't killed anyone.'

'So Veyrenc just came to find out the name of the fifth boy?'

'Yes, I think so. And to let the fifth boy know that he knows.'

'I'm not sure you're right.'

'Me neither. Let's say that's what I hope.'

'What about the other two? We don't warn them, then?'

'Not for the moment.'

'And what about number five?'

'I would say that number five's big enough to look after himself.'

Danlgard got lethargically to his feet. His anger with first Brézillon, then Devalon, then Veyrenc, and the horrors of another open grave, plus an excess of alcohol, had left him feeling weak.

'And you know number five, do you?' he asked.

'Yes,' said Adamsberg putting his finger back in the empty glass.

'It was you.'

'Yes, *capitaine.*'

Danglard nodded and said goodnight. Sometimes one can be sure of something but still find it unbearable when it's confirmed. Adamsberg waited five minutes after Danglard had left. Then he put his glass on the bar and climbed the stairs himself. He stopped at Veyrenc's bedroom door and knocked. The *lieutenant* was on his bed, reading a book.

'I've got some sad news for you, *lieutenant.*'

Veyrenc looked up, expectantly.

'I'm listening.'

'Fernand the little chap, and Big Georges – remember them?'

Veyrenc shut his eyes rapidly.

'Well, they're both dead.'

The *lieutenant* nodded a brief acknowledgement but did not speak.

'You going to ask me how they died?'

'How did they die?'

'Fernand drowned in a swimming pool and Georges was burnt alive in his shack.'

'Accidents, then.'

'Fate caught up with them, in a manner of speaking. A bit like in Racine, don't you think?'

'Maybe.'

'Goodnight, *lieutenant.*'

Adamsberg closed the door and stood outside in the corridor. He had to wait almost ten minutes before he heard Veyrenc's melodious voice.

> *'Cruelty damns sinners to the dark of the grave.*
> *Was it vengeance divine or the burden they bore*
> *That turned these young villains to shadows on the shore?'*

Adamsberg plunged his fists into his pockets and tiptoed away. He had tried to appear cool to calm Danglard. But Veyrenc's words were far from reassuring. Cruelty, vengeance, war, treason and death – that's Racine for you.

XXIX

'WE'LL HAVE TO BE DISCREET,' SAID ADAMSBERG, PARKING IN FRONT OF THE priest's house in Le Mesnil. 'We don't want to upset a man who's mourning the relics of Saint Jerome.'

'I wonder,' said Danglard, 'whether the fact that his church in Opportune appears to have let a stone fall and kill a parishioner might not also have shaken him.'

The curate, who was not best pleased at their arrival, showed them into a small, dark but warm room, with low ceiling beams. The priest in charge of the fourteen parishes did indeed look like any other man. He had abandoned clerical garb for ordinary clothes and sat peering into a computer screen. He got up to greet them, a rather ugly man but healthy and ruddy-complexioned, looking more as if he were on holiday than suffering from depression. However, one of his eyelids was twitching like the heartbeat of a small creature, suggesting a troubled soul, as Veyrenc would have put it. In order to obtain the interview, Adamsberg had had to make a fuss about the theft of the relics.

'I don't imagine the Paris police would normally come as far as Le Mesnil-Beauchamp just because some holy relics go missing,' said the priest as they shook hands.

'No, you're right,' Adamsberg admitted.

'And you're in charge of Serious Crime, as I discovered. Am I supposed to have done something?'

Adamsberg was relieved to find that the priest did not express himself in the customary hermetic and mournful sing-song of some churchmen. This chant tended to inspire in him an irresistible melancholy, inherited from the interminable services in the freezing-cold village church of his childhood. Those were some of the only moments when his indomitable and indestructible mother had allowed herself to sigh and dab her eyes with a handkerchief, thus revealing to him, in a spasm of embarrassment, painful intimate feelings that he would rather not have witnessed. And yet it was during those Masses that he had also had the most intense daydreams. The priest now motioned them to sit opposite him, on a long wooden bench, with the result that the three policemen lined up like so many schoolboys in class. Adamsberg and Veyrenc were both wearing white shirts, thanks to the unpredictable contents of the emergency packs. Adamsberg's was too big and the cuffs were slipping down over his hands.

'Your curate wanted to keep us out,' said Adamsberg, twitching his sleeves. 'So I thought Saint Jerome would get us in.'

'The curate is protecting me from the outside world,' replied the priest, as he gazed at an early bluebottle flying round the room. 'He doesn't want me to be seen. He's ashamed, so he's keeping me hidden. If you'd like something to drink, it's in the sideboard. I don't drink now. I don't know why, it just doesn't interest me.'

Adamsberg made a negative sign to Danglard. It was only nine o'clock in the morning. The priest looked up, surprised not to hear questions coming from them in return. He was not a Norman, and seemed able to speak quite openly. This embarrassed the three police officers. To discuss the mysteries of a priest – which they assumed to be sensitive matters – was more difficult than to interview a criminal suspect across a table. Adamsberg felt he was being obliged to walk over a delicate patch of lawn in hobnailed boots.

'The curate's hiding you,' he ventured, using the Norman device of the statement-containing-a-question.

The priest lit his pipe, still following with his gaze the fly that was swooping low over his keyboard. He cupped his hand ready to catch it, brought it down on the table, missed.

'I'm not trying to kill it,' he explained, 'just to catch it. I take an interest in the frequency of the vibrations of flies' wings. They're much more rapid and loud when they're caught in a trap. You'll see.'

He puffed out a large smoke ring and looked at them, his hand still cupped like a lid.

'It was my curate who had the idea to put it about that I was suffering from depression,' he went on, 'to let things settle down. He practically placed me in solitary confinement, at the request of the diocesan authorities. I haven't seen anyone for weeks, so I don't mind talking about it, even if it is to policemen.'

Adamsberg hesitated at this puzzling remark, unselfconsciously offered by the priest. The man needed to be listened to and understood, why not? After all, priests spent their lives listening to the problems of their parishioners without ever having the right to complain themselves. The *commissaire* envisaged various hypotheses: a love affair, regrets of the flesh, the loss of the relics, or the accident that had happened in the Opportune church.

'Loss of vocation?' guessed Danglard.

'You've got it,' said the priest, nodding towards Danglard as if to give him a good mark.

'Sudden or gradual?'

'Is there any difference? If something feels sudden, it's only the end of a long hidden process that one may not have been aware of.'

The priest's hand came down on the fly, which once again managed to escape between the thumb and the index finger.

'A bit like a stag's antlers, when they show through its hide,' suggested Adamsberg.

'If you like. The idea grows, like a larva inside its hiding place, and then it suddenly emerges and takes off. You don't just mislay your vocation one day, like you lose a book. Anyway, you generally find the book again, but you never get your vocation back. That proves that the vocation had been dwindling away for a long time, without drawing attention to itself. Then one morning it's all over, you've gone past the point of no return during the night without even realising it: you look out of the window, a woman goes past on a bicycle, there's snow lying on the apple trees, and you feel a terrible sickness, life outside is calling you.'

> *'Yesterday I still loved this great calling of mine*
> *I rejoiced to break bread, I rejoiced to serve wine.*
> *But now on a sudden, all is ashes and dust*
> *And I must leave the church to another man's trust.'*

'Pretty much, yes.'

'So these lost relics weren't really worrying you, after all?' asked Adamsberg.

'Do you want me to start worrying about them?'

'Well, I was thinking of doing a deal: I would have tried to get Saint Jerome back for you, and in exchange you could tell me something about Pascaline Villemot. I suppose the deal wouldn't appeal to you now.'

'Oh, I don't know. My predecessor, Father Raymond, was very attached to the relics, the ones in Le Mesnil or indeed relics in general. I wasn't up to his level of scholarship, but I remember quite a lot about it. Even if it's just for his sake, I'd like to get Saint Jerome back.'

The priest turned to indicate the bookshelf behind him, as well as a weighty volume on a lectern, protected by a plexiglas cover. This ancient book had already irresistibly attracted Danglard's attention.

'All that stuff comes from him. The book too, of course,' he said, gesturing respectfully towards the lectern. 'Given to Father Raymond by a certain Father Otto who died during the bombing of Berlin. Are you interested?' he asked Danglard, who was gazing hungrily at the book.

'Yes, I admit I am. If it's what I think it is.'

The priest smiled, recognising a connoisseur. He puffed at his pipe, making the silence last, as if to herald the arrival of a famous person.

'It's the *De sanctis reliquis*,' he said, savouring his announcement, 'in the unexpurgated edition of 1663. You can consult it if you like, but please use the tongs to turn the folios. It's open at the most famous page.'

The priest gave a curious snort of laughter, and Danglard headed immediately for the lectern. Adamsberg watched him raise the lid and lean over the book, and realised that Danglard would not hear another word they said.

'It's one of the most famous books on relics,' the priest explained, with a casual wave of his hand. 'Actually, it's worth a lot more than any bones belonging to Saint Jerome. But I'd only sell it in a case of dire necessity.'

'So you *are* interested in relics, then.'

'I do have a weakness for them. Calvin described the people who hawked relics around as "traffickers in ordure", and he wasn't entirely wrong. But that ordure gives a bit of spice to a holy place, helps people to concentrate. It's hard to concentrate in a vacuum. That's why it doesn't bother me that in our reliquary of Saint Jerome, most of the bones came from sheep, and there's even one from the snout of a pig. Father Raymond used to laugh at that. He would only tell the secret, with a twinkle in his eye, to certain people, the ones strong enough to stomach such a down-to earth revelation.'

'You mean to say there's a bone in a pig's snout?' asked Adamsberg.

'Yes,' the priest replied, smiling. 'Just a little bone, quite elegant and symmetrical, a bit like a double heart in shape. Not a lot of people know that, which explains why there's one among the Le Mesnil relics. It used to be thought of as a mysterious bone, and people thought it had special qualities. Like a narwhal's tusk gave rise to the idea of the unicorn. The world of fantasy fills the gaps in people's knowledge.'

'And you knowingly left these animals' bones in the reliquary?' asked Veyrenc.

The fly went past again and the priest raised his arm, ready to pounce.

'What difference would it make?' he replied. 'The human bones were unlikely to be Saint Jerome's either. In those days, relics were bandied about like sweets. Supply expanded to meet demand. Seems that Saint Sebastian had four arms, Saint Anne three heads, Saint John six index fingers, and so on. In Le Mesnil, we're not so presumptuous. Our sheep's bones date from the late fifteenth century, which is already pretty good. Remains of men or animals, what does it really matter in the end?'

'So the guy who robbed the church has just got the remains of someone's Sunday joint?' said Veyrenc.

'No, because funnily enough, the thief seemed to pick and choose. He only took the human fragments, a bit of a tibia, a second cervical vertebra, and three ribs. Must have been either an expert, or else somebody local who knew all about the shameful secret of the reliquary. That's why I'm trying to find him,' he added, pointing to the computer screen. 'I just wonder what he has in mind.'

'You think he'll try to sell them?'

The priest shook his head.

'I've been scanning offers on the Internet, but I can't find anyone selling Saint Jerome's tibia. Obviously not for sale. But what are *you* looking for? They tell me you've been digging up Pascaline's body. The gendarmes have already finished their inquiry about the stone that killed her. A sad accident, it seems, nothing suspicious. Pascaline never hurt a fly, and she didn't have any money to leave.'

The priest brought down his hand on to the table. This time the fly was trapped, and immediately started buzzing more loudly.

'Hear it?' he said. 'Its response to stress?'

'Yes,' said Veyrenc politely.

'Is it sending a message to its friends? Or working up the energy to escape? Do insects have emotions? That is the question. Have you ever listened to a fly when it's dying?'

The priest had put his ear to his hand, appearing to count the thousands of beats per second of the fly's wings.

'We didn't dig her up,' said Adamsberg, attempting to bring the conversation back to Pascaline. 'But we do want to know why someone took the trouble to open her coffin three months after her death, to get at the head.'

'Good Lord!' gasped the priest, letting the fly disappear vertically into the air. 'What an abomination!'

'The same thing has happened to another woman. Elisabeth Châtel from Villebosc-sur-Risle.'

'I knew Elisabeth as well. Villebosc is one of my parishes. But she wasn't buried there. She was buried in Montrouge, in Paris, because of a family quarrel.'

'That's where her grave was opened.'

The priest pushed away his computer screen, then rubbed his left eye, to try and stop the tic in his eyelid. Adamsberg wondered whether, apart from his loss of vocation, the man was perhaps genuinely suffering from depression, and whether his odd behaviour was an indication of that. Danglard, who was wholly absorbed in consulting his treasure trove, using the tongs, was no help in trying to get their host to concentrate on the matter in hand.

'To the best of my knowledge,' the priest went on, lifting up his thumb and index finger, 'profanation of the dead has only two causes, each of them extremely repugnant. Either violent hatred, in which case the body is attacked.'

'No,' said Adamsberg. 'They weren't damaged.'

The priest lowered his thumb, abandoning this theory.

'Or else passionate love, which is, alas, very close to hate, with a morbid sexual fixation.'

209

'And did Elisabeth and Pascaline inspire anyone with unbridled passion?'

The priest lowered his finger, abandoning the second theory as well.

'Both of them were virgins, and very determined to remain so, believe me. They were both women of absolutely unassailable virtue, no need to preach it to them.'

Danglard pricked up his ears, wondering how to interpret that 'believe me'. His eyes met those of Adamsberg, but the latter signalled to him not to say anything. The priest pressed his finger on his eyelid again.

'Some men are particularly attracted to women of great virtue,' said Adamsberg.

'Well, there is a challenge there,' the priest agreed. 'The temptation of an unusually difficult conquest. But neither Elisabeth nor Pascaline ever complained of anyone harassing them.'

'So what did they come and tell you so often at confession?' the *commissaire* asked.

'Secrets of the confessional,' the priest replied, raising his hand. 'Sorry.'

'So they did have *something* to say?' put in Veyrenc.

'Everyone has something to say. That doesn't mean that it's worth passing on, still less that graves should be profaned. You stayed at Hermance's house, didn't you? So you heard what she has to say? She doesn't have a life, as most people would see it, but that doesn't stop her talking about it all day long.'

'You know as well as I do, Father,' said Adamsberg gently, 'that maintaining the secrecy of the confessional is not sustainable or even legal in certain circumstances.'

'Only in the case of murder,' the priest objected.

'I think that's what we are dealing with.'

The priest relit his pipe. They could hear Danglard turning over another thick page of the book, while the fly, which seemed no calmer than before, continued to buzz loudly, hurling itself at the window. Danglard knew that the *commissaire* was putting on pressure to overcome the priest's reluctance. Adamsberg was excellent at eliminating obstacles, slipping inside the resistance of other people with the treacherous power of a trickle of water. He would have made a formidable priest, midwife or purger of souls. Veyrenc got up in turn and walked round the table to look at the book which was so absorbing Danglard's attention. The *commandant* let him see it, but with a bad grace, like a dog unwillingly sharing a bone: '*On sacred relics and all the uses that may be made of them, whether for the health of the body or the salubrity of the mind, and the useful medicines which may be derived from them to lengthen life: edition purged of past errors.*'

'What's so special about the book?' Veyrenc asked in a low voice.

'The *De reliquis*,' Danglard whispered, 'has been famous since the mid-fourteenth century. The Church condemned it, which made it very popular at once. Many women were burnt at the stake for consulting it. This is the 1663 edition, which is a collector's item.'

'Why?'

'Because it re-established the original text, including a diabolical potion banned by the Church. Read it for yourself, Veyrenc.'

Danglard watched as the *lieutenant* struggled in front of the page that was open in front of him. The text was in French, but an antiquated and very obscure version.

'Complicated, huh?' said Danglard, with a thin smile of satisfaction.

'I can't understand it, and you're not about to explain it to me, I suppose.'

Danglard shrugged.

'There are some other things I ought to explain to you first.'

'I'm listening.'

'Well, you'd do better to leave the squad, Veyrenc,' Danglard whispered. 'Nobody catches Adamsberg, any more than they can catch the wind. And if you're trying to have a go at him, you'll have to reckon with me first.'

'I'm sure I would, *commandant*. But I'm not trying to do anything.'

'Kids are kids. You're past the age of bothering about their fights and so is he. Stay with us and get on with the job, or else push off.'

Veyrenc closed his eyes quickly and went back to his seat on the bench. The conversation with the priest had progressed, but Adamsberg looked disappointed.

'Nothing else at all?' he was saying.

'No, nothing, except that pathological dislike of homosexuality in Pascaline's case.'

'So you reckon they they didn't sleep together or anything?'

'They didn't sleep with *anyone*, man or woman.'

'Did either one ever talk to you about stags?'

'No, never. Why on earth would they?'

'It's just Oswald. He gets everything mixed up.'

'Oswald, and this isn't a secret of the confessional, is a bit special. He's not as daft as his sister, but he talks off the top of his head, if you see what I mean.'

'What about Hermance? Did she come and see you?'

The fly, being either provocative or careless, was once more approaching the warm computer top, distracting the priest.

'She often did, long ago, when the villagers used to say she brought bad luck. Then she lost her wits and she's never really got them back.'

Like your vocation, thought Adamsberg, wondering whether one morning, if he himself looked out and saw the snow on the branches and a woman on a bicycle, he would leave the squad and never return.

'So she doesn't come any more.'

'Yes, of course she does,' said the priest, watching the fly again as it moved over his keyboard. 'But that reminds me of something. Just a little thing. It was about six or seven months ago. Pascaline used to have several cats. One of them was killed and left bleeding on her porch.'

'Who did that?'

'Nobody ever owned up. Probably kids, like in every village. I'd forgotten all about it, but it upset her a lot. And she wasn't just upset, she was frightened.'

'How do you mean?'

'Frightened that someone would suspect her of being a lesbian. Like I said, she had a thing about it.'

'I don't see the connection,' said Veyrenc.

'Yes, there was one,' said the priest, sounding a trifle irritated. 'It was a tomcat, but they'd cut off its male parts.'

'A bit violent for kids messing about,' observed Danglard, pulling a face.

'Did Elisabeth have cats too?'

'Just the one. But nothing ever happened to it, nothing like that.'

The three men sat in silence on the way back to Haroncourt. Adamsberg was driving at a snail's pace, as if the car needed to go at the same slow speed as his thought processes.

'What do you think of him, *capitaine*?' Adamsberg asked at last.

'A bit on edge, a bit weird, but that's understandable if he's going to take a big step like that. Still, it was worth the trip.'

'Because of the book? Is it an inventory of relics?'

'No, it's the best-known treatise on how to use them. '*On sacred relics and the uses that may be made of them.*' The priest's copy is in very good condition. I couldn't possibly afford it – it'd cost four years of my pay.'

'Relics were used for something?'

'For everything. For stomach upsets and earache, fever, piles, weakness, the vapours.'

'Ah, we should offer some to Dr Roman, then,' said Adamsberg with a smile. 'So why is this edition so valuable?'

'I already told Veyrenc. Because it contains the most famous potion, one the Church outlawed for centuries. It's a bit disconcerting, in fact, to find it in the possession of a priest. And he's left it open at exactly that page, oddly enough. A sort of provocation, I suppose.'

'My guess is he's the best-placed person to have taken Saint Jerome's bones himself. But what was this medicine supposed to do, Danglard? Give him back his vocation? Remove all devilish temptations?'

'No – it's a potion for acquiring eternal life.'

'On earth or in heaven?'

'On earth, for centuries and centuries.'

'Go on then, *capitaine*. Tell me what it contains.'

'How do you expect me to remember that?' Danglard grumbled.

'Actually, I remember it,' said Veyrenc, discreetly.

'OK, *lieutenant*, I'm listening,' said Adamsberg, still smiling. 'Maybe it'll tell us what the priest had in mind.'

'All right,' said Veyrenc, hesitantly, not yet able to guess whether Adamsberg was serious or just joking. '*Sovereign remedy for the lengthening of life, through the quality possessed by sacred relics to weaken the miasmas of death, preserved from the truest processes and purged of former errors.*'

'Is that it?'

'No, that's just the heading.'

'It's after that that it gets more complicated,' said Danglard, stupefied and offended.

'*Five times cometh the age of youth, till the day thou must invert it, pass and pass again, out of reach of the thread of life. Sacred relics thou wilt crush, taking three pinches, mixed well with the male principle which must not bend, and with the quick of virgins, on the dexter side, sorted by three into equal quantities, and grind these with the living cross from the heart of the eternal branches, adjacent in equal quantity, kept in the same place by the valency of the saint, in the wine of the year, and thus wilt thou lay its head on the ground.*'

'Did you know about this before, Veyrenc?'

'No, I just read it today.'

'Do you understand it?'

'No.'

'Neither do I.'

'It's about acquiring eternal life,' commented Danglard sulkily. 'You won't manage that with a couple of spoonfuls of something.'

Half an hour later, Adamsberg and his colleagues were putting their bags back in the car and heading for Paris. Danglard complained about the fireguard, not to mention the stag's antlers which were taking up the back seat.

'There's only one solution,' said Adamsberg. 'We'll put the antlers in front and the two passengers in the back, with the fireguard between us.'

'We'd do better to leave the antlers here.'

'You must be joking, *capitaine*. You drive, you're the tallest, Veyrenc and I will sit either side of the fireguard. It'll be fine.'

Danglard waited until Veyrenc was sitting in the car, before drawing Adamsberg aside.

'He's got to be lying, *commissaire*. Nobody could memorise a text like that. Nobody.'

'I've already told you, Danglard, he's got special gifts. Nobody else can make up verses like he does.'

'It's one thing to make stuff up, and another to remember it. He recited that damned text pretty well word-perfect. He's lying. He must already have known that recipe off by heart.'

'Why would that be, Danglard?'

'No idea. But it's been a potion known to damned souls for centuries and centuries.'

XXX

'SHE DID WEAR NAVY-BLUE SHOES,' RETANCOURT ANNOUNCED, PLACING A plastic bag on Adamsberg's desk.

Adamsberg looked at the bag, then at the *lieutenant*. She was carrying the cat under her arm, and the Snowball, looking blissful, was allowing himself to be carried round like a rag doll, head and paws hanging down. Adamsberg had not been expecting such rapid results, nor indeed any result at all. But now here were the shoes belonging to the angel of death, sitting on his table: worn, out of shape, and definitely navy blue.

'There's no sign of shoe polish on the soles,' Retancourt added. 'But that's not surprising, because they've been worn a lot over the last couple of years.'

'Tell me about it,' said Adamsberg, hoisting himself on to one of the Swedish bar stools he had brought into his office.

'The estate agent just left the nurse's house as it was, knowing it would be impossible to sell. Nobody went round to clean it after the arrest. But when I got there it was empty – no furniture, no crockery, no clothes.'

'Why? Looters?'

'Yes. In the neighbourhood, everyone knew the nurse had no family, and that she had some stuff in good condition. Gradually people started taking things. I had to go round a few squats and a travellers' camp. With the shoes I found one of her blouses and a blanket.'

'Where?'

'In a caravan.'

'With people living in it?'

'Yes. But you don't need to know who they are, do you?'

'No.'

'I promised this lady I'd get her another pair of shoes. She doesn't have any others, just bedroom slippers. So she'll miss these ones.'

Adamsberg swung his legs.

'This district nurse,' he mused, 'went around knocking off old people with her injections for forty years. It was virtually her mission in life for about half a century, almost a tradition. Why would she suddenly turn to the occult, and start hiring ruffians to dig up graves belonging to virgins? I don't get it, the switch just isn't logical.'

'The nurse wasn't logical either.'

'Yes, she was. All forms of mania have a certain rigidity, they follow a pattern.'

'Maybe being in prison threw her off balance.'

'That's what the pathologist suggested.'

'Why did you say "virgins"?'

'Because they both were, Pascaline and Elisabeth. And I'm supposing that had some significance for the grave-robber. The nurse never had a husband or partner either.'

'She would have needed to find out if it was true of Pascaline and Elisabeth.'

'Yes, so she would have had to spend some time in Upper Normandy. Nurses get told a lot of things they don't ask about.'

'Have we any record of her being there?'

'No, no victims towards the west at all, except for one in Rennes in Brittany. But that might not mean anything. She travelled a lot from place to place, staying a few months, then moving on.'

'What are those doing here?' asked Retancourt, pointing to the two large antlers taking up space on the office floor.

'A trophy. Someone gave me them the other night. I cut them off myself.'

'Ten points, eh?' said Retancourt approvingly. 'And what did you do to deserve them?'

'They asked me to go up there and I went. But I'm not sure that I was really being called there for him. He was known as the Red Giant.'

'Who?'

'Him. The stag.'

'Why would someone do that? Do you think it was a lure, to get you to go to the graveyard at Opportune?'

'Possibly.'

Retancourt lifted up one of the antlers, weighed it and put it down delicately.

'You're not supposed to separate them,' she said. 'So what else did you pick up there?'

'I learned that there's a bone in the snout of a pig.'

Retancourt let this remark pass, hoisting the cat up on her shoulder.

'It's in the shape of a double heart,' Adamsberg went on. 'I also learned that one could cure the vapours with a saint's relics, and acquire eternal life for centuries and centuries, and that the remains of Saint Jerome might include some sheep's bones.'

'Anything else?' asked Retancourt, patiently waiting for the information that really interested her.

'That the two men who dug out the grave of Pascaline Villemot were probably our Diala and La Paille. That Pascaline died of a fractured skull, caused by a stone falling from the church, that one of her cats was slaughtered and emasculated three months before her death, and had been left in that state on her doorstep.'

Adamsberg suddenly raised his hand, twined his legs round the foot of the stool and called up a number on his mobile.

'Oswald? Did you know that Pascaline's cat had been left bleeding at her door?'

'Narcissus? Reckon everyone knew about him in Opportune. Famous for his weight, he was. Over eleven kilos. He nearly won a prize at the show. But that was last year. Hermance gave her a new cat. Hermance likes cats, they're nice clean creatures.'

'Were Pascaline's other cats male too, do you know?'

'No, all girls, they were. Narcissus's daughters. Not important, is it?'

Another trick of the Normans, Adamsberg reflected, consisted of putting a question while apparently not being interested in the reply. As Oswald just had.

'I was just wondering why whoever killed Narcissus went to the trouble of cutting his balls off.'

'Whoever told you that don't know his arse from his elbow. Narcissus was neutered, oh, years ago. He used to sleep all day. A cat that weighs eleven kilos, ever seen that happen by chance?'

'Are you sure about that?'

'Course I am, 'cos Hermance chose a tomcat for her, so the other cats could have kittens.'

Frowning, Adamsberg called another number, while Retancourt picked up the bag of shoes, looking annoyed. After twelve hours of difficult investigation, she had turned up a spectacular link between the district nurse and the recent deaths in La Chapelle, but the *commissaire* was off on quite a different track, wandering down country lanes.

'This cat's balls are a matter of urgency, are they?' she asked sharply.

Adamsberg motioned her to take a seat. He had the parish priest of Le Mesnil on the line.

'Listen, Oswald tells me that that cat, Narcissus, had already been neutered. So he couldn't have been castrated when he was killed.'

'Well, I tell you I saw it with my own eyes, *commissaire*. Pascaline brought his body up to the church in a cat basket, to ask me to bless it. I had to have a long argument with her, to explain why I couldn't do it. The cat had had its throat cut and its parts were a bloody mess. What else do you want me to say?'

Adamsberg heard a sharp slap at the other end and wondered whether the priest was still catching flies.

'In that case, I don't understand,' he said. 'In Opportune, apparently everyone knew that the cat had been neutered.'

'Maybe whoever did it didn't know that, perhaps they weren't from the village. Or it could be this person had a thing against males, if I can add an opinion to your investigation.'

Adamsberg snapped off his phone and started swinging his legs again in perplexity.

'*A thing against males*,' he repeated to himself. 'The trouble is, Retancourt, that even people who don't know anything about it would guess that a cat weighing eleven kilos and sleeping all day would have to have been neutered.'

'Not the Snowball.'

'The Snowball's a special case, let's leave him out of it. The problem's still the same. Why did Narcissus's killer try to castrate a cat that had already had its balls cut off?'

'What if we were to concern ourselves more with whoever killed Diala?'

'We are. Being fixated on virgins and castrating a male must have some connection. This cat belonged to Pascaline, and only the tom was killed. As if someone wanted to eliminate all masculine presence surrounding Pascaline. To purify her environment, perhaps. Maybe they were trying to purify the graves as well, by putting some invisible potion in there.'

'As long as we don't know whether these two women were deliberately killed, we won't get anywhere. Accidents or murders, a killer or a grave-robber, that's a huge difference. But we've no way of telling.'

Adamsberg slid off the stool and paced round the room.

'There is a way,' he said. 'If you can face it.'

'Carry on.'

'If we could find the stone that fractured Pascaline's skull. If it was an accident, it must have been loose and got dislodged from the wall of the church. But if it was a murder, the stone could already have been on the ground, and the killer would have used it to hit her with. Either a falling stone or a murder weapon. If it was the latter, the stone would surely show some sign of having been exposed to the air. The accident is supposed to have happened on the south side of the church. So there would be no reason for a stone out of the wall to have any moss on it. But if it was lying in the grass, some moss might have grown on its north face. It rains a lot up there, so that would be bound to happen quite quickly. Knowing Devalon, I doubt whether he would have looked for lichen on the stone.'

'So where's the stone now?' asked Retancourt.

'It must either be in the *gendarmerie* in Evreux or have been thrown out. Devalon's an aggressive cop, Retancourt, and an incompetent one. You might have to fight your way to get to the stone. Best not to give him any warning, he's quite capable of getting rid of it just to bugger us up. Especially since he's already made some mistakes in this inquiry.'

The cat miaowed anxiously. The Snowball could always sense the moment when his preferred shelter was going to disappear. Three hours later, while Retancourt was making her inquiries in Evreux, the cat was still mewing, its nose glued to the front door of the squad's office, an obstacle between its little body and the absent woman to whom it was devoted. Adamsberg forcibly dragged the animal over to Danglard.

'*Capitaine*, since you seem to have some pull over this creature, can you tell it that Retancourt will be back soon? Give it a glass of wine or something, but for pity's sake stop it making this din.'

Adamsberg broke off sharply.

'Shee-it,' he muttered, letting the Snowball fall heavily to the ground with another pitiful mew.

'What is it?' asked Danglard, by now preoccupied with the despairing cat, which had jumped on to his knee.

'I've suddenly understood the story about Narcissus.'

'About time,' muttered the *commandant*.

Just then Retancourt called in. Her voice could be heard clearly on the mobile, and Adamsberg couldn't guess which of the two, Danglard or the cat, was listening more attentively.

'Devalon didn't want me to see the stone. He's an obstinate man – he would have fought me with his bare fists to stop me getting to it.'

'You'll have to find a way, *lieutenant*.'

'Don't worry, the stone's safe in the boot of my car. One of its surfaces is covered in lichen.'

Danglard wondered whether Retancourt's methods had been even more physical than Devalon's fists.

'I'm on to something else,' said Adamsberg. 'I know what happened to Narcissus.'

Yes, thought Danglard resignedly, everybody has known that for about two thousand years. Narcissus fell in love with his reflection in the water, and drowned when he tried to get close to it.

'It wasn't his balls they cut off, it was his penis,' Adamsberg explained.

'Ah,' said Retancourt. 'So where does that get us, sir?'

'To the very centre of an abomination. Get back here quickly, *lieutenant*, the cat's pining for you.'

'That's because I went without saying goodbye. Put him on the line.'

Adamsberg knelt down and put the mobile close to the cat's ear. He had once met a shepherd who telephoned to his bell-wether to keep it calm, so this kind of thing no longer surprised him. He could even remember the ewe's name: George Sand. Maybe one day George Sand's bones would find their way into a sacred reliquary. Lying on its back, the cat listened while Retancourt explained that she was on her way home.

'Can you tell me what this is all about?' asked Danglard.

'Both those women were murdered,' said Adamsberg, getting to his feet. 'Call everyone together. Conference in two hours.'

'Murdered? Just for the pleasure of opening their graves three months later?'

'I know, Danglard, it doesn't make sense. But it doesn't make sense to cut off a cat's penis, either.'

'That makes more sense,' retorted Danglard, who always retreated into his bottomless fund of knowledge when he was lost, as another might retreat to a convent. 'I've known zoologists who would think it quite important.'

'Why?'

'To get at the bone. There's a bone in a cat's penis.'

'Danglard, you're having me on.'

'There's a bone in a pig's snout, isn't there? Well, then.'

XXXI

ADAMSBERG ALLOWED HIMSELF TO WANDER DOWN TO THE SEINE, FOLLOWING the seagulls wheeling in the distance. Paris's river, although polluted and evil-smelling on certain days, was his watery refuge, the place where he could allow his thoughts to float free. It released them like a flock of birds, and they scattered into the sky, enjoying themselves, allowing the wind to blow them here and there, disorganised and unconscious. Paradoxical though it might sound, producing disorganised thoughts was Adamsberg's most important activity. It became particularly necessary when too many elements were blocking his mind, piling up in compact bundles and petrifying his actions. The only thing to do then was to open his head and let everything spill out. This happened effortlessly as he walked down the steps to the waterside.

In this general release, there was always one idea more tenacious than the others, like the seagull that marshals the rest of the group. A sort of head prefect, or gendarme, spending all its energy supervising the others and stopping them flying outside the boundaries of the real. The *commissaire* looked up into the sky to identify which gull was currently acting as this single-minded gendarme. He quickly found one, harrying a giddy juvenile that was playing at confronting the wind instead of its responsibilities. Then the gendarme swooped down on another thoughtless bird that was skimming over the dirty waters. The gendarme-gull was screaming without intermission. Just now his own gendarme-thought, equally monomaniac, was flying to and fro inside his head, squawking, 'There's a bone in the snout of a pig, and there's a bone in the penis of a cat.'

These new pieces of knowledge were preoccupying Adamsberg greatly as he strolled along beside the river, which today was dark green, its surface ruffled with waves. There couldn't be that many people who knew about the bone in a cat's penis. What was it called? No idea. What shape was it? Again, no idea. Perhaps it was odd, like the one in the pig's snout. So people who found one must have wondered where to place it in the great jigsaw puzzle of nature. On the animal's head, perhaps. Or they thought it was sacred, like the narwhal's tusk that people used to think grew on the head of the unicorn. Whoever had taken it from Narcissus must obviously be a specialist, possibly a collector, like some people collect shells. But what for? And why do people collect shells, for that matter? For their beauty? Their rarity value? To bring good luck? Adamsberg decided to take the advice he had given his son, and pulled out his mobile to call Danglard.

'*Capitaine*, can you tell me what it looks like, this bone from a cat's penis? Does it have some special beautiful shape?'

'No, not particularly. It's just odd, like all penile bones.'

'*All* penile bones?' said Adamsberg to himself, disconcerted by the thought that some element of human anatomy might also have eluded him. He could hear Danglard tapping on his keyboard, probably writing up the trip to Opportune. It wasn't a good moment to disturb him.

'Good grief,' Danglard was saying. 'We're not going to have to deal with this wretched cat for ever, are we? Even if his name was Narcissus.'

'Just a few minutes. This thing is worrying me.'

'Well, it doesn't worry cats. In fact, it makes life easier for them.'

'That wasn't what I meant. Why did you say "all penile bones"?'

Resignedly, Danglard tore himself away from the computer screen. He could hear the cries of seagulls at the other end of the phone and knew perfectly well where the *commissaire* was, and in what state of mind, his thoughts blowing about over the river.

'Like all penile bones, that is to say the penile bones of all carnivorous animals,' he said, enunciating clearly as if talking to a dull schoolboy. 'All carnivores have one,' he went on, underlining the point. 'Pinnipeds, felids, viverids, mustelids . . .'

'Stop, Danglard, you've lost me.'

'All carnivores, then: walrus family, weasel family, badgers, polecats, bears, lions, what have you.'

'So why isn't this generally known?' Adamsberg asked, for once feeling shocked at his own ignorance. 'And why is it just carnivores?'

'That's just how it is – it's nature's way. And nature knows what it's doing: it's giving a bit of help to the carnivores. They're rare, so they have to spend a lot of energy reproducing and surviving.'

'And why is this bone so special?'

'Because it's unique, it doesn't have any symmetry, bilateral or axial. It's twisted, a bit curved, has no articulation at top or bottom, and it has a swelling at its distal extremity.'

'What's that mean?'

'At the end.'

'Would you say it was as bizarre as the one in the pig's snout?'

'Yes, if you like. Because there isn't an equivalent in humans, so when medieval people found the penile bone of a walrus or a bear, they were puzzled by it. Just like you are.'

'Why a bear or a walrus?'

'Because they're big animals it's a bigger bone, and turns up more easily. In a forest, on a beach. But they weren't any better at identifying the penile bone of a cat. Since cats aren't eaten for food, their skeleton is less well known.'

'But people eat pork. Why don't they know about the one in the snout of the pig?'

'Because it's enclosed inside cartilage.'

'*Capitaine*, do you think the person who stole Narcissus's penis was a collector of some kind?'

'No idea.'

'Let me put it another way: do you think this bone might be thought valuable by certain people?'

Danglard made a sound that might have indicated doubt, or weariness.

'Well, like anything that's rare, or puzzling, it might have *some* value. There are some people who pick up pebbles out of streams. Or cut antlers off stags. We're never very far away from superstition. Which is the glory and the tragedy of the human race.'

'You don't like your pebble, then, *capitaine*?'

'What bothers me is that you picked one with a black stripe down the middle.'

'It's because of the line on your forehead when you're worried.'

'Are you coming back for the conference?'

'See, you're worried now. Of course I am.'

Adamsberg climbed back up the stone steps, hands in pockets. Danglard wasn't mistaken. What had he been doing when he'd picked up the pebbles? And what value had he attached to them, being himself a freethinker, who had never been tempted by superstition? The only times when he thought of a god was when he felt godlike himself. It happened on very rare occasions, when he found himself out alone during a violent thunderstorm, preferably at night. Then he liked to rule the sky, directing thunderbolts, summoning up torrential rain, conducting the music of the cloudburst. These were passing crises, exhilarating, and perhaps convenient outlets for the masculine libido. Adamsberg stopped suddenly in the street. Masculine libido. The male principle. The cat. the pig. The reliquary. His thoughts once more shot up into the air like a flock of birds.

XXXII

THE OFFICERS IN THE SERIOUS CRIME SQUAD WERE ARRANGING THE CHAIRS in the Council Chamber when Adamsberg walked across the large communal room without saying a word. Danglard gave him a quick look, and from the glow circulating under the *commissaire*'s skin like radioactive material he deduced that something critical had happened.

'What is it?' asked Veyrenc.

'He's plucked an idea out of the air,' Danglard explained, 'from the seagulls. You could call it a celestial bird-dropping. It falls on him, with a flurry of wings, between earth and heaven.'

Veyrenc glanced admiringly at Adamsberg, momentarily unsettling Dangard's suspicions. But the *commandant* quickly corrected the impression. Admiring one's enemy doesn't make him any less an enemy, on the contrary. Danglard remained convinced that Veyrenc had found in Adamsberg his quarry of choice, an enemy to be reckoned with, the little gang-leader of long ago, standing in the shade of the walnut tree, and the chief of the squad today.

Adamsberg opened the meeting by distributing to everyone the photographs of the exhumation at Opportune, which were particularly horrific. His movements were quick and concentrated, and everyone understood that the investigation had taken a new turn. Their chief rarely made them stay for conferences at the end of the afternoon.

'We didn't have victims, murderer, or motive with these graves. Now we have all three.'

Adamsberg rubbed his cheeks, wondering how to proceed. He didn't like summing up, not being gifted at the task. Danglard always helped him out in this respect, rather like the punctuator in the village, providing links, transitions and repetitions in the conversation.

'The victims,' Danglard proposed.

'Neither Elisabeth Châtel nor Pascale Villemot died by accident. Both of them were murdered. Retancourt has brought the evidence back from the Evreux *gendarmerie* this afternoon. The stone which had supposedly "fallen" out of the south wall of the church, fracturing Pascaline's skull, had been lying on the ground for at least a couple of months. While it was there, it had acquired a deposit of dark lichen on one of its surfaces.'

'And the stone couldn't have jumped up off the ground to hit her,' observed Estalère attentively.

'Correct, *brigadier*. Someone used it to bash her head in. That enables us to deduce that someone had most likely tampered with Elisabeth Châtel's car as well, causing a fatal accident once she drove it on the main road.'

'Devalon's not going to be happy about this,' observed Mercadet. 'It's what you could call rubbishing his investigation.'

Danglard smiled as he chewed his pencil, feeling pleased that Devalon's aggressive refusal to listen had led him straight into trouble.

'But why didn't Devalon think of examining the stone?' Voisenet asked.

'Because he's as thick as two planks, according to local opinion,' explained Adamsberg. 'But also because there was no reason in the world to think anyone would murder Pascaline.'

'How did you find her grave?' asked Maurel.

'By chance, apparently.'

'That's impossible.'

229

'Correct. I think we were deliberately pointed in the direction of the graveyard at Opportune. The murderer is telling us where to look, but from way ahead.'

'Why?'

'I don't know.'

'Back to the victims, then,' prompted Danglard. 'Pascaline and Elisabeth.'

'They were about the same age. They both led very quiet lives and there was no man in sight. Both of them were virgins. Pascaline's grave had been treated in exactly the same way as Elisabeth's. The coffin had been broken open, but the body hadn't been touched.'

'Was their virginity something to do with the motive for the killings?' asked Lamarre.

'No, it was the criterion for choosing the victims, but not the motive.'

'I don't get it,' said Lamarre, frowning. 'This murderer, she kills virgins, but her aim isn't to kill virgins?'

The interruption had disturbed Adamsberg's concentration, so he signed to Danglard to carry on.

'Remember what the pathologist told us,' the *commandant* said. 'Diala and La Paille were killed by a woman, measuring about one metre sixty-two or so, someone who was a perfectionist, who knew how to use both a scalpel and a syringe, and wore navy-blue leather shoes. The shoes had been polished under the soles, indicating a possible dissociative pathology, or at least a desire to provide a protective layer between herself and the ground on which the crimes were committed. Claire Langevin, the angel of death, presents all these characteristics.'

Adamsberg had opened his notebook without noting anything in it. He doodled as he listened to the summary by Danglard, who would, in his opinion, have made a better chief of squad than him.

'Retancourt has found a pair of shoes that belonged to her,' Danglard added. 'They were made of navy-blue leather. That's not enough to provide any certainty, but in the meantime we're still closely investigating this nurse.'

'She finds everything, Retancourt,' muttered Veyrenc.

'She can channel her energy,' Estalère responded passionately.

'This angel of death is a fantasy,' said Mordent irritably. 'Nobody ever saw her talking to Diala or La Paille at the Flea Market. She's invisible, she's vanished into thin air.'

'That's how she used to operate all her life,' said Adamsberg. 'Like a ghost.'

'No, it doesn't fit,' Mordent persisted, stretching his long heron-like neck out of his grey pullover. 'This woman killed thirty-three old people, always the same method, never changing it at all. And suddenly she's transformed herself into a different kind of monster, she goes chasing after virgins, opens graves, cuts the throats of two big lads. No, it just doesn't fit. You can't change a square into a circle, and someone who goes round quietly killing off helpless elderly folk doesn't turn into a wild necrophiliac. Shoes or no shoes.'

'I agree it doesn't fit,' said Adamsberg, nodding. 'Unless, that is, some profound shock might have opened up a different crater in the volcano. The lava of madness might have flowed in a different direction. Maybe her stay in prison could have had a strong effect, or the fact that her Alpha caught sight of her Omega.'

'I know about Alpha and Omega,' piped up Estalère. 'They're the two halves of a dissociating murderer, one each side of the wall.'

'The angel of death is a dissociator. Her arrest may have broken down her inner wall. After that, any kind of change is conceivable.'

'All the same,' said Mordent, 'it doesn't tell us what she's after with her virgins, or what she's looking for in their graves.'

'That's the black hole,' said Adamsberg. 'To get in there, we can only work backwards, since we have traces of her actions. Pascaline owned four cats. Three months before her death, one of them was killed. The only male among them.'

'Was that some kind of early threat to Pascaline?' asked Justin.

'No, I don't think so. It was killed to get at its genitals. Since it was already a neutered tom, its penis was the part that was taken. Danglard, explain about the bone.'

The *commandant* repeated his lesson about penile bones in carnivores – all pinnipeds, felids, etc.

'Anyone else here know about that before?' asked Adamsberg.

Only Voisenet and Veyrenc raised their hands.

'Voisenet, that figures, since you're a zoologist. But Veyrenc, how did you know that?'

'My grandfather told me. When he was a boy, a bear was killed in the valley. Its corpse was dragged around the villages. My grandfather kept the bone from its penis. He said it shouldn't be lost or sold at any price.'

'Do you still have it?'

'Yes, it's still there, back home.'

'Do you know why he valued it so much?'

'He just said it kept the house standing and the family safe.'

'How big is the penile bone of a cat?' asked Mordent.

'This big,' said Danglard, showing about two or three centimetres between finger and thumb.

'Not enough to keep a house standing,' remarked Justin.

'It's symbolic,' said Mordent.

'I dare say,' said Justin.

Adamsberg shook his head, without pushing back the hair that was falling into his eyes.

'No, I think this cat's bone has some precise significance for whoever took it. I think it's something to do with the male principle.'

'Contradiction with the value of the virgins, then,' objected Mordent.

'Depends what she's looking for,' said Voisenet.

'She's looking for eternal life,' said Adamsberg. 'And that's the motive.'

'I don't get it,' said Estalère after a silence.

And for once, something Estalère didn't get corresponded to incomprehension all round.

'At the same time the cat was mutilated,' Adamsberg said, 'it was discovered that a reliquary had been looted, in the church at Le Mesnil, just a few kilometres away from Opportune and Villeneuve. Oswald was right, that's a lot of disturbance for a small area. From the reliquary the thief took only the human bones belonging, supposedly, to Saint Jerome, but left behind various sheep bones, plus the bone from the snout of a pig.'

'Must have been a connoisseur, then,' remarked Danglard. 'It's not everyone who could recognise the bone from a pig's snout.'

'There's a bone in a pig's snout?'

'So it would seem, Estalère.'

'The same way, it's not everyone would know that the cat has a penile bone. So one way or another, we're dealing with a woman who knows what she's doing.'

'I don't see the link,' Froissy said, 'between the relics, the cat and the graves. Except that there are bones in all three cases.'

'That in itself is something,' said Adamsberg. 'The relics of the saint, the relics of a male animal, and the relics of virgins. In the priest's residence in Le Mesnil, alongside Saint Jerome, they have a very old book, which is open and available for anyone to see, where these three elements are combined in a kind of recipe.'

'More like a remedy or a potion,' Danglard corrected.

'What for?' asked Mordent.

'To obtain eternal life, with various ingredients. In the priest's house, the book was open at the page of this recipe. He's very proud of it, and I think he shows it to all his visitors. So did his predecessor, Father Raymond. This recipe must have been known to about thirty parishes in the area, and over many generations.'

'And nowhere else?'

'Oh yes,' said Danglard. 'The book's famous, and especially this concoction. It's the *De sanctis reliquis*, in the 1663 edition.'

'Never heard of it,' said Estalère.

And, once more, something that Estalère had never heard of corresponded to ignorance all round.

'Personally, I wouldn't want eternal life,' said Retancourt, in a low voice.

'Wouldn't you?' asked Veyrenc.

'Just imagine living for ever. You'd end up flinging yourself on the ground and being bored to death.'

> *'Carpe diem, Madame:*
> *The span of a lifetime flies as a summer day,*
> *Much more cruel though would be for ever here to stay.'*

'Yes, you could put it like that,' nodded Retancourt.

'So we need to analyse what's in this book, is that it?' asked Mordent.

'I think so,' replied Adamsberg. 'Veyrenc has memorised the recipe.'

'The potion,' Danglard corrected him again.

'Go on, Veyrenc, but not too fast.'

'Sovereign remedy for the lengthening of life, through the quality possessed by sacred relics to weaken the miasmas of death, preserved from the truest processes and purged of former errors.'

'That's just the title,' Adamsberg explained. 'Now for the rest, *lieutenant.'*

'Five times cometh the age of youth, till the day thou must invert it, pass and pass again, out of reach of the thread of life.'

'I don't understand a word of it,' said Estalère, this time with a note of panic in his voice.

'No one really understands it,' Adamsberg reassured him. 'But I think it means something about the age you have to be to take the remedy. Not when you're young.'

'That's quite possible,' agreed Danglard. 'When you've seen the age of youth pass five times. One could say five times fifteen, if you took the average age of marriage in the late Middle Ages in Western Europe. That would make it seventy-five.'

'Which is exactly the age of the angel of death now,' said Adamsberg slowly.

There was a silence and Froissy raised her elegant arm to say something.

'We can't carry on like this. I propose we continue the discussion across the road.'

Before Adamsberg could say anything there was a general move to adjourn to the *Brasserie des Philosophes*. The discussion could not begin again until everyone was seated in the bay with the stained-glass windows, in front of a plateful of food and a glass.

'Right,' said Mordent. 'Maybe when she reached the age of seventy-five, it opened up another crater.'

'The nurse can't see herself joining the common herd of old folk she's been bumping off,' said Danglard. 'She's not an ordinary mortal any more. One might imagine that she wants to find the secret of eternal life and hold on to her powers.'

'And that she's been preparing for it for some time,' said Mordent. 'So she'd need to have got out of prison before her seventy-fifth birthday whatever happened, in order to get the recipe together.'

'The potion.'

'I guess that makes sense,' said Retancourt.

'Give us the rest of the text, Veyrenc,' said Adamsberg.

'*Sacred relics thou wilt crush, taking three pinches, mixed well with the male principle which must not bend, and with the quick of virgins, on the dexter side, sorted by three into equal quantities, and grind these with the living cross from the heart of the eternal branches, adjacent in equal quantity, kept in the same place by the valency of the saint, in the wine of the year, and thus wilt thou lay its head on the ground.*'

'I didn't understand that,' said Lamarre, getting in before Estalère.

'Let's take it again slowly,' said Adamsberg. 'Start again, Veyrenc, bit by bit.'

'Sacred relics thou wilt crush, taking three pinches.'

'That's easy enough,' said Danglard. 'Three pinches of bones that have been reduced to powder. Saint Jerome would fill the bill.'

'*. . . Mixed well with the male principle which must not bend . . .'*

'A phallus,' suggested Gardon.

'That doesn't bend,' added Justin

'Well, a penis with a bone in it, for example,' confirmed Adamsberg. 'In other words the penile bone of a cat. And since cats have nine lives, that would give a special little eternity as a bonus.'

'Yes, OK,' said Danglard, who was taking notes.

'And with the quick of virgins, on the dexter side, sorted by three into equal quantities.'

'Look out,' said Adamsberg, 'here come our virgins.'

'Sorted?' asked Estalère. 'Does that mean three by three?'

'No, it means "matching" – you have to take the same quantities as for the relics.'

'But what are you supposed to take, for heaven's sake?'

'Well, that's the question,' said Adamsberg. 'What is "the quick of virgins"?'

'Blood?'

'Genitals?'

'Heart?'

'I'd say blood,' said Mordent. 'That's the most logical, if you're seeking eternal life. Virgin's blood, mixed with a male principle which would fertilise it and create eternity.'

'Why blood "on the dexter side", though?'

'It means on the right,' said Danglard.

'Since when is there right-hand and left-hand blood?'

'Don't know what that means,' said Danglard, serving more wine all round.

236

Adamsberg had put his chin in his hands.

'None of that fits the opening of a grave,' he said. 'You could easily take any of these things from the corpse of a virgin who had recently died. That's not what happened. And as for blood, you can't extract blood or indeed any vital part from a body that's been three months in the ground.'

Danglard pulled a face. He liked the intellectual element of the discussion, but the subject matter was abhorrent to him. The sordid dissection of the potion was making him now find repugnant the great *De sanctis reliquis* which he had once loved,

'So what's left in the tomb that might appeal to our angel?' Adamsberg was asking.

'Nails, hair, perhaps?' Justin asked.

'But to get them you wouldn't need to kill anyone. They could have been taken from living women.'

'The only thing left in the grave is bones,' said Lamarre.

'What about the pelvis?' suggested Justin. 'The basin of fertility. To sort of complement the "male principle".'

'That sounds a good idea, Justin, but only the head end of the coffins was opened, and the robber didn't take any bones, not even a splinter.'

'We've reached a dead end,' said Danglard. 'How does the text go on?'

Veyrenc obediently recited it: '*Now grind these with the living cross from the heart of the eternal branches, adjacent in equal quantity.*'

'Well, that's clear, at any rate,' said Mordent. 'The living cross that lives in the eternal branches must mean Christ's cross.'

'Yes,' said Danglard. 'So-called fragments of the True Cross were sold by the thousand as sacred relics. Calvin calculated that there must have been more wood than three hundred men could carry.'

'Well, it gives us something to aim for,' said Adamsberg. 'Can one of you check whether there has been any theft from a reliquary containing fragments of the Cross since the nurse escaped from prison.'

'OK, I will,' said Mercadet, taking notes.

On account of his narcoleptic tendencies, Mercadet was often asked to do research in the files, since he was virtually incapable of fieldwork.

'We should also see whether she ever practised in the Le Mesnil-Beauchamp region, possibly under a different name from Clarisse Langevin, and possibly a long time ago. Take her photo with you.'

'OK,' said Mercadet, with the same ephemeral show of energy.

'"Clarisse" is the name of your bloodthirsty nun, *commissaire*,' whispered Danglard. 'The district nurse's name is Claire.'

Adamsberg turned to him with a vague and astonished look.

'You're right,' he said. 'How odd that I mixed them up. As if they're two kernels of a walnut inside the same shell.'

Adamsberg signalled to Veyrenc to carry on.

'. . . *kept in the same place by the valency of the saint.*'

'That's easy, too,' said Danglard, confidently. 'It must mean the geographical sector, the zone of influence of the sacred relics. That would be the unity of place, so that all the ingredients came from the same area.'

'Does a saint have a zone of influence?' asked Froissy. 'Like a radio transmitter?'

'It isn't written down anywhere, but that was the general feeling. If people took the trouble to go on pilgrimages, it was with the idea that the closer you got, the greater the influence of the saint.'

'So she had to find all the ingredients in an area not too far from Le Mesnil,' said Voisenet.

'Logical,' said Danglard. 'In the Middle Ages, it was important to ensure the compatibility of the constituent parts, if a potion was going to be successful. They also took climate into consideration when balancing mixtures. So the bones of a Norman saint would mix better with some bones from a Norman virgin and a cat from the same place.'

'OK,' said Mordent. 'So what comes next. Veyrenc?'

'. . . *in the wine of the year, and thus wilt thou lay its head on the ground.*'

'Wine,' said Lamarre. 'That must be to mix it together.'

'It means blood, too.'

'Christ's blood. That ties it all together.'

'Why "of the year"?'

'Because in those days,' Danglard explained, 'wine didn't keep. You always drank it the same year. Like when we drink Beaujolais Nouveau.'

'So what's left?'

'. . . *thou wilt lay its head on the ground.*'

'It means laying it low,' said Danglard.

'So it must mean to overcome,' put in Mordent. 'You'll overcome death, I suppose, or the death's head.'

'So,' said Mercadet, consulting his notes, 'the killer has put together all these elements: some quick of virgins, whatever that may be, some saint's relics, a cat's bone. But perhaps not yet the wood of the Cross. All she needs is the wine of the year to mix it all up.'

Several glasses were emptied at the mention of wine, which seemed to conclude the conference. But Adamsberg had not moved, so no one else dared to get up. They did not know whether the *commissaire* was about to nod off, with his cheek on his hand, or whether he was about to close the session. Danglard was about to nudge him, when he suddenly came to the surface like a sponge.

'I believe that a third woman is going to be killed,' Adamsberg said, without moving his cheek from his hand. 'I think we'd better order some coffee.'

XXXIII

'THE QUICK OF VIRGINS, SORTED BY THREE IN EQUAL QUANTITIES,' SAID Adamsberg. 'By three. We ought to take notice of that.'

'It must be the dosage,' said Mordent. 'Three *pinches* of powdered saint's bones, three pinches of the penile bone, three pinches of the wood of the cross, and three of some sort of virgin principle.'

'No, *commandant*, I don't think so. We've already had two virgins being dug up. Whatever they wanted to find there, it seems to me that one would have been quite enough to get three pinches. And it would have been enough to write "in equal quantities". Instead of that the recipe says "by three".'

'Yes, three pinches.'

'No, three virgins. Three pinches from three virgins.'

'You don't have to take it that far, surely. It's both a recipe and a sort of poem.'

'No,' said Adamsberg, 'Just because the language seems complicated to us, we don't have to regard it as a poem. It's an old cookbook, nothing else.'

'That's correct,' said Danglard, although he was a bit shocked by the casual way Adamsberg referred to the *De reliquis*. 'It *is* just a plain compendium of medical recipes. It's not meant to be in code, it's meant to be easily understood.'

'Well, that's just what it isn't,' said Justin.

'It's not all that obscure,' said Adamsberg. 'We just have to take care to read each word carefully, and not miss anything out. In these ghoulish mixtures, just like any cookery recipe, every word counts. "Sorted by three." That's the danger area. That's where we have to start work.'

'Where?' asked Estalère.

'With the third virgin.'

'Yes, it's quite possible,' agreed Danglard.

'We'll have to go and look for her,' said Adamsberg.

'Yes?' said Mercadet, lifting his head.

Lieutenant Mercadet was taking plentiful notes, as he did every time he was wide awake enough to compensate by redoubled zeal for his previous absences.

'The first thing we need to do is check whether any other virgin from Upper Normandy has been recently killed, or has died in an apparent accident.'

'How big do you reckon the saint's zone of influence would be?' asked Retancourt.

'The best thing would be to draw up a radius of fifty kilometres around Le Mesnil-Beauchamp.'

'Seven thousand, eight hundred and fifty square kilometres,' said Mercadet, making a rapid calculation. 'And how old would our victim be?'

'Symbolically,' said Danglard, 'one could guess a minimal age of twenty-five. That was the age of Saint Catherine, when adult virginity is supposed to start. And we could use a cut-off date of forty, because after that both men and women were considered old.'

'That's a bit too broad,' said Adamsberg. 'We need to move more quickly. Let's start with the age of our existing two victims, somewhere between thirty and forty. About how many women would that give us in the area, Mercadet?'

The *lieutenant* was given a few moments to do his calculations in

241

silence, surrounded by his cups of coffee, sorted in threes. It was a pity, Adamsberg reflected, that Mercadet was so given to drowsiness. He had a remarkable head for figures and lists.

'Very roughly, I'd say about a hundred and twenty to two hundred and fifty women in the area who might possibly be virgins.'

'That's still too many,' said Adamsberg chewing his lip. 'We need to make the area smaller. Let's target an area of, say, twenty kilometres around Le Mesnil. What does that give?'

'Between forty and eighty women,' Mercadet replied promptly.

'And how are we going to identify these forty virgins?' asked Retancourt, sharply. 'It's not a crime, so it won't show up on any database.'

A virgin, thought the *commissaire,* glancing quickly at his large but pretty *lieutenant.* Retancourt kept her private life very private, hermetically sealed against any inquiries. Perhaps this detailed discussion of virgin women was exasperating her.

'We'll consult the local priests,' Adamsberg said. 'Starting with the one in Le Mesnil. Work quickly, all of you. Overtime if necessary.'

'*Commissaire,*' said Gardon, 'I don't think it's as urgent as all that. Pascaline and Elisabeth were killed three and a half months ago and four months ago respectively. The third virgin is almost certainly already dead.'

'I don't think so,' said Adamsberg, looking up at the ceiling. 'Because of the new wine which has to be the final liquid binding the whole mixture. It has to mix all the ingredients. So it will be the November vintage.'

'Or October,' said Danglard. 'They used to do the first pressing earlier than we do today.'

'All right,' said Mordent, 'So what does that mean?'

'Well, if we follow what Danglard told us,' Adamsberg went on, 'you have to respect the harmonious balance for the mixture to succeed. If I was making this mixture, I'd arrange for regular intervals between taking the ingredients so that there wasn't too long a gap. Like a sort of relay race.'

'It's compulsory, even,' said Danglard, chewing his pencil. 'In medieval times irregularity and interruptions were a sort of obsession. They brought bad luck, broke the spell. Whatever the line was, a real or an abstract one, it shouldn't be interrupted or broken. In all things, it was essential to follow an orderly and continuous development, in a straight line without hiccups.'

'Now,' said Adamsberg, 'the killing of the cat and the looting of the relics happened three months before Pascaline's death. Then the "quick of virgins" was taken three months *after* their deaths. Three, like the number of pinches, the number of virgins, three months, like the length of a season. So the last "quick" will be collected either three months before the new wine, or just before it. And the virgin will be killed three months before that.'

Adamsberg interrupted himself and counted on his fingers, several times.

'So it's quite probable that this woman is still alive, but that her death is programmed for some time in the next three months, most likely either early April or late June. And today's the twenty-fifth of March.'

Three months, two weeks – or even one week. In silence, everyone was considering the urgency and the impossibility of their task. Because even if they did manage to establish a list of virgin women in the circle around Le Mesnil, how could they possibly guess which one the angel of death would choose? And how on earth could they protect her?

'All this is just speculation on a massive scale,' said Voisenet, shaking himself as if coming round at the end of a film and abruptly tearing himself away from the fiction that had engaged him up till then. 'Like everything else.'

'Yes, that's all it is,' said Adamsberg.

A flurry of wings between heaven and earth, thought Danglard anxiously.

XXXIV

THE DISCUSSION HAD LASTED SO LONG THAT ADAMSBERG WAS RUNNING LATE and had to take his car to go to Camille's studio. He certainly wouldn't tell Tom the story about the nurse and the ghastly mixture. Eternal life, he thought, as he parked in the rain. Omnipotence. The recipe in the *De reliquis* seemed ridiculous, a real hoax. But a hoax that had haunted humans since their first steps in the cosmic wilderness which so worried Danglard. A murderous hoax, in search of which which men had elaborated religions and killed each other since time immemorial. This was essentially what the nurse had been looking for, throughout her life. To have the power of life or death over others, to be able to dispose of other people's existences, was already to be some kind of goddess, weaving the web of their destinies. And now she was taking care of her own. Having reigned over other lives, she couldn't allow death to catch up with her like any normal old woman. She would use her immense power of life and death for herself, gaining the power of the Immortals and reaching her true throne, from where she would continue her lethal work. She had reached the age of seventy-five and it was time, now that the cycle of youth had passed five times. This was the moment and she had always known it. Her victims had been singled out far in advance, the times and methods of killing had been worked out in minute detail. This woman was meticulous, the plan had been worked out step by step, without leaving anything to chance. She didn't have a few months' advance over the police, but ten or fifteen years. The third virgin had been doomed in advance. And he couldn't see how he, Adamsberg, with his twenty-seven officers, or even with a hundred, could block the implacable advance of the Shade.

No, he would tell Tom the rest of the story of the two ibex instead.

Adamsberg climbed the seven flights of stairs and rang the bell, ten minutes late.

'If you remember, can you give him his nose drops?' asked Camille, giving him a small bottle.

'Of course I'll remember,' said Adamsberg, putting the bottle in his pocket. 'Off you go. Play beautifully.'

'Yes.'

Just a basic exchange of words between friends. Adamsberg lay on the bed, with Tom lying on his stomach.

'Remember where we'd got to? Remember the nice brown ibex, who loved birds, but didn't want the other ginger one to come and annoy him on his bit of the mountain? Well, he did come along, just the same. He came along with his big horns flashing around. And he said: "You were nasty to me when I was a kid, and now you're going to be sorry." "It was just kids' games," the brown ibex said, "Nothing serious. Go home and stop bothering me." But the ginger one wouldn't listen. Because he'd come a long, long way to get his revenge on the brown one.'

Here Adamsberg stopped and the child signified by moving his foot that he wasn't asleep.

'So the one who'd come a long, long way said, "You poor sap, I'm going to take your territory, and I'm going to take your job." Just then a very wise chamois, who was passing, and who had read all the books there are, said to the brown one: "Watch out, this ibex has already killed two other ibex and he's out to get you as well." "No, I don't believe you," said the brown one to the wise old chamois. "You're just exaggerating because you're jealous." But he was left feeling uneasy. Because this ginger ibex was very clever and what's more he was very good-looking. The brown one decided to fence the ginger one in with a fireguard, while he had a serious think. No sooner said than done. The fireguard was perfect. But the brown ibex had one failing: he wasn't very good at having a serious think.'

By the child's weight, Adamsberg felt that Tom had gone to sleep. He put his hand on the baby's head and closed his eyes, breathing in his smell of soap, milk and sweat. And something else.

'Surely your mother doesn't spray perfume on you,' he whispered. 'That's silly, babies shouldn't wear perfume.'

No, the delicate smell didn't come from Tom, it was coming from the bed. Adamsberg sniffed in the dark, like the brown ibex, suddenly alerted. It was a scent he knew from somewhere. But it wasn't Camille's.

He got up gently, and laid Tom in his cot. He walked around the room, sniffing the air. The scent was localised, it was on the sheets. A man, for God's sake, a man had been sleeping there, leaving his smell.

Well, so what? he thought, switching on the light. How many women's beds did *you* jump into, before it turned Camille into a friend? He lifted the covers in a swift movement, looking at them as if finding out more about the intruder would soothe his anger. Then he sat on the disturbed bed and breathed in deeply. It wasn't important. One lover more or less, what difference would that make? Nothing serious. Not a reason to be angry. Feelings of revenge like those of Veyrenc were not in his nature. Adamsberg knew the sensation would pass, and waited for it to subside, while he withdrew to the protection of his own private shore, where nothing and no one could reach him.

Calmly, he folded the covers back, tucked them in properly on both sides, and smoothed the pillows with the palm of his hand, not quite knowing whether with this gesture he was wiping out the unknown man or his own anger, which had already passed. He found under his hand a few hairs, which he examined under the lamp. Short hairs, masculine hairs. Two black and one ginger. He clenched his fingers round them abruptly.

Breathing fast, he paced from wall to wall, images of Veyrenc tumbling into his head. A torrent of mud, in which he saw the *lieutenant*'s face from every angle, sitting in the blasted broom cupboard: the silent face, the provocative face, the verse-spouting face, the obstinate face, just like a Béarnais. Fucking bastard of a Béarnais. Danglard was right, this mountain dweller was dangerous, he had seduced Camille on to his wavelength. He had come to exact vengeance, and had started right here. In this bed.

Thomas made a sound in his sleep, and Adamsberg laid his hand on his head.

'It's that ginger ibex, little one,' he whispered. 'He's on the attack, and he's taken the other one's wife. And that means war, Tom.'

Adamsberg sat motionless for the next two hours, alongside his son's cot, waiting for Camille to return. He departed quickly, hardly speaking to her, his attitude bordering on discourtesy, and went out into the rain. Behind the wheel, he reviewed his strategy. It looked good: it would be silent and efficient. If one can play at bastards, so can two. He looked at his watches by the overhead light and nodded. By five o'clock tomorrow, the system would be in place.

XXXV

Lieutenant Hélène Froissy, so self-effacing, quiet and gentle that she tended to melt into the background, a woman with unremarkable features but a very shapely figure, had three special qualities. The first was that she could be seen eating from morning to night, without putting on any weight; secondly, she painted in watercolours, the only hobby she was known to have. Adamsberg, who filled entire notebooks with sketches during meetings, had taken over a year to notice Froissy's little paintings. One night the previous spring, he had been looking in the *lieutenant's* cupboard for something to eat. Froissy's office was considered by the whole squad as a back-up supply of groceries and you were sure to find a great variety of foodstuffs there: fresh and dried fruit, biscuits, dairy products, cereal, pâté, Turkish delight – a resource in cases of unforeseen pangs of hunger. Froissy was well aware of these depredations and laid in stocks accordingly. When foraging about, Adamsberg had stopped to leaf through a sheaf of watercolours and had discovered the darkness of her colours and subjects, the desolate silhouettes and mournful landscapes under lowering skies. Since then, they had occasionally exchanged paintings and drawings without speaking, slipped into a report here and there. Froissy's third characteristic, however, was that she had a degree in electronics and had worked for eight years in the transmission-reception services, otherwise known as telephone tapping, and had accomplished marvels of speed and efficiency in this post.

She joined Adamsberg at seven in the morning, as soon as the rather scruffy little bar opposite the *Brasserie des Philosophes* opened its doors. The *Brasserie*, being opulent and catering for a largely bourgeois clientele, never opened before nine, whereas the workmen's cafe raised the blinds at dawn. The croissants had just appeared in a wire basket on the counter and Froissy took advantage of this to order her second breakfast.

'It's illegal, of course,' she said.

'Naturally.'

Froissy pulled a face as she dipped her croissant in her cup of tea.

'I need to know a bit more,' she said.

'Froissy, I can't take the risk that a rogue cop has infiltrated the squad.'

'What would he be up to?'

'That's what I don't know. If I'm wrong, we'll forget it – you know nothing about it.'

'But I'll still have placed bugs without knowing why. Veyrenc lives alone. What do you expect to get by listening in?'

'His telephone conversations.'

'So what? If he's plotting anything, he's hardly going to talk about it on the phone.'

'If he *is* plotting anything, it would be extremely serious.'

'All the more reason for him to keep quiet.'

'All the less. You're forgetting the golden rule of secrecy.'

'And that is?' asked Hélène, sweeping up her crumbs into one hand with the other, so as to leave the table looking clean.

'Someone who has a secret, a secret so important that this person has sworn by all that's holy not to tell a single soul, always does in fact tell *one* other person.'

'Where does that rule come from?' asked Froissy, rubbing her hands together.

'From human nature. Nobody, with very rare exceptions, can keep a secret entirely to themselves. The bigger the secret, the more reliable the rule. That's how secrets leak out, Froissy, being passed from one person who's sworn not to tell to another person who swears not to tell, and so on. If Veyrenc has a secret, at least one other person must be in on it. And he'll talk to that person, which is what I want to hear.'

That and something else, thought Adamsberg, feeling uncomfortable at misleading an honest person like Hélène Froissy. His resolve of the previous evening had not diminished, and he had only to think of Veyrenc laying hands on Camille – or, worse still, their inevitable coupling – for his entire being to be transformed into a war machine. In his dealings with Froissy, though, he simply felt a bit shabby, and he could deal with that.

'Veyrenc's secret,' Froissy repeated, dropping her crumbs neatly into her empty cup. 'Does it have anything to do with his poems?'

'No, not at all.'

'With his stripy hair?'

'Yes,' admitted Adamsberg, realising that Froissy would not cross over the bounds of legality unless he gave her a bit of help.

'He was attacked?'

'Perhaps.'

'And he's looking for revenge?'

'Possibly.'

'Deadly revenge?'

'That I can't say.'

'I see,' said the *lieutenant*, continuing to smooth the table with her hand, and looking vaguely puzzled to find nothing left there. 'So it amounts to protecting him from himself in the end?'

'You've got it,' said Adamsberg, delighted that Froissy had managed unaided to find that the end might justify the means. 'Afterwards, we'll dismantle the listening equipment and everyone will be OK.'

'All right, then,' said Froissy, pulling out her notebook and pen. 'Let's go. Targets? Objectives?'

In an instant, the self-effacing and morally anxious woman had disappeared, transformed into the formidable technician that she could be.

'It would be enough for me if you bug his mobile. Here's the number.'

While he was feeling in his pocket for Veyrenc's number, Adamsberg found the little bottle Camille had given him. Contrary to his promise, he had failed to remember to give Tom his nose drops.

'Bug all his calls and have them connected through to my home number.'

'I'll have to make them transit through the squad headquarters, then be transferred to you.'

'Where will the transmitter be at headquarters?'

'In my cupboard.'

'But everyone goes looking in there for food, Froissy.'

'I'm talking about the *other* food cupboard, to the left of the window. I keep it locked.'

'So the first one is a decoy, is it? What do you keep in the other one?'

'Turkish delight, direct from Lebanon. I'll give you a spare key.'

'Fine. Here are the keys to my house. Install the speaker in the bedroom upstairs, away from the window.'

'Obviously.'

'I don't just need sound, I need a screen too, to follow where he goes.'

'Long distances?'

'Could be.'

To see whether Veyrenc would take Camille away somewhere. A weekend in the country, a fairytale inn in the woods, the baby playing happily in the grass at their feet. Oh no, no *fucking* way! The bastard was not going to take Tom away from him.

'Is it important to follow his movements?'

'Essential.'

'Well, in that case, we'll have to do more than bug the mobile. We'll put a GPS under his car. And do you want a mike in the car too?'

'While we're at it. How long do you need?'

'I'll have it done by five this evening.'

XXXVI

BY FOUR-FORTY THAT AFTERNOON HÉLÈNE FROISSY WAS FINE-TUNING THE reception for the receiver she had installed in Adamsberg's bedroom. She could hear Veyrenc's voice quite well, although it was overlaid by the voices around and by sounds of chairs scraping, footsteps and papers rustling. The microphone was too powerful, the bug on the mobile only needed to pick up sound from a radius of five metres. That would be enough to cover Veyrenc's small flat, and it would allow her to tune out much of the interference.

Now she could hear Veyrenc's voice quite distinctly. He was talking to Retancourt and Justin. Froissy listened in for a few moments to the light tone and husky sound of the *lieutenant*'s voice while eliminating the last remnants of outside interference. Now Veyrenc was sitting down at his desk. She heard the click of a keyboard and then he said quietly to himself: '*I have no place to go to bury deep my pain.*' Froissy glanced angrily at the bug she had just installed, at the diabolical device that could pour Veyrenc's innermost thoughts direct into Adamsberg's room. There was something violent about putting these tracking devices on Veyrenc. Froissy hesitated before setting everything to 'go', then turned all the switches on, one by one. A battle between macho boys, she thought as she closed the door, and she had been drawn into it on her full responsibility.

XXXVII

ON MONDAY, 4 APRIL, DANGLARD PINNED UP A MAP OF THE EURE *département* in Normandy on the wall of the Council Chamber. In his hand he was holding a list of the twenty-nine women assumed to be virgins, aged between thirty and forty, living within twenty kilometres of Le Mesnil-Beauchamp. Their addresses had been located, and Justin was marking their homes on the map with red drawing pins.

'You should have used white ones,' said Voisenet.

'Oh, bugger off,' said Justin. 'Haven't got any.'

The men were all tired. They had spent a week checking lists and combing the area, interviewing all the parish priests. One thing seemed certain. No other woman corresponding to their criteria had died accidentally in recent months. So the third virgin must still be alive. This certainty weighed as heavily on the shoulders of the officers as their doubts concerning the direction in which their boss had taken the investigation. They were inclined to question the very basis of their work – namely the link between the profanation of the graves and the recipe in *De reliquis*.

The opposition had divided into different groups. The most hard-nosed among them thought that traces of lichen on a stone were insufficient evidence of murder. And that, seen from one point of view, the whole structure which Adamsberg had built up was as flimsy as a dream, a fantasy into which he had drawn them all during that extraordinary conference. Others, more hesitant, were prepared to accept that both Pascaline and Elisabeth had been murdered, and agreed that their deaths might somehow be related to the mutilated cat and the theft of the relics. But they refused to follow the *commissaire* in his view of the medieval potion. And even among those, finally, who accepted the *De reliquis* theory, its interpretation was subject to much discussion and analysis. After all, the text didn't say anything about cats, and the male principle could just as well, for all they knew, refer to the semen of a bull. There was nothing to indicate the contrary, just as there was no precise indication that three separate virgins were required to provide ingredients. Maybe two were enough, and all this labour was for nothing. And nothing proved, either, that the third virgin would be killed three months, or six months, before the new wine was ready. The whole thing, from insubstantial beginnings to improbable reasoning, made a completely unbelievable farrago, detached from reality.

With the passage of time, an unprecedented rebellion was brewing in the squad, drawing in more recruits as the hours passed and their fatigue grew. People remembered the hasty rustication of *Lieutenant* Noël, from whom nothing had been heard. And this punishment appeared all the more incomprehensible since Adamsberg was now treating the New Recruit very offhandedly, and avoiding him as much as possible. Murmurings were heard that the *commissaire* had still not recovered from his traumatic Quebec experience, from his separation from Camille, or from the death of his father and the birth of his son, events which had suddenly precipitated him into the the ranks of older men. People remembered the pebbles he had placed on their desks, and somebody suggested that Adamsberg was veering towards mysticism. Once he was on such slippery territory, he would send the whole investigation plunging into the abyss, with all hands.

Such discontent would not have gone beyond the usual level of grumbling if Adamsberg had seemed his normal self. But since the day after the conference about the Three Virgins, the *commissaire* had become inaccessible, sending out brief, morose messages, never setting foot in the Council Chamber. It was as if his veins had frozen. The rebellion had revived the old debate between the positivists and the cloud shovellers, the latter becoming fewer in number as Adamsberg remained cold and distant.

Two days earlier, a fierce argument over whether they ought simply to stop looking for the damned relics and all the rest of the ridiculous ingredients had once more stimulated these antagonisms. Mercadet, Kernorkian, Maurel, Lamarre, Gardon, and Estalère were, of course, solidly behind the *commissaire*, who did not himself appear to be preoccupied by the potential mutiny in the squad. Danglard, stony-faced, was still holding the bridge, although he was one of those who had the gravest doubts about Adamsberg's orders. But in the face of a mutiny, he would have allowed himself to be chopped into tiny pieces rather than admit this; and he continued stolidly defending the *De reliquis* theory, though without placing any faith in it. Veyrenc had not taken sides, contenting himself with carrying out his duties and trying to keep a low profile. Since the conference of the Three Virgins, he and the *commissaire* had suddenly been placed on a war footing, but he had no idea why.

Strangely enough, Retancourt, one of the leading positivists in the squad, had remained neutral throughout, like a blasé supervisor on duty in a rowdy playground. Quieter than usual and deep in concentration, Retancourt had appeared to be absorbed in a problem known only to herself. She had not even turned up for work on Monday morning. Puzzled at this, Danglard had consulted Estalère, who was reckoned to be the expert on the polyvalent goddess.

'She's channelling all her energy in one direction,' was Estalère's diagnosis. 'There's not an ounce left for us, and hardly any for the cat.'

'And what's she channelling it into, in your opinion?'

'It's not administrative, not family, nothing physical. Not technical,' said Estalère, ticking off the possibilities, I think it's, how shall I put it . . . ?' Estalère pointed to his forehead.

'Intellectual,' said Danglard

'Yes,' said Estalère. 'It's something she's thinking about. Something's intrigued her.'

Adamsberg was in fact acutely conscious of the climate which he had produced in the squad, and he was attempting to control it. But the recordings of Veyrenc had seriously upset him, and he was having difficulty regaining his equilibrium. The phone-tapping had not taken him one step further in his research into the war of the two valleys and the deaths of Fernand and Big Georges. Veyrenc called nobody except one or two relatives and friends, and never commented on his work with the squad. On the other hand, Adamsberg had twice overheard Veyrenc and Camille in bed, and was crushed by the thought of their two bodies, wounded by the crudity of real lives when they are those of other people. And now he deeply regretted his action. Their relationship, far from enabling him to get close to them and control them, was in fact driving him ever further from them. He wasn't there in that bedroom, it wasn't his space. He had invaded it like an intruder and he would have to leave it. The disappointed recognition that there was an inaccessible space belonging only to Camille and which did not concern him at all was gradually beginning to replace his anger. All that was left for him to do was return to his own territory, chastened and soiled, encrusted with memories that he would have to destroy. He had spent a long time walking around listening to the seagulls, in order to understand that he would have to give up his siege of an imaginary citadel.

Feeling relieved and as if recovering from a fever which had left him drained, he crossed the Council Chamber and looked at the map which Justin was completing. On seeing him come in, Veyrenc had immediately withdrawn into a defensive posture.

'Twenty-nine,' said Adamsberg, reckoning up the red drawing pins.

'We'll never manage it,' said Danglard. 'We'll have to narrow down the criteria to keep it more controllable.'

'What about their way of life?' suggested Maurel. 'We could rule out the ones who live with someone else – parents, brother, aunt – because they'd be less accessible to a killer.'

'No, we can't assume that,' said Danglard. 'Elisabeth was killed on her way to work.'

'What about the wood of the Cross? Any joy there?' wondered Adamsberg in a husky voice, as if he had had a cough for a week.

'There are no other relics in the whole of Upper Normandy,' replied Mercadet. 'And there've been no thefts during the period in question. The last dodgy sale reported was of some relics of Saint Demetrius of Salonika, fifty-four years ago.'

'And the angel of death. Any sightings of her in the area?'

'There is one possibility,' said Gardon. 'But we've only got three witnesses. A district nurse came to live in Vecquigny six years ago. That's only three kilometres north-east of Le Mesnil. The description's a bit vague. A woman between sixty and seventy, small, neat, chatty. Could be just about anyone. They remembered her in Le Mesnil, Vecquigny and Meillères. She was practising there about a year.'

'Long enough to pick up information, then. Do we know why she left?'

'No.'

'Let's just drop it,' said Justin, who had crossed over into the positivist camp during the rebellion.

'Drop what, *lieutenant*?' said Adamsberg in a faraway voice.

'Everything. The book, the cat, the third virgin, the bits of bone, the whole bloody lot. It's a complete load of bollocks.'

'I don't need any more men on this business,' said Adamsberg, sitting down in the middle of the room with everyone looking at him. 'All the facts have been assembled. We can't do any more, either through the files or on the ground.'

'Well, how do we proceed, then?' asked Gardon, still hoping for a lead.

'Intellectually,' hazarded Estalère, imprudently joining the discussion.

'You're the intellectual genius who's going to find the solution, are you, Estalère?' asked Mordent.

'Anyone who wants to be taken off this case can go,' said Adamsberg in the same tired voice. 'In fact, they're needed elsewhere. We need someone to look at the death in the rue de Miromesnil and the fight at Alésia. And there needs to be an inquiry into the outbreak of food poisoning at the nursing home in Auteuil. We're behind on all these cases.'

'I think Justin's got a point,' said Mordent, in a level tone. 'I think we're on the wrong track, *commissaire*. After all, if you take the long view, it started with a cat that some kids could have been tormenting.'

'A penile bone taken from a cat,' said Kernorkian defensively.

'I just don't believe in the third virgin,' said Mordent.

'I don't even believe in the first,' said Justin gloomily.

'Oh, come on,' said Lamarre. 'That Elisabeth woman was dead all right.'

'I meant the Virgin Mary.'

'I'll leave you to it,' said Adamsberg, putting on his jacket. 'But the third virgin's out there somewhere, drinking her little cup of coffee, and I'm not going to let her die.'

'What little cup of coffee?' asked Estalère, but Adamsberg had already left the building.

'Nothing,' said Mordent. 'It's just a way of saying she's carrying on with her life.'

XXXVIII

FRANCINE DIDN'T LIKE OLD THINGS. THEY WERE DIRTY AND RICKETY. SHE really felt happy only in the immaculate universe of the pharmacy where she did the cleaning and laundry and stacked the shelves. But she didn't like returning to the old family home, which was dirt-encrusted and tumbledown. When he was alive, Honoré Bidault wouldn't let anyone touch it, but now what difference could it make? For the last two years, Francine had been planning her move away, far from the old farmhouse, to a brand-new flat in town. And she would leave everything here – the crocks, the battered saucepans, the big old wardrobes – everything.

Half past eight in the evening was the best moment of the day. Francine had finished the dishes, closed the plastic rubbish bag firmly and taken it out to the doorstep. Dustbins attracted any number of insects – best not to keep them inside the house at night. She checked the kitchen, always with the fear that she might find a mouse or some disgusting insect, a caterpillar or spider – the house was crawling with nasty creatures like this that kept making their way in and out when you weren't looking, and there was no way of getting rid of them because of the fields outside, the attic up above and the cellar down below. The only bunker which she had succeeded in protecting from these intruders was her bedroom. She had spent months blocking the chimney, cementing up all the cracks in the walls and the gaps under the windows and round the doors, and had put her bed up on bricks. She preferred to leave the room unaired rather than let anything get in while she was asleep. But there was nothing she could do about the woodworms which were eating their way through the ancient beams overhead all night. Every evening, Francine watched the little holes over her bed, fearing to see the head of a worm poking out. She didn't know what the horrid creatures looked like – earthworms? centipedes? earwigs? But every morning she had to brush away in disgust the little piles of sawdust that had fallen on her bedspread.

Francine poured some hot coffee into a large cup, added a lump of sugar and two capfuls of rum. The best moment of the day. Then she carried the cup into the bedroom, with the little bottle of rum, ready to watch two films one after the other. Her collection of eight hundred and twelve tapes, all labelled and in order, was stacked in the other room, her father's bedroom, and sooner or later the damp would start to damage them. She had decided to leave the farm the day a wood-work expert had come to inspect the house, five months after her father's death. In the cross-beams he had detected seven holes made by death-watch beetles. Seven. Huge holes you could put your little finger into. 'If you listen hard, you can hear them munching away,' the man had said with a laugh.

It ought to be treated, the expert had said. But as soon as she had seen the size of the beetle holes, Francine had made up her mind. She would move out. She sometimes wondered, with horror, what a death-watch beetle looked like. Like a big worm, or a beetle with a drill in its head?

* * *

At one in the morning, Francine looked up at the woodworm holes and checked, thanks to the marks she had made, that they had not moved too much further across the beam. She put out the light, hoping not to hear the snuffling of the hedgehog outside. It was a horrid sound, almost like a human being snorting away in the night. She lay on her stomach, pulling the blankets over her head, just leaving a little space to breathe through. 'Francine, you're thirty-five years old and you still act like a child,' the priest had said. Well, so what? In another two months, she wouldn't have to see this house, or the priest in her village of Otton, ever again. She wouldn't spend another summer here. It was even worse in summer, with the big moths that came in – goodness knew how – banging their huge floppy bodies against the blinds and lampshades. And then there were bluebottles, hornets, horseflies, field mice and harvest-mites. People said that harvest mite larvae dug little holes in your skin and laid eggs in them. Yuk.

In order to get to sleep, Francine went through the countdown to her removal day, the first of June. She had been told over and over that she was getting a bad deal, exchanging this enormous eighteenth-century farmhouse for a two-room balcony flat in Evreux. But as far as she was concerned, it was the best deal she'd made in her life. In two months' time she'd be safe with her eight hundred and twelve films in a clean white apartment, just along the street from the pharmacy. She'd be sitting on a nice new blue cushion on a floor covered with shiny lino, in front of her TV set, with her coffee and her rum, and without the least little woodworm to bother her. Only two months to go. She'd sleep in a high bunk bed, away from the wall, with a varnished ladder to climb into it. There would be pastel-coloured sheets, which would stay clean without flies coming and leaving spots on them. Acting like a child or not, she'd be happy at last. Francine snuggled under the bedclothes and put her fingers in her ears. She didn't want to hear the hedgehog.

XXXIX

As soon as he had closed his front door behind him, Adamsberg made for the shower. He shampooed his hair, rubbing as hard as he could, then leaned against the tiled wall and let the warm water run over his closed eyes and dangling arms. Stay in the river like that, his mother used to say, and you'll come out white as snow.

An image of Ariane flashed across his mind, refreshingly. Good idea, he said to himself, turning off the taps. He could invite her out to dinner, and then see if anything happened, yes or no. He dried himself quickly, put his clothes back on over his still-damp skin, and went past the tracking console which was at the end of his bed. Tomorrow he would ask Froissy to come and disconnect this infernal machine and carry off in its wires the image of the damned Béarnais with his crooked smile. He picked up the pile of recordings of Veyrenc, and broke the disks one by one, throwing the shiny fragments round the room. Then he put them all in a bag which he carefully sealed. Next, he ate some sardines, tomatoes and cheese. Feeling both purified and well fed, he decided to call Camille as an indication of his goodwill, and enquire about Tom's cold.

The line was engaged. He sat on the edge of the bed, chewing the rest of his bread, and tried again ten minutes later. Still engaged. Chatting to Veyrenc, no doubt. The transmitter with its regularly flashing red light offered a last temptation. He switched it on with a brusque gesture.

Nothing, except the sound of the television and a vacuum cleaner. Adamsberg turned up the sound. Veyrenc was listening to a discussion about jealousy, by some irony of fate, while vacuuming his room. To be listening to this programme in his house through Veyrenc's set, and indirectly in his company, seemed somewhat pernicious. A psychiatrist was explaining the causes and effects of compulsive possessiveness and Adamsberg, stretching out drowsily on his bed, was relieved to find that in spite of his recent attack of jealousy he displayed none of the symptoms described.

A shout awoke him suddenly. He jumped up to turn off the television in his room, which was now blaring out.

'Don't move, motherfucker!'

Adamsberg took three paces into the room, having already realised his mistake. It wasn't his own television but the transmitter which was sending him a gangster film directly from Veyrenc's flat. Sleepily, he reached out to turn it off, but halted when he heard Veyrenc reply to the previous speaker. And Veyrenc's voice was too distinctive to be that of a television actor. Adamsberg looked at his watches. Two in the morning. Veyrenc had a nocturnal visitor.

'You gotta gun?'
'My service revolver.'
'Where?'
'On the chair.'
'We're taking that, right?'
'Is that what you want? Weapons?'
'What do you think?'
'I don't think anything.'

Adamsberg hurriedly rang the squad.

'Maurel, who's there with you?'

'Mordent.'

'Get over to Veyrenc's flat this instant – he's had a break-in, there are two of them, they're armed. Quick as you can, Maurel, they're threatening him.'

He rang off and called Danglard, while trying to do up his shoelaces with the other hand.

'Well, think a bit, then, mate.'

'Can't remember, eh?'

'Sorry, am I supposed to know you?'

'Well, we'll soon get your memory back for you. Put your clothes on, it'll look better.'

'What for?'

'We're going for a little ride. You're going to drive, and we'll tell you where to go.'

'Danglard? Two guys are threatening Veyrenc in his flat. Get over to the squad and take over the phone tap. Don't leave it on any account. I'm on my way.'

'What phone tap?'

'Bloody hell, the one on Veyrenc!'

'I don't have his mobile number – how can I put a tap on him?'

'I'm not asking you to do it but to take it over. The gear's in Froissy's cupboard, the one on the left. Get a move on, for Christ's sake, and call Retancourt.'

'Froissy's cupboard's locked, commissaire.'

'Get the spare key from my drawer, for God's sake,' cried Adamsberg, as he ran downstairs.

'Right,' said Danglard.

There was a phone tap, there was a hold-up, and as he hurriedly pulled on his shirt Danglard trembled, as he understood why. Twenty minutes later, he was switching on the receiver, kneeling in front of

Froissy's cupboard. He heard running footsteps as Adamsberg arrived behind him.

'Where are they now?' the *commissaire* asked. 'Have they left the house?'

'No, not yet. Veyrenc's deliberately taking his time getting dressed and finding his car keys.'

'They're taking his car?'

'Yes. He's found the keys now, the men were getting –'

'Shut up, Danglard.'

The two men knelt down and leaned to listen to the transmitter.

'No, sonny, just leave your mobile here. Think we're stupid?'

'They've ditched the mobile,' said Danglard. 'We'll lose their signal now.'

'Switch on that other mike.'

'What other mike?'

'The one for the car, dammit! And switch on the screen – we'll be able to follow them with the GPS.'

'Nothing showing. They must be between the flat and the car.'

'Mordent?' Adamsberg was calling. 'They're down in the street outside his house.'

'We're only just getting to the corner of the street, sir.'

'Shit.'

'There was an accident at Bastille and a big tailback. We put on the siren but it was chaos.'

'Mordent, they're going to take him in his car. You're going to follow them via the GPS.'

'But I don't have his wavelength.'

'No, but I do. I'll guide you. Keep the line open. Which car are you in?'

'The BEN 99.'

'I'll send you the sound through your radio.'

'What sound?'

'Their conversation inside the car.'

'Right.'

'There they are,' whispered Danglard, 'They're moving off now, east towards the rue de Belleville.'

'I can hear them,' said Mordent.

'And not a peep out of you, you little shit. Put your seat belt on, and keep both hands on the wheel. Go to the ring road. We're going out to the suburbs – you'll like that, won't you?'

'Not a peep out of you, you little shit.' Adamsberg recognised this sentence. From a long time ago, in a high meadow. He clenched his teeth and gripped Danglard's shoulder.

'Sweet Jesus, *capitaine*, they're going to kill him.'

'Who is?'

'Them. The Caldhez gang.'

'Step on it, Veyrenc, faster'n that! It's a cop car isn't it, motherfucker? You can go fast as you like! Put the lights and siren on so they get out of our fucking way.'

'How do you know who I am?'

'Don't try to be smart, motherfucker, we're not going to fuck about all night.'

'Motherfucker, fucking, that's all they can say,' groaned Danglard, sweating profusely.

'Shut up, Danglard. Mordent, they're on the ring road, heading north. They've got the lights flashing, you should be able to spot them.'

'I can hear the siren, yeah.'

'*. . . Fernand and Big Georges. Remember now? Or did you forget you bumped them off?*'

'*I'm just remembering.*'

'*Took your time, didn't you? Need us to remind you who we are now?*'

'*No. You've got to be the other little bastards from Caldhez. Roland and Pierrot. But anyway, I didn't kill those other pieces of shit. Your Fernand and Big Georges.*'

'*You won't get out of it like that, Veyrenc. We told you we weren't going to fuck about. Straight on, we're going to Saint-Denis. You bumped them off, and Roland and me, we're not going to twiddle our fucking thumbs waiting for you to come after us.*'

'*I told you, I did not kill them.*'

'*Shut your face. We've got ways of knowing, don't try and tell me different. Turn right here and shut the fuck up.*'

'Mordent, they're going past the cathedral in Saint-Denis.'

'We're just reaching it now.'

'Keep north, Mordent, north.'

Adamsberg, still on his knees in front of the receiver, was pressing his fist against his lips, pushing at his teeth.

'We'll get them,' said Danglard mechanically.

'They're fast workers, *capitaine*. They can kill without even noticing it. Shit, now due west, Mordent. They're going towards those big building sites.'

'OK, *commissaire*, I can see their lights. They're about two hundred and fifty metres ahead.'

'Get ready – they're probably going to drag him on to some building site. Once they're out of the car I won't be able to hear them.'

Adamsberg pressed his fist against his mouth again.

'Danglard, where's Retancourt?'

'Don't know, she wasn't at home.'

'I'm going to Saint-Denis. Keep track of the GPS and switch it to my car.'

Adamsberg ran out of the building, while Danglard tried to stretch his aching knees. Without taking his eyes off the screen, he limped to a chair and pulled it over towards the little cupboard. A pulse was beating in his temples, giving him a piercing headache. He was going to be responsible for Veyrenc's death, just as surely as if he had pulled the trigger. It was he who had taken the decision, on his own initiative, to warn Roland and Pierrot to be on guard, telling them that their two friends had been killed. He hadn't mentioned Veyrenc's name, but even people of their limited intelligence wouldn't take long to put two and two together. Not for a moment had Danglard imagined that they would take the risk of going for Veyrenc. The real idiot was him, Danglard. And he was the real bastard, too. Contemptible jealousy at being ousted had driven him to a lethal decision, taken without foreseeing the consequences. Danglard jumped as he saw the luminous dot on the screen come to a stop.

'Mordent, they've stopped. Rue des Ecrouelles, about halfway along. They're still in the car. Don't show yourself.'

'We're forty metres behind. We'll do the rest on foot.'

'It's not going to hurt you one little bit. Pierrot, wipe the prints off the car. Nobody'll know what the fuck you were doing out at Saint-Denis, nobody'll know why you died on a building site. And that'll be the last we hear of you, Veyrenc, and your fucking hair. And if you make a sound, it's quite simple – you're dead sooner.'

Adamsberg was driving at top speed, sirens screaming, along the almost empty ring road. Oh God, please let him . . . For pity's sake. He didn't believe in God. OK, the third virgin, then, the one he did believe in. Please get Veyrenc out of this alive. Please, please. It must have been Danglard, Christ Almighty, there couldn't be any other explanation.

Danglard, who had thought he had to go and warn the other two in the Caldhez gang, to protect them. Without telling him. Without knowing what they were capable of. He, Adamsberg, would have been able to tell him that Roland and Pierrot were not the sort to sit and wait for someone to threaten them. They were bound to react immediately and blindly.

'Mordent?'

'They're into the site. We're going in. Bit of a struggle. Veyrenc's elbowed one of them in the belly, he's down. No, he's up, again, still got the gun. The other's grabbed Veyrenc.'

'Shoot, Mordent.'

'Too far away. Fire in the air?'

'No – if they hear that they'll shoot too. Get closer. Roland likes talking, he likes showing off, it'll slow them down a bit. At twelve metres, shine a torch and fire.'

Adamsberg came off the ring road. If only he hadn't told this damned story to Danglard. But he had done the same as everyone else. He had revealed his secret to one person. One too many.

'What I'd really like, I'd like to get you back on the High Meadow. But I'm not that fucking stupid, Veyrenc, I'm not going to help the cops to work it out. And what about your boss, eh? Did you ask him what he was doing there? Wouldn't you like to know, eh? You make me laugh, Veyrenc, you've always made me laugh.'

'Thirteen metres,' whispered Mordent.

'Go for their legs.'

Adamsberg heard three shots over his car radio. He hurtled into Saint-Denis at a hundred and thirty kilometres an hour.

Roland had collapsed, hit in the back of the knee, and Pierrot had wheeled round. The gamekeeper was facing them, brandishing his gun. Roland let off a clumsy shot, hitting Veyrenc in the thigh. Maurel aimed at the gamekeeper and hit his shoulder.

'The two men are down and held, sir. One hit in the arm, the other in the knee, Veyrenc's taken a hit in the leg. Situation under control.'

'Danglard, send two ambulances.'

'They're already on their way,' said Danglard in a hollow voice. 'Bichat Hospital.'

Five minutes later, Adamsberg raced on to the muddy building site. Mordent and Maurel had dragged the three wounded men on to dry ground, and laid them on sheets of corrugated iron.

'That's a nasty wound,' said Adamsberg, leaning over Veyrenc. 'Bleeding like hell. Give me your shirt, Mordent, I'll try and tourniquet it. Maurel, you take Roland, he's the bigger one, immobilise his knee.'

Adamsberg tore Veyrenc's trouser leg and tied the shirt tightly round his thigh above the wound.

'That'll probably wake him up at least,' said Maurel.

'Yeah, he always faints, but he'll come out of it, he's like that. Veyrenc, can you hear me? Grip my hand if you can.'

Adamsberg repeated it three times, before at last feeling Veyrenc's fingers tighten.

'OK, Veyrenc, now open your eyes,' Adamsberg said, tapping his cheeks. 'Come on, open your eyes. Tell me if you can hear me.'

'Yeah.'

'Say something.'

Veyrenc opened his eyes wide. His gaze fell on Maurel, then on Adamsberg, uncomprehendingly, as if he was expecting his father to take him to hospital in Pau.

'They came for me,' he said, 'the Caldhez gang.'

'Yes, Roland and Pierrot.'

'They came over the rocks by the chapel in Camalès, they came to the High Meadow.'

'We're in Saint-Denis,' Maurel broke in anxiously. 'We're in the rue des Ecrouelles.'

'Don't worry, Maurel,' said Adamsberg. 'It's a childhood memory.

Come on, Veyrenc,' he went on, shaking him. 'High Meadow, is it? Remember now?'

'Yes.'

'Four boys. What about the fifth, where is he?'

'Up by the tree, he's their leader.'

'Yeah, right,' said Pierrot, with a cackle. 'Their leader. Ha!'

Adamsberg left Veyrenc and approached the two men, who were lying down handcuffed a few feet away.

'Well, well, look who's here,' said Roland.

'Glad to see me, are you?'

'You bet. Always in the fucking way.'

'Tell him the truth about the High Meadow. Tell Veyrenc what I was doing under the tree.'

'He knows, doesn't he?' Roland said tauntingly. 'Wouldn't be here otherwise, would he?'

'You've always been a little shit, Roland. And that's God's truth.'

Adamsberg saw the blue lights of the ambulances approach, lighting up the fence of the site. The paramedics loaded the men on to stretchers.

'Mordent, I'm going with Veyrenc. Can you go with the others? They've got to be put under police guard.'

'*Commissaire*, I'm minus my shirt.'

'Take Maurel's. Maurel, you can take my car back to headquarters.'

Before the ambulances had left, Adamsberg had time to call Hélène Froissy.

'Froissy, I'm sorry as hell to get you out of bed. But can you go and strip out all the bugging equipment, first from the office, then from my house. Then go out to Saint-Denis, rue des Ecrouelles. You'll find Veyrenc's car there – clean it all out.'

'Can't it wait a few hours?'

'Froissy, I wouldn't be calling you at three in the morning if it could wait a single minute. Lose the lot.'

XL

THE SURGEON WALKED INTO THE WAITING ROOM AND LOOKED AROUND TO see which one was the *commissaire de police* waiting for news of the three men with bullet wounds.

'Where is he?'

'Over there,' said the anaesthetist, pointing to a small dark man who was fast asleep, stretched out across two chairs, with his head resting on his jacket for a pillow.

'If you say so,' said the surgeon, and shook Adamsberg by the shoulder.

The *commissaire* sat up, felt his aching back, rubbed his face, and ran his hands through his hair. Ready for the day, thought the surgeon, but then he hadn't had time to shave either.

'They're OK, all three of them. The knee injury will need physiotherapy, but the kneecap wasn't touched. The shoulder wound's almost nothing, he can go home in a couple of days. The one with the thigh injury's lucky, it was pretty close to an artery. He's feverish, and he's talking in verse.'

'What about the bullets?' asked Adamsberg, shaking out his jacket. 'I hope they haven't been mixed up?'

'No, each one in a box, labelled with the bed number. What happened?'

'Hold-up at a cash machine.'

'Oh,' said the surgeon, disappointed. 'Money's the root of all evil, I suppose.'

'Where's the knee injury?'

'In Room 435 with the shoulder.'

'And the thigh?'

'Room 441. What happened to him?'

'The one with the knee injury shot him.'

'No, I meant his hair.'

'Oh, that's natural. Well, a sort of natural accident.'

'I'd call that an intradermic keratin variation. Very rare – exceptional, really. Do you want some coffee? A bit of breakfast? You look rather pale.'

'I'll find a machine,' said Adamsberg, standing up.

'The coffee in the machine's horse piss. Come with me, I'll fix you up with something.'

As doctors tend to be obeyed, Adamsberg went off docilely behind the man in the white coat. Have something to eat. Have something to drink. You'll feel better soon. Stumbling a little, Adamsberg had a quick thought for the third virgin. It was midday, nearly time for lunch. No need to feel scared now, things would be all right.

The *commissaire* walked into Veyrenc's hospital room at lunchtime. The patient was gloomily considering a bowl of soup and a pot of yogurt on a tray in front of him.

'Got to eat,' said Adamsberg, sitting down by the bed. 'No choice.'

Veyrenc nodded and picked up a spoon.

'When your childhood memories come to the surface, Veyrenc, it gets risky. For everyone. You had a narrow escape.'

Veyrenc lifted the spoon, then put it down again, staring at his bowl of soup.

> *My soul is divided by a cruel stroke of fate.*
> *My honour persuades me to bless the man who rode*

To save me from the blows of unspeakable hate.
Yet my heart still rebels and cannot shed its load
Of resentment at him, from whom this bounty flowed.'

'Yes, that is indeed the problem. But I'm not asking for anything from you, Veyrenc. And I'm no better placed than you are. I've saved the life of a man who may ruin my own.'

'What do you mean?'

'Because you've taken from me what I hold most dear.'

Veyrenc raised himself on one elbow, with a grimace of pain that pulled his crooked lip upwards.

'Your reputation? I haven't done anything to harm that yet.'

'What about my woman? Seventh floor, door facing the stairs.'

Veyrenc fell back against the pillows, open-mouthed.

'I wasn't to know,' he said in a low voice.

'No. Nobody knows everything, perhaps you should try to remember that.'

'It's like in the story,' said Veyrenc after a silence.

'What story?'

'The king, who sent one of his generals into battle and certain death, because he loved his wife.'

'I don't understand,' said Adamsberg, sincerely. 'I'm tired. Who loved who?'

'Once upon a time, there was this king,' said Veyrenc.

'Yes.'

'And he was in love with the wife of this other guy.'

'Right.'

'So the king sent the other guy off to war.'

'Right.'

'And the guy got killed.'

'I see.'

'So the king took the woman.'

'Well, that's not the same as me.'

The *lieutenant* stared at his hands, concentrating and far away. 'But you could have.

> *In the dark of the night, my lord, there came a time*
> *To rid your sight of one whose presence was a crime.*
> *Death lay in wait at last for him who wished you ill,*
> *And who in love and war, is now your rival still.'*

'Yeah, right,' said Adamsberg.

> *'What pity, what concern, made you reign your wrath in,*
> *And led you to rescue the man behind the sin?'*

Adamsberg shrugged his shoulders, which were aching with fatigue.

'You were *tailing* me?' asked Veyrenc. 'Because of her?'

'Yes.'

'You recognised the guys in the street?'

'When they pushed you into the car,' Adamsberg lied, choosing to keep quiet about the microphones.

'I see.'

'We're going to have to understand each other, *lieutenant*.'

Adamsberg got up and closed the door.

'We're going to let Roland and Pierrot get away. Without a policeman on duty outside their room, they'll take the first opportunity to make a run for it.'

'A present?' asked Veyrenc, with a fixed smile.

'Not for them, for us, *lieutenant*. If we press charges, there'll be accusations and a trial, yes? You agree?'

'I should certainly hope there *will* be a trial. And sentences.'

'They'll defend themselves, Veyrenc. Their lawyers will argue for self-defence.'

'How could they make that out? They held me up at gunpoint in my flat.'

'By claiming that it was you who killed Fernand and Big Georges and that you were planning to kill them too.'

'But I didn't kill those others,' said Veyrenc sharply.

'And I didn't attack you on the High Meadow,' said Adamsberg, equally sharply.

'I don't believe you.'

'Nobody's prepared to believe anyone else. And none of us can prove any of the accusations we make – it's one man's word against another's. The jury will have no more reason to believe you than them. Roland and Pierrot could get away with it, believe me, and that could leave you in even bigger trouble.'

'No,' said Veyrenc. 'They wouldn't be able to prove it, so there would be no verdict against me.'

'No, but you'd have a new reputation, *lieutenant*, and there'd be rumours. Did he kill those two other guys or not? The suspicion will stick to you like a tick. And you'll still be scratching away at it in sixty years' time, even if you're acquitted.'

'I see,' said Veyrenc, after a pause. 'But why should I trust you? What's in this for you? You want to fix their escape, so they can start again another time?'

'You're still harking back to that, Veyrenc? Do you really think it was me that sent Roland and Pierrot after you last night? And that that's why I was downstairs outside your house?'

'Well, I have to consider the possibility.'

'Why would I have saved you, then?'

'In order to cover yourself, for a second attack that would succeed.'

A nurse breezed in and put two tablets in a cup on the night table.

'Painkillers,' she said. 'To be taken with meals, there's a good boy.'

'Come on, swallow them down,' said Adamsberg, handing them over. 'Take them with a spoonful of soup.'

Veyrenc obeyed, and Adamsberg put the cup back on the tray.

'Yes, that does make sense,' said the *commissaire*, returning to sit down and stretching his legs. 'But it's not true. Sometimes an untruth can be very convincing, and still not be true.'

'Well, what *is* the truth?'

'I've got a personal reason for wanting them to escape. I didn't tail you, *lieutenant*, I put a bug on you. I bugged your mobile phone and your car.'

'You went that far?'

'Yes. And I should prefer that not to get known. If there's a prosecution, it will all come out – phone-tapping, the lot.'

'Why, who's going to tell them?'

'The officer who installed it on my orders. Hélène Froissy. She trusted me and did what I asked. She thought she was acting in your own best interests. She's an honest woman and she'll tell the truth if the magistrate asks her.'

'I see,' said Veyrenc carefully. 'So it's in both our interests.'

'Yes.'

'But it's not so easy, escaping from here,' objected Veyrenc. 'They can't get out of the hospital without attacking the duty policemen. That wouldn't look good. And you'd be suspected, or at best accused of negligence.'

'Yes, they will attack a couple of policemen. I've got a couple of youngsters who'll swear blind that the criminals knocked them to the ground.'

'Estalère?'

'Yes, and Lamarre.'

'But why would Roland and Pierrot try to escape? They probably think it's impossible to get out of the hospital. There could be more police at the exits.'

'They'll escape because I'll tell them to.'

'And they'll obey you.'

'Of course.'

'And who says they won't try it on again?'

'I do.'

'So you're still giving them orders, *commissaire*?'

Adamsberg stood up and went round the bed. He looked at the temperature chart: 38.8 degrees.

'We'll talk about it again, Veyrenc, when we can each listen to what the other one's saying. When your fever has gone down.'

XLI

THREE DOORS AWAY FROM VEYRENC, IN ROOM 435, ROLAND AND PIERROT were bargaining aggressively with the *commissaire*. Veyrenc had dragged himself painfully, step by step, to the doorway and, sweating with pain, strained his ears to pick up snatches of their conversation.

'You're bluffing,' said Roland.

'You ought to be thanking me for offering you a way out. Otherwise you're looking at ten years minimum for you, and three for Pierrot. Shooting at a policeman's a serious offence – they won't show you any mercy.'

'Carrot Top was out to kill *us*,' said Pierrot. 'It was legitimate self-defence.'

'Anticipated self-defence,' said Adamsberg. 'And where's your proof, Pierrot?'

'Don't listen to him, Pierrot,' said Roland. 'Carrot Top's going to jail for murdering the others, plus intent to murder us, and we'll get off with compensation, plenty of cash.'

'No, that's not what's going to happen,' said Adamsberg. 'You're going to make yourselves scarce, and you're going to keep your mouths shut.'

'Why?' asked Pierrot, distrustfully. 'What's the catch, if you get us out of here? I smell a bloody great rat.'

'Course you do. But the rat's my business. You disappear, a long way off, and we hear no more from you, that's all I'm asking.'

'What's the catch?' Pierrot repeated.

'I'll tell you what the catch is. If you don't do as I say, I'll make public the name of the guy who paid you off all those years ago. And I don't think he'll much appreciate the publicity, thirty-four years on.'

'What do you mean, paid us off?' asked Pierrot, in genuine surprise.

'Ask Roland,' said Adamsberg.

'Don't listen to him,' said Roland. 'He's a fucking tosser, always was.'

'The deputy mayor in those days, remember him? In charge of planning and also a wine-grower. You know who I mean, Pierrot. And now he's boss of a big building firm, isn't he? He paid the gang a big advance to beat up the Veyrenc kid. With the rest to come after you got out of the reformatory. That's why Roland's got a chain of hardware stores, and that's why Fernand was swanning about in the South of France.'

'What money? I didn't get any!' yelled Pierrot.

'No, neither did Big Georges. Roland and Fernand pocketed the lot.'

'You bastard,' hissed Pierrot.

'Shut up, motherfucker,' growled Roland.

'Say it isn't true, then,' Pierrot demanded.

'He can't,' said Adamsberg. 'Because it is true. The deputy mayor was after all the vines of the Veyrenc de Bilhc appellation. He wanted to force a sale and threatened Veyrenc's father if he wouldn't play ball. But Veyrenc Senior hung on. So our man organised a gang attack on the little kid, knowing that the father would give in out of fear.'

'I don't have to listen to this bullshit,' said Roland. 'You can't know all that stuff.'

'I wouldn't normally, no. Because you'd sworn secrecy to that bastard in the town hall. Only everyone always tells *one* person their secret, Roland, so you told your brother. Who told his girlfriend. Who told her cousin. Who told her best friend. Who told her boyfriend. Who happened to be my brother.'

'Roland, you fucking bastard,' said Pierrot from his bed.

'I couldn't put it better myself,' said Adamsberg. 'So now do you understand that if you don't do as I say, and if you touch a hair of Veyrenc's head, brown or ginger, I'll publicise the name of your contact in the town hall. Who will have ways of taking care of you. So what's your decision?'

'We'll go,' muttered Roland.

'Good. And you'd better not damage the looks of the two cops on duty, because they know the score. You can make it look convincing, but don't hurt them.'

In the corridor, Veyrenc shrank back inside his door. He managed to reach his bed just before Adamsberg came out of Room 435. Veyrenc lay back on the bed, exhausted. He had never known exactly why his father had agreed to sell the vineyard in the end.

XLII

'And now the wise old chamois did something monumentally stupid, out of jealousy, although he'd read all the books there were. He went and found two big wolves, who were unfortunately very mean and nasty. "Watch out for the ginger ibex," he said, "he's going to attack you with his horns." No sooner said than done. The two wolves attacked the ginger ibex. They were very hungry and would have gobbled him all up, and he would never have been heard of again. And then the brown ibex would have been able to get on with his life in peace, without his rival, and had fun with the marmots and squirrels. And the girl ibex. But no, Tom, that's not how it worked out, because life is more complicated and so is the inside of an ibex's head. So the brown one went charging after the two wolves, and smashed their jaws. And they ran away without asking for more. The ginger one had been bitten on his leg, so the brown one had to look after him. He couldn't let him die, now could he, Tom? And all this time, the girl ibex was hiding. She didn't want to have to choose between the brown ibex and the ginger one, that upset her. So the two ibex sat down on their chairs and smoked their pipes and had a chat. But all the same, they would have attacked each other with their horns over the slightest thing. Because one thought he was right and the other one was wrong. And the other one thought *he* was telling the truth and the other one was lying.'

The baby put a finger on his father's eye.

'Yes, Tom, it is difficult. It's a bit like the *opus spicatum*, with fish-bones going one way and another. And then Third Virgin, who lived all by herself in a nice little rabbit hole with her gerbils, appeared on the scene. She lived on dandelions and plantains, and she was very scared, because a tree had nearly fallen on her. Third Virgin was very tiny, she drank a lot of coffee, and didn't know how to protect herself against the evil spirits of the forest. So Third Virgin called for help. But some of the other ibex got cross, they said Third Virgin didn't exist, and they weren't going to get involved. So the brown ibex said, "OK, let's just drop it." Look, Tom, I'm going to do it again.'

Adamsberg rang Danglard's number.

'*Capitaine*, I'm still educating my little one. Once upon a time, there was a king.'

'Yes.'

'Who was in love with the wife of one of his generals.'

'Yes.'

'So he sent his rival off into battle, knowing that he would be killed.'

'Correct.'

'Danglard, what was the king called?'

'David,' said Danglard, in a hollow voice, 'and the general he sacrificed was called Uriah. David married his widow, who became Queen Bathsheba, mother of the future King Solomon.'

'See, Tom, how simple it is,' said Adamsberg to his son, who was snuggled up on his stomach.

'Are you saying that for my benefit?' asked Danglard.

Adamsberg sensed the lifelessness in his deputy's voice.

'If you think it was me that got Veyrenc set up to be killed,' Danglard went on, 'you're quite right. I could say I didn't mean it to happen, and I could swear that I had no idea that's how it would turn out. But so what? Who would ever know whether I didn't really want it to happen, deep down?'

'*Capitaine*, don't you think we worry enough about what we really *do* think, without having to worry about what we might have thought if we did think it?'

'Maybe,' said Danglard, in a barely audible voice.

'Listen, Danglard, he's not dead, nobody's dead. Except perhaps you, drinking yourself to death in your sitting-room.'

'I'm in the kitchen.'

'Danglard?'

No answer.

'Danglard, get a bottle of wine and come over here. I'm on my own with Tom. Saint Clarisse has popped out for a walk. With the tanner, I dare say.'

The *commissaire* hung up so that Danglard couldn't refuse. 'Tom,' he said, 'remember the very wise chamois, who had read all those books? And had done something very stupid? Well, the inside of his head was so complicated that he got lost inside it himself in the evenings. And sometimes during the day as well. And not all his wisdom and knowledge helped him to find a way out. So then the ibex had to throw him a rope and pull hard to get him out of it.'

Adamsberg suddenly looked up at the ceiling. From the attic came a slight sound, as of a robe swishing over the ground. So Saint Clarisse had not popped out to see the tanner after all.

'It's nothing, Tom. A bird or the wind. Or a rag blowing over the floor.'

In order to sort out the inside of Danglard's head, Adamsberg made a good fire in the grate. It was the first time he had used the fireplace, and the flames rose up high and clear without smoking out the room. This was how he intended to burn the Unsolved Question about King David, which was clogging up his deputy's head, spreading doubts into all its corners. As soon as he came in, Danglard sat down by the fire alongside Adamsberg, who added log after log to the fire to reduce his anguish to ashes. At the same time, without telling Danglard, Adamsberg was burning the last traces of his resentment of Veyrenc.

Seeing the two ruffians from Caldhez again, hearing Roland's vicious voice, had brought the past back to mind, and the cruel attack in the High Meadow reappeared to him in full colour. The scene played itself out from start to finish before his eyes, in screaming detail. The little kid on the ground, held down by Fernand, while Roland approached with a piece of broken glass. 'Not a peep out of you, you little shit.' The panic of little eight-year-old Veyrenc, his head bleeding, his stomach slashed, in unspeakable pain. And himself, young Adamsberg, standing motionless under the tree. He would give a lot not to have lived through that scene, so that this unfinished memory would stop pricking him thirty-four years later. So that the flames would burn away Veyrenc's persistent trauma. And, he caught himself thinking, well, if being in Camille's arms could help Veyrenc get rid of it, so be it. On condition that the damned Béarnais didn't take his territory. Adamsberg threw another log on the flames and smiled vaguely. The territory he shared with Camille was out of Veyrenc's reach. He needn't worry.

By midnight, Danglard, at last feeling calmer about King David, and soothed by the serenity emanating from Adamsberg, was finishing the last of the bottle he had brought with him.

'Burns well, your fire,' he commented.

'Yes, that was one of the reasons I wanted this house. Remember old Clémentine's fireplace? I spent night after night in front of it. I would light the end of a twig and make circles in the dark, like this.'

Adamsberg put out the overhead light and plunged a long twig into the flames, then traced circles and figures-of-eight in the near-darkness.

'Pretty,' said Danglard.

'Yes, pretty, and mesmerising.'

Adamsberg gave the twig to his deputy and rested his feet on the brick surround, pushing his chair back.

'I'm going to have to drop the third virgin, Danglard. Nobody seems to believe in her, nobody wants to know. And I haven't the slightest idea how to find her. I'll have to abandon her to her fate and her cups of coffee.'

'I don't think so,' said Danglard, blowing gently on the end of the twig to rekindle it.

'No?'

'No, I don't believe you're going to let her drop. Nor am I. I think you'll go on looking. Whether the others agree or not.'

'But do you think she even exists? Do you think she's in danger?'

Danglard drew a few figures-of-eight.

'The hypothesis based on the *De Reliquis* is very fragile,' he replied. 'It's like a thread of gossamer, but the thread does exist. And it links together all these odd elements in the story. It even links up to the business of shoe polish on the soles of the shoes and dissociation.'

'How?' asked Adamsberg, taking back the twig.

'In medieval incantatory ceremonies, people drew a circle on the ground. In the middle of it would be the woman who would dance and call up the devil. The circle was a way of separating off one piece of ground from the rest of the earth. Our killer is working on a piece of ground that belongs just to her, spinning her thread inside her own circle.'

'Retancourt hasn't gone along with me about this thread,' said Adamsberg, rather grumpily.

'I don't know where Retancourt is,' said Danglard, pulling a face. 'She didn't come into the office again today. And there's still no reply from her home.'

'Have you called her brothers?' asked Adamsberg with a frown.

'Called her brothers, called her parents, called a couple of her friends I had the numbers of. Nobody's seen her. She didn't let us know she wouldn't be in. And nobody in the squad has any idea what she's up to.'

'What was she working on?'

'She was supposed to be on the Miromesnil murder with Mordent and Gardon.'

'Have you listened to her answering machine?'

'Yes, but there are no particular messages about meeting anyone.'

'Are any of the squad cars missing?'

'No.'

Adamsberg threw down the twig and stood up. He paced around the room for a few moments with folded arms.

'*Capitaine*, raise the alarm.'

XLIII

NEWS OF THE DISAPPEARANCE OF *LIEUTENANT* VIOLETTE RETANCOURT FELL like a bombshell in the offices of the Serious Crime Squad, immediately repressing any rebellious mutterings. In the ominous panic which began to spread, everyone realised that the absence of the large blonde officer deprived the building of one of its central pillars. The dismay of the cat, who had gone to curl up between the photocopier and the wall, reflected fairly accurately the morale of the staff, with the difference that the officers, armed with her description, were engaged in non-stop searching, inquiring at all the hospitals and *gendarmeries* in the country.

Commandant Danglard, only just recovering from his own moral crisis over King David, and prey to his usual pessimism, had taken refuge quite openly in the basement where he was sitting on a chair near the boiler, knocking back white wine in full view of anyone who cared to look. Estalère, at the opposite extremity of the building, had gone up to the coffee-machine room and, rather like the Snowball, had curled up on *Lieutenant* Mercadet's foam cushions.

The shy young receptionist, Bettina, who had only recently started working at the switchboard, walked across the Council Chamber, which seemed to be plunged in mourning, and where the only sound was the clicking of telephones and a few repeated words – yes, no, thanks for calling back. In one corner, Mordent and Justin were talking in low voices. Bettina knocked quietly at Adamsberg's door. The *commissaire*, hunched on his high stool, was staring at the ground without moving. The young woman sighed. Adamsberg urgently needed to get some sleep.

'Monsieur le *commissaire*, she said, sitting down discreetly. 'When do we think *Lieutenant* Retancourt went missing?'

'Well, she didn't come in on Monday morning, Bettina, that's all we know. But she could have gone missing on Saturday, Sunday or even Friday evening. It could be three days ago, or five.'

'Just before the weekend, on Friday afternoon, she was smoking a cigarette out in the entry with the new *lieutenant*, the one with fancy hair, in two colours. She said she was going to leave the office early, because she had a visit to make.'

'A visit or an appointment?'

'Is there a difference?'

'Yes. Try to remember, Bettina.'

'Well, I think she used the word visit.'

'Anything else?'

'No. They went off towards the big room, so I didn't hear any more.'

'Thanks,' said Adamsberg, blinking his eyes.

'You ought to get some sleep, sir. My mother says that if you don't sleep, the mill starts grinding its own stone.'

'*She* wouldn't go to sleep. She'd look for me day and night, without eating or sleeping till she found me. And she would find me.'

Adamsberg slowly pulled on his jacket.

'If anyone asks, Bettina, I'm at the Bichat Hospital.'

'Ask one of them to drive you. That way you could nap for twenty minutes in the car. My mother says snatching forty winks here and there is the secret.'

'But all the officers are busy looking for her, Bettina. They've got better things to do.'

'I haven't,' said Bettina. 'I'll drive you over.'

Veyrenc was taking his first tentative steps in the corridor, leaning on a nurse's arm.

'We're improving,' said the nurse. 'We've got less of a temperature this morning.'

'Let's go back to his room,' said Adamsberg, taking Veyrenc's other arm.

'How's the leg?' he asked, once they had got Veyrenc on to the bed.

'Not bad. Better than you,' said Veyrenc, struck by Adamsberg's exhausted features. 'What's happened now?'

'She's vanished. Violette. For either three or five days. She's nowhere to be found, she hasn't given any sign of life. It can't have been intentional, because all her stuff's still there. She was just wearing her ordinary jacket and had her little backpack.'

'Dark blue?'

'Yes.

'Bettina told me that you were talking to her on Friday afternoon in the hall. And apparently Violette said something about a visit she had to make, that she was going to leave early.'

Veyrenc frowned.

'A visit? And she told me about it? But I don't know who her friends are.'

'She told you about this, and then you both walked into the Council Chamber. Try and remember, please, *lieutenant* – you may have been the last person to see her. You were smoking.'

'Ah,' said Veyrenc, lifting his hand. 'Yes, she had promised she'd call in on Dr Roman. She said she went in about once a week, to try and distract him. She kept him up to date with the investigations, showed him photos, sort of trying to bring him up to speed.'

'What photos?'

'Forensic photos, *commissaire*, the ones of corpses. That's what she was showing him.'

'OK, Veyrenc, I see.'

'You're disappointed.'

'Well, I'll go and see Roman. But he's completely vague, with his vapours as he calls them. If there had been anything to take notice of, he'd be the last to realise it.'

Adamsberg sat for a moment without moving, in the comfortable padded hospital chair. When the nurse came in later with his supper tray, Veyrenc put his finger to his lips. The *commissaire* had been asleep for about an hour.

'Shouldn't we wake him?' whispered the nurse.

'He couldn't have held out a minute longer. We'll let him sleep another hour or two.'

Veyrenc telephoned the squad while examining his tray.

'Who am I talking to?' he asked.

'Gardon,' said the *brigadier*. 'Is that you, Veyrenc?'

'Is Danglard there?'

'Well, he is, but he's practically out of commission. Retancourt's disappeared, *lieutenant*.'

'Yes, I know. Can you get me Dr Roman's phone number?'

'Yeah, coming up. One of us was going to come and see you tomorrow. Do you need anything?'

'Something to eat, *brigadier*.'

'You're in luck. It's Froissy who'll be coming.'

At least that's one bit of good news, thought Veyrenc, as he called the doctor. A very distant voice answered. Veyrenc had never met Roman, but he was obviously in some kind of fog of absent-mindedness.

'*Commissaire* Adamsberg will be round to see you at about nine o'clock, doctor. He asked me to warn you.'

292

'Er, yes, if you say so,' said Roman, who seemed supremely indifferent to the news.

Adamsberg opened his eyes a little after eight.

'Oh shit,' he said. 'Why didn't you wake me, Veyrenc?'

'Even Retancourt would have let you sleep. *Victory comes only to the man who has slept.*'

XLIV

DR ROMAN SHUFFLED OVER TO OPEN THE DOOR, THEN SHUFFLED BACK TO his armchair, as if he were on skis.

'Don't ask how I am, Adamsberg, it annoys me. Do you want a drink?'

'I wouldn't mind a coffee.'

'Can you get it yourself? I'm just not up to it.'

'Come and keep me company in the kitchen, then.'

Roman sighed and shuffled on his skis to a chair in the kitchen.

'Do you want a cup?' asked Adamsberg.

'Yes, put in as much as you like, nothing stops me sleeping, twenty hours out of twenty-four. A lot, eh? I don't even have time to get bored.'

'Like a lion. You know a lion sleeps twenty hours a day?'

'It has vapours too?'

'No, it's just made that way. Doesn't stop it being king of the animals.'

'But a deposed king. You've found a replacement for me, Adamsberg.'

'I didn't have any choice.'

'No,' said Roman, closing his eyes.

'Don't the medicines help?' asked the *commissaire*, looking at the pile of boxes on the table.

'They're stimulants. They wake me up for about a quarter of an hour, long enough to work out what day it is. What day is it?'

The doctor's voice was thick, dragging out the vowel sounds as if something was stopping him articulating clearly.

'This is Thursday. And last Friday night, six days ago, you were visited by Violette Retancourt. Do you remember?'

'I haven't lost my wits, you know – it's just that I don't have any energy. Or taste for anything.'

'But Retancourt brought you some stuff you like to see. Forensic pictures, photos of corpses.'

'That's right,' smiled Roman. 'She's very considerate.'

'She knows what keeps you happy,' said Adamsberg, pushing a bowl of coffee towards the doctor.

'You look all in, *mon vieux*,' commented the doctor. 'Exhausted physically and mentally.'

'You haven't lost your touch, have you? I'm in the middle of an investigation that's like a horror movie, and it's slipping away from me. I've got a Shade that won't leave me alone, a nun in my own house and a new *lieutenant* who's biding his time till he nails me. I've just spent all night rescuing him from a gang who were after him. And then, the next day, I find out that Retancourt has vanished into thin air.'

'Thin air? Has she got the vapours too?'

'She's disappeared, Roman.'

'Yes, I heard what you said.'

'Did she say anything to you last Friday? Anything that might give us a lead? Did she say she was worried about anything?'

'No. I don't see what could ever worry Retancourt, and the more I think about it, the more I think I ought to have got her to try and deal with my own vapours. No, *mon vieux*, we talked shop. At least we pretended to. After three-quarters of an hour, I tend to drop off.'

'Did she tell you about the district nurse? The angel of death?'

'Yes, she told me all about that, and the graves that had been opened. She comes quite often, you know. Heart of gold, that girl. She even left me some of the photos, to give me something to do if I could work up any interest.'

Roman extended a limp arm over the mass of papers on the kitchen table and pulled out a bundle which he slid over to Adamsberg. Some enlarged colour photographs showed the faces of La Paille and Diala, the details of their wounds, the traces of injections in their arms, and the photographs of the two corpses of Montrouge and Opportune. Adamsberg pulled a horrified face at the last two and put them at the botttom of the pile.

'Very good-quality prints, as you see. Retancourt has been spoiling me. You really have got a heap of shit here,' observed the doctor, tapping the pile of photographs.

'Yes, I realise that, Roman.'

'There's no one harder to catch than these methodical maniacs, until you've cottoned on to their obsession. And since their obsession is always completely crazy, you're always in the dark.'

'Is that what you said to Retancourt? You discouraged her?'

'I'd never dare try to discourage your *lieutenant.*'

The *commissaire* saw Roman's eyelids start to droop, and filled up his bowl of coffee again at once.

'Give me a couple of uppers as well. The red and yellow box.'

Adamsberg put two capsules in the hollow of Roman's hand, and the doctor swallowed them.

'OK,' said Roman, 'where were we?'

'What you said to Retancourt the last time you saw her.'

'Same as I said to you. Your murderer is completely insane and very dangerous.'

'Do you agree it's a woman?'

'Obviously. Ariane's the best. If that's what she says, you can be absolutely sure of it.'

'I know what the killer is after, Roman. She wants absolute power, divine potency, eternal life. Didn't Retancourt tell you that?'

'Yes, she read out to me the old recipe for the potion,' said Roman, tapping the photos. 'And yes, you're spot on with that, "the quick of virgins".'

'The quick of virgins,' Adamsberg murmured. 'She couldn't have told you much about that, because that's the one bit we didn't understand.'

'You didn't understand?' asked Roman, looking stunned, and seeming to come back to life as he talked shop. 'But it's staring you in the face. It's as obvious as your mountain.'

'Forget my mountain. What do you mean? Tell me what it is, this "quick".'

'What do you think, slowcoach? The quick and the dead. The quick is what remains alive even after death: it defies death and even old age. Hair, of course. When you're an adult and your body has stopped growing, the only thing that carries right on growing all the time is your hair.'

'Unless it falls out.'

'Well, women don't go bald, stupid. Hair, nails. Both the same thing anyway, both keratin. The quick of the virgins must be their hair. Because, in the grave, it's the only part of the body that doesn't decay. It's anti-death, an antidote to death if you like. It isn't rocket science. Are you following me, Adamsberg, or have you got the vapours as well?'

'I'm following you,' said Adamsberg, looking amazed. 'It's clever, Roman, and more than probable.'

'Probable? Don't you believe me? It's absolutely certain – it's in the photos, for pity's sake.'

Roman pulled over the pile of photos, then yawned and rubbed his eyes.

'Get some cold water from the tap on the dishcloth. Rub my head with it.'

'The dishcloth's filthy.'

'Never mind. Hurry up.'

Adamsberg obeyed and rubbed Roman's head hard with the cold

cloth, as one might rub down a horse. Roman emerged from the treatment looking red-faced.

'Better?'

'It'll do. Give me the rest of the coffee and pass me the photo.'

'Which one?'

'The first woman, Elisabeth Châtel. And fetch me my magnifying glass from my desk.'

Adamsberg placed the glass and the ghastly photo in front of the doctor.

'There,' said Roman, pointing to the right temple on Elisabeth's skull. 'Some locks of her hair have been cut off.'

'Are you sure?'

'Absolutely.'

'The quick of virgins,' said Adamsberg, looking at the photo. 'This crazy woman has killed them to get at their hair.'

'Which had resisted death. On the right of the skull, you'll note. Remember the text?'

'The quick of virgins, on the dexter hand, sorted by three in equal quantities.'

'Dexter, on the right. Because the left, sinister, is the dark side, in Latin. The right means life. The right hand leads to life. You follow?'

Adamsberg nodded silently.

'Ariane did think it might be hair,' he said.

'I think you're a bit sweet on Ariane.'

'Who told you that?'

'Your blonde *lieutenant*.'

'So why didn't Ariane notice if the hair had been cut?'

Roman laughed, rather cheerfully.

'Because she wasn't as good at spotting it as I am. Ariane's very good, but her father wasn't a barber. Mine was. I can spot when a lock of hair has been freshly cut. The ends are different – clean, not split. Can't you see that here?'

298

'No.'

'Well, your father wasn't a barber either.'

'No.'

'Ariane has another excuse. Elisabeth Châtel, from what I'd guess, didn't pay much attention to her looks. Am I right?'

'Yes. She didn't use make-up, didn't wear jewellery.'

'And she didn't go to the hairdresser. She cut her hair herself and made a bit of a mess of it. If her fringe was in her eyes, she picked up the scissors and cut it, just like that. So her hair is all different lengths, some long, some short, some medium. It would be pretty impossible for Ariane to spot which locks had been freshly cut in the middle of that mishmash.'

'We were working at night under arc lamps.'

'That would be another reason. And in the case of Pascaline, it's hard to see anything.'

'And you told Retancourt all this on Friday?'

'Yes, of course.'

'And what did she say?'

'Nothing. She looked thoughtful, like you. I don't think it makes that much difference to your inquiry, though.'

'Except that now we know why she opens graves. And why she needs to kill a third virgin.'

'You really think that?'

'Yes. By three, the number of women.'

'Possibly. You've identified the third?'

'No.'

'Well, look for a woman with a good head of hair. Both Elisabeth and Pascaline had plenty of hair. Get me to my bedroom, *mon vieux*, I can't take any more.'

'I'm really sorry, Roman,' said Adamsberg, standing up abruptly.

'Doesn't matter. But while you're looking through those old remedies, try and find one against the vapours for me.'

'I promise,' said Adamsberg as he helped Roman towards the bedroom. The doctor turned his head, intrigued by Adamsberg's tone.

'Are you serious?'

'Yes, I promise.'

XLV

RETANCOURT'S DISAPPEARANCE, PLUS THE NIGHT-TIME COFFEE HE HAD drunk with Roman, the tender lovemaking of Camille and Veyrenc, the quick of virgins, and Roland's thuggish face had all disturbed Adamsberg's sleep. Between two shuddering bouts of wakefulness, he had dreamed that one ibex – but which one, the brown or the ginger? – had gone crashing down the mountain. The *commissaire* woke feeling sick and aching. An informal conference, or rather a sort of funeral session, had spontaneously opened that morning at the Serious Crime Squad. The officers were all hunched over on their seats, cramped with anxiety.

'None of us has voiced it,' Adamsberg began, 'but we all know Retancourt hasn't wandered off, or been hospitalised, or lost her memory. She's fallen into the hands of our maniac. She left Dr Roman knowing something we didn't know. That the "quick of virgins" means their hair, and that the murderer opened the graves to cut it off their corpses, because it's the only part of the body that resists decomposition. On the dexter, in other words on the right side of the skull, which is positive compared with the left. And she hasn't been seen since. So we might deduce that, after leaving Roman, she understood something that took her straight to the killer. Or else something that sufficiently worried the angel of death that she decided Retancourt must disappear.'

Adamsberg had deliberately chosen the word 'disappear' as being more evasive and optimistic than 'die'. But he had no illusions about the nurse's intentions.

'With that stuff about the "quick of virgins", said Mordent, 'and nothing else, Retancourt must have understood something we still haven't worked out.'

'That's what I'm afraid of. Where did she go next, and what did she do to alert the killer?'

'Well, the only way is to try and work out what she understood,' said Mordent, rubbing his forehead.

There was a discouraged silence and several hopeful faces turned towards Adamsberg.

'I'm not Retancourt,' he said, with a shake of his head. 'I can't reason as she would, nor can any of you. Even under hypnosis, or catalepsy, or in a coma, nobody knows how to merge themselves with her in spirit.'

The word 'merge' sent Adamsberg's thoughts back to the Quebec expedition, when he had indeed had to merge his body with his *lieutenant*'s impressive bulk. The memory made him tremble with chagrin. Retancourt, his tree. He had lost his tree. Suddenly he raised his head and looked round at his motionless colleagues.

'Yes,' he said in a near-whisper, 'there is just one of us who might have merged in spirit with Retancourt, to the point of being able to find her.'

He stood up, still hesitating, but a kind of light dawned on his face.

'The cat,' he said. 'Where's the cat?'

'Behind the photocopier,' said Justin.

'Hurry up,' said Adamsberg in a frantic voice, going from chair to chair and shaking his officers as if he were waking soldiers in his exhausted army. 'We're all so stupid. I'm so stupid. The Snowball will lead us to Retancourt.'

'The Snowball?' said Kernorkian. 'But that cat's a waste of space.'

'The Snowball,' Adamsberg pleaded, 'is a waste of space who adores Retancourt. The Snowball wants nothing more than to find her. And the Snowball is an animal. With a nose, sensory organs, a brain as big as an apricot, stuffed with a hundred thousand smells.'

'A hundred thousand?' said Lamarre sceptically. 'Could the Snowball cope with a hundred thousand smells?'

'Yes, perfectly. And if he remembered only one, it would be Retancourt's.'

'Here's the cat,' announced Justin, and doubt returned to all minds as they saw the beast draped like a flaccid dishcloth over the *lieutenant*'s arm.

But Adamsberg, who was pacing up and down at a frantic speed in the hall, refused to give up his idea, and was issuing his battle orders.

'Froissy, put a transmitter round the cat's neck. You haven't taken the material back yet?'

'No, sir.'

'Good, go ahead. Powerful as you can make it, Froissy. Justin, organise two cars and two motorbikes, on the right frequency. Mordent, call the *préfecture* and get them to send a helicopter to our courtyard, with all the necessary. Voisenet and Maurel, move all the cars out of the yard so it can land. We'll need a doctor with us and an ambulance following us.'

He looked at his watches.

'We've got to be ready to go in an hour. Me, Danglard and Froissy in the helicopter, two teams in the cars, Kernorkian and Mordent, Justin and Voisenet. Bring something to eat, we won't be stopping. Two men on bikes, Lamarre and Estalère. Where is Estalère, anyway?'

'Up there', said Lamarre, pointing to the ceiling.

'Well, fetch him down here,' said Adamsberg, as if referring to a parcel.

A febrile physical agitation, a chaos of rapid movements and shouted orders, nervous queries and footsteps thundering up and down stairs transformed the squad's headquarters into a battle station before an assault. The sounds of people puffing, snorting and running about were drowned by the throbbing of the fourteen police cars as they were driven out of the large courtyard to make room for the helicopter. The old wooden staircase leading to the top floor had one step at the turn a couple of centimetres lower than the others. This anomaly had caused many a fall when the squad had first moved in, but people had got used to it. Now, in their impatience, two men, Maurel and Kernorkian, crashed downstairs.

'What the heck's all that din?' asked Adamsberg, hearing the fracas above his head.

'Just someone falling downstairs,' answered Mordent. 'The chopper'll be here in fifteen minutes. Estalère's on his way down.'

'Has he eaten?'

'No. Not since yesterday. He slept here.'

'Give him something to eat, then. Have a look in Froissy's cupboard.'

'Why do you need Estalère?'

'Because he's a specialist on Retancourt, a bit like the cat.'

'Estalère did say something about it,' Danglard confirmed. 'He said she was looking for something intellectual.'

The young *brigadier* approached the group. He was trembling. Adamsberg put his hand on his shoulder.

'She's already dead,' said Estalère in a defeated voice. 'After all this time, it stands to reason she's dead.'

'Yes, it stands to reason, but Retancourt's a woman beyond the bounds of reason.'

'But she's *mortal*.'

Adamsberg bit his lip.

'What's the chopper for?' asked Estalère.

'The Snowball won't stick to roads. He'll go through houses and gardens, and across roads, fields and woods. We won't be able to keep up with him in a car.'

'She's far away,' said Estalère. 'I can't feel her near us any more. The

Snowball won't be able to go that far. He's got no muscles, he'll just collapse on the way.'

'Have something to eat, *brigadier*. Do you feel strong enough to ride a motorbike?'

'Yes.'

'Good. Give the cat something to eat, too. Plenty of it.'

'There's another possibility,' said Estalère, in a tragic voice. 'We don't actually know that Retancourt was on to something. The maniac might not have been after her just to shut her up.'

'What for, then?'

'I think she's a virgin,' whispered the *brigadier*.

'I thought of that too, Estalère.'

'She's thirty-five, and she was born in Normandy. and she has lovely hair. I think she could be the third virgin.'

'But why her?' asked Adamsberg, though he already knew the answer.

'To punish us. By taking Violette, the killer would get hold of . . .'

Estalère hesitated and hung his head.

'. . . the material she needs,' Adamsberg completed his sentence. 'And at the same time, she'd be striking us in the heart.'

Maurel, his knee still sore after falling downstairs, was the first to stop his ears as the helicopter arrived, flying in over the roof. The other officers all lined up at the windows, hands over ears, watching the large grey and blue machine gently lower itself into the courtyard. Danglard went over to Adamsberg.

'I'd rather go in the car,' he said, looking embarrassed. 'I'd be no use to you in the helicopter, I'd just be ill. I have enough problems in lifts.'

'Swap with Mordent, then, *capitaine*. Are the men ready with the cars?'

'Yes. Maurel's waiting for a word from you to open the door and let the cat out.'

'What if he just goes for a piss in the yard?' said Justin. 'That's the kind of thing he'd normally do.'

'He'll get back to his normal self when he finds Retancourt,' Adamsberg pronounced.

'Forgive me for raising this', said Voisinet, with some hesitation. 'But if Retancourt's already dead, will he still be able to smell his way towards her?'

Adamsberg clenched his fists.

'Look, I'm sorry,' said Voisenet. 'But it really is important.'

'There are still her clothes, Justin.'

'Voisenet,' Voisenet automatically corrected him.

'Clothes keep their smell for a long time.'

'Yes, OK.'

'She may be the third virgin. That may be why she's been taken.'

'Yes, I thought of that too,' said Voisenet. 'But if so, you could call off the search in Normandy.'

'Already done.'

Mordent and Froissy joined Adamsberg, ready for the signal to leave. Maurel was carrying the cat in his arms.

'He won't be able to damage the transmitter with his claws, will he, Froissy?'

'No, I've protected it.'

'Right, Maurel, get ready. As soon as the chopper's gained some height, release the cat. And as soon as the cat goes, give the signal to the cars.'

Maurel watched the team go out, bowing their heads as they ran under the rotor blades of the helicopter, which had begun to rev up. The machine hoisted itself jerkily into the air. Maurel put the Snowball down so that he could cover its ears from the noise of the engine and the cat flattened itself against the ground like a pool of fur. Adamsberg had said 'release the cat' the same way one might say 'release the torpedo.' But the *lieutenant* was sceptical as he picked the animal up and headed for the doorway. The soft mass in his arms didn't exactly look like a guided missile.

XLVI

FRANCINE NEVER GOT UP BEFORE ELEVEN. SHE LIKED TO LIE FOR A LONG time under her blankets in the morning, when all the night-time creatures were back in their holes.

But a sound had bothered her last night, she recalled. She pushed back the old eiderdown – that would have to go as well, with all the dust mites that must be living under its yellow silk – and looked round the room. She immediately discovered what it was. A sliver of cement blocking a crack under the window had fallen out and was lying in fragments on the floor. Daylight was visible between the wall and the wooden surround of the window.

Francine went to take a closer look. Not only would she have to block the hateful crack up again but she would have to think. How and why had the cement fallen out? Could some creature from the outside have pushed its snout into the crack, or tried to break in by knocking the wall? If so, what could it be? A wild boar, perhaps?

Francine sat back on the bed, with tears in her eyes and her feet lifted well off the floor. If only she could go to a hotel until the flat was ready. But she had done her sums and it would be far too dear.

She wiped her eyes and put on her slippers. She'd lived for thirty-five years in this tumbledown old farm, so she'd manage for another two months. She didn't have any choice. She would have to wait, counting the days. She cheered herself up with the thought that it would soon be time to go to the pharmacy. And this evening, after blocking up the hole, she'd go to bed with her coffee and rum and watch another film.

XLVII

IN THE HELICOPTER HOVERING OVER THE ROOFS OF THE OFFICE, ADAMSBERG was holding his breath. The little red light from the cat's transmitter was quite visible on the screen, but it wasn't moving an inch.

'Shit,' muttered Froissy through clenched teeth.

Adamsberg spoke into his radio.

'Maurel? Have you let him go?'

'Yes, *commissaire*. He's sitting on the pavement. He went about four metres to the right of the door, then he sat down. He's watching the traffic.'

Adamsberg let the mike fall on to his knees and bit his lip furiously.

'Look, he's moved,' announced the pilot, Bastien, a man overweight to the point of obesity but who was flying the helicopter with the casual grace of a pianist.

Adamsberg leaned towards the screen, his gaze riveted to the little red light which was indeed starting to move off slowly.

'He's going towards the Avenue d'Italie. Keep following him, Bastien. Maurel, tell the cars to start.'

At ten past ten, the helicopter was flying due south over the southern part of Paris, like a great insect tied to the movements of a soft furry cat, quite unfitted to the outdoor life.

'He's turning south-west, he's going to cross the ring road,' said

Bastien. 'The traffic's at an absolute standstill, there's a big tailback.'

'Please don't let Snowball get run over,' prayed Adamsberg rapidly, addressing his prayer to he knew not who, now that he had lost sight of his third virgin. 'Let him be a cunning animal.'

'He's across,' announced Bastien. 'He's going into the suburbs. He's found his cruising rhythm now, he's almost running.'

Adamsberg glanced in wonder at Mordent and Froissy, who were craning over his shoulder to see the red point moving on the screen.

'He's almost running,' he repeated, as if to convince himself of this unlikely development.

'Nope, now he's stopped,' said Bastien.

'Cats can't run for long,' said Froissy. 'He might do it a bit now and then, but no more.'

'He's off again, steady rhythm again.'

'How fast?'

'Two, three kilometres an hour. He's heading for Fontenay-aux-Roses at a steady trot.'

'Cars, make for the D77, Fontenay-aux-Roses, still south-west.'

'What's the time?' asked Danglard as he took the car on to the D77.

'Eleven-fifteen,' said Kernorkian. 'Perhaps he's just looking for his mother.'

'Who?'

'The cat.'

'Grown-up cats don't recognise their mothers, they don't give a damn.'

'Well, what I mean is that the Snowball could be taking us absolutely anywhere. Perhaps he's taking us to Lapland.'

'Not if he's going south.'

'All right, keep your hair on,' said Kernorkian. 'All I meant was –'

'Yes, I know what you meant,' Danglard cut him off. 'You just meant we don't know where the fucking cat's going, we don't know if he's going after Retancourt, we don't know if Retancourt's alive or dead. Hell's bells, Kernorkian, we don't have any choice.'

'Head for Sceaux,' came Adamsberg's voice over the radio. 'Take the D67 via the D75.'

'He's slowing down,' said Bastien. 'He's stopping. Perhaps he's taking a rest.'

'If Retancourt's in Narbonne,' muttered Mordent, 'we've got a long way to go yet.'

'Hell, Mordent,' said Adamsberg. 'She might not even be in Narbonne, at that.'

'Sorry,' said Mordent. 'It's just nerves.'

'I know, *commandant*. Froissy, have you got anything to eat there?'

The *lieutenant* felt in her backpack.

'What do you want? Sweet or savoury?'

'What kind of savoury?'

'Paté?' guessed Mordent.

'That'd be nice.'

'He's still taking a nap,' reported Bastien.

In the cockpit of the helicopter, as it circled in the sky above the place where the cat was sleeping, Froissy prepared sandwiches of duck liver and green pepper paté. All four munched in silence, taking as long as possible, as if to suspend time. If you have something to do, anything can happen.

'He's off again, he's trotting along,' said Bastien.

Estalère, having stopped his bike, was listening to the instructions over the radio as he gripped the handlebars. He felt he was in some ghastly horror film. But the determined onward journey of the little animal encouraged him more than any other thought. The Snowball was heading for some unknown destination, without hesitating or weakening, crossing industrial zones, bramble patches, fields, railway tracks. Estalère admired the cat. It had been six hours now since it had begun its odyssey and they'd gone about eighteen kilometres. The police cars were moving slowly, halting for long stretches at the side of the road before making for the next point identified by the helicopter, and getting as close as possible to the route of the cat.

'Off you go again,' Adamsberg was saying to the cars. 'Go towards Palaiseau, on the D988. He's heading for the Ecole Polytechnique, south side.'

'He's going to get an education,' said Danglard, starting the engine. 'Nothing but cotton wool in that little head.'

'We'll see about that, Kernorkian.'

'The speed we're going now, we could stop off for a drink.'

'No,' said Danglard, whose head was still aching from the amount of wine he had drunk in the basement the day before. 'Either I drink to get drunk, or I don't touch the stuff. I don't like just having a glass. Today's a non-drinking day.'

'I get the impression that the Snowball likes a drink,' said Kernorkian.

'Yes, he's a bit inclined that way,' agreed Danglard. 'Have to keep an eye on him.'

'If he doesn't drop dead on this trek.'

Danglard checked the dashboard. Four-forty p.m. The time was dragging, making everyone feel nervy and at the end of their tether.

'We're going to refuel at Orsay, then we're back,' announced Bastien over the radio.

The helicopter moved off quickly, leaving the little red dot behind. Adamsberg had the feeling briefly that he was abandoning the Snowball in his quest.

At half past five, after seven hours on the move, the cat was still going strong and determinedly heading south-west, though stopping to rest every twenty minutes. The procession of vehicles followed it from stop to stop. By eight-fifteen, they were going through Forges-les-Bains on the D 97.

'He can't hold out much longer,' said Kernorkian, who was encouraging Danglard's pessimism. 'He's clocked up thirty-five kilometres on his little paws.'

'Shut up! He's still moving, so far.'

At eight-thirty-five, with darkness now fallen, Adamsberg came back on the radio.

'He's stopped. On a minor road, the C12 between Chardonnières and Bazoches, about two and a half kilometres from Forges. He's in a field, north of the road. He's off again. No, he's turning round and round.'

'He's going to drop dead,' said Kernorkian.

'Give it a rest!' cried Danglard, exasperated.

'He's hesitating,' came Bastien's voice.

'Perhaps he's going to stop for the night,' suggested Mordent.

'No,' said Bastien. 'He's looking round for something. I'm going down.'

He brought the helicopter down about a hundred feet, hovering over the cat which was sitting still.

'There's a big hangar over there,' said Adamsberg, pointing to a long roof of corrugated iron.

'Used-car dump,' said Froissy. 'Seems to be abandoned.'

Adamsberg clenched his fingers on his knees. Froissy silently passed him a mint, which the *commissaire* accepted without query.

'Well,' said Bastien, 'if you ask me, there are dogs in there, and the cat's frightened. But I think that's where he wants to go. I've had eight cats myself.'

'Go towards the used-car dump,' said Adamsberg to the cars. 'You can reach it via the C8 where it meets the C6. We're landing.'

'Good,' said Justin, driving off again. 'We're going to meet up.'

Grouped round the helicopter in an uncultivated field, Bastien, the nine police officers and the doctor were peering through the darkness at an old hangar surrounded by abandoned cars, with vegetation growing thickly around the rubbish. The dogs had seen the intruders and were approaching, barking furiously.

'Three or four of them,' commented Voisenet. 'Big ones.'

'That's why the Snowball won't move,' said Froissy. 'He doesn't know how to get past them.'

'We neutralise the dogs and keep watching the cat,' decided Adamsberg. 'Don't go too near him, though – we don't want him distracted.'

'He looks in a strange state,' said Froissy, who was sweeping the field with her night-vision binoculars and had them trained on the Snowball as he sat about forty metres away.

'I'm scared of dogs,' said Kernorkian.

'Stay back, then, but don't shoot. We'll just try and knock them out.'

Three large dogs, apparently surviving in a semi-wild condition in the huge building, were by now charging at the police, well before they had reached the doors of the hangar. Kernorkian shrank back against the warm body of the helicopter, near the large reassuring bulk of Bastien, who was smoking a cigarette, while the other officers floored the dogs. Adamsberg looked at the hangar with its opaque broken windows and rusty half-open doors. Froissy started to move forward.

'Don't go far yet,' said Adamsberg. 'Wait for the cat to make a move.'

The Snowball, now encrusted with dirt up to his neck, and looking thinner as his bedraggled fur clung to him, was sniffing at one of the unconscious dogs. Then he sat down and started washing one paw carefully, as if he had all the time in the world.

'What the fuck's he up to?' said Voisenet, shining his flashlight across.

'Maybe he's got a thorn in his paw,' said the doctor, a quiet, patient man, who was entirely bald.

'I'm walking wounded, too,' said Justin, showing his hand, which had been grazed by the teeth of one of the dogs. 'But I'm not taking time off.'

'It's just an animal, Justin,' said Adamsberg.

The Snowball finished that paw, washed another, then set off towards the hangar, suddenly breaking into run for the second time that day.

Adamsberg punched one fist into the other hand.

'She's got to be in there,' he said. 'Four men round the back, the rest with me. Doctor, come with us.'

'Dr Lavoisier,' said the doctor. 'Like Lavoisier the chemist, you know.'

Adamsberg looked at him blankly. He didn't know, and certainly didn't care, who Lavoisier the chemist was.

XLVIII

IN THE DARKNESS INSIDE THE INDUSTRIAL BUILDING, EACH OF THE TWO groups moved forward in silence, flashing their torches across broken furniture, piles of tyres and bundles of rags. The hangar seemed to have been abandoned for about ten years but still smelled strongly of diesel oil and burnt rubber.

'He knows where he's going,' said Adamsberg, as he focused his torch on the little round pawprints that the Snowball had left in the thick dust.

Head down, and breathing with difficulty, Adamsberg followed the cat's tracks very slowly, and none of the others tried to move ahead of him. After eleven hours of the chase, no one was now eager to reach their goal. The *commissaire* concentrated on putting one foot in front of the other as if he were wading through mud, hauling his stiff legs along with every pace. His group met up with the second team at the entry to a long dark corridor, lit only by a high window through which the moon was shining. The cat had stopped about twelve metres along it, and was crouching in front of a door. Adamsberg caught its luminous eyes with a sweep of the torch. It was now seven days and seven nights since Retancourt had been brought to this burial pit, in which three dogs were somehow surviving.

Adamsberg advanced heavily along the corridor, turning round after he had gone a few steps. None of the others had followed him. They were all massed at the end of the corridor, a frozen group, unable to face the last stretch.

I can't face it either, thought Adamsberg. But they couldn't stay there, clinging to the walls, abandoning Retancourt because they were unable to bear the sight of her body. He stopped in front of the metal door guarded by the cat, which was now sniffing along the ground, unconcerned by the terrible excremental smell coming from it. Adamsberg took a deep breath and put out his hand to release the hook that secured the door, then pulled it open. Forcing himself to look down, he made himself see what he had to: Retancourt's body, lying on the floor of a dark and tiny room, huddled against old car tools and petrol cans. He stood quite still, his gaze fixed on the sight, tears spilling freely from his eyes. It was the first time he had wept for anyone, except his brother Raphaël or Camille. Retancourt, his tree, his mainstay, was on the ground, struck down. Running the beam of the torch across her, he could see her dust-covered face, the nails on her hands already turning blue, her open mouth and her blonde hair, across which a spider ran.

He stood leaning against the dark brick wall, while the cat, unafraid, went into the tiny room and jumped on to Retacourt's body, lying down on her filthy clothes. The smell, Adamsberg thought. All he could smell was diesel, motor oil, urine and shit. Just regular animal and mechanical fluids. What was missing was the stench of decomposition. He took a couple of steps towards the body again, and knelt down on the sticky concrete floor. Holding his torch over Retancourt's face, which looked like a dirt-encrusted marble statue, all he could see was the immobility of death. The lips were open and fixed, not reacting to the spider as it ran over them. He slowly stretched out his hand and laid it on her forehead.

'Doctor!' he called, beckoning him on.

'He's calling you, doctor,' said Mordent, not moving an inch himself.

'Lavoisier, like the chemist.'

'Go on, he's calling you,' said Justin.

Still on his knees, Adamsberg moved back to make room for the doctor.

'She's dead,' he said, 'and yet she isn't dead.'

'One or the other, *commissaire*,' said Lavoisier, opening his bag. 'I can't see anything.'

'Torches, please,' called Adamsberg.

The group gradually approached, Mordent and Danglard in front with their flashlights.

'Still slightly warm,' said the doctor, after a rapid examination. 'She must have died less than an hour ago. I can't find a pulse.'

'She *is* alive,' said Adamsberg.

'Just a minute, *mon vieux*, don't get excited,' said the doctor, pulling out a mirror and placing it in front of Retancourt's mouth.

'OK', he said after several long seconds. 'Get the stretcher. She's still alive. I don't know how, but she's alive. In a para-lethal state, subnormal temperature – I've never seen anything like it before.'

'Seen what?' asked Adamsberg. 'What state is she in?'

'The metabolic functions are operating at minimum level,' said the doctor, still pursuing his examination. 'Her hands and feet are freezing cold, the circulation's very slow, the intestines have emptied and the eyes are unfocused.'

The doctor rolled up the sleeves of Retancourt's sweater and felt her arms. 'Even her forearms are already cold.'

'Is she in a coma?'

'No. It's a form of lethargy, below the normal vital thresholds. She could die at any minute with the stuff she must have been injected with.'

'What?' asked Adamsberg, who was holding Retancourt's large arm in both hands.

'Well, as far as I can tell, she's been injected intravenously with a dose of sedatives strong enough to kill a horse.'

'The syringe,' whispered Voisenet.

'She must have been hit on the head first,' said the doctor, feeling under her hair. 'There's possible concussion. She's been tied up tightly, hands and feet, the rope's bitten into the skin. I think she was injected with the stuff here. She should have died almost immediately. But according to the dehydration rate and the excretion, she must have survived six or seven days. It's not normal. I confess, I don't really understand it.'

'She isn't a normal person, doctor.'

'Lavoisier, like the chemist,' said the doctor automatically. 'Yes, I can see that, *commissaire*, but her size and weight alone wouldn't explain it. I just don't know how her organism managed to fight against the toxins, as well as hunger, thirst and cold.'

The paramedics arrived, put a stretcher on the ground and began trying to transfer Retancourt on to it.

'Gently,' said Lavoisier. 'Don't oblige her to breathe more deeply, it could be fatal. Put straps round her and move her a centimetre at a time. Let go her arm, *mon vieux*,' he said to Adamsberg.

Adamsberg removed his hands from her arm and told the officers to move back into the corridor.

'She's channelled her energy,' said Estalère as he watched the slow transfer of the large body on to the stretcher. 'She must have channelled it into stopping that sedative invading her bloodstream.'

'If you say so,' said Mordent. 'But we'll never really know.'

'Take the stretcher straight to the helicopter,' Lavoisier ordered. 'We've got to move quickly now.'

'Where will they take her?' asked Justin.

'The hospital in Dourdan.'

'Kernorkian and Voisenet, can you go to Dourdan and find a hotel for everyone to stop in tonight,' said Adamsberg. 'Tomorrow we'll have to go through this shed with a fine-tooth comb. They must have left some traces in all this sticky dust.'

'There weren't any prints in the corridor,' Kernorkian said. 'Just those of the cat.'

'They must have come from the other end. Lamarre and Justin, stay here to guard the exits until I can send some officers over from Dourdan to take over for the night.'

'Where's the cat?' asked Estalère.

'On the stretcher. Go and get it, *brigadier* – take care of it and help it recover.'

'There's a very good restaurant in Dourdan,' said Froissy calmly, '*La Rose des Vents*. Old beams and candlelight, speciality seafood, excellent wine – they do sea bream in a pastry crust, if they can get it. Of course, it's not cheap.'

The men all turned towards their quiet colleague, stunned that Froissy could be thinking about food while one of the team was at death's door. Outside, the revving-up of the helicopter indicated that Retancourt's removal was imminent. The doctor didn't think she would regain consciousness. Adamsberg could read it in his eyes.

He looked over the exhausted faces before him, shining palely in the torchlight. The incongruous prospect of a good dinner in a high-class restaurant seemed as remote to them as it was desirable, in some other life; an ephemeral bubble in which the artifice would help to suspend the horror.

'Right you are, Froissy,' Adamsberg said. 'We'll meet up at *La Rose des Vents* and get some supper there. Come on, doctor, we're going with Retancourt.'

'Lavoisier, like the chemist,' said the doctor.

XLIX

VEYRENC HAD NOT COME TO PARIS IN ORDER TO BECOME ABSORBED IN THE day-to-day affairs of the Serious Crime Squad. But at nine-thirty that night, having swallowed down his hospital supper hours before, he could no longer concentrate on the TV film. With an irritable gesture, he reached for the remote control and switched it off. Lifting his leg with both hands, he swivelled on the bed, grabbed his crutch and made his way slowly to the telephone in the corridor.

'*Commandant* Danglard? Veyrenc de Bilhc here. What's the latest?'

'We've found her, thirty-eight kilometres outside Paris, by following the cat.'

'The cat? What do you mean?'

'The . . . cat . . . wanted . . . to . . . find . . . Retancourt. Get it?'

'OK, OK,' said Veyrenc, sensing that his colleague was stressed-out.

'She's more dead than alive. We're on the road to Dourdan and she's in a para-lethal state of suspension.'

'Can you explain a bit what's happened? I need to know.'

Why, I wonder? thought Danglard.

Veyrenc listened to Danglard's account, which was much less coherent that it would normally be, and hung up. He pressed the wound on his thigh, exploring the degree of pain with his fingers, and imagined Adamsberg leaning over Retancourt, trying desperately

321

to find a means of bringing his stalwart *lieutenant* back into the land of the living.

> *The one who in the past had brought you back to life*
> *Lies now in sore distress, victim of deadly strife.*
> *Do not surrender, lord, to the call of despair,*
> *The gods may look kindly, if you venture to dare,*
> *And letting fall their wrath, will forthwith grant her breath,*
> *If with courage and strength you draw her back from death.*

'What, not asleep yet? Come on, time for bed,' said a nurse, taking him by the arm.

L

ADAMSBERG WAS STANDING BY RETANCOURT'S BED, HIS HANDS GRIPPING the sheets, but could still not see whether she was breathing. For all the injections, pumps and cleansing processes applied by the doctors, he could sense no change in her appearance, except that the nurses had washed her thoroughly and cut her hair, which had been infested with fleas. The dogs, of course. Over the bed, a screen was giving out weak vital signals. But Adamsberg preferred not to look at it, in case the green line should suddenly go flat.

The doctor took him by the arm and pulled him away from the bed.

'Go and see the others, get a bite to to eat, and think about something else. You can't do any more here. She just needs rest.'

'She's not resting doctor, she's dying.'

The doctor looked away.

'It's not looking good,' he admitted. 'She's had a massive dose of Novaxon and it's paralysed her whole organism. The nervous system has closed down, but the heart's somehow managing to hold out. I really don't understand how she's surviving. Even if we manage to save her, *commissaire*, I can't be certain she'll have all her mental faculties. There's only a minimal flow of blood to the brain. It's in the hands of fate now – try to understand.'

'A few days ago,' said Adamsberg, having difficulty articulating through clenched teeth, 'I saved a guy whose fate had dictated that he was going to die. There isn't such a thing as fate. She's survived this long, she'll hold out. You'll see, doctor, it'll be one for your record books.'

'Go and see the others. She could last for days in this state. I'll call you if anything changes, I promise.'

'You can't take everything out, clean it and put it back in?'

'No, we can't.'

'Sorry, doctor,' said Adamsberg, letting go his arm, which he had been clutching. He went back to the bed and ran his hands over Retancourt's cropped hair.

'I'll be back, Violette,' he said softly.

That was what Retancourt always said to the cat when she went out, so that it wouldn't worry.

The crude and explosive hilarity reigning in the restaurant sounded more like a birthday party than a team of police officers plunged in the deepest anguish. Adamsberg looked at them from the doorway, the candlelight making all their faces deceptively young and beautiful, their elbows resting on the white cloth, glasses passing from hand to hand and jokes being cracked. Yes, it was the right thing to do, as he had hoped; it was best, after all, that they should have this brief respite outside real time, and enjoy it to the full, because they knew it couldn't last. He was afraid that his arrival might break the mood of fragile happiness behind which their worries could be seen as if through glass. He forced a smile as he joined them.

'She's a bit better,' he announced as he sat down. 'Pass me a plate.'

Even Adamsberg, whose mind was still clinging on to Retancourt's body, benefited a little from the food, wine and laughter. He had never been very good at meals in company, still less jolly ones, since he was incapable of cracking jokes quickly or making clever repartee. Like an ibex watching a train speed by in the valley, he sat peaceably like a foreign observer, watching his colleagues exchange excited remarks. Froissy, curiously, was on top form at times like this, helped by the food and drink and a wicked sense of humour which one wouldn't have suspected from seeing her in the office. Adamsberg let himself be carried along by the mood, while constantly keeping an eye on the screen of his mobile. Which rang at eleven-forty.

'She's going downhill again,' said Dr Lavoisier. 'We're going to try a total blood transfusion: it's the last hope. The problem is that she's group A negative and, God help us, our reserves were used up yesterday for a road-crash victim.'

'What about donors?'

'We've only got one here, and we need three. The two other regulars are on holiday. It's Easter weekend, *commissaire*, half the town's away. I'm so sorry. By the time we find donors from other centres it'll be too late.'

A sudden silence fell over the table at the sight of Adamsberg's devastated face. He left the room at a run, followed by Estalère. The young man returned a few minutes later and collapsed into his seat.

'Urgent blood transfusion,' he said. 'Group A negative, but they haven't got the right donors on hand.'

Sweating from his run, Adamsberg came into the white-walled room where the only A-negative donor in Dourdan was finishing giving blood. It seemed to him as though Retancourt's cheeks had turned blue.

'I'm Group O,' he announced to the doctor, pulling off his jacket.

'Right, we can use you, you can be the next.'

'I've drunk two glasses of wine.'

'Never mind. The state she's in, that's the least of our worries.'

A quarter of an hour later, his arm numbed by the tourniquet, Adamsberg could sense his blood flowing into Retancourt's body. Lying on his back alongside her bed, he kept his eyes fixed on her face, waiting for any sign of a return to life. Please. But try as he might to concentrate and pray to the third virgin, he couldn't give more blood than anyone else. And the doctor had said he needed three. Three donors. Three virgins. Three.

His head was starting to spin, since he had scarcely touched his food. He accepted the vertigo without displeasure, feeling that his train of thought was slipping away from him. Still forcing himself to keep watching Retancourt, he noticed that the roots of her hair were fairer than the ends. He had never noticed before that Retancourt dyed her hair a darker blonde than the natural colour. What an odd aesthetic idea. There was a lot he didn't know about Retancourt.

'Are you all right?' asked the doctor. 'Not going to pass out?'

Adamsberg made a negative sign and returned to his vertiginous thoughts. Light blonde and dark blonde in Retancourt's hair, the quick of the virgin. Therefore, he calculated with difficulty, the *lieutenant* must have dyed her hair in December or January, since the fairer roots had grown about two or three centimetres, an odd idea in wintertime, and he had not noticed. He had lost his father about then, but that had nothing to do with it. It seemed to him that Retancourt's lips had moved, but he couldn't see very well. Perhaps she wanted to tell him something, to talk about the quick growing on her head, coming out of her skull like the horns of the ibex. Good God, the quick. From a long way off, he heard the doctor saying something.

'Stop now,' said a voice, that of Dr Lariboisier, or whatever his name was. 'We don't want two corpses instead of one. That's as much as we can take from him.'

At the hospital reception desk, a man was asking:

'Violette Retancourt, where is she?'

'Sorry, you can't see her now.'

'I'm a donor, Group O, universally compatible.'

'She's in resuscitation,' said the woman at the desk, jumping up. 'I'll take you there.'

Adamsberg was talking to himself when they took off the tourniquet. Hands helped him up, and someone made him drink some sugary water, while another medic was giving him an injection in his other arm. The door opened, and a large shape wearing a leather jacket burst into the room. '*Lieutenant* Noël,' said the large shape. 'Group O.'

LI

IN FRONT OF THE HOSPITAL, AS A CONTRAST WITH THE BLEAK CONCRETE surroundings, the planners had put a little green space, to indicate that some flowers ought to be included somewhere. In his comings and goings, Adamsberg had spotted this concession to nature, fifteen metres square, with two benches and five flower baskets arranged around a little fountain. It was now two in the morning, and the *commissaire*, feeling better with his sugar balance restored, was resting and listening to the plashing of the water, a comforting sound that he knew medieval monks had valued for its soothing qualities. After Noël had finished the final transfusion, the two men had stood and looked at Retancourt's inert body, one each side of her bed, as if they were supervising a risky scientific experiment.

'It's coming through now,' said Noël.

'Not yet,' said the doctor.

From time to time, Noël would impatiently and fruitlessly grip Retancourt's arm to try and hurry up the process, stir her blood, get the system going again, restart the engine.

'Come on, big girl, for Chrissake, get moving!'

On edge and unable to stand still without moving and speaking, Noël paced from one end of the bed to the other, rubbing Retancourt's feet to warm them up, then tried her hands, checked the drip, patted her head.

'That's not helping,' said the doctor irritably.

The heartbeat on the screen suddenly accelerated.

'Here she comes now,' said the doctor, as if announcing the arrival of a train.

'Come on, big girl,' repeated Noël for the tenth time. 'Make an effort.'

'We have to hope,' said Lavoisier, with the involuntary brutality that doctors display, 'that she's not going to wake up with brain damage.'

Retancourt opened her blue eyes weakly and looked blankly at the ceiling.

'What's her first name?' asked Lavoisier.

'Violette,' said Adamsberg.

'Like the flower,' added Noël.

Lavoisier sat on the bed, turned Retancourt's face towards him and took her hand.

'Is your name Violette?' he asked. 'If yes, blink your eyes for me.'

'Come on, big girl,' said Noël.

'Don't try to help her, Noël,' said Adamsberg.

'Nothing to do with help or not,' said Lavoisier, running out of patience. 'She's got to understand the question. For pity's sake, shut up – she's got to concentrate. Violette, tell me, is that your name?'

Ten agonising seconds passed before Retancourt unmistakably blinked her eyes.

'She's understood,' said Lavoisier.

'Of course she understood,' said Noël. 'You should make the question harder, doc.'

'That's already a hard question, when you're coming back from where she's been,' said the doctor.

'Look, I think we're in the way,' said Adamsberg.

Lieutenant Noël was incapable of sitting and listening to the sound of the fountain like Adamsberg. The *commissaire* watched him pacing up and down the little garden, where the two policemen seemed to be in a tiny circus ring, lit from ground level by blue lights.

'Who told you, *lieutenant*?'

'Estalère phoned me from the restaurant. He knew my blood group would be compatible. He's the kind of guy who remembers personal details. Whether you take sugar in your coffee, whether you're A, B or O. Tell me what's happened, *commissaire*, I've missed out on a lot of this.'

Adamsberg summarised, in his own haphazard fashion, the elements Noël had missed while he was out consulting the seagulls. Curiously, the *lieutenant*, who was in theory a hardcore positivist, asked him to repeat twice the *De sanctis reliquis* recipe. And he was opposed to Adamsberg's proposal to give up on the third virgin. Nor did he make any inappropriate jokes about the cat's penile bone or the quick of virgins.

'We can't just allow some girl to get knocked off without lifting a finger, *commissaire*.'

'But I was probably mistaken when I thought the third virgin had already been chosen.'

'Why?'

'Because in the end, I think the killer chose Retancourt for that.'

'But that wouldn't make sense,' said Noël, stopping short.

'Why not? She meets the requirements of the recipe.'

Noël looked across at Adamsberg through the darkness.

'Well, for a start, *commissaire*, Retancourt would have to be a virgin.'

'Yes, well, I think she is.'

'I don't.'

'You'd be the only one to think that, Noël.'

'I don't think. I know. She's not a virgin. Not at all.'

Noël sat down on the bench, looking pleased with himself, while Adamsberg in turn started walking round the garden.

'Surely you're the last person Retancourt would take into her confidence.'

'We yell at each other so much that we end up telling each other the story of our lives. She's not a virgin, full stop.'

'So that means that there is a third virgin. Somewhere else. And that Retancourt did understand something we didn't.'

'And before we find that out,' said Noël, 'a lot of water's going to flow under the bridge.'

'We'll have to wait a month for her to recover properly, according to Lariboisier.'

'Lavoisier,' said Noël. 'Maybe a month for someone normal, but probably a week for Retancourt. Funny to think of your blood and mine circulating through her veins.'

'And the blood of the third donor.'

'Who's the third donor, anyway?'

'He's a cattle farmer, I believe.'

'That'll be a weird mixture,' said Noël, with a pensive shake of his head.

In his chilly hotel bed, Adamsberg could not close his eyes without seeing himself once more lying wired up alongside Retancourt and going back over the vertiginous thoughts that had flashed through his head during the transfusion. Retancourt's dyed hair, the quick of virgins, the horns of the ibex. There was a persistent alarm bell ringing through this combination of ideas, which would not be silenced. It must be something to do with the blood passing from him into her, recharging her heartbeats, rescuing her from the clutches of death. It must be something to do with the virgin's hair, of course. But what was the ibex doing there? That reminded him that the horns of the ibex were simply the same thing as hair in a very compressed form, or, looking at it another way, that his own hair was simply a very dispersed kind of horn. They were all the same thing. But so what? He would have to try and remember tomorrow.

LII

A PEAL OF CHURCH BELLS WOKE ADAMSBERG AT MIDDAY. *NO PEACE FOR the wicked*, his mother used to say. He called the hospital at once and listened as Lavoisier gave a positive report.

'She's talking?' he asked

'No, she's sleeping soundly now,' said the doctor, 'and probably will for some time. Remember, she's also got concussion.'

'Is she saying anything in her sleep?'

'Yes, she mutters stuff from time to time. But it's not really conscious or even intelligible. Don't get excited.'

'I'm quite calm, doctor. But I just want to know what she says.'

'She keeps saying the same thing over and over. A bit of poetry that everyone knows.'

Poetry? Was Retancourt dreaming about Veyrenc? Or had he somehow infected her? Seducing all the women into his entourage one after the other?

'So what poetry would that be?' asked Adamsberg, with some annoyance.

'Lines by Corneille we all learned at school:

> To see the last Roman, as he draws his last breath,
> Myself to die happy, as the cause of this death.'

They were indeed two of the few lines of verse that even Adamsberg knew by heart.

'That's not her style,' he muttered. 'Is that really what she's saying?'

'Oh, if you heard what people sometimes say under sedatives or anaesthetic, you'd be astonished. I've heard blameless people come out with unbelievable obscenities.'

'Is that what she's doing?'

'Like I said, she recites Corneille. Nothing surprising about that. Mostly people in her state say things they remember from their childhood, especially stuff they learned at school. She's just going back to what she was made to learn for homework, that's all. Once I had a government minister who was in a coma for three months, and he went through his primary education, multiplication tables and all. He could still remember it pretty well.'

As he listened to the doctor, Adamsberg was staring at a sentimental picture over his hotel bed, a forest glade in which a mother deer was being followed by a cute little fawn through the ferns. 'An accompanied hind,' Robert would call her.

'I've got to go back to Paris today, to my own hospital team,' the doctor was saying. 'It won't hurt to move her now, so I'm taking her in the ambulance. We'll be at Saint-Vincent-de-Paul Hospital by this evening.'

'Why are you taking her with you?'

'Because it's such an extraordinary case, *commissaire*. I'm going to see this one through.'

Adamsberg hung up, still looking at the painting. The tangled skein was in there too, the quick of virgins and the 'living cross from the heart of the eternal branches'. He looked for a long time at the hind as if hypnotised, trying to touch something just beyond his reach. An element he still had not grasped. *There's a bone in the snout of a pig, and a bone in the penis of a cat.* And if he was not much mistaken, and unlikely though that seemed, maybe there was *a bone in the heart of a stag*. A bone in the form of a cross, which would take him straight to the third virgin.

LIII

THE TEAM HAD BEEN WORKING IN THE HANGAR SINCE TEN IN THE morning, with the help of two technicians and a photographer recruited from the local force at Dourdan. Lamarre and Voisenet had been in charge of searching the surrounding area, looking for tyre tracks in the field. Mordent and Danglard had each taken half the hangar. Justin was checking the tool cupboard where Retancourt had been found. Adamsberg joined them as they were starting a picnic lunch, sitting in the field under a pleasant April sun: sandwiches, fruit, beer, and hot drinks from a thermos, all impeccably organised by Froissy. There were no chairs in the hangar, so they sat on old car tyres, forming a curious circular convention in the field. The cat, which had not been allowed to travel in the ambulance, was curled up at Danglard's feet.

'The vehicle must have come in this way,' explained Voisenet, his mouth full, pointing to a gap leading from the road. 'It stopped by the side door at the end of the hangar, after reversing to have the boot facing the entry. There are plants everywhere, it's impossible to find tracks. But judging by the way the grass is crushed down, it would be some kind of transit van, probably with a capacity of nine cubic metres. I don't think the nurse has anything like that. She must have hired it. We might be able to trace it via agencies specialising in freight vehicles. An old woman renting a big van can't be that common.'

Adamsberg had sat down cross-legged in the warm grass, and Froissy had laid out an ample supply of food beside him.

'The transport of the body was carefully organised,' said Mordent, taking over. Perched on a large tyre, he looked more than ever like a heron on its nest. 'The nurse must have had a trolley, or hired it with the van. It looks as if there was a ramp you could let down. All she had to do was roll the body down the slope and put it on the trolley. Then she pushed the trolley through the hangar to the tool cupboard.'

'Can you see tracks from its wheels?'

'Yes, they go through the hall. She must have neutralised the dogs with meat laced with Novaxon. Then the tracks turn, and we can see them going along the corridor. Partly covered by the return trip.'

'Footprints?'

'You're going to like this,' said Lamarre, with the smile of a child who has been hiding a present behind his back to increase the surprise. 'The angle of the corridor wasn't easy to negotiate, so she had to lean hard on the trolley and pivot on her feet – see what I mean?'

'Yes.'

'And the concrete floor is rough there.'

'Yes?'

'And just there we found traces . . .'

'Of navy shoe polish,' said Adamsberg.

'You've got it.'

'Isolated from the ground on which her crimes are committed,' said the *commissaire* slowly, 'but still leaving traces behind. Nobody can really be a Shade. We'll get her through these blue marks.'

'There aren't any full prints anywhere, so we can't be sure about the size. but it looks as if they were women's shoes, flat-heeled and solid.'

'Now the cupboard,' said Justin. 'That's where she injected the dose of Novaxon, before shutting the door on its hook.'

'Nothing of significance in the cupboard?'

A short silence punctuated Justin's report.

336

'Yes,' he said. 'The syringe.'

'You can't be serious, *lieutenant*! She surely didn't leave her syringe behind?'

'Yes, absolutely. On the floor. Wiped completely clean, of course – no prints.'

'So now she's signing her work,' said Adamsberg, getting to his feet as if the nurse was openly challenging him.

'That's what we thought too.'

The *commissaire* paced around for a few moments on the grass, his hand behind his back.

'Right,' he said. 'She's crossed some kind of threshhold. She thinks she's invincible, and she's telling us so.'

'Seems logical,' said Kernorkian, 'for someone who wants a recipe for eternal life.'

'But she still hasn't laid hands on the third virgin,' said Adamsberg.

Estalère did his round of the officers, pouring coffee into the plastic cups they held out. The makeshift picnic site and the absence of milk made it impossible for him to conduct his usual complicated ceremony.

'She'll get there before we do,' said Mordent.

'Don't be too sure,' said Adamsberg.

He returned to the circle of officers and sat down cross-legged in the centre.

'The quick of virgins,' he said, 'didn't just mean the dead women's hair.'

'But Roman settled that for us,' said Mordent. 'We know this maniac cut off some locks of hair.'

'If she cut off some locks of hair, it was in order to gain access.'

'To what?'

'To the *real* hair of death. To the hair that goes on growing *after* death.'

'Oh, of course!' exclaimed Danglard ruefully. 'The quick. The part that keeps on living – and growing – even after death.'

'That's the reason,' Adamsberg went on, 'why it was essential for the nurse to come back and dig up her victims a few months later. The *quick* needed time to grow. And that's what she was after, the two or three centimetres of hair growing out from the root, in the grave. It was more than a symbol of eternal life. It was a concrete example of vital resistance, life refusing to stop after death.'

'Ugh, sickening,' said Noël, summing up the general reaction.

Froissy packed up the food, which no longer tempted anyone.

'But how will that help us identify the third virgin?' she asked.

'Now that we understand that, Froissy, the rest will follow logically: it has to be crushed with the "*living cross in the heart of the eternal branches*", adjacent in equal quantity.'

'We'd already settled that,' said Mordent. 'It must mean wood from the Holy Cross.'

'No,' said Adamsberg. 'That doesn't fit. Like the rest, the text has to be read absolutely literally, word for word. Christ's cross can't live *in* the heart of anything, it doesn't make sense.'

Danglard, sitting sideways on his tyre, screwed up his eyes, on alert.

'The recipe says,' Adamsberg went on, 'that it's a *living* cross.'

'That's just what doesn't make sense,' commented Mordent.

'A cross, living inside a body that represents eternity,' said Adamsberg slowly, pronouncing every word clearly. 'A body related to eternal branches.'

'In the Middle Ages,' said Danglard, 'the creature that signified eternity was the stag.'

Adamsberg, who up to this point hadn't been entirely sure of his ground, smiled across at his deputy.

'Why was that, *capitaine*?'

'Because the stag's antlers reach up to heaven. Because the antlers die and fall, then grow again every year, like the leaves of trees, with an extra point, getting more powerful, year by year. It's an amazing phenomenon, to do with the beast's vital force. It was once considered a symbolic representation of eternal life, always beginning again, and always growing larger, like the antlers. Sometimes one finds representation of stags with Christ on their heads, or a cross between the antlers.'

'The stag's antlers grow out of its skull,' said Adamsberg. 'Like hair.'

The *commissaire* ran his hand over the spring grass.

'The *eternal branches* could be a metaphor for the stag's antlers.'

'Do they have to be in the mixture, then?'

'No, because we need a cross. And every word in the recipe counts, like I said. The cross that lives *in the heart of the eternal branches*. So the cross must be inside the stag. It must be a bone, like the antlers, and incorruptible.'

'Perhaps the bone at the base of the antlers, where it makes an angle,' said Voisenet.

'It doesn't look to me as if deer's antlers make a cross,' said Froissy.

'No, no,' said Adamsberg. 'I think the cross is somewhere else. I think it's a secret bone that you have to know about, like the cat's. The penile bone represents the male principle. We need something of the kind in the stag. A bone in the shape of a cross, that would represent the stag's links with eternity, but hidden inside its body. A living bone.'

Adamsberg looked round at his colleagues, waiting for a response.

'I don't see it,' said Voisenet.

'Well, I think,' Adamsberg went on, 'that we'll find this bone in the heart of a stag. The heart is the symbol of life, it beats. A cross that lives, a cross inside the heart of the stag with eternal antlers.'

Voisenet turned to Adamsberg.

'It sounds good, *commissaire*,' he said. 'The only problem is that there isn't a bone in the heart of a stag. Or in anyone else's heart. Not in the shape of a cross or anything else.'

'Well, Voisenet, there has to be something like that.'

'Why?'

'Because in the forest of Brétilly, and then again in the forest near Opportune, two male stags were slaughtered last month and left lying on the ground. The only thing that had been done to them was that their hearts had been cut out. These killings were carried out by the same person. They were in the same place, that is within the zone of the saint's influence, and they were killed near the two women who were sacrificed. They must have been shot by our angel of death.'

'That makes sense,' said Lamarre.

'The stags were cut open after death in a particular place. Exactly like what happened to the cat, Narcissus. They were *operated on* in some sense. With a definite aim, to get something out. What? The living cross in the heart. So it must be inside the stag's heart, in some form.'

'That's impossible,' said Danglard, shaking his head. 'We'd know about it.'

'We didn't know about the cat, or the pig's snout,' said Kernorkian.

'Yes, I knew about those all right,' said Voisenet. 'But I also know there's no bone in the heart of a stag.'

'I'm sorry, *lieutenant*, but there really has to be one.'

At this point there were some mutterings and doubtful glances, as Adamsberg got up to stretch his legs, It did not seem evident to the positivists that reality should reshape itself to meet the strange ideas that the *commissaire* was putting forward, inventing a bone in the heart of the stag.

'No,' insisted Voisenet. 'It's the other way round. There is no bone in the heart. So we have to work around that, because it's the truth.'

'Voisenet, there's got to be something, or none of these actions would make sense. And if there is, we need to watch for the next stag to be slaughtered. The third virgin the nurse has picked out will be in the nearby area. The cross in the heart must be as close as possible to the quick of the virgin. "Adjacent in equal quantity." It doesn't mean "joined with it", it means "close by".'

'Adjacent,' said Danglard, 'means lying alongside, or lined up against.'

'Thank you, Danglard. For the virgin and the stag to be close together looks right: the female and male essences giving birth to life, in this case eternal life. When we find another stag with its heart cut out, we'll know the name of the virgin out of all those you've got on your lists.'

'All right,' admitted Justin. 'But how do we find this stag? Will we have to keep a watch on the forests?'

'Someone's already doing that for us.'

LIV

ADAMSBERG WAITED IN THE RAIN FOR THE ANGELUS TO BE RUNG IN THE church at Haroncourt before he pushed open the door of the café. This Sunday evening, he found the assembled men all present and correct, and about to begin the first round of drinks.

'Ah, you'll be wanting a drink then, man from the Béarn,' said Robert, without letting his surprise show.

A rapid glance at Anglebert told Adamsberg that the outsider was still welcome to sit down, even if he had dug up a grave at Opportune-la-Haute eighteen days earlier. As in the past, a place was made for him alongside the elder of the tribe, and a glass pushed towards him.

'You've been busy,' observed Anglebert, pouring out the white wine.

'Yes, I've had problems, police problems.'

'Ah, that's life,' said Anglebert. 'Robert's a roofer, he gets roof problems, Hilaire's got pork-butcher problems, Oswald's got farmer's problems, and I've got the problem of getting old. And that's no fun, believe me. Drink up.'

'I know now why those two women were killed,' said Adamsberg, obeying the command. 'And I know why their graves were opened as well.'

'So now you're satisfied.'

'No, not really,' said Adamsberg, grimacing. 'This killer is a fiend from hell, and she hasn't finished yet.'

'But she's going to?' said Oswald.

'Or so you think,' punctuated Achille.

'Yes, she does intend to finish the job,' said Adamsberg, 'by killing a third virgin. I'm looking for this third virgin. And I need some help.'

All eyes swivelled towards him, surprised at such an open appeal.

'Well, not wishing to cause offence,' said Anglebert, 'but that's *your* job.'

'Not ours,' punctuated Achille.

'You're wrong, it does concern you. Because it's the same woman who slaughtered your stags.'

'Told you so,' breathed Oswald.

'How do you know?' asked Hilaire.

'That's his business,' Anglebert interrupted. 'If he tells you he knows, then he knows, that's all.'

'Stands to reason,' punctuated Achille.

'Both the human victims were linked with the death of a stag,' Adamsberg went on. 'Or, more precisely, an attack on the heart of the stag.'

'What's the point of that?' asked Robert

'To get at the bone in the heart, the bone that's shaped like a cross,' said Adamsberg, staking everything on this throw.

'Ah, could be,' said Oswald. 'That's what Hermance thought. She's got one of them, Hermance has.'

'A bone in her heart?' asked Achille in astonishment.

'No, in her sideboard drawer. She's got a stag's heartbone.'

'Going after the cross in a stag, this day and age, you've got to be a bit cracked,' said Anglebert. 'That's stuff they did in bygone times.'

'Kings of France used to collect 'em, though,' said Robert. 'To bring them good health.'

'Like I said, it's stuff from the olden days. Nobody collects them now.'

Adamsberg drank a glass to his own health, secretly celebrating the fact that there really was a bone like a cross in the heart of a stag.

'But what did he want with the cross, this murderer of yours?' asked Robert.

'I told you, she's a woman.'

'Aargh,' said Robert, with a look of disgust. 'But anyway, you know why, do you?'

'It was to put this cross alongside hair taken from the virgins.'

'Well,' said Oswald, 'that proves she's crazy. What's that supposed to be about?'

'It's part of a recipe to give you eternal life.'

'God's sakes,' spluttered Hilaire.

'Eternal life, eh?' observed Anglebert. 'All right for some, but then again, you wouldn't really want it, would you?'

'Why not?'

'C'm on, Hilaire, just think if you had to live for ever. What on earth would you do all day? You can't sit around drinking for thousands of years.'

'That's a long time, all right,' said Achille.

'She plans to kill the next woman,' Adamsberg went on, 'after she's killed the next stag. Or maybe the other way round, I don't know. But all I can do is follow the cross in the heart. So that's why I want you to tell me as soon as another stag is found dead.'

An ominous silence suddenly fell, such as only Normans can create or tolerate. Anglebert poured another round of drinks, making the neck of the bottle clink against each glass.

'Well, my friend, it's already happened,' said Robert.

There was another silence, while everyone swallowed a mouthful, except Adamsberg who was staring at Robert with a stricken expression.

'When?' he asked.

'About six days back.'

'Why didn't you call me?'

'You didn't seem interested any more,' said Robert sulkily. 'All you cared about was Oswald's ghost.'

'Where was this?'

'At Le Bosc des Tourelles.'

'Was it killed the same way as the others?'

'Yeah, just the same. Heart on the ground beside it.'

'Which are the nearest villages to it?'

'Campenille, Troimare, Louvelot. Then a bit further away, Longeney one way and Coucy the other. Couple more. Plenty of choice.'

'And no woman has been killed or had an accident round there?'

'No.'

Adamsberg breathed in relief and took another sip of wine.

'Well, there was that old Yvonne who fell over on the bridge,' said Hilaire.

'Is she dead?'

'You've got death on the brain as usual,' said Robert. 'No, she broke her hip.'

'Can you take me there tomorrow?'

'Where? To see Yvonne.'

'No, the stag.'

'He's already been buried.'

'Who's got the antlers?'

'Nobody, he'd already lost 'em.'

'I'd still like to see the spot.'

'Could be done,' said Robert, holding out his glass for a third helping. 'But where will you sleep? In the hotel, or at Hermance's?'

'Best be the hotel,' said Oswald quietly.

'Yes, that'd be best,' said the punctuator.

Nobody expained why it was no longer possible to stay with Oswald's sister.

LV

WHILE HIS COLLEAGUES WERE CHECKING THE AREA SURROUNDING LE BOSC des Tourelles, Adamsberg had been hospital visiting. He had seen both Veyrenc, who was now hobbling around at Bichat, and Retancourt, who was still asleep at Saint-Vincent-de-Paul. Veyrenc was due to be discharged the next day, and Retancourt's sleep appeared to be more like a natural state. She's returning to the surface quite fast, Lavoisier had said. He was taking quantities of notes on the polyvalent goddess. Veyrenc, once he had been brought up to date on the rescue of the *lieutenant* and the cross inside the stag, had formulated some advice which Adamsberg was chewing over as he walked back to the headquarters.

Her strength brought from the brink one who was close to death.
But another's weakness threatens her every breath.
Make haste, the time draws near. The great stag died at last,
The virgin is at risk, her hour is almost past.

'We've got a Francine Bidault here,' said Mordent, passing over an index card to Adamsberg. 'Aged thirty-five. Lives outside Clancy, a hamlet, population two hundred, seven kilometres from the edge of the Bosc des Tourelles. The other two nearest women live fourteen or nineteen kilometres away, and they're both closer to another forest, La

Chataigneraie, which is big enough to have deer in it. Francine lives alone, in an isolated farmhouse, almost a kilometre away from the nearest neighbours. Her garden wall is easy to climb, and the house is very old. Rickety wooden doors, simple locks, easy to force.'

'Right,' said Adamsberg. 'Does she go out to work? Does she have a car?'

'She's got a part-time job, cleaning in a pharmacy in Evreux. She goes there by bus every day except Sunday. Any attack would most likely come between seven at night and one the next afternoon, which is when she leaves home.'

'And she's a virgin? They're sure about that?'

'Well, according to the priest at Otton, yes. "A little cherub," he calls her. Pretty, childlike, not quite all there, according to some other reports. Mind you, the priest says there's nothing really wrong with her head, but she's afraid of almost everything, specially creepy-crawlies. She was brought up by her father after her mother died, and he was a brute. He died a couple of years back.'

'There's a problem,' said Voisenet, whose positivist credentials had been been severely dented when Adamsberg had guessed at the existence of a bone in the heart of a deer, simply by shovelling clouds. 'Devalon's found out we're operating in Clancy, and why. He's looking bad, because he failed to spot that Elisabeth and Pascaline had been murdered. He's insisting that his outfit take charge of protecting Francine Bidault.'

'All the better,' said Adamsberg. 'As long as Francine's under police guard, that's all we're asking. Call him, Danglard. Tell Devalon he's got to have three men in shifts, armed, between seven at night and one p.m. next day, without leaving her unprotected for a moment. They should begin tonight. The guard should be *inside* the house and, if she doesn't object, in the bedroom. We'll send Evreux a photograph of the nurse. Who's been checking the van-hire firms?'

'I did,' said Justin, 'with Lamarre and Froissy. Nothing so far in the whole Ile-de-France region. Nobody remembers a woman of seventy-five hiring a van that big. They're quite positive.'

'And the blue stains?'

'Yes, they're definitely shoe polish.'

'Retancourt came out with something else this afternoon,' said Estalère, 'but it didn't amount to much.'

Intrigued faces turned towards him.

'Did she quote Corneille again?' Adamsberg asked.

'No, she talked about shoes. She said, "*Send some shoes to the caravan.*"'

The men looked at each other in puzzlement.

'The big girl's losing it again,' said Noël.

'No, Noël. She promised this lady, who lives in a caravan, that she'd give her another pair of shoes to replace the blue ones she took away, the nurse's. Lamarre, can you take care of that? You'll find the address in Retancourt's files.'

'After all she's been through, that's the first thing she thinks about telling us?' said Kernorkian.

'That's the way she is,' said Justin with a shrug. 'Nothing else?'

'Yes, she said: "*But he needn't give a damn. Tell him that. He needn't give a damn.*"'

'Does she mean about this lady? And her shoes?'

'No, no,' said Adamsberg. 'She wouldn't say that about the lady.'

'Who's "him"?'

Estalère jerked his chin towards Adamsberg.

'Yeah, probably,' said Voisenet.

'But what?' murmured Adamsberg. 'What is it that I needn't give a damn about?'

'Well, *I* reckon she's losing it,' said Noël, anxiety in his voice.

LVI

FOR THE FIRST TIME IN HER LIFE, AND FOR TWENTY-TWO DAYS NOW, Francine had not been pulling the blankets over her face at night. She went to sleep with her head calmly resting on the pillow, which was much more comfortable than being curled up under her sheets with a tiny opening to breathe through. Not only that, but she had been making only the most cursory checks on the woodworm holes, hardly bothering to count the new perforations moving towards the south end of the beam, and not worrying about what the nasty little creatures looked like.

This police protection was a gift from the gods. Three men came in turns every night and watched over her, even in the morning, until she went to work. It was a dream come true. She had asked no questions about the reason why she was under guard, for fear her curiosity might annoy the gendarmes and then they would abandon their bright idea. From what they had given her to understand, it was something to do with recent burglaries, so Francine didn't find it at all odd that the gendarmes should be keeping an eye on all the women locally who lived alone. Others might have protested, but she was far from doing so. On the contrary, she gratefully cooked supper every evening for the gendarme on duty, and a much better supper than she had ever made for her father.

The rumours of these good suppers – and of Francine's pretty face –

had spread in the Evreux brigade, so although Devalon did not know why, there was never any problem finding volunteers to guard Mademoiselle Bidault. Devalon had no time at all for the cock-and-bull investigation being led by Adamsberg, which he thought was a complete waste of time. But there was no way this Paris police chief, who had already demolished the Evreux reports on Elisabeth Châtel and Pascaline Villemot because of a bit of lichen on a stone, was going to trespass on his patch. His men would be the ones to guard the farm, and not a single cop from Adamsberg's outfit would set foot there. Adamsberg had had the cheek to insist that the men doing shifts would have to be sitting up and awake. Well, he could stuff that. He wasn't going to have his team short-manned for this ridiculous enterprise. He would send his men over to Francine's after their normal day's work, with orders to eat and sleep there, without trying to stay awake.

During the night of 3 May, at three-thirty-five in the morning, only the woodworms were awake in the bedrooms where Francine and *Brigadier* Grimal were sleeping. The insects were quite uninhibited by the presence of an armed man in the house as they munched their thousandth of a millimetre of wood. Woodworms being deaf, they did not react to the creak of the scullery door. Grimal, who was sleeping in the bedroom of Francine's late father, tucked in under a purple eiderdown, sat up in the dark, unsure what kind of sound had woken him, or whether his gun was on the left or right of the bed, on the chest of drawers or on the ground. He felt blindly on the table, then crossed the room, wearing only his T-shirt and shorts, and opened the door leading to Francine's bedroom. Empty-handed, he watched as a long grey shadow approached him in a strangely slow and silent way, without stopping when the door opened. The shadow didn't approach normally, it slid and stumbled, passing over the floor in a hesitant but unstoppable progress. Grimal had just time to shake Francine awake, without knowing whether he was trying to save her or to ask her for help.

'A ghost, Francine! Get up, run!'

Francine screamed, and Grimal, although terrified, approached the shadow to cover the flight of the young woman. Devalon had not prepared him to deal with this, and he cursed his boss with his last thought. To hell with him, and the ghost as well.

LVII

ADAMSBERG GOT THE CALL FROM THE EVREUX BRIGADE AT EIGHT-TWENTY in the morning, as he was sitting in the workmen's café opposite the sleeping *Brasserie des Philosophes*. He was drinking a coffee there with Froissy, who had embarked on her second breakfast. *Brigadier* Maurin, who had arrived at Clancy to take over from Grimal, had found his colleague dead with two bullets in the chest, one of them through the heart. Adamsberg slammed his cup down on his saucer.

'And the virgin?' he asked.

'Disappeared. It looks like she jumped out of the back window. We're looking for her.'

The gendarme's voice was broken with sobs. Grimal had been forty-two years old, and more concerned with clipping his garden hedge than with upsetting people.

'What about his gun?' asked Adamsberg. 'Couldn't he have used it?'

'He was in bed, asleep, sir. His gun was on the chest in the bedroom – he can't have had time to pick it up.'

'But that's impossible,' muttered Adamsberg. 'I particularly asked that the guard should be sitting up, awake, fully dressed and armed.'

'Devalon didn't bother with all that, sir. He sent us over there after work. We couldn't stay awake all night.'

'Tell your boss he can go roast in hell.'

'Yes, I know, *commissaire*.'

Two hours later, gritting his teeth with fury, Adamsberg was leading his men into Francine's farmhouse. The young woman had been found in tears, her feet bleeding, in a neighbour's hay barn, where she had taken refuge between two bales of straw. A grey shape that wobbled like a candle flame was all she had seen, that and the arm of the gendarme who had pulled her out of bed and pushed her towards the back bedroom. She was already running towards the road when the two shots had rung out.

The *commissaire* felt Grimal's cold forehead, kneeling by his head so as not to tread in his blood. Then he called a number, and heard a sleepy voice at the other end.

'Ariane, I know it's not eleven yet, but I need you.'

'Where are you?'

'In a village called Clancy in Normandy, on the Chemin des Biges, number four. Please hurry. We won't touch anything till you get here.'

'Who's this technical team you've got here?' asked Devalon, indicating with a sweep of his hand the small group who had accompanied Adamsberg. 'And who are you bringing in now?' he added, jerking his chin at the telephone.

'I'm bringing in my forensic pathologist, *commandant*. And I don't advise you to raise any objections.'

'Go fuck yourself, Adamsberg – this is one of my men.'

'A man you sent to his death.'

Adamsberg glanced at the two gendarmes who had accompanied Devalon. Their body language indicated that they agreed with him.

'Stay here to guard your man's body,' he said to them. 'And don't let anyone approach him until the doctor gets here.'

'Don't you give orders to my men, Adamsberg. We don't have to take any shit from a Paris cop.'

'I'm not from Paris. And you haven't got any men any longer.'

Adamsberg went out, dismissing Devalon's fate from his mind immediately.

'What have you found?'

'I think I can piece it together,' said Danglard. 'The killer came in over the north wall, crossed the grass, that's about fifty metres, then came in though the scullery door, which is the most dilapidated.'

'The grass isn't very long. No footmarks, then.'

'The outside wall's banked with earth, so there are some prints. A lump of clay's fallen out, showing where the killer came over.'

'What else? asked Adamsberg, sitting down and half-sprawling across the kitchen table.

'Forced the door, went through the scullery, then the kitchen, and into the bedroom through this door. No prints there, there isn't a speck of dust on the tiles. Grimal must have been coming out of the back room, and the shooting took place near Francine's bed. He was shot at point-blank range, apparently.'

Devalon had been obliged to leave the farmhouse, but he was refusing to cede the territory to Adamsberg. He was walking up and down in the road, cursing as he waited for the arrival of the doctor from Paris, firmly intending to use his own pathologist for the post-mortem. He saw a car screech to a halt in front of the old wooden gate of the farm, and a woman got out and turned towards him. He had his last shock that day when he recognised the well-known features of Ariane Lagarde. He retreated and saluted without a word.

'Yes, point-blank,' said Ariane. 'Must have been between about three and four-thirty, at a guess. The shots were fired during a fight, they must have been struggling. He didn't have time to resist much. And I think he was scared stiff, you can see it in his expression. On the other hand,' she said, sitting down next to Adamsberg, 'the murderer took her time. She's even signed it.'

'You mean she injected him like the others?'

'Yes, on the left arm – it's almost invisible. We can check it later, but I think it's like for Diala and La Paille: a make-believe injection, with nothing going in at all.'

'It's her trade mark,' said Danglard.

'Can you make a guess at the killer's height?'

'I need to check the direction of the bullets. But at first sight, not anyone very tall. And the weapon was small-calibre. One of those deadly little handguns.'

Mordent and Lamarre returned from the bedroom.

'That sounds right, *commissaire*,' said Mordent. 'In the struggle, they trod on each other's feet. Grimal was barefoot, so he left no marks, but she did. Just a little, but there's a slight trace of blue.'

'Are you sure, Mordent?'

'You have to look for it, but when you see it it's obvious. Come and have a look – take the magnifying glass. It's not so easy on this old floor with its tiles.'

With the extra light provided by the technician, and using the magnifier, Adamsberg looked at a streak of blue on the terracotta tiling, about five or six centimetres long. There was a clearer trace on the join, and a further patch of polish on the next tile. Frowning, he came back into the dining room without speaking, opened the cupboards one by one, then went into the kitchen and found some shoe polish and an old rag on a shelf.

'Estalère,' he said, 'take this. Go back to the wall where she came in. Put polish all over the soles of your shoes, then come back here.'

'But this polish is brown.'

'Never mind, just go and do it.'

Five minutes later, Estalère was back at the kitchen door.

'Stop, *brigadier*. Take your shoes off and give them to me.'

Adamsberg examined the soles by the light of the window, then put his hand into one of them and pressed it to the floor, turning it on the spot. He looked at the spot with the magnifying glass and then did the same with the other shoe.

'Nothing,' he said. 'The wet grass has washed it all off. There are a few traces of polish on the sole, but not enough to have left it on the floor. You can put your shoes back on, Estalère.'

He came back to sit in the other room with his three colleagues and Ariane. His fingers smoothed the oilcloth on the table, as if trying to find something invisible.

'No,' he said. 'It's too much.'

'Too much polish?' asked Ariane. 'Is that what you mean?'

'Yes, too much, in fact it's impossible. But it *is* polish all the same. Only not from the soles of the shoes.'

'Do you think she's just signing it?' asked Mordent. 'Like with the syringe? Does she spread the shoe polish around, so as to leave her mark?'

'Something like that, to pull us along in her wake. To guide us.'

'Along the wrong track, you mean?' asked the doctor, blinking her eyes.

'Precisely, Ariane. Like wreckers who used to imitate lighthouses, to lure ships on to the rocks. We've got a false lighthouse here.'

'A lighthouse that's sending us to the nurse?' said Ariane.

'Yes, that must be what Retancourt meant. "Tell him not to give a damn." She must have meant about the blue shoes. That they don't matter.'

'How is she?' asked Ariane.

'She's recovering quite quickly. Enough to tell us that it didn't matter, anyway.'

'You mean the shoes and all the rest of it?' asked Ariane.

'Yes. The injections, the scalpel, the shoe polish. It's a plausible trail, but it's false. A real decoy. For weeks now, this killer's been playing games with us. And all of us, myself included, have been stupidly chasing after this lantern that someone is waving in the woods ahead of us.'

Ariane folded her arms and dropped her chin. She hadn't had time to put on her full make-up, and Adamsberg found her more beautiful than ever.

'It's all my fault,' she said. 'It was me that said it could be a case of dissociation.'

'Yes, but I was the one who identified the nurse as our suspect.'

'Yes, but I went along with it,' Ariane insisted. 'I told you a lot of back-up stuff about psychological profiling.'

'Well, this killer certainly knows all about female psychology. Everything was set up so we would make this mistake, Ariane. And if the murderer wanted us to think it was a woman, then it must be a man. A man who took advantage of Claire Langevin's escape to push us towards her. He knew I'd react to the hypothesis that it was the nurse. But it isn't her. And that's why these murders don't correspond to her psychology, the angel of death. You said so yourself, Ariane, that night after Montrouge. There wasn't a second lava-flow out of the volcano. It must be a quite different volcano.'

'Well, if so, it's someone very clever,' sighed the doctor. 'The wounds on Diala and La Paille really do indicate a killer who isn't tall. But I suppose it would always be possible to fake that. A man of average height could always calculate how to angle the knife to make it look that way. Of course, he'd really have to know what he was doing.'

'The syringe in the hangar was already over the top,' said Adamsberg. 'I should have reacted sooner.'

'A man,' said Danglard, sounding discouraged. 'We'll have to start all over. From the beginning.'

'No, Danglard, that won't be necessary.'

Adamsberg saw a rapid and focused look cross his deputy's face, then an expression of resigned sadness. Adamsberg gave him a slight nod. Danglard knew. As he did himself.

LVIII

WITHOUT STARTING THE CAR, ADAMSBERG SAT ALONGSIDE DANGLARD AS THEY both watched the wipers try to deal with the torrential rain battering the windscreen. Adamsberg liked the regular sound they made as they groaned against the deluge.

'I think we're thinking the same thing, *capitaine*,' said Adamsberg.

'*Commandant*,' corrected Danglard gloomily.

'To try and send us on the trail of the nurse, the killer must have known a lot about me. He had to know I'd arrested her, and that I'd be upset to learn she was out of jail. And he also had to be able to follow the investigation, step by step. To know that we were looking for navy-blue shoes and traces of polish from the soles. He also had to be well-informed about Retancourt's movements. He must have wanted to destroy me. He provided everything – the syringe, the shoes, the scalpel, the shoe polish. An extraordinary manipulation of the inquiry, Danglard, carried out by someone of remarkable intelligence and efficiency.'

'By a man in our squad.'

'Yes,' said Adamsberg sadly, leaning back in his seat. 'By one of our own, a black ibex on the mountain.'

'What's it got to do with an ibex?'

'Oh, nothing.'

'I don't want to believe this.'

'We didn't want to believe there was a bone in a pig's snout, but there is one. Like there's a bone in the squad, Danglard. Stuck in its throat.'

The rain slackened off and Adamsberg slowed the pace of the windscreen wipers.

'I did tell you he was lying,' Danglard went on. 'Nobody could have remembered that text from the *De reliquis* unless they already knew it. He must have known the recipe for the potion by heart.'

'But in that case, why did he tell us it?'

'Provocation. He thinks he's invincible.'

'The child on the ground,' murmured Adamsberg. 'The lost vineyard, poverty, years of humiliation. I used to see him around, Danglard. He used to pull a beret right down to his nose to cover up the ginger streaks. He used to limp after the accident with the horse, he would blush to meet people, and he skulked along by the walls, with other boys calling him names.'

'He can still get to you, then.'

'Yes.'

'But it's the child that touches you. And the adult has grown up twisted. He's trying to turn the tables on you, because you were the little gang-leader of the village, responsible for his tragic lot, as he would put it in his verses. He's making the wheel of fortune spin round. It's your turn to fall, while he's moving up the ranks. He's turning into what he spouts about all day long, a Racinian hero, caught in a torrent of hate and ambition, plotting the deaths of other people and the day of his own apotheosis. From the start, you knew he'd come here to get his revenge for the fight between the two valleys.'

'Yes.'

'He's put his plan into action, one thing after another, driving you in the wrong direction, sending the investigation off track. He's killed seven times now: Fernand, Big Georges, Elisabeth, Pascaline, Diala, La Paille, Grimal. He almost killed Retancourt. And he's going to kill the third virgin.'

'No, Francine's safe enough.'

'So you think. But this man's tough. He'll kill Francine, then he'll get you, once you've been disgraced. He hates you.'

Adamsberg lowered the window and stretched his arm out of the car palm up, as if to catch the rain.

'You're unhappy about it,' said Danglard.

'Yes, I am rather.'

'But you know we're right.'

'When Robert called me about the second stag, I was tired and couldn't really be bothered. It was Veyrenc who offered to drive me up there. And in the cemetery at Opportune it was Veyrenc who pointed out the short grass on Pascaline's grave. He encouraged me to open it, just as he'd encouraged me to carry on in Montrouge. And he intervened with Brézillon, so that we could continue our investigation. So that he could keep track of it, while I was getting deeper and deeper in the shit.'

'And,' Danglard pointed out gently, 'he took Camille from you. That's high-level vengeance, like in a play by Racine.'

'How did you know about that, Danglard?' said Adamsberg, clenching his fist in the rain.

'When I had to take over the listening device in Froissy's cupboard, I had to play a bit of the previous tape to get the soundtrack tuned. I did warn you about him. Intelligent, strong and dangerous.'

'All the same, I liked him.'

'Is that why we're sitting here in Clancy in this car? Instead of getting back to Paris?'

'No, *capitaine*. For one thing, it's because we've got no absolute proof of all this. An examining magistrate would release him after twenty-four hours. Veyrenc could tell him about the war between the valleys and say that I was bent on destroying him for private reasons. So that no one would ever know who was the fifth boy under the tree.'

'Yes, I suppose so,' agreed Danglard. 'He's got that over you.'

'Secondly, I still don't understand what Retancourt was trying to tell me.'

'Well, I can't fathom how the Snowball was able to do those thirty-eight kilometres,' remarked Danglard, looking thoughtful about this new Unsolved Question.

'That was an example of the miracles of love, Danglard. And maybe the cat had also picked up some tips from Violette. How to save your strength, bit by bit, to commit it to a single mission, overcoming any obstacle in your path.'

'She was partnered with Veyrenc at work. That's why she must have guessed about that damned thing we couldn't see. He knew she was going to see Roman. He must have waited for her on the way out. And she was rather taken by him, so she would have followed him. The only time in her life when Violette's instincts let her down.'

'Love and its disasters, Danglard.'

'Even Violette can be tricked. By a smile or the sound of a voice.'

'I want to know what she was trying to tell me, Danglard,' Adamsberg insisted, pulling his now soaking-wet arm back into the car. 'In your view, *capitaine*, what would be the first thing she would do, once she was able to articulate at all?'

'She'd try to talk to you.'

'To tell me what?'

'The truth. And that's what she did. She talked about the shoes. She said they didn't matter. So she was telling us it wasn't the nurse.'

'But that wasn't the *first* thing she said. It was the second.'

'Before that she didn't say anything that made sense, just quoted a line or two from Corneille.'

'Who speaks those lines in Corneille?'

'Camille. It's in his play *Horace*.'

'Ah, you see, Danglard, that proves it. Retancourt wasn't just reciting stuff from school. She was trying to send me a message through another Camille. But I don't know what it means.'

'Because it wasn't clear. Retancourt was still only semi-conscious. You can't treat what she said to an interpretation, like you can for dreams.'

Danglard thought for a few moments.

'The play goes like this,' he said. 'Camille is caught up in a fight between two sets of brothers, who are enemies. The Horatii on one hand and the Curiatii on the other. She's in love with one of them, but he wants to kill a man from the other side, who's her brother. Well, around your Camille, we have the same thing, sort of. Two cousins who are enemies, you and Veyrenc. But Veyrenc stands for Racine. And who was Racine's big enemy and rival? Corneille.'

'Really?' asked Adamsberg.

'Really. Because Racine's terrific success as a playwright pushed poor old Corneille out of the limelight. They hated each other. Retancourt has chosen Corneille, and is pointing at his enemy: Racine. It must mean Veyrenc. That's why she spoke in verse, so that you would immediately think of Veyrenc.'

'Well, that's just what I did. I wondered if she was dreaming about him, or if he'd infected her with his verse-speaking.'

Adamsberg put the window back up and fastened his seat belt. 'Let me have a word with him alone first,' he said, starting the engine.

LIX

VEYRENC WAS CONVALESCENT NOW. SITTING ON HIS BED, WEARING SHORTS, and leaning back on two pillows, with one leg bent and the other stretched out, he watched as Adamsberg, arms folded, paced up and down at the foot of the bed.

'Does it hurt to stand on it?' Adamsberg asked.

'It stings a bit, I can feel it, but it's not too bad.'

'Are you OK to walk, drive a car?'

'Yes, I think so.'

'Good.'

> 'Now speak to me, my lord: I see from your pale face
> That a worry torments you in some secret place.'

'Correct, Veyrenc. This killer who murdered Elisabeth, Pascaline, Diala, La Paille, the gendarme Grimal, this person who opened graves and nearly killed Retancourt, who cut up three stags and a cat and stole the relics, it's not a woman at all. It's a man.'

'Is that just a hunch? Or have you got some new elements?'

'What do you mean by "elements"?'

'Well, evidence.'

'No. But I know this man knew enough about the angel of death to send us off on a wild-goose chase after her, stopping us looking elsewhere, while he was calmly going about his business.'

Veyrenc screwed up his eyes and reached for his cigarettes.

'The investigation was dragging on,' said Adamsberg, 'and these women had been killed, and I was getting nowhere. A pretty good form of revenge for the killer. Can I have one?' he added, pointing to the cigarette packet.

Veyrenc passed him the packet and lit both cigarettes. Adamsberg watched his hands. No trembling or sign of emotion.

'And this man,' said Adamsberg, 'is someone in our squad.'

Veyrenc ran his fingers through his variegated hair and exhaled rapidly, a stunned expression on his face.

'But I don't have a single tangible element of proof. My hands are tied. What would you do, Veyrenc?'

The *lieutenant* flicked some ash into his hand, and Adamsberg passed him an ashtray.

> '*When we searched far afield, sending forth all our men*
> *Into distant domains in search of this our prey,*
> *He was here, in our midst, and our quest went astray.*'

'Yes. Some victory, eh? One intelligent killer manipulating twenty-seven idiots.'

'You surely can't be thinking of Noël? I don't really know him, but I can't see it. He's aggressive but not a killer.'

Adamsberg shook his head.

'Well, who then?'

'I was thinking about what Retancourt said when she was semiconscious.'

'Ah,' said Veyrenc, with a smile. 'When she quoted Corneille, those lines from *Horace*.'

'How did you know?'

365

'Because I've been asking for news of her. Lavoisier told me about it.'

'You're very considerate, for a newcomer.'

'Retancourt's my partner at work.'

'I think she tried hard to point the finger at the killer, but she hadn't the strength to do it.'

> *'Did you doubt it, my lord?*
> *Since you waited so long, to give her words their weight*
> *Neglecting their meaning, until it was too late?'*

'So have *you* discovered it, Veyrenc? What she meant?'

'No, I haven't' said Veyrenc, looking away to tap off his ash. 'So what are you going to do, *commissaire*?'

'Something very obvious. I'm going to lie in wait for the killer. Things are moving faster. He knows that Retancourt is bound to talk soon. He doesn't have much time, since she's recovering quite well – about a week, maybe. He absolutely has to finish the potion, before he's intercepted. So we'll expose Francine, without any obvious protection.'

'Pretty classic,' said Veyrenc.

'A race against time isn't original, *lieutenant*. Two guys run neck and neck around a track and the fastest one wins. That's all. And yet thousands of people have been racing each other for thousands of years. Well, it's just the same with this. The killer's running, so I'll run too. Not a matter of doing anything tricksy, just trying to get there before he does.'

'But the killer's sure to suspect that you're going to try and trap him.'

'Of course. But he'll keep running, because he doesn't have any choice either. He's not trying to be original at this point, just trying to succeed. And the more elementary the trap, the less the murderer will suspect anything.'

'Why?'

'Because, like you, he'll think I'm plotting something more intelligent.'

'Ye-es,' Veyrenc admitted. 'So if you choose the elementary method, you put Francine back in her house? Discreetly protected this time?'

'No, no. No one in their right mind would think we could get Francine to set foot in that farmhouse again.'

'So where'll you put her? In a hotel in Evreux? And let the information leak out?'

'Not quite. I've chosen a place that I think is reasonably safe and secret but which the murderer might be able to guess, if he has his wits about him. Which he generally has.'

Veyrenc thought for a few moments.

'So it's got to be a place you know quite well,' he said, thinking aloud. 'A place that won't frighten Francine too much, but that you can protect without your policemen being obvious.'

'For instance?'

'For instance, the inn in Haroncourt.'

'See, it was quite easy. In Haroncourt, where the whole thing started, but under the protection of Robert and Oswald. They'll be a lot less obvious than a bunch of cops. Cops are always easy to spot.'

Veyrenc looked doubtful.

'Even a cop who's come down out of the mountains and hasn't bothered to do up all his shirt buttons or to get rid of the mist in his eyes?'

'Yes, even me, Veyrenc. And do you know why? Why do you think an ordinary customer sitting in a café drinking his beer doesn't look like a policeman sitting at a table and drinking his beer? Because the policeman's on duty and the other isn't. Because a man on his own thinks, daydreams, and wonders about things. But the cop is watching the whole time. The ordinary guy's eyes are looking in at himself, but the cop's eyes are always flicking round his surroundings. He might as well put up a sign. So we won't put an officer in the bar at the hotel.'

'I see. Not bad,' said Veyrenc, stubbing out his cigarette.

'Well, anyway, I hope so,' said Adamsberg, getting up.

'What did you really come here for, *commissaire*?'

'To ask you whether any more details had come back to you, now you've remembered where it really happened, the attack: in the High Meadow.'

'Just one.'

'And that is?'

'That fifth boy, the one under the tree, standing looking at the others getting to work on me.'

'Yes.'

'He had his hands behind his back.'

'So?'

'So I'm wondering what he was holding in his hands, or hiding. A weapon, perhaps?'

'You're getting warm. Keep on thinking, *lieutenant*.'

Veyrenc watched as the *commissaire* picked up his jacket, of which one sleeve was inexplicably soaking wet, and went out, slamming the door. He closed his eyes and smiled.

> *You lie to me, my lord, but your tricks help me know*
> *To what strange final end you wish my steps to go.*

LX

CROUCHING IN A DARK CORNER OF THE LINEN STORE, THE SHADE WAS waiting for the evening routines to be over. The night shift would soon be there, and the nurses were going round the rooms, emptying bedpans, putting out lights, and getting ready to return to their lodgings. Getting into Saint-Vincent-de-Paul Hospital had been even easier than expected. No distrust, no questions, not even from the *lieutenant* on duty on the first floor, who tended to drop off to sleep every now and then but who had saluted pleasantly and reported that all was well. The hypersomniac idiot, that was a piece of luck. He had gratefully accepted a cup of machine coffee, containing two sleeping pills, which meant he'd be out for the count till tomorrow morning. When people don't suspect you, it's all quite simple. Soon now, the incredible hulk would be unable to say anything: it was about time she was shut up for good. Retancourt's unpredictable survival capacity had been an unexpected setback. And those damned lines from Corneille that she had stammered out. Luckily none of the imbeciles in the squad had understood, not even their resident intellectual, Danglard, never mind an airhead like Adamsberg. Retancourt, though, was dangerous, as smart as she was strong. Still, tonight there would be a double dose of Novaxon, and in her present condition she'd croak at the first intake of breath.

The Shade smiled, thinking of Adamsberg, who right now would be setting up his gimcrack little trap in the inn at Haroncourt. A pathetic little trap, which would close on him, making him look ridiculous and humiliated. In the distress that would be caused by the incredible hulk's death, the Shade would have no trouble getting to the goddamn third virgin, who had escaped by a hair's breadth last time. What a pathetic halfwit – and they were protecting her as if she were a precious vase. That had been the Shade's only mistake. Who would have thought that anyone would guess there was a bone like a cross in the heart of a stag? Or that such an ignorant and vague mind as Adamsberg's would find the link between the stags and the virgins, between Pascaline's cat and the *De reliquis*. But by some monumental bad luck, that's what he had done, and he'd identified the third virgin quicker than might have been expected. It was also bad luck that Danglard was well-read enough to want to see the book at the priest's house and had recognised the 1663 edition. Typical that fate should throw some cops like this in the way.

But, after all, these obstacles weren't serious: Francine's death was only a matter of weeks away and there was still plenty of time. By the autumn the mixture would be ready and both time and the enemy would be powerless.

The ancillary staff were leaving the kitchens on the first floor, the nurses were going round saying their usual goodnights to each patient (close your eyes now, try to get a good night's rest). The night lights in the corridor had been lit. Best to wait a good hour, so that the insomniacs had time to drop off. But by eleven o'clock the hulk would be asleep for good.

LXI

ADAMSBERG CONSIDERED THAT HE HAD LAID HIS TRAP WITH CHILDLIKE
simplicity and he was quite pleased with it. It was a classic mousetrap,
of course, but it ought to be secure, complete with the slight twist he
was banking on. Sitting behind the door of the bedroom, he was waiting
for the second consecutive night. Three metres to his left sat Adrien
Danglard, an excellent exponent of the speedy assault, unlikely though
that might seem. In action, his lethargic body snapped into movement
like a rubber band. Danglard was wearing a particularly elegant suit this
evening. His bulletproof vest affected its lines somewhat, but Adamsberg
had insisted on his wearing it. To his right was Estalère, whose qualities included seeing uncommonly well in the dark, like the Snowball.

'It won't work,' said Danglard, whose pessimism always got the better
of him at night.

'Yes, it will,' said Adamsberg for the fourth time.

'It's ridiculous. The Haroncourt inn. He's sure to smell a rat.'

'No. Hush, Danglard. Estalère, take care – I can hear you breathing.'

'Sorry,' said Estalere. 'It's hay fever.'

'Well, blow your nose once for all, then keep quiet.'

Adamsberg rose silently one last time and twitched the curtain another
few centimetres along. He had to have the dark absolutely under control.
The killer would be completely silent, as the cemetery keeper at

Montrouge had described, and as Gratien and Francine had confirmed. There would be no heavy footsteps to give warning of approach. They would have to be able to see the killer before the killer saw them. The darkness in the corners where they were posted would have to be denser than the light round the door. He sat back down and gripped the light switch. His job was to switch it on the moment the killer got inside the door. Then Estalère would block the exit while Danglard pulled his gun. Perfect. He looked at the bed where the woman he was protecting was peacefully asleep.

As Francine slept under her guard in the inn at Haroncourt, the Shade checked the time in Saint-Vincent-de-Paul, a hundred and thirty-six kilometres away. At ten fifty-five, the Shade silently opened the door of the linen store and slipped along the corridor, syringe in hand, checking the numbers of the rooms. Retancourt's room, number 227, had its door open, being guarded by the sleeping Mercadet. As the Shade tiptoed round him, he did not stir. In the middle of the room the large body of the *lieutenant* was visible under the sheets, her arm hanging down vulnerably at the side of the bed.

LXII

ADAMSBERG WAS THE FIRST TO SEE THE SHADE COME INTO HIS FIELD OF vision. His heart did not miss a beat. He pressed the switch with his thumb, Estalère barred the doorway, Danglard pushed the gun into the back of the figure, which did not cry out or utter a word as Estalère rapidly put the handcuffs on it. Adamsberg went over to the bed and stroked Retancourt's hair.

'OK, let's go,' he said.

Danglard and Estalère dragged their prisoner out of the room and Adamsberg took care to switch the light off on the way out. Two squad cars were waiting outside the hospital.

'Wait for me back at headquarters,' said Adamsberg. 'I won't be long.'

At midnight he was knocking at the door of Dr Roman. Five minutes later the doctor opened the door, looking pale and dishevelled.

'You're mad,' said Roman. 'What are you getting me up for?'

The doctor could hardly stand and Adamsberg pulled him along in his slippers into the kitchen, where he sat him down in the same place as he had on the evening of their conversation about the 'quick of virgins'.

'Do you remember what you asked me for?'

'I didn't ask you for anything,' said Roman, looking dazed.

'You asked me to find you an old recipe against the vapours. And I promised I would.'

Roman blinked and rested his heavy head on his hand.

'So what did you find me? Eye of newt and toe of frog? Gall of pig? Or some recipe that tells you to cut up a chicken and lay it on my head? I know those old wives' tales.'

'And what do you think of them?'

'Are you waking me up in the middle of the night for rubbish like that?' said Roman, reaching out sleepily for his stimulant pills.

'Listen to me,' said Adamsberg, holding back his arm.

'All right, but put some cold water on my head.'

Adamsberg once more rubbed the doctor's head with the wet and still grubby dishcloth. Then he looked in the drawers for a plastic bin bag, which he opened and put down between them.

'They're here, your vapours,' he said, putting his hand on the table.

'In the bin bag?'

'You're not with it, Roman.'

'No.'

'They're here,' said Adamsberg, showing him the packet of red and yellow stimulants, which he dropped into the bag.

'Hey, give me back my stuff.'

'No.'

Adamsberg got up and opened all the medicine packs he could see, looking for capsules.

'What's this one?' he asked when he found some.

'It's Gavelon.'

'Yes, I can see that, but what's it for?'

'It's for stomach relief. I've always taken it.'

Adamsberg made one pile with the boxes of Gavelon and another with the stimulants, Energyl, and swept the lot into the bin bag. 'Have you taken many of these?'

'As many as I could. Give me back my pills.'

'Your pills, Roman, are what were giving you the vapours. It was in the capsules.'

'I know what Gavelon is, don't be silly.'

'You don't know what's inside these capsules.'

'Gavelon, of course, *mon vieux*.'

'No, some ghastly stuff, eye of newt and toe of frog, ground up with pig's gall and chicken's blood. We'll get it analysed.'

'You're the one who's not with it now, Adamsberg.'

'Listen carefully, and concentrate as hard as you can,' said Adamsberg, taking the doctor's wrist. 'You've got plenty of friends, haven't you, Roman? Plenty of excellent women friends too, like Retancourt, who run errands for you and help you out, don't they? Like going and fetching your prescriptions from the pharmacy because you can't go yourself.'

'Yes.'

'Someone comes to see you every week and brings you your pills?'

'Yes.'

Adamsberg closed the bin bag and put it down beside him.

'Are you taking that lot away?' asked Roman.

'Yes. And now you've got to drink as much fluid as you can and piss it out. In a week's time, you should almost be yourself. Don't worry about your supplies of Gavelon and Energyl, I'll get you some. The genuine article. Because what you've been taking is really eye-of-newt stuff. Or your vapours, if you want to put it like that.'

'You don't know what you're saying, Adamsberg. You don't know who has been bringing me them.'

'Oh yes, I do. One of your contacts for whom you have great esteem.'

'How do you know?'

'Because your contact is sitting in my office this minute, with handcuffs on. Because she's killed eight people.'

'You can't be serious, Adamsberg,' said Roman after a shocked silence. 'Are we talking about the same person?'

'A very sharp mind, with a head screwed on to her shoulders. And one of the most dangerous killers I've come across. Ariane Lagarde, the most famous pathologist in France.'

'You must be out of your mind.'

'No, *she* is. She's a dissociator, Roman.'

Adamsberg helped the doctor up and took him to his bed.

'Get the dishcloth,' said Roman. 'You never know.'

'OK.'

Roman sat down on the bed, looking both tired and stunned, gradually remembering all the times Ariane had been to visit him.

'But we've known each other for ever,' he said. 'I can't believe you, *mon vieux* – she would never try to kill me.'

'No, she wasn't trying to *kill* you. She just needed you out of circulation, so that she could take your place for as long as was necessary to carry out her plans.'

'Plans for what?'

'Her plans to examine her own victims, so that we wouldn't know what she was after. She told us it was a female killer about one metre sixty-two tall, so I'd go chasing off after that district nurse. She didn't mention that Elisabeth and Pascaline had had their hair scalped at the root. You didn't tell me the whole truth, Roman.'

'No, all right, I didn't.'

'You realised that Ariane had made a serious professional mistake if she hadn't noticed that the hair had been shaved. But if you told me that, you'd get your friend into trouble. On the other hand, if you said nothing you'd be hampering the investigation. You wanted to be sure before acting, so you asked Retancourt for enlargements of the photographs of Elisabeth.'

'Yes.'

'Retancourt wondered why, and she started looking at the enlargements differently. She saw the marks on the right side of the skull, but she didn't know what they meant. It bothered her and she came back to ask you. What was it you were looking for? What had you seen? What you'd seen was that a small section of the skull had actually been scalped, but you hadn't said so. You decided to help us as much as you could, without betraying Ariane. So you gave us the information, but you altered it a bit. You told us the hair had been cut, but not that it had been *shaved*. After all, what difference could that possibly make to our investigation? It was hair, just the same. And that way you got Ariane off the hook. By saying that you were the only person who could spot it. Your story about hair being recently cut and having different-shaped ends – that was rubbish, wasn't it?'

'Yes.'

'You couldn't have told from an ordinary photograph a detail like the cut ends. Was he really a barber, your father?'

'No, he was a doctor. But whether the hair was cut or shaved, I couldn't see that it made any difference. I didn't want to get Ariane into trouble, five years off retirement. I thought she'd simply made a mistake.'

'But Retancourt wondered how Ariane Lagarde, supposedly the best forensic pathologist in the country, could have missed this finding. It seemed to her impossible that Ariane should miss it if *you* were able to guess at it just from an ordinary photo. She concluded that Ariane had not seen fit to tell us about it. But why? So, after she left you, she went round to the morgue to see Ariane and ask questions. Ariane realised the danger. It was in one of the morgue's vans that she transported Retancourt to the hangar.'

'Put some more cold water on my head.'

Adamsberg wrung out the cloth and once more gave Roman's head a good rub.

'There's something that doesn't fit,' said Roman from under the cloth.

'What?' asked Adamsberg, stopping what he was doing.

'I felt the first vapours long before Ariane took this job in Paris. She was still in Lille. So how come?'

'She must have travelled to Paris, got inside your flat and replaced all your regular pills with whatever she used.'

'The Gavelon, for instance.'

'Yes, because she could inject capsules with some concoction of her own. She's always been fond of mixing peculiar drinks, do you remember that? Then all she had to do was wait in Lille until you were too unwell to work.'

'Did she tell you that? That she'd put me out of action?'

'She hasn't said a word yet.'

'How can you be so sure, then?'

'Because it was the first thing Retancourt said to me:

"To see the last Roman as he draws his last breath,
Myself to die happy, as the cause of this death."

It wasn't because of Camille or Corneille that she chose these lines, but because of *you*. Retancourt was thinking about you, with your vapours and your problem having enough breath to cross the room. *Roman*, that's you, made short of breath by a woman.'

'Why did Retancourt talk in verse?'

'Because of her partner at the office, the New Recruit, Veyrenc. His way of talking is infectious and she was very drawn to him. And because she was only half conscious with all the drugs, she regressed to being a schoolgirl, and the name "Roman" must have brought the line swimming to the surface. Lavoisier says that one of his patients spent three months repeating his times tables.'

'I don't see what Lavoisier has to do with it. He was a chemist who was guillotined in 1793. More cold water.'

'I'm talking about Lavoisier the doctor, who accompanied us to Dourdan,' said Adamsberg, giving Roman's head another rub.

'He's called Lavoisier, like the chemist?' asked Roman indistinctly, from under the cloth.

'Yes, as he never stops telling us. Once we realised that Retancourt was trying to say something about *you*, and not some Ancient Roman, and that a woman had caused your problems, the rest was easy. Ariane had put you out of action in order to take your place. I didn't ask for her, Brézillon didn't ask for her. She applied for it herself. Why? For prestige? But she already had that.'

'So that she could run the investigation herself,' said Roman, emerging from the cloth with his hair standing on end.

'And, by the same token, she could engineer my fall from grace. I once humiliated her professionally, long ago. She never forgets and never forgives.'

'Are you going to question her now?'

'Yes.'

'Take me with you.'

Roman had been too weak to go out for months now. Adamsberg wondered whether he could even manage the three flights of stairs to get down to the car.

'Take me with you,' Roman insisted. 'She was my friend. I'll have to see it to believe it.'

'Well, all right,' said Adamsberg, lifting him up under the arms. 'Hold on to me. If you go to sleep at the office, there are some cushions upstairs, for the benefit of Mercadet.'

'Does Mercadet eat pills full of unspeakable things, then?'

LXIII

ARIANE'S BEHAVIOUR WAS THE MOST EXTRAORDINARY THAT ADAMSBERG HAD ever seen in an arrested suspect. She was sitting on the other side of his desk, and should have been facing him. But she had turned her chair through ninety degrees and was looking at the wall, as if it was the most natural thing in the world. So Adamsberg had gone round to the wall to face her, whereupon she had immediately turned her chair through a right angle again, to face the door. This was neither fear, nor provocation, nor ill will on her part. But just as one magnet repulses another, so the *commissaire*'s approach made her swivel round. It was just like a toy one of his sisters had had, a little dancer who could be made to turn around when you put it close to a mirror. It was only later that he had understood that two contrary magnets were hidden, one inside the dancer's pink tights and one behind the mirror. So Ariane was the dancer and he was the mirror. A reflective surface that she was instinctively avoiding, so as not to see Omega in Adamsberg's eyes. As a result, he was obliged to keep moving round the room, while Ariane, oblivious of his movements, spoke into empty space.

It was equally clear that she did not understand what she was being accused of. But without asking questions or rebelling, she sat, docile and almost consenting, as if another part of her knew perfectly well what she was doing and accepted this for the moment, a mere twist of fate which she could handle. Adamsberg had had time to skim some of the chapters in her book and recognised in this conflicted yet passive attitude the disconcerting symptoms of the dissociated criminal. A split in the individual, which Ariane knew so well, having spent years exploring it with fascination, without realising that her own case had been the motive behind her research. Faced with an interrogation by the police, Ariane understood nothing, and Omega was prudently lying low, waiting for conciliation and a way out.

Adamsberg imagined that Ariane must be a hostage to her incalculable pride: this woman, who had never forgiven even the offence of the twelve rats, had been unable to bear the humiliation caused by the paramedic who had tempted her husband away so publicly. That or something else. One day the volcano had erupted, setting free a torrent of rage and punishments in a sequence of unbridled attacks. Ariane the pathologist remained ignorant of these murderous outbreaks. The paramedic had died a year later, in a climbing accident, but the husband had not returned to his wife. He had found a new partner, who in turn died on a railway line. Murder after murder: Ariane was already on her way to her ultimate aim, acquiring powers superior to those of all others of her sex. An eternal dominion which would preserve her from the threatening encirclement of her fellow women. At the centre of this journey lay an implacable hatred of other people which no one would understand – unless Omega revealed it one day.

But Ariane had had to bide her time for ten years, since the recipe in the *De sanctis reliquis* was clear: 'Five times cometh the age of youth, till the day thou must invert it, pass and pass again.'

On this point, Adamsberg and his colleagues had made a serious miscalculation, by choosing to take fifteen as the age to be multiplied five times. Having identified the district nurse as their suspect, they had all interpreted the text to correspond to the seventy-five years of her age. But at the time the *De reliquis* was being copied, fifteen was seen as adulthood, when a girl could already be a mother and a boy ride on horseback. *Twelve* was when young people left behind the age of their youth. So the time to reverse the approach of death and escape its grasp came at the age of sixty. Ariane had been on the eve of her sixtieth birthday when she had embarked upon the series of crimes she had long been planning.

Adamsberg had started the tape officially recording the interrogation of Ariane Lagarde on 6 May at one o'clock in the morning: she was being held on suspicion of premeditated homicide and attempted homicide, in the presence of officers Danglard, Mordent, Veyrenc, Estalère and Dr Roman.

'What's all this about, Jean-Baptiste?' asked Ariane amiably, speaking to the wall.

'I'm reading you the charge in its first draft,' Adamsberg explained gently.

She knew everything and knew nothing, and her gaze, if one managed to catch it, was difficult to bear, both pleasant and arrogant, understanding and vindictive, as Alpha and Omega battled it out. An unconscious gaze, which disconcerted her questioners, referring them to their own demons and the intolerable idea that perhaps behind their own walls there lurked monsters of which they were unaware, ready to burst open the swelling crater of an unsuspected volcano inside them. As Adamsberg read out the long charge sheet of her crimes, he watched for any quiver, any sign that one of them might elicit a response from Ariane's imperial expression. But Omega was far too cunning to reveal herself. Hidden behind her impenetrable veil, she waited, smiling in the shadows. Only the rather stiff and mechanical smile hinted at her secret existence.

'. . . You are charged with the murders of Jeannine Panier, aged twenty-three, and Christiane Béladan, aged twenty-four, both mistresses of Charles André Lagarde, your husband; with encouraging and organising the escape of Claire Langevin, aged seventy-five, incarcerated at Freiburg Prison in Germany; with the murder of Otto Karlstein, aged fifty-six, warder at the same prison; with the murders of Elisabeth Châtel, aged thirty-six, secretary; of Pascaline Villemot, aged thirty-eight, shop assistant; of Diala Toundé, aged twenty-four, unemployed; of Didier Paillot, aged twenty-two, unemployed; you are further charged with the attempted murder of Violette Retancourt, aged thirty-five, police officer; with the murder of Gilles Grimal, aged forty-two, gendarme; with the attempted murder of Francine Bidault, aged thirty-five, pharmacy assistant; with the attempted murder for a second time of Violette Retancourt, in front of witnesses; with the desecration of the graves of Elisabeth Châtel and Pascaline Villemot.'

Adamsberg, dripping with sweat, put down the sheet of paper. Eight murders, three attempted murders, two exhumations.

'Not to mention the mutilation of Narcissus, cat, aged eleven,' he murmured, 'or the evisceration of the Red Giant, stag, ten points, and two anonymous members of the same species. Have you heard what I'm saying, Ariane?'

'I wonder what you are doing, that's all.'

'You've always disliked me, haven't you? You've never forgiven me for invalidating your results in the Hubert Sandrin case in Le Havre.'

'Gracious. I don't know what's given you that idea.'

'When you hatched your plan, you decided to target my squad. To succeed while making me fail would be exactly what you wanted.'

'I was assigned to your squad.'

'Because there was a vacancy and you applied for it. You made Dr Roman ill by making him eat capsules full of pigeon shit.'

'Pigeon shit? Really?' asked Estalère in an undertone. Danglard shrugged to indicate he didn't know what that meant. Ariane took a cigarette from her handbag and Veyrenc gave her a light.

'As long as I can smoke,' she said graciously, addressing the wall, 'you can talk as much as you like. I was warned about you. You're crazy. Your mother was right: everything goes in one ear and out the other.'

'Let's leave my mother out of it, Ariane,' said Adamsberg evenly. 'Danglard, Estalère and I saw you creep into Retancourt's room at eleven tonight, with a syringe full of Novaxon. What was that for?'

Adamsberg had gone round to the wall and Ariane had immediately turned towards the desk.

'You'll have to ask Roman that,' she said. 'What he told me was that the syringe contained a powerful *antidote* to Novaxon, which would have helped her to recover. You and Lavoisier had said she wasn't to have it, because it was still an experimental drug. I was just doing a good turn for Roman. I had to, because he couldn't get to the hospital himself. I never suspected there was an affair going on between Roman and Retancourt. Or that she was drugging him, so that she would have him at her mercy. She was always round at his place, clinging on to him. I suppose he realised what she was doing, and seized the chance to get rid of her. In the state she's in, her death would just have looked like a relapse.'

'In the name of God, Ariane,' cried Roman, trying to get up.

'Let it go, *mon vieux*,' said Adamsberg, returning to his seat, which had the effect of making Ariane pivot round again.

Adamsberg opened his notebook, leaned back and scribbled for a few moments. Ariane was very strong. In front of a magistrate, her version might look convincing. Who would doubt the word of the famous pathologist Ariane Lagarde, as opposed to that of the humble Dr Roman who was losing his wits?

'You knew the nurse,' Adamsberg began again. 'You had often interrogated her for your research. You knew who had arrested her. It didn't take much to send me on her track. Of course, she had to be out of prison first. So you killed the guard and got her out of jail dressed as a doctor. Then you installed yourself at the heart of the investigation, with a plausible scapegoat all ready to take the blame. All you had to do then was make up the potion, your most ambitious cocktail.'

'You've never liked my cocktails, have you?' Ariane said, indulgently.

'No, not much. Did you copy out the recipe, Ariane? Or did you know it by heart from your childhood?'

'Which one? Beer and crème de menthe? Coffee and grenadine?'

'Did you know that there's a bone in a pig's snout?'

'Yes,' said Ariane, looking surprised.

'Yes, you did know, because you left it behind in the reliquary of Saint Jerome, along with the sheep's bones. You'd always known about the reliquary, as you had about the *De reliquis*. And did you know there was a bone in the penis of a cat?'

'No, I have to confess I didn't know that.'

'And a bone shaped like a cross in the heart of a stag?'

'No, I didn't know that, either.'

Adamsberg tried another gambit and went to the door. But the pathologist just turned calmly to look at Danglard and Veyrenc, staring right through them.

'Once you found out that Retancourt was recovering, you knew you didn't have much time to stop her talking.'

'A remarkable case. Apparently Dr Lavoisier doesn't want to send her back to you. Or that's what they say in Saint-Vincent-de-Paul.'

'How do you know what they say?'

'Hospital gossip, Jean-Baptiste. It's a small world.'

Adamsberg took out his mobile. Lamarre and Maurel were searching the flat Ariane had rented in Paris.

'We've found the shoes,' said Lamarre. 'Beige espadrilles that lace up high on the ankle, and they have a big platform sole, about ten centimetres high.'

'Yes, she's wearing a pair like that tonight, but black.'

'This pair was with a long grey woollen coat, carefully folded. But there isn't any polish on the soles.'

'That's normal, Lamarre. The polish is part of the trick, to direct us towards the nurse. What about the potion?'

'Nothing so far, sir.'

'What are they doing in my flat?' asked Ariane, looking slightly shocked.

'They're searching it,' said Adamsberg, putting the mobile back in his pocket. 'They found your other pair of espadrilles.'

'Where?'

'In the fuse cupboard on the landing, safe from Alpha's eyes.'

'Why should I put any of my things out there? The fuse cupboard on the staircase doesn't belong to me.'

He still had no serious material evidence, Adamsberg thought, and with someone like Lagarde it would take more than her showing up in Saint-Vincent-de-Paul at night to make anything stick. There remained the slender hope of a confession, of a personality crash, as Ariane would say herself.

He rubbed his eyes.

'Why are you wearing those shoes? Isn't it very awkward to walk in platform soles?'

'It makes you look slim. It's a question of style. Not that you'd know anything about style, Jean-Baptiste.'

'I know what you told me yourself. The dissociator isolates herself from the ground her crimes are committed on. With soles like that, you're high up above the ground, almost as if you were on stilts, aren't you? And it makes you look taller. The guard at Montrouge and Oswald's nephew both saw you as a tall grey shape on the nights you were prospecting for the site of the graves, and Francine said the same thing. But it didn't make it easy to walk. You have to go a step at a time, so it looked as though you were slipping and tottering, as all three of them said.'

Tired of going round in circles like the mirror, Adamsberg sat down at his desk again, settling for speaking to the right shoulder of the in-accessible dancer.

'Of course,' he went on, 'it looked like a coincidence that took me to the village of Haroncourt. Was that a twist of fate? No, you were manipulating fate. You got Camille that invitation to play in the concert. She never could understand why the orchestra from Leeds asked her to join them. That way, you drew me up there too, so I was on the spot. After that, you could guide me where you wanted to, following events, and making sure you were there to prevent any accidental obstacle arising. You asked Hermance to call me in to look at the graveyard in Opportune. Then you asked her not to put me up again, in case she said too much. A woman like you can manipulate poor Hermance like putty. Because you know that area well, it's where you grew up and spent the time of your youth, "pass and pass again". The former priest at Le Mesnil, Father Raymond, was your cousin twice removed. Your adoptive parents brought you up in the manor at Ecalart, only four kilometres from the relics of Saint Jerome. And the old priest used to spend so much time with you, letting you look at his old books, even letting you touch Saint Jerome's ribs, that they whispered in the village that you were his daughter, the daughter of sin. Do you remember him?'

'He was a family friend,' she replied, smiling at the wall and at her childhood memories. 'He was a bit boring, always going on about that old stuff. Still, I was fond of him.'

'He was interested in the *De reliquis* recipe?'

'I think that was *all* he was interested in. And in me. He had got it into his head that he was going to make up the potion. He was crazy, really, with all his fads. A very special man. For a start, he had a penile bone.'

'What, the priest?' asked Estalère, scandalised.

'He got it from the curate's cat,' replied Ariane, with a near-laugh. 'And then he wanted some stag's bones.'

'Which bones?'

'From the heart.'

'You said you didn't know about that.'

'*I* didn't, but he did.'

387

'And he got hold of them? He prepared the potion with you?'

'No, no, the poor man was gored by the second stag. One of its antlers opened up his belly and he died.'

'So you wanted to start again, after him?'

'Begin what?'

'The potion, the mixture?'

'What mixture? Grenadine and beer?'

Back to square one, thought Adamsberg, drawing a figure eight on his notebook, as he had with the twig in the fire. A long silence followed.

'Anyone who says Father Raymond was my father is talking rubbish,' said Ariane unexpectedly. 'Have you ever been to Florence?'

'No, I go to the mountains if I need a break.'

'Well, if you went there you would see two figures, all in red, covered with scales and boils, with drooping breasts and testicles.'

'Maybe so.'

'There's no "maybe" about it, Jean-Baptiste. You'd see them, that's all.'

'What about them?'

'They're in a picture by Fra Angelico. You're not going to argue with a picture, are you?'

'No, OK.'

'They're my parents.'

Ariane gave a tremulous smile at the wall.

'So stop harassing me about them, please.'

'I didn't say anything about them.'

'That's where they are, so leave them there.'

Adamsberg glanced at Danglard, who conveyed by signs that yes, Fra Angelico was a painter, and there were some figures in his paintings covered with pustules, but that nothing indicated they were Ariane's parents, given that the artist had lived in the fifteenth century.

'What about Opportune?' Adamsberg began again. 'You remember the people there – you know them all like the back of your hand. It was easy for you to appear in the graveyard to the impressionable young Gratien, who went up there every Tuesday and Friday evening at midnight. And easy to guess that Gratien would tell his mother, who'd tell Oswald. Easy enough to control Hermance. You took me where you wanted, sending me like a guided robot through this series of corpses that you were creating and I was finding and handing over to you, because I trusted your autopsies to be competent. But you couldn't guess that the new priest would mention the *De reliquis*, or that Danglard would take a look at it. Even so, what would that matter? Unfortunately for you, Ariane, Veyrenc has a photographic memory and he remembered the whole recipe. He's got this odd, unforeseeable but genuine gift. And you didn't imagine that Pascaline would take her poor mutilated cat to the priest to get his blessing. That was an odd and unforeseeable act, but it happened. Nor could you have imagined that Retancourt would survive the dose of Novaxon. Her stamina was something odd and unforeseeable, too. And you couldn't guess that the death of a stag would so distress that group of men. Or that Robert, who was particularly upset, would drag me off to see the corpse of the Red Giant, so that that stag's heart remains engraved in my memory, and I've still got his antlers. The peculiarities of all these people – their talents, their interests, their unpredictable actions, – are not things you've ever concerned yourself with. You never suspected they could exist. You've only ever liked other people when they're dead, haven't you? Other people? What are they? Contemptible and insignificant beings, the whole negligible human race. But neglecting them was what brought about your downfall, Ariane.'

Adamsberg stretched out his arms and closed his eyes, realising that Ariane's incredulity and refusal to speak were creating impenetrable barriers between them. Their conversation was running along two parallel tracks that never met.

'Tell me about your husband,' he said, putting his elbows on the table. 'What's become of him?'

'Charles?' said Ariane, raising her eyebrows. 'I haven't seen him for years. And the less I see of him, the better, actually.'

'Are you sure about that?'

'Quite sure. Charles is a failure who just chases paramedics in skirts. As you know.'

'But you didn't marry again after he left you. No boyfriends?'

'What the fuck has that got to do with anything?'

The first crack in Ariane's façade. Her voice had dropped in register and she wasn't censoring her speech. Omega was advancing along the top of the wall.

'Apparently, Charles is still in love with you.'

'Gracious. Still, that wouldn't surprise me – he's so pathetic.'

'Apparently, he has realised that the paramedics aren't a patch on you.'

'Obviously. You're not going to compare me with fat sows like that, are you, Jean-Baptiste?'

Estalère leaned towards Danglard.

'Is there a bone in the snout of a sow?' he whispered.

'Suppose so,' said Danglard, indicating that this wasn't the moment.

'Apparently, Charles wants to get back together with you,' Adamsberg was saying. 'At least, that's what the gossip is in Lille.'

'Gracious.'

'But are you perhaps afraid that you'll be too old, when he does come back?'

Ariane gave a small, almost flirtatious laugh.

'Ageing, Jean-Baptiste is a perverse idea, arising in God's vicious imagination. How old do you think I am? Sixty?'

'Oh no, nothing like that,' said Estalère spontaneously.

'Shut up,' said Danglard.

'See? Even that youngster knows.'

'What?'

Ariane took another cigarette, and the veil of smoke protected her once more from Omega.

'You came to my new house,' Adamsberg continued, 'just before I moved in, to check it out and unblock the door to the attic. You gave quite a scare to the old man, Lucio Velasco. What did you put on your face? A mask? A stocking?'

'Who's Lucio Velasco?'

'My neighbour. He's Spanish. Once you had the attic door unblocked, you could get in there whenever you wanted. You sometimes came at night and walked about up there, then you got out quickly.'

Ariane let her ash fall to the floor.

'You've heard footsteps in your attic?'

'Yes.'

'That was her, Jean-Baptiste. Claire Langevin. She's after you.'

'Yes, that's what you wanted us to think. I was supposed to tell people about these nightly sounds, to foster the myth of this nurse prowling about ready to strike. And she would have, in the end, by *your* hand, with a syringe and a scalpel. But do you know why it didn't worry me? No, you can't know that.'

'You *should* worry. She's dangerous, as I have told you many times.'

'Well, you see, Ariane, I already had a ghost in the house, Saint Clarisse. How peculiar is that?'

'Killed by the tanner in 1771,' said Danglard.

'With his bare hands,' Adamsberg added. 'Don't lose the thread, Ariane – you don't know everything in this world. I thought it was Clarisse walking about in the attic. Well, to be honest, I really thought old Lucio was on his rounds, checking up. He has a sort of special aura too. He used to worry about the ghost when I had little Tom staying overnight. But it wasn't him I could hear. It was you, up there.'

'No, it was her.'

'You're not going to talk, are you, Ariane? About Omega?'

'Nobody talks about Omega. I thought you had read my book.'

'In some dissociators, you wrote, a crack can open up.'

'Only if they're flawed.'

*　　*　　*

Adamsberg pursued the interrogation until far into the night. Roman had been allowed to stretch out on the cushions in the coffee-machine room and Estalère on a camp bed. Danglard and Veyrenc backed up the *commissaire* with their cross-questioning. Ariane, although tired, remained steadfastly in Alpha mode, without resisting the endless session or abandoning her stance of denying or claiming not to understand anything about Omega.

At four-forty in the morning, Veyrenc staggered to his feet and fetched four coffees.

'I take my coffee with a drop of barley-water,' Ariane explained politely, without turning to face the desk.

'We don't have any,' said Veyrenc. 'We can't make cocktails here.'

'Pity.'

'I don't think there'll be any barley-water in prison,' murmured Danglard. 'The coffee's undrinkable. And the food's fit for animals. It's really filthy stuff, what they give the prisoners.'

'And why in the name of all that's holy are you talking to me about prison?' asked Ariane, with her back to him.

Adamsberg closed his eyes and prayed to the third virgin to come to his assistance. But just then the third virgin was fast asleep in the hotel in Haroncourt between clean, pale blue sheets, and blissfully ignorant of the troubles of the man who'd saved her. Veyrenc gulped his coffee and put the cup down, with a discouraged shrug.

'Cease the struggle, my lord!
With cunning and brute strength you have fought the good fight;
Ramparts and battlements have fallen to your might.
But the wall that resists, the prize you cannot claim,
Will block you for ever, for madness is its name.'

'I agree, Veyrenc,' said Adamsberg, without opening his eyes. 'Take her away, with her wall and her cocktails and her hatred. Get her out of my sight!'

'Six syllables,' Veyrenc noted. '*Get her out of my sight.* A hemistich. Not bad.'

'At that rate, Veyrenc, all cops would be poets.'

'If only,' muttered Danglard.

Ariane snapped her cigarette lighter shut and Adamsberg opened his eyes.

'I need to go to my flat, Jean-Baptiste. I don't know what you're up to, or why, but I'm professional enough to guess. You're holding me for more questioning, aren't you? So I need to get my things.'

'We'll fetch anything you need.'

'No. I want to look for them myself. I don't want your men putting their great paws all over my clothes.'

For the first time, Ariane's expression, which Adamsberg could see only in profile, became set and anxious. She would herself have diagnosed this as Omega moving on to the attack. Because Omega needed to do something vital.

'They'll have to come with you, while you pack a case. But they won't touch anything.'

'I don't want them to be there, I want to be on my own. It's private, it's intimate. You can understand that, surely, can't you? If you're scared I'll try to escape, you can station as many fuckwits as you like outside.'

As many fuckwits as you like. Omega was coming to the surface. Adamsberg watched Ariane's profile, her eyebrow, her lip, her chin, and detected there a tension caused by some fresh thought.

No cordials in prison, just piss-awful coffee. No more cocktails in prison, neither the *violine* nor the *grenaille*, no crème de menthe, no marsala. Above all, no magic potion. But the mixture was almost ready. All she needed was the quick of the third virgin and the wine of the year. Well, the matter of wine could easily be fixed, it was simply there to bind the mixture together, and water would do at a pinch. The third virgin was out of reach, of course, so there was no question of eternity. But since the mixture was almost complete, it might provide long life. How much? A hundred years? Two hundred? A thousand? That would keep you going in prison, without needing to worry or start over. But where was the mixture? It was the fear of never being able to drink it that was making her clench the cigarette between her teeth. Between Ariane and the hard-won treasure there were now several ranks of policemen.

And the treasure was the only proof of the murders. Ariane would never confess. The mixture, the mixture alone, with its hairs from the heads of Pascaline and Elisabeth, its remains of cat, stag and human bones, would demonstrate that Ariane had followed the dark path of the *De reliquis*. To get hold of it now was as essential for her as it was for the *commissaire*. Without the potion, he wouldn't have much chance of making a charge stick. These are just the fantasies of a cloud shoveller, the examining magistrate would say, and Brézillon would back him up. Dr Lagarde was so famous that the threads painfully pulled together by Adamsberg would look flimsy indeed.

'So the potion's in your flat,' said Adamsberg, his eyes not leaving Ariane's taut profile. 'Probably in some hiding place where Alpha's ordinary habits wouldn't find it. You want it and I want it, but I'm the one who'll find it. I'll take my time and I'll pull the building apart if I have to, but I'll find it.'

'Whatever you say,' said Ariane, dragging on her cigarette, then exhaling the smoke, once more looking indifferent and relaxed. 'May I have your permission to visit the lavatory, *commissaire*?'

'Veyrenc, Mordent, go with her. Stay close to her.'

Ariane went out of the room, slowly, on her platform shoes, and held tightly by her two guards. Adamsberg followed them with his eyes, puzzled by her sudden about-turn and the pleasure she had taken from her cigarette. You smiled, Ariane. I'm going to take your treasure and you smiled.

I know that smile. It was the same one as in that café in Le Havre, after you'd thrown my beer away. And the same one when you persuaded me to go after the nurse. The smile of the victor to the one who's about to lose. A triumphant smile. I'm going to get hold of your fucking potion, yet you're smiling.

Adamsberg leapt to his feet and pulled Danglard by the sleeve.

LXIV

DANGLARD RAN AFTER THE *COMMISSAIRE* WITHOUT UNDERSTANDING, HIS LEGS stiff with fatigue, and followed him to the door of the staff washroom where Mordent and Veyrenc were standing guard.

'Go on, *commandant*,' Adamsberg ordered. 'Kick the door in.'

'But . . . but I can't . . .' Mordent began.

'Kick the door in, for God's sake! Veyrenc, help me.'

The lavatory door gave in after three shoves from the shoulders of Veyrenc and the *commissaire*. The ibex charging in unison, Adamsberg had time to think as he grabbed Ariane's arm and took hold of the thick brown phial she was holding. The pathologist screamed. And in that long, ferocious and nerve-rending scream, Adamsberg at last understood what the real nature of an Omega could be. He would never witness it again. Ariane collapsed into unconsciousness, and when she came to, a few minutes later in the cells, Alpha was back in place, calm and sophisticated.

'The potion was in her handbag,' said Adamsberg, staring at the little bottle. 'She took some water from the basin to mix it up and she was just going to drink it.'

He raised his hand and looked carefully at the phial by the light of the lamp, examining the thick liquid inside. The men looked at the small bottle with a certain reverence, as if it were holy oil.

'She's very clever,' said Adamsberg. 'But she wasn't able to hide that cunning little smile of her Omega, a smile of victory. And she smiled when she was sure I thought the potion was in her flat. So it had to mean the bottle was somewhere else. About her person, obviously.'

'Why didn't you confiscate her bag before?' asked Mordent. 'It was a big risk – those toilet doors are solid.'

'I simply never thought of it before, Mordent. I'll put this bottle in the safe. I'll be with you in a minute, and we can all go home.'

Half an hour later, Adamsberg stood inside his front door and locked it firmly. He carefully extracted the brown phial from his jacket pocket and placed it in the centre of the table. Then he emptied the remains of a small bottle of rum into the sink, rinsed it out, found a funnel, and slowly poured half the mixture into it. Tomorrow, the brown phial would go to the lab, and there was plenty of the potion left for analysis. Nobody else had seen through the dark glass exactly how much liquid was inside it, so no one would know that he had taken a generous dose out of it.

Tomorrow, he would visit Ariane in her cell. And he would discreetly pass over the rum bottle. Then the pathologist would remain completely serene in prison, being certain she would survive long enough to complete her project. She would swallow the revolting mixture as soon as he had his back turned and would go to sleep like a devil sated.

And why, Adamsberg wondered, as he put the two small bottles back into his jacket, should he care that Ariane should remain serene in prison? When he could still hear that harsh scream in his ears, full of madness and cruelty? Because he had once been a little in love with her, had once desired her? No, it wasn't even that.

He went to the window and looked out into the garden in the night. Lucio was taking a leak under the hazel tree. Adamsberg waited a few moments, then went out to him. Lucio was looking up at the cloudy sky and scratching the spider's bite.

'Can't sleep, *hombre*?' he asked. 'Have you finished the job?'

'Almost.'

'Difficult nut to crack, eh?'

'Yes.'

'Ah, what men will do,' sighed Lucio. 'And women.'

The old man walked off towards the hedge and came back with two cold bottles of beer, which he opened with his teeth.

'Don't tell Maria, will you?' he said, handing one to Adamsberg. 'Women get so het up. That's because they're perfectionists, you understand, they have to see the whole job through. Whereas a man, he'll do a bit here, a bit there, and then botch it together, or even just leave it half-done. But a woman has to follow her idea through for days and months, without even a drop of beer.'

'I've arrested a woman tonight who was just about to finish the task she'd set herself.'

'A big one?'

'Gigantic. She was preparing a diabolical potion that she wanted to swallow. And I thought it was probably best in the end that she should swallow it. So that her task is pretty much finished. Right?'

Lucio drained his bottle and threw it over the wall.

'Yes, of course, *hombre*.'

The old man went back home and Adamsberg took a leak under the tree himself. 'Yes, of course, *hombre*.' Otherwise the bite would itch till the end of her days.

LXV

'THIS IS WHERE WE'RE GOING TO END THE STORY, VEYRENC,' SAID ADAMSBERG, stopping under a large walnut tree.

Two days after the arrest of Ariane Lagarde, and faced with the scandal which the news had caused, Adamsberg had felt a pressing need to go and cool his feet in the waters of the Gave. He had bought two tickets to Pau, and dragged Veyrenc off with him, without consulting him. They had now arrived in the Ossau valley and Adamsberg made his colleague climb the rocky path up to the chapel of Camalès. They had just come out on to the High Meadow. Veyrenc looked around with a dazed expression, at the field and the mountain tops. He had never been back to this meadow.

'Now that we're free of the Shade, we can sit down in the shade of the walnut tree. But not for too long, because we know it's unlucky. Just long enough to deal with this itch from the past. Sit down, Veyrenc.'

'Where I was, that day?'

'For instance?'

Veyrenc walked about five metres and sat cross-legged in the grass.

'The fifth boy, under the tree, can you see him?'

'Yes.'

'Who is it?'

'You.'

'Yes, me. I'm thirteen years old. Who am I?'

'A gang leader from the village of Caldhez.'

'Correct. And what do I look like?'

'You're standing up. You're watching the whole thing, but you don't intervene. You have your hands behind your back.'

'Why?'

'Because you're hiding some sort of weapon, a stick or something, I don't know.'

'You saw Ariane the other night, when she got to my office. She had her hands behind her back too. Was she carrying a weapon?'

'No, of course not, that was quite different. She was handcuffed.'

'An excellent reason to have your hands behind your back. I was tied up, Veyrenc, like a goat at the end of its chain. My wrists were tied to the tree. I hope you'll understand now why I didn't intervene.'

Veyrenc ran his hand through the grass several times.

'Tell me what happened.'

'There were two rival gangs in Caldhez. The gang from the bottom of the village, by the fountain, with Fernand as its leader; and the gang at the top of the village by the wash house, which was led by me and my brother. We used to fight all the time – wars, plots, battles, it was all we thought about. Just kids' games, until Roland and a few other boys arrived. At that point, the fountain gang turned into a really nasty outfit. He wanted to wipe us out and run the village. It was like gang warfare in the city. We resisted as best we could, but he hated me more than anyone else, he really had it in for me. The day they went after you, Roland came and cornered me, with Fernand and Big Georges. "We're taking you to watch something, motherfucker," he said. "Keep your eyes open, and after that you'll keep your mouth shut, because if you don't, motherfucker, we'll do the same to you." They dragged me up here and tied me to the tree. Then they went into the chapel to wait for you. It was your usual route home from school. They jumped you, and you know the rest.'

Adamsberg realised that he had started to call Veyrenc 'tu' without realising it. As kids do. Both of them, up on the High Meadow, were kids again.

'We-ell,' said Veyrenc, pulling a face and not looking entirely convinced.

> '*Give me leave to show doubt, to my ears this is new.*
> *How can I be convinced that what you say is true?*'

'I managed to pull my penknife out of my back pocket. And because I'd seen lots of films, I tried to cut the cords. But we're never in a film, Veyrenc. If we were in a film now, Ariane would have confessed. In real life, her wall has remained intact. So I was getting nowhere, sweating away, trying to get through the cord. The blade slipped and my knife fell on the ground. When you passed out, they untied me quickly and dragged me off down the path at a run. It was a long time before I dared try and go back to the High Meadow to find my knife. Winter was over, the grass had grown. I looked everywhere but I never found it.'

'Does that matter?'

'No, Veyrenc. But if the story's true, there's a good chance the knife's still here, stuck somewhere in the ground. The song of the earth, remember? That's why I brought the pickaxe along. You're going to look for the knife. It should still be open, just as it fell. My initials are carved on the wooden handle, JBA.'

'Why don't we both look?'

'Because you're not sure if you believe me. You might still accuse me of dropping it in the earth while I was digging. No, I'm going to walk away, with my hands in my pockets and I'm going to watch you. We're going to open another grave, looking for a *living* memory. But it would surprise me if it's more than a few inches from the surface.'

'It might not be there at all,' said Veyrenc. 'Someone might have come along a few days later and picked it up.'

'If they had, we'd have heard about it. Remember that the cops were looking for the fifth boy. If someone had found my knife, with my initials on it, I'd have been caught. But they didn't find the fifth boy, and I kept my mouth shut. I couldn't prove anything. If the story's true, the knife should still be there, thirty-four years later. I wouldn't ever have dropped my precious knife on purpose. If I didn't pick it up myself, it's because I couldn't. I was tied up.'

Veyrenc hesitated, then stood up and took the pickaxe while Adamsberg walked off a little distance. The surface was hard, and the *lieutenant* spent over an hour under the walnut tree, at regular intervals picking up clods of earth and crumbling them in his fingers. Then Adamsberg saw him drop the pickaxe and pick something up from the ground, wiping the earth off it.

'Find it?' he asked, coming up. 'Can you read anything on it?'

'JBA,' said Veyrenc, as he finished cleaning the handle with his thumb.

He handed the knife to Adamsberg without a word. The blade was rusty, the handle's varnish worn away, and the carved initials were full of black earth – and perfectly legible. Adamsberg turned it over in his hand, his penknife, the damned penknife which hadn't managed to cut the cords, and hadn't helped him to come to the rescue of a little kid bleeding from an attack by the vicious Roland.

'It's yours if you want it,' said Adamsberg, offering it, taking care to hold it by the blade. 'It's a male principle, a symbol of how both of us were impotent that day.'

Veyrenc nodded and accepted it.

'Now you owe me ten centimes,' Adamsberg added.

'Why?'

'It's a tradition. If you give a sharp object to anyone, the other person has to give you a coin to prevent it cutting him. I wouldn't like you to have bad luck on my account. You keep the knife, I'll take the ten centimes.'

LXVI

IN THE TRAIN ON THE WAY BACK, VEYRENC WAS TROUBLED BY ONE LAST IDEA.

'Someone who's a dissociator,' he said, looking grave, 'doesn't know what they've done, right? They repress the memory.'

'That's the theory, according to Ariane. We'll never know whether she was just play-acting when she refused to confess, or whether she's a genuine dissociator. Or indeed if such a thing really exists.'

'If it did exist,' said Veyrenc, with a crooked smile, 'would I have been able to kill Fernand and Big Georges and then wipe it from my memory?'

'No, Veyrenc.'

'How can you be sure?'

'Because I checked. I got your employment records and your worksheets from Tarbes and Nevers, which was where you were at the time of the murders. The day Fernand was murdered, you were accompanying someone to London. When Big Georges was killed, you were under arrest.'

'I was?'

'Yes, for insulting a superior officer. What was that about?'

'What was his name?'

'Pleyel, like the pianos.'

'Yes,' Veyrenc said, remembering. 'He was someone like Devalon. We had a scandal on our hands, political corruption. Instead of doing his job, he did what the government told him, provided false documents and got the main offender out of trouble. I wrote a few harmless lines about him, and he didn't like that.'

'Remember them?'

'No, not any more.'

Adamsberg got out his notebook and leafed through it.

> '"*The pride of the powerful corrupts men without cease,*
> *And makes a cringing slave of a chief of police.*
> *The Republic turns pale and slides into despair,*
> *While criminal tyrants profit without a care.*"

Result, fifteen days confined to barracks.'

'Where did you find that?' asked Veyrenc, smiling.

'It's in the station records. Your lines saved you from killing Big Georges. You didn't kill anyone, Veyrenc.'

The *lieutenant* squeezed his eyes shut and relaxed his shoulders.

'You still haven't given me my ten centimes,' said Adamsberg, holding out his hand. 'I've been working hard on your behalf. You gave me a lot of trouble.'

Veyrenc dropped a copper coin into Adamsberg's hand.

'Thank you,' said Adamsberg, pocketing the coin. 'And when are you going to give up Camille?'

Veyrenc turned his head away.

'OK,' said Adamsberg, leaning against the window and falling instantly asleep.

LXVII

DANGLARD HAD TAKEN ADVANTAGE OF RETANCOURT'S RETURN FROM hospital, earlier than expected, to decree a break in honour of the third virgin, after bringing up some bottles from the basement. In the resulting festivity, only the cat remained calm, sleeping peacefully curled up on Retancourt's powerful forearm.

Adamsberg walked slowly across the room, feeling awkward, as usual when there was some kind of celebration. He took the glass that Estalère held out for him as he passed, pulled out his mobile and called Robert's number. In the café in Haroncourt, the second round of drinks had just begin.

'It's the Béarnais cop,' Robert announced to the evening assembly, covering the telephone with his hand. 'He says his troubles are over and he's going to have a drink and think of us.'

Anglebert considered his reply.

'You can tell him that's fine by us.'

'He says he's found two of Saint Jerome's bones in a flat in Paris in a toolbox,' reported Robert, covering the phone again. 'And he'll come and put them back in the reliquary at Le Mesnil. Because he doesn't know what else to do with 'em.'

'Well, neither do we, for God's sake,' said Oswald.

'He says we should tell the priest anyway.'

'Makes sense,' commented Hilaire. 'Just because Oswald can't be bothered with them, don't mean to say the priest won't. Got his own worries, the priest, hasn't he? Got to reckon with that.'

'You can tell him that will be fine by us,' Anglebert commanded. 'When's he coming?'

'Saturday.'

Robert returned to the telephone, and concentrated in order to transmit the response of the elder of the tribe.

'Now he's saying he's got some stones from his river back home, and he wants us to have them, if we've no objection.'

'What the heck are we supposed to do with them?'

'I get the feeling it's like the antlers of the Red Giant. It's sort of an honour in return.'

Undecided faces turned to Anglebert.

'If we refuse,' said Anglebert, 'he might be offended.'

'Stands to reason,' punctuated Achille.

'You can tell him that's fine by us too.'

Leaning against the wall, Veyrenc watched as the members of the squad circulated. This evening they had been joined by Dr Roman, who had also returned to earth, and Dr Lavoisier, who was closely monitoring Retancourt's case. Adamsberg was walking quietly from place to place, here now, then absent, like a lighthouse going on and off. The strain of his long pursuit of Ariane, the Shade, had left dark traces on his face. He had spent three hours walking in the waters of the Gave and picking up pebbles before he'd joined Veyrenc to take the train back to Paris.

The *commissaire* took a crumpled piece of paper from his pocket and motioned to Danglard to come over. Danglard well knew that smile and that twitch of the head. He went across, looking suspicious.

'Veyrenc would say that fate likes to play games with us. You know that there are ironies of fate, and that's how we recognise it.'

'Veyrenc's going away, it seems.'

'Yes, he's going back to his mountains. He's going to have a think with his feet in the river and his hair blowing in the wind, to work out whether he'll come back to us or not. He hasn't decided.'

Adamsberg held out the paper.

'Got that this morning.'

'I can't understand a word of it,' said Danglard looking down.

'Naturally – it's in Polish. Apparently it informs us that the district nurse has just died, *capitaine*. It was a straightforward road accident. She was knocked over by a car in Warsaw. Squashed flat by a driver who didn't stop at the lights and couldn't tell the road from the pavement. And we know who the driver was.'

'A Pole, I presume.'

'Yes, but not just any Pole.'

'A Pole who was drunk?'

'No doubt. But what else?'

'I don't know what you're getting at.'

'An *old* Pole. Ninety-two years old. The woman who killed old people was killed by one of them.'

Danglard thought for a moment.

'That makes you laugh?'

'Yes, Danglard.'

Veyrenc saw Adamsberg grip the *commandant*'s shoulder, he saw Lavoisier fussing over Retancourt, he saw Roman coming back to life, Estalère running round filling glasses, Noël bragging about his blood donation. None of it concerned him. He hadn't come to Paris to get interested in people's lives. He had come to sort out once and for all the matter of his hair. Which he had.

> '*It is over, soldier, the tragedy is run.*
> *You are free to go now where you please 'neath the sun.*
> *What sorrowful regret holds you here in this hall?*
> *Why do you not make haste, bid farewell to them all?'*

Yes, why not? Veyrenc drew on his cigarette and watched as Adamsberg left the hall, discreet and light-footed, carrying the great stag's antlers, one in each hand.

'O ye Gods,
I beseech you, indulge the charm that holds me here.
Their vain humanity is both tragic and dear.'

Adamsberg walked home along the darkened streets. He would not tell Tom a word about Ariane's atrocities. He had no wish that such horrors should reach the child so early in life. In any case, there was no such thing as a dissociated ibex. Only human beings have a talent for bringing about this kind of calamity. Whereas ibex can make their horns grow out of their skulls, just like stags. That's something humans can't do. So we'll stick to stories about the ibex.

Then the wise old chamois who'd read lots of books realised that he had made a big mistake. But the ginger ibex never found out that the wise chamois had thought he was wicked. And then the ginger ibex realised that he'd made a big mistake too and that the brown ibex wasn't wicked, either. Right you are, said the brown ibex, that's ten centimes you owe me.

In the little garden, Adamsberg put the antlers down while he looked for his keys. Lucio appeared immediately from the darkness and joined him under the hazel tree.

'All right, *hombre*?'

Lucio slipped across to the hedge without waiting for a reply and came back with two beers, which he opened. His radio was hissing away in his pocket.

'This woman,' he said, passing Adamsberg a bottle. 'The one who hadn't finished her task. You gave her the potion?'

'Yes.'

'And she drank it?'

'Yes.'

'Good.'

Lucio took a few mouthfuls, before pointing to the ground with the tip of his walking stick.

'What's that you're carrying around?'

'A ten-pointer from Normandy.'

'Live or cast?'

'Live.'

'Good,' said Lucio again. 'But don't separate them.'

'Yes, I know.'

'You know something else too?'

'Yes, Lucio, the Shade has gone. Dead, finished, out of the way.'

The old man stood for a moment without speaking, tapping the top of the little bottle against his teeth. He looked at Adamsberg's house, then turned to the *commissaire*.

'How?'

'Guess.'

'They used to say she could only be killed by an old man.'

'Well, that's what happened.'

'Tell me.'

'It happened in Warsaw,'

'The day before yesterday, in the evening?'

'Yes, why?'

'What happened?'

'An old Polish man, aged ninety-two, ran her over. She went under the front wheels of his car.'

Lucio thought, and rolled the bottle across his mouth.

'Just like that?' he said, gesturing with his only fist.

'Just like that,' Adamsberg said.

'Like the tanner, with his bare hands.'

Adamsberg smiled and picked up his antlers.

'Stands to reason,' he punctuated.

www.vintage-books.co.uk